THE TRAJECTORY

MW00473342

"*The Trajectory of Dreams* is unsettling, beautifully written, and truly original. In Lela White, Nicole Wolverton has created one of the most haunting characters in contemporary fiction. This is a remarkable debut."
—Emily St. John Mandel, author of
The Lola Quartet, The Singer's Gun, and *Last Night in Montreal*

"This novel is a free dive into the bottomless ocean of insanity. With every chapter, every kick of the fins, you're sucked in deeper as the darkness mounts and the pressure builds. And like the ocean, The Trajectory of Dreams gives up its secrets grudgingly, so you'll continually be stunned as the protagonist, Lela, falls to her inevitable implosion."
—Mike Mullin, author of
Ashfall and *Ashen Winter*

"Nicole Wolverton's *The Trajectory of Dreams* leads readers into a seemingly orderly world that spirals into madness. Just when you think you understand—you hope you don't!"
—Jenny Wingfield, author of
The Homecoming of Samuel Lake

"This is a psychological thriller of epic proportions. [...] 5 out of 5 stars for its crazy twists and exhilarating ending. This is a gripping, disquieting look at mental illness that will cause you to question how well you can truly know a person, especially those with something to hide."
-Literary R&R

THE TRAJECTORY OF DREAMS

NICOLE WOLVERTON

Published by Bitingduck Press
ISBN 978-1-938463-44-0
For information contact
Bitingduck Press, LLC
Montreal • Altadena
notifications@bitingduckpress.com
http://www.bitingduckpress.com
Cover image by Lance Schriner,
http://www.stingraydesign.net

Publisher's Cataloging-in-Publication
Wolverton, Nicole [1972-   ]

The Trajectory of Dreams/by Nicole Wolverton –1st
ed.—Altadena, CA: Bitingduck Press, 2013
p. cm.
ISBN 9781938463440

[1. Psychological Thriller—Fiction 2. Murder—Serial
Murder—Fiction 3. Astronautics, accidents—Fiction
4. Sleep disorders, insomnia—Fiction] I. Title

LCCN 2012952699

For Craig

Chapter One

GODSPEED

BREAKING INTO AN ASTRONAUT'S HOME TOOK TIME. THERE WERE research and preparation to account for. An assassination plan in case the subject failed my testing. And even establishing a schedule and behavioral pattern for each astronaut could take weeks.

My investigation of Robert Jeffrey Meehan, Ph.D., was no exception.

It had taken five visits to his apartment building, logging his routine and determining his usual bedtime, before I felt comfortable enough to pick the lock on his door the first time.

During every visit I stood at the foot of his bed. Now I clocked each twitch of his leg, hitch in his breath, and the time at which he appeared to descend into REM sleep. I recorded everything on the polysomnography observation report attached to my clipboard.

Not for the first time, I wished for the equipment in the sleep lab at work—an EEG, EKG, nasal airflow sensor—but none of those were portable. Not exactly the kind of machines that lent to criminal trespass on the sly.

Even without them, though, no detail escaped my notice. I watched. Always, I watched.

Meehan lay on his back, deep in sleep. He twisted his head to the side and smacked his lips. Nothing out of the ordinary; common sleep behavior.

Benjamin Franklin said he considered death as necessary as sleep: *We shall rise refreshed in the morning.* Meehan very well might, at that. Only death was inevitable—sleep was a luxury or a curse, a thing some people yearned for and went to great lengths to get. But the astronauts were different. Sleep was their gift. Their talent.

Meehan's dark skin shined in the dim glow of the moon through the gap in the curtains hung across the window. The t-shirt he wore to bed bunched around his neck like waves lapping at the shore of his chin. His foot poked out from the bottom of the comforter, long toes slack.

The almost uncontrollable urge to run my fingers through the coarse hair at his ankle seized me, but doing so might wake him. The idea was to check for sleep disorders and ensure he could sleep on the shuttle during liftoff, not interfere.

I glanced at my watch. I'd been rooted to the same spot for over four hours.

I flipped to the final evaluation sheet and wrote:

Subject continues to engage in deep sleep with only momentary lapses that do not appear to be cause for concern. His sleep duration on this last night of observation conforms with previous studies.

Total recording time: 257 minutes
Total sleep time: roughly 256 minutes
PLM index: 2.2
Total REM events: 5 est.

Dr. Meehan appears to be well-qualified for the upcoming shuttle mission. He has what appears to be normal sleep architecture and excellent sleep efficiency. – recorded at 4:17 a.m., Lela White

I tucked the clipboard under my arm and picked up my camera.

Time for one last sweep of his apartment.

There was a pattern when it came to how astronauts lived. Not all, of course, but most. So many had been in the military, and it showed in the way they folded their socks and underwear. T-shirts were a precision operation, creased exactly and stacked in a drawer.

I raised the camera and took a shot of his nightstand. Meehan had never been in the military, so his living space was messier. A bowl with the remains of an orange lay on top of a stack of books. Mysteries, mostly. A worn copy of *Crime and Punishment* topped the pile, and at the bottom was an Amelia Earhart biography.

There were photographs, too. In one, a close-up shot, he stood with his arm around a slight woman with straight brown hair that fell to her clavicles, a soft chin on a thin face, and bony shoulders. If her eyes had been hazel instead of brown, almond-shaped instead of slanted, she could have been me.

A pile of still-smelly workout clothes moldered in a puddle in front of Meehan's closet. True, he'd been to the gym just before returning home, but it was unsanitary to let them sit like that. My fingers crooked with wanting to pick them up and sort them for the washing machine.

At least his closet looked tidy. A row of pressed dress shirts hung in a row—white, light blue, and light pink—and his pants lined up as file folders in a drawer. Several NASA polo shirts lay beyond that. The camera's click was almost silent.

But not silent enough.

Meehan twitched, and my heart stuttered. The movement was unlike the normal jerks he'd experienced during sleep: He was more alert. I should have known better—he was probably coming out of a sleep cycle.

I lowered the camera, each second passing in slow motion, and retrieved the clipboard from under my arm. Would he wake?

The assassination plan for Meehan was well thought out. NASA contracted the Forty Winks Sleep Lab to run sleep studies on all candidates for the shuttle program, so I had access to medical records. Meehan's severe shellfish allergy wouldn't keep him out of space. But if he didn't pass my more personalized sleep observation (outside lab protocol), I planned to sneak powdered shrimp in the oatmeal he ate every morning. His phone would be incapacitated to prevent a call for help. He'd be dead within minutes.

It would look like a natural death, an unfortunate accident. Something that could happen to anyone.

Simple.

Of course, the emergency plan was far different.

I fumbled with the autoinjector attached to the clipboard, hoping it wouldn't come to that. The shot was my backup, but it wasn't particularly artful or subtle. My nose wrinkled.

The word—*kill*—flopped around in my brain. It was precaution, not practice. The idea flooded my veins with an apprehension that prickled and stung. Maybe it should have gotten easier over the years, the idea that I might have to carry out an assassination plan one day. Every event planner had a plan B and a plan C, a worst-case scenario type of thing. Of course, none of those plans ended with a corpse.

Meehan jerked again and rolled away. Had his eyelashes fluttered? I held my breath and counted backward from thirty. The temperature in the room seemed to plummet by twenty degrees, which made my face all the hotter.

His hand floated back to scratch his hip, and he half-hummed, half-groaned.

If my stomach grumbled, he'd hear me. If he flopped over again, he'd see me.

I stood in front of his closet, as far away from the bedroom door as possible.

If I made a run for it, there was no doubt he'd catch me. He'd been a soccer star in high school, and I was just some skinny woman who'd never been athletic.

I could see it in my head. How wide his eyes would be when he saw me standing over his bed. The soft *sniiiick* the autoinjector would make when the needle entered his flesh. The way Meehan's muscles would soften and go slack. The blank expression in his eyes when his heart stuttered and finally stopped.

NASA would delay the shuttle mission out of respect for his family, of course, but it ultimately would go on. They'd replace him, and I'd have to complete an additional observation.

For the good of the shuttle launch and the astronauts, I would kill him. Years prior, the shuttle program had languished on hiatus for forty-nine months—shut down after the last incident. It was my responsibility to ensure it never happened again.

Meehan rolled again, this time onto his stomach. His arms tightened around his pillow in a bear hug. Within seconds he snored. Not loud—it was more of a wispy grumble. Not the type indicative of obstructive sleep apnea.

All the while adrenaline roller-coastered through me, up the steep beginning incline and wailing around the curves and dips.

His breathing evened out and deepened. I tried to control my own, finally sucking in a quiet lungful of air.

I stepped closer, raising the autoinjector. All it would take was a quick jab. He stayed asleep, though, sinking deeper and deeper with each rise of his lungs. My feet moved of their own accord, carrying me around his bed and out his bedroom door.

Some animals are more equal than others. It was definitely true in my case. Years of creeping around, dealing with security systems, and digging into blue prints had left me with skills on par with any professional burglar. They were just animals, though. I was *more*. I had purpose.

The astronauts I'd studied had gone up and come down—safely. Without my vigilance, the time would come when they might not be so lucky. A disaster would happen again. We must study the past to predict the future.

I still remembered the last time in vivid detail. I'd been ten—just turned, in fact, several days prior.

The fireball and puffy cloud trail on the television screen in my elementary school hallway turned my fascination to stomach-churning terror, then back to serrated prickles of dread as the smoky streams from the space shuttle split apart, curling and expanding into antennae. A giant, roiling snail head in a sky so blue it hurt to look at.

A gravelly "major malfunction" oozed out of the speakers.

The picture went dead, thanks to a quick-thinking teacher, but not before the announcer intoned, "And our prayers are with the *Constitution* astronauts."

I hope the astronauts were asleep, I'd thought, rubbing my eyes like I'd just woken myself. The hallway and everyone in it had been so clear. So vivid.

The astronauts had to have been asleep. God simply plucked them out of the shuttle, dreaming their dreams, and took them to Heaven. They hadn't felt a thing. I was sure of it.

Every night I lay awake, fighting the pull of my eyelids, and stared at the ceiling while hoping this time the boosters would fall away. Praying this time the fiery rockets would fade to pinpricks of light as the shuttle disappeared into space.

Meehan's living room was a tomb: silent and still. The knob of the door leading to the hallway was cool under my hand. It didn't make a sound and neither did the door itself. Even when I relocked the deadbolt with the lock pick, the quiet was complete.

"Godspeed," I whispered before padding down the corridor.

Meehan would never know I'd been watching over him, recording his sleep. He'd never know I ensured the safety of his mission by carrying out the job the universe had tasked me with.

He'd never know.

Chapter Two

ALL LIVING IS DYING

No living thing can exist without sleep. Not for long, anyway. As a certified polysomnographic technician, a woman of science, I understood clearly the importance of rest. Go without dreams, without the beautiful mechanism of circadian rhythms, and the body withers. The mind withers.

I was the lone exception.

Even after staying up all night to observe Meehan, my thoughts were shark's tooth sharp. Not that I needed a razor focus to shelve books on my Saturday morning volunteer shift at the library down the street from my house.

Mrs. Gerhardt had sent me off with a cart full of returns. In the psychology section, I was hunting the spot for *When She Was Bad: Violent Women and the Myth of Innocence* when the librarian's unmistakable shuffling echoed among the stacks.

She rounded the corner at a clip, which for her was the speed of an eighty year old arthritic, despite the fact that she couldn't have been any older than sixty-five. "Bad ticker," she'd once explained to me. "Nothing to worry about."

It wasn't like I didn't understand the severity of having a heart condition. I'd spent time trying to guess what hers might be, whether it was something straightforward or something more complicated, like a congenital heart defect. I'd once caught her reading an article about tetralogy of Fallot, but there was no evidence one way or another.

"Now *there's* an interesting book, Lela" she said, nodding to my hand.

"Living a secret life as an abnormal psychologist?" I asked. I slid the book into its place.

She leaned against the cart and sighed through lips the color of a fire engine, her signature. I'd never seen her without the lipstick. It made her pale skin even whiter.

The ends of her mouth turned up into a prim smile. "I've nearly adopted you, haven't I?"

"I'm as normal as they come. You should know."

"Hmph. At the very least, you're one of the best volunteers I ever had. Well, you and your dad. Speaking of which, are you doing anything next week?"

"Next week?" I'd be starting my observation of the final astronaut for the upcoming *Empire* shuttle mission, but I couldn't tell her that.

I pushed the cart into the aisle and shambled toward the front of the library. Mrs. Gerhardt followed, one hand gripping the end of the handle.

Her thin brows drew together. "Your father's death?"

"No. I mean, am I supposed to do something? Is that normal?"

"Oh, well…some people mark the passage of a year, but it's not about what you're *supposed* to do. It's about what you *feel* like doing. My mother passed twenty years ago, but my father and I still visit her grave every year on her birthday and lay flowers. My Edgar was cremated, of course, so there's no grave for him, but I make his favorite dinner on our wedding anniversary."

"Why do you take your mother flowers? It's not like she needs them or knows you're there."

"We do those types of things because it makes us feel better. I miss her, and I miss my husband. Don't you miss your parents?"

My eyes cut toward her, but I forced my head to stay put. "I miss Dad."

And I did, although my astronaut observations were easier with him gone. When I returned from Meehan's apartment that morning, there was no one but Nike to ask questions about where I'd been. No lies to invent. I still kept my bedroom closet door padlocked, but with no one to stumble on files and supplies, I didn't have to.

"But not your mother?" she asked.

"Have I ever?"

"No, but you're old enough to understand that people have reasons for the things they do. Maybe not good reasons or sane reasons, but there you go."

I positioned the now-empty cart next to the circulation desk, and Mrs. Gerhardt edged behind it and shifted up onto a stool. I said, "Thirty-two is not some magical age at which I suddenly figure out why she abandoned us. And it's not like I'm going to start caring about it, either."

She patted my hand. Hers were cold. "No, of course not. But she was sick, your mo—"

"What do you know about it?" I asked. A tense static roared in my ears. Behind my lids, Dad's face loomed, urging me to calm myself, to be pleasant.

No one likes a sour puss, Lela. I forced a tooth-crammed smile and turned to Mrs. Gerhardt.

Her entire body twitched. "Nothing. Just things your father said over the years."

Keeping the smile in place, I said, "Maybe I *will* go to the cemetery. What do you say when you go? Is there something special I should do?"

"No, of course not. You do what feels right. In Mexico they remember those who have passed on the Day of the Dead, or some celebrate the memory of their dead on Halloween. You know, my mother used to say that Halloween is the day when the veil between living and dead is thinnest—it originated as a pagan celebration, you know. It was a common thing to leave an offering of some sort in case one of your ghosts came back, sort of like when you leave cookies for Santa on Christmas Eve."

"I'm supposed to leave cookies out for Dad?" I asked. I hoped he didn't want anything homemade.

Mrs. Gerhardt laughed. "No, that's not what I mean." The wrinkles in her face shook. "He was very proud of you, you know."

"Dad?"

She nodded. "You're so driven. Even when you were a little girl, you knew exactly what you wanted. Everything was all about sleep. He was always worried about you, worried you were too serious for your own good."

"There's nothing wrong with knowing what you're meant to do with your life."

"Oh, I know," she said. "And so did your dad. He talked about you so much, Lela. His daughter, the big scientist." She smiled.

Maybe he'd been proud, but he hadn't been happy. "Lela," he said before he died, "almost everything about this life has been a pile of donkey crap."

I hadn't taken it personally, not even when he'd had an aneurysm that night.

"He never saw it coming," the doctor had said.

Mrs. Gerhardt's smile thinned. "He wouldn't like you being alone so much of the time, though. I always thought you'd settle down with a nice boy after you put in your time at the lab."

"I'm not alone," I said. "I've got Nike. And you. I can't really say I'm too motivated to get involved with anyone, *especially* since Mom ran off."

"A cat and an old woman are not exactly scintillating company," she said in a dry voice. "What about Trina? You could pal around together. Everyone needs friends." She glanced up. "Speak of the devil."

I could feel the woman's presence behind me even before she said a word. It was like a fleet of crabs had crawled up my back, pinching at my skin.

Trina Shook had always reminded me of my mother: vicious and hateful with a veneer of goodness. It was more than just the faux little girl lilt of Trina's voice. They also shared the same head of hair—dark blonde, parted over the left eye. Trina's hung straight to her shoulders while my mother's had curled around her face like snakes with broken necks.

"Hey, Mrs. Gerhardt! And Lela! Long time, no see!" she joked. Behind her eyes, the disgust lurked. It shone like a gemstone, some dark and terrible thing that only wanted to consume. A short chin belied the roundness of her face: she was all cheekbones and forehead

My mouth tightened, but I schooled my own face into a pleasant mask before turning around.

"How's the reading coming, Trina?" Mrs. Gerhardt asked. Out of the corner of my eye, I could see her face twitch, like she was trying not to laugh.

Traitor.

"Oh, it's naptime. We just finished reading the second book and serving snacks. Most of the kids are dead asleep already. I just wanted to say hello to my favorite cubicle-mate." She hit me in the shoulder just a little too hard. She wasn't heavy, by any means, but she was solidly built.

"That's so nice," I said, hoping my voice circled the approximation of perky. "What did you read today?"

I stared at the clock over her head and counted the time it took her to babble out the answer. Two hundred and forty seconds later, give or take, she was still talking. I was about to ask what she'd read next, but Mrs. Gerhardt butted in.

"I think I see Yolanda waving you back, Trina."

"Oh! Well, see you on Monday. Or maybe later!" She waved over her shoulder, gave her hair a perky toss, and trotted back toward the children's reading area.

"She sure does have a lot of spirit," Mrs. Gerhardt said, chuckling.

I raised one eyebrow, frowning. "That's one way to look at it."

"Can't really turn down a volunteer, now can I?"

"I'm on to you, lady," I said, lowering my voice but attempting to mimic the teasing tone she always used. Dad would have liked that. He could have confessed to burglary in that kind of a voice, and people would have laughed and assumed he was kidding. "All this talk about Trina, me being friends with Trina. I don't want anything to do with her. Keep it up, and I can't be held responsible for my actions."

She grinned. "I don't know what you're talking about." She slid a paper across the desk. "Can you take that to Trina? I *must* help Mr. Charles with the Internet again."

I rolled my eyes and bared my teeth at Mrs. Gerhardt, who was now walking away. If this was what my volunteer experience was going to be like from here on out, maybe I'd think about changing my hours. At least I was getting better at pretending to joke.

With the paper curled in my fist, I wandered toward the children's section. It was hidden behind a low partition, the walls painted blue—probably in an effort to soothe the savage beasts it was meant to contain. Short bookshelves lined the walls. I hadn't spent an inordinate amount of time there, even when I was a kid. I could still remember following Mrs. Gerhardt around the stacks in the adult section, my head barely reaching her shoulder. The first novel she ever demanded I read was *Lord of the Flies*, but only after I told her I had no interest in *Little Women* or books for little kids. That'd been a long time ago.

Trina and another volunteer sat together at the front of the children's section, watching the kids. For all I knew, they'd been plotting to slash my tires. I was relatively certain they weren't planning a sophisticated reading program. Neither could probably envision anyone, let alone younger people, having an interest in science or philosophy.

I waved the paper at Trina and folded my arms across the divider, resting my chin on my forearm.

A little girl in a yellow sweater curled up on a rubber mat with a book—something about bubbles—clutched tight against her chest. Her mouth puckered, the shine of saliva rich on the lips. She scrunched her face once before the outline of an eyeball beneath the lid shifted from side to side. Her body jerked in time before she woke with a gasp and stared at the ceiling. Probably not a great sleeper, although it was hard to tell from just a single observation.

A boy behind her scratched at his nose, lips puckering in his sleep. A moment later his entire body spasmed, as though he dreamed of hitting the ground after a long fall. That was supposed to indicate anxiety. He was young, maybe eight years old. I hoped he didn't have a lot to be stressed out about at that age.

I watched them all, inspecting their dream cycles and noting their sleep disturbances. Not one of them seemed truly unable to sleep, something I found miraculous. Studies showed that hyperactive children often also had sleep problems—and judging by the yelling and running and fighting I'd seen during the reading hour over the years, well…still, the unconscious ballet tiptoed all around me while I wondered if any of them would one day join the space program.

Sleep patterns changed throughout a lifetime, so there was no way of catching someone with a disqualifying disorder early on. Too bad—it would have been so much easier to assassinate a child. Even with my skinny arms, it wouldn't be hard to overpower one of them. No need for more complicated schemes.

All it would take was to catch one of them in the stairway or the bathroom, cut off air flow. Simple and beautiful.

Agitation burned my esophagus. Even though it'd be necessary if the universe demanded it, there was relief in not having to kill a child. I was a hero, not a monster.

"They're so peaceful when they're asleep, aren't they?" Trina leaned next to me, smiling. Her black diamond eyes glittered. I hadn't even seen her cross the room. "God, don't you just want a half dozen of them? I haven't told my boyfriend yet, but I want to start having kids as soon as we get married."

I shuddered. "All that screaming and crying makes me crazy."

"You'd be a good mother." She paused, setting a doll on the counter, its lashes drifting to kiss its apple red cheeks. "You're always so nice. And you always listen to what people are saying. Kids have a lot to say, you know?"

My fingers crept closer to the doll, poking at its hip with my nail. The pink dress belled out from the waist, ending in frayed lace at the hem. Rage burned in my stomach. How dare she make assumptions about me? She'd been my officemate for years, almost as long as I'd been employed at the Forty Winks Sleep Lab, but she hardly knew anything about me.

"Well, bless your heart," I said. The cold air of the library hit my teeth; I smiled harder. "What do you like about children?"

Always keep them talking about themselves. That had been Dad's motto.

"Just look at them!" Trina hissed. "Little angels. And the babies have that smell."

"Yes, I would imagine the diapers…"

"No," she said. Her pinched face morphed into a dreamy, dopey expression. "I mean, yeah. The diapers are rank, but there's something about the way their skin smells. Like the air hasn't had a chance to pollute them yet."

"Pollute them? What do you mean?"

I imagined the oxygen and hydrogen molecules attacking a newborn, turning the skin against itself, setting the organs on their eventual path to decay. All living is dying. Not a second went by when some part of a human being wasn't one step closer to the end. And at the end came sleep, deeper and more satisfying than anyone could ever imagine.

"Just that they're so innocent and sweet at this age."

Innocent. Right. When was anyone innocent?

I stood the doll upright, closing my own eyes when the doll's popped open, the distinctive *sllliccck* of the lids pounding in my ears.

✳✳✳

IKE'S PUFFY YELLOW TAIL BUSHED AND SHOOK, CURLING AROUND the leg of the table in the front hallway when I walked in the door after my shift. He blinked up at me, his own form of Morse code. We'd always communicated this way.

"Yes, I know," I said. "I'll finish the report right now."

After arriving home from my final observation at Meehan's apartment, I'd arranged all the evidence on my bed and dove into a review. Of course, by the time I came up for air I'd only had enough time to shower, eat a quick breakfast, and leave for the library.

But anyone could have broken in, Nike fluttered. *Seen your research.*

"No one would dare, not while you're here." Agitation seared my stomach, blistering it to charcoal. He was right; I should have been more circumspect.

It was careless.

"I said I'd do it now. And everything was locked up in my closet. It was safe."

He followed me into the kitchen like a magnet, my satellite. I filled his dish on the worn linoleum floor with milk and checked his food levels.

You seem disturbed.

"Mrs. Gerhardt is trying to set me up with Trina. She thinks I need to make friends. I'm trying out Dad's trick, though—the whole thing about asking lots of questions and smiling for no reason. A rule of two questions minimum seems like a good idea, right? Trina might take it the wrong way, of course, like I really want to be friends. I'll have to observe reaction to the questions. I may need to revise the number up or down."

You're a great mind doing important work. Trina would only interfere.

"It's not like I'm going to suddenly start hanging out with her. It was just irritating. She kept looking at me, like she was picturing what my intestines looked like," I said. The light streamed into the kitchen from the small window above the sink. I held my hand into the beam, swirling my fingers and casting shadows. Dust motes eddied on the breeze like insects fighting to the death. "And Mrs. Gerhardt kept going on and on about my dad. And then Mom."

Nike glanced up from his milk, squinting through topaz marble eyes. A shudder traversed his lanky body.

I left him there, abandoning him for the quiet sanctity of my bedroom. The closet door was padlocked, the key hidden on my dresser, under the urn that no longer held my father's ashes.

It took only a few moments to access the closet. The sick turbulence in my chest lifted, and a true smile crawled across my face. It was my proximity to the work itself. Somehow it always made everything less stressful.

Meehan's file (royal blue in color, as were all the files for male astronauts. The female astronauts got blood red files) lay in the wire in-box on top of the filing cabinet wedged right inside the closet door. On the wall above the storage, I'd hung a to-do board. The interior of my closet was painted bright white, the landscape so clean that I could conduct autopsies if need be.

I drew a line through Meehan's name with the dry-erase marker. He was the fifth astronaut to pass muster for this mission, which left just one. Of the other four I'd already approved, three were astronauts who'd flown before. It hadn't taken much time to investigate the other, a woman with a strict schedule and the most elegant sleep I'd ever seen.

It was hard to explain Colonel Janet Markowitz. She was tall and willowy, yes, but even when she slept there was a grace about her. Every breath seemed choreographed to the subtle shiver of her eyes beneath her lids during REM cycles. I found myself waxing poetic while writing her final observation report, as though attempting to force the artistry I saw in her body through the nib of my pen. Even her house exuded a calm confidence.

The final astronaut to study was really a cosmonaut. The Russian space program had lent two of their people to NASA for upcoming missions: Zory Korchagin and Yuriy Amanov. I had files on them both, things I'd gleaned from various sources, but NASA hadn't released official biographies yet. No photos, either, and my research had come up fruitless on that. Still, it wouldn't take much effort to procure address information through the lab and begin my investigation of Korchagin. Amanov could wait—he wasn't scheduled to fly for another six months.

I fanned out the photographs from the file before connecting my camera to the laptop and printing the pictures I'd taken that morning. Nike slinked into the room and settled on the desk amid a cloud of long, shedding fur and twitched his pink nose.

Nicely done, he blinked out.

"The new camera lens really helps with the low light conditions, don't you think?" I asked.

Yes, and you were very thorough. Do you think there's any significance to his choice of vitamins?

"I seriously doubt it," I said. "Zinc is pretty common, particularly if he's trying to ward off colds before the launch."

Zinc deficiency can mean a few things. Impotence. Hair loss.

"Does it matter? It's not any of my business whether Meehan can get an erection, and he has a full head of hair. Neither one of those things impact whether he can sleep during liftoff."

Nike's baleful glare made me turn away to again study the photographs I'd taken. There was nothing new in any of them—I hadn't glossed over anything. After my printer stopped buzzing, I shuffled through the new photos as well.

I'd snapped close-ups of the photographs Meehan kept on a table in his living room. The first was of him with an older couple—his parents. Another included Meehan with his arm around the same woman from his bedside table frame, the two of them grinning into the camera. On second glance she didn't look so much like me: she had the well-rested look of someone who sleeps ten hours each night.

A third picture had Meehan in a uniform of some sort with a cluster of little boys around him. His Boy Scout troop, perhaps. The background check I'd done indicated that he'd acted as a troop leader in his hometown.

"He'll be fine if anything happens during liftoff," I announced while pausing to scratch Nike behind the ears. Thin lines of darker yellow fur marred the top of his head and ran down his back. "A little messy, maybe, but he's a sleeper."

What will you ask your janitor friend to teach you this week?

"I'd like to know more about some of his cleaning chemicals. Maybe I can use them in an assassination plan. So far I've been unable to find out much about this Korchagin's medical history, so the plan will have to be something more creative."

You do not need his expertise on the chemicals. You should break things off with him before your dalliances become too personal. What if he's talking about you to someone?

I stacked the photographs and numbered each one in the back upper right corner, ignoring Nike. He was an elderly cat—he'd been my constant companion since he was a kitten. He'd grown a bit whiter through the face over the years, but his coat was still silky and bright, almost the color of maize. He could be cranky, especially when he thought something was interfering with my observations.

After flipping through the pictures again, I was positive there was nothing in any of them to change my mind about my final observation report. Meehan would sleep during liftoff. And Nike worried for no good reason.

A drift of bees vibrated behind my eyes, and my lids drooped. All at once the air inside my head expanded and contracted in waves. I'd slept for an hour, maybe three, four nights ago. I'd be good with another forty-five minute nap. But first I had to complete the investigation.

I sandwiched the photos into a white envelope and sealed it shut. Those went in the back of the folder. In front were the observation reports in chronological order, with the final report clipped to the inside of the file. I clicked out a label (Robert Jeffrey Meehan, Ph.D.: approved) and slid it into the clear plastic sleeve to attach to the top of the Pendaflex folder.

The file drawer slid open. My finger dragged along the files. I closed my eyes—the *thwap thwap* as each one popped off my short nail quieted the volcano in my stomach. All told, my files held the sleep history and surveillance notes on three dozen people or so who might one day die on the space shuttle if I didn't carry out my observations to the universe's satisfaction.

Most slept as if they'd bitten into a cursed apple like in a fairy tale. The rest were still acceptable, lacking any discernible sleep disorders.

Good, sound sleepers.

Chapter Three

UGLY LIARS

BLUE SPARKLES SHIMMERED, MASHED INTO THE CREASES OF MY mother's closed eyelids, more saturated than the color on the rest of her skin. A light snore dribbled out of her. Her curly hair tangled across her face and dipped into the sockets of her deep-set eyes.

The thick smacking of Mom's lips muted against the nubby couch. I cocked my head to the side. She rooted deeper under the blankets, the tip of her mauve turtleneck poking over the edge.

I hoped the shuttle astronauts slept better than Mom. Panic shot through my belly button, sizzling my spine and docking at the back of my neck. It made me feel like throwing up, but I'd gotten yelled at last time. I'd promised to make it to the toilet if it happened again.

Taking a deep breath, just the way Dad told me, the vinegar feeling in my throat backed down. I held my body stiff, imagining I was strapped into the shuttle, measuring the air in and out. Four-three-two-one-in, four-three-two-one-out. Just like sleep. It didn't match to Mom's snuffling, though.

She coughed, writhing as though I'd coated her in itching powder. I waited for the coughing to subside, then matched her breath for breath, grasping the hem of my shirt the way my mother clutched at the edge of the blanket.

The coarse fabric of an imagined astronaut suit rubbed across my shins. I didn't know if they wore their helmets during takeoff, but the air would probably be hot with the gases fueling their ascent. Maybe it would smell like whatever the astronauts ate for breakfast.

A yawn, and then her lashes flapped against her cheek before drifting up to hide the eyeshadow. Her olive green eyes widened. My eyes went to the chip in her front tooth.

"What are you doing?"

"Nothing." The pattern from the couch cushion crimped the skin of her neck.

"How long you been standing there?"

"Not long."

She pushed off the arm of the couch, levering her thin torso to slump upright. She repositioned the glittery barrette in her hair. "You're pulling a face like a lying liar. Jesus hates ugly liars."

She didn't need to know a thing. Everything I did was silly or stupid or trifling, so saying anything was useless.

"Are you just going to stand there and eyeball me?" Mom hissed. "Go get me a beer."

When I returned she sat with her head in her hands, chanting over and over again: "Burn burn burn burn burn burn burn burn."

"Mom?" I said. She glanced up, and I shoved the beer at her.

"I killed them all," she hissed, a thin-lipped smile on her mouth. "I burned those astronauts up."

I turned and fled to the safety of the kitchen.

Chapter Four

TUMULTUOUS SEAS

THE REMAINDER OF THE WEEKEND PASSED IN A PLEASANT, SLOW motion loop. By Monday morning a sense of dread over having to deal with Trina competed with the excitement of getting back to the sleep lab.

"Miles to go before I sleep," I muttered. Faint light burned through the window in the front door, casting shards across the floor.

Nike pawed my calf while I locked my briefcase, then nudged me with his nose.

"I should be home at the normal time," I said, "but if I can get Korchagin's home address today, I'll do some reconnaissance later."

With one final head butt, Nike stalked away, bottle-brush tail swishing.

Outside the house, the thick, wet air descended, squelching in my shoes during the walk to the car. The sky above was clouded over and gray. It was a relief to slide over the well-worn seats, shut the door behind me, and set the air conditioner to high. My mind emptied on the drive, only the pleasant hum of the highway beneath the tires to break the silence.

My first client of the week already waited at the reception area inside the four-story, glass-faced building that housed the Forty Winks Sleep Lab. Mrs. Hernandez, her dark hair tied back in a loose ponytail and eyes bright, looked more well-rested than the last time she'd been in the office several weeks prior.

I caught a glimpse of The Chin pushing a bucket and mop into a closet at the end of the hall. He hadn't seen me.

"How's your treatment going?" I asked Mrs. Hernandez in the elevator. I forced myself to breathe, to think calm thoughts. Dad had always coaxed me to work through the panic that caught me around people I didn't know very well. She stood too close.

"Fine. I cut out all caffeine, and I do twenty minutes of yoga before going to bed," she said.

I glanced at her chart, edged away, and gave her my biggest smile. "Dr. DeFinnis prescribed weekly therapy for your depression as well. Has that helped?"

She side-eyed me. "I think so. I haven't been waking up nearly as much during the night."

"But you *have* been waking? How often?"

"Not a lot. And not every night."

The elevator doors peeled back, revealing a shiny white corridor lined with doors. She followed at an acceptable distance, and I led her to the last room on the right. It smelled of bleach, reminding me again of The Chin. His presence was everywhere in the building, like a ghost. At every corner, he was there, staring at me with his small dark eyes.

"Are you still taking anti-depressants?" I asked. Turn on the charm, be folksy, that was Dad's way. "They sure can make a difference, can't they?"

"Yeah. Dr. DeFinnis spoke to my shrink, I guess, and suggested he put me on something else."

"You were taking Celexa."

"Right. Now I'm on Normontil," she said.

"That can still cause insomnia. A real bugger to get to sleep," I said, adding a wink. "It's too early to really tell, though. What we're concerned with now is measuring your alertness during the day. As we discussed, we'll run a Maintenance of Wakefulness Test today. But only if you had a good night's sleep last night."

Her answering smile was relaxed. Maybe I'd keep the wink, but only after I studied it in a mirror. Sometimes that kind of thing could look like a facial tic or the beginnings of a mild epileptic seizure. "I did," she said. "Didn't wake up once that I can remember."

Every case was critical. While curing the masses of their sleep disorders didn't play into mission goals, success still weighed on me.

Each month I measured the number of labs I'd run, the number of patients now able to sleep or sleep better. The tally made the difference—a negative number meant I'd have to work harder, and a positive number correlated to a personal reward. An extra hour or two at the library, additional time to read for pleasure.

I pointed toward the chair next to the bed, and she perched on the edge of it. "Here's how this is going to go: we do four sleep trials of up to forty minutes each with two hours between each one. You don't have to stay here during the breaks, but you can't sleep. Maybe go shopping. Do you like shopping? The idea for these in-office tests is to lie in bed but stay awake for as long as you can." Several follow-up sentences ran through my head, none of them appropriate for the office.

Mrs. Hernandez slipped off her shoes and climbed past the safety railing, settling in the middle of the mattress. It was hard work trying to come up with good conversation for conscious people. The sleeping and the dead were less fraught with danger and opinions.

The door to the observation room opened, and Trina stepped through. She'd pulled her hair up into a bouncy ponytail that swung back and forth. "Good morning, Lela! Hey there, Mrs. Hernandez! How's everything going?"

A well of irritation scratched inside of my throat. Working with Trina was always a negative on the points scale. "What are you doing here?" I asked, barely able to control the tone of my voice, and flashed a smile.

"I'm your co-pilot on the study," she said. She was like an over-excited puppy—I half expected her to sit at my feet and wiggle her nonexistent tail, begging for a treat while secretly thinking about sinking its teeth into my jugular.

"Oh, that's great," I said, faking enthusiasm. "Why don't you take Mrs. Hernandez's belongings to the locker?"

She grinned and looped the purse handles over her arm. "You bet! Don't worry about a thing," she said to Mrs. Hernandez. "Lela's the best we have." Under her white lab coat, she wore a mauve sweater. I couldn't take my eyes off it.

After Trina left the room, Mrs. Hernandez asked, "Was I supposed to be worried? Is this going to hurt?"

I suppressed the urge to roll my eyes.

"Not at all. This is just like your polysomnogram, except you stay awake instead of sleep. We'll use the same types of sensors," I said and held them up, "on your head, face, and chin to monitor when you're awake and when you're asleep. Think of it as a really weird facial."

I attached the sensors and checked their connection to the computer by her bedside. Yes, a facial that left circular indentations in her skin. It might be mistaken for an enormous ringworm infection. I smiled, hoping the gesture was comforting.

"Now, I need to get you propped up a little more," I said. "Slide up a little onto the support pillow. Yes, just like that. You see the camera at the foot of your bed. Stay still, look directly ahead of you, and try to stay awake."

"What happens if I don't?" she asked. Her left eye twitched.

A sign of someone's death.

"We post it to the Internet with commentary about how much you drool. Kidding!" I said. Even the giggle sounded rehearsed. I loathed myself at that moment. "We allow you to sleep for ninety seconds to see if you wake on your own. If you continue to sleep, we get you up and conclude the first trial. Sleep is really important, you know? During that time your brain is at work, helping to prepare you for learning and memorization. It boosts your ability to be creative. Wouldn't want to be a zombie now, would you?" She was starting to give me that look, the one that told me I was rambling. "Anyway, don't use extreme measures to stay awake, all right? No slapping or pinching yourself, and I'll refrain from slapping or pinching you, too. Just look ahead, try to stay awake, and smile."

"Ready for patient calibration?" Trina's chirping voice asked over the intercom.

"Yes, please," I said.

"Okay," she said. "Let's lower the lights a bit."

The room went dim, and I flicked on the light behind the bed. Trina ran the woman through the commands—*clench your teeth, move your eyes, turn your head*. And when she gave the approval, I patted Mrs. Hernandez's shoulder (the lab manual suggested this maneuver to calm the patient, although I hated touching the clients) and joined Trina in the observation room.

Even the ski slope of her nose reminded me of my mother.

"How was your weekend?" she asked.

"Fine." I pretended to flip through Mrs. Hernandez's chart in the hopes that maybe we'd get through the first trial without Trina's incessant chatter, even as I encouraged it. "How about you? What did you do?"

"Mine was great! My boyfriend—I think I told you he lives in Austin—he surprised me after my shift at the library by showing up. It was so great. We went to Traders Village flea market and out to dinner. Do you have a boyfriend? You've never mentioned anyone."

I shook my head and checked the occipital electroencephalogram reading. A high-pitched voice chanted in my head: *shut up, shut up, shutup, SHUT UP.* My fists clenched.

Breathe. Just like Dad taught me. Keep it at bay. Push for control. Four-three-two-one-in, four-three-two-one-out.

"Hey, Mrs. Gerhardt said you still live in your childhood home. I didn't know that. Did you buy your parents' old house?"

"My father left it to me in his will."

Mrs. Gerhardt had been discussing me with Trina? My lips drew back involuntarily with the urge to growl.

"Oh, that's so nice! Did you ever live anywhere else?" she asked.

The sensors registered some eye movement. I glanced into the camera display—Mrs. Hernandez was still awake, so that was good news. Even with Trina's constant verbal assault, my points for the month were in the positive. Trina was probably collecting information, looking for a way to use it against me.

My mother's cackling laugh ricocheted around the inside of my skull.

"No," I said. "I've always lived there. I've always lived in that house." In that bedroom. With the same furniture, the same closet. "What about you?"

Trina continued to babble throughout the entire forty minutes, and with each word her voice sounded more and more like my mother's; it morphed from childlike to almost a high-pitched shriek. I could feel my blood pressure escalating, my heart muscle fighting to contain the tension, my lips trembling with the effort of smiling.

The clock ticked down the minutes, the seconds. Mrs. Hernandez hung on. I envied her the silent, dark room. Almost like being buried, an avalanche of dirt separating her from any stimuli. Away from the chalkboard-on-nails of Trina's words and questions and thoughts.

For just a second, I fantasized about slipping my hands around

Trina's neck, feeling the cords of muscle strain against my palm while I bore down. She'd gasp and claw at my fingers, and I'd squeeze, squeeze, squeeze.

Breathe. Four-three-two-one-in, four-three-two-one-out.

The timer went off, jolting me out of my daydream.

"I'll get her," I said. I jumped out of my chair before Trina could answer, but more of her words floated after me through the door: "See you back at your desk."

The threat was enough to prompt a raft of goose flesh over my arms.

✳✳✳

I INHALED A BLAST OF FIRE, THICK IN MY THROAT AS THOUGH I'D digested a ball of lava. The humidity had gotten no better since that morning. Sweat plastered my shirt to the small of my back.

Mrs. Hernandez would return to the office at two, so I had time to take a lunch away the building. Trina had all but invited herself along, but I'd waited until she excused herself to the restroom and escaped.

The dark walls closed in when the door hurled me into the Russian tearoom. The owner's short, limp hair bobbed over the divider to the dining room, and I waited, inhaling chilly air into my lungs.

The owner released a gap-toothed grin and showed me to my favorite table. My hands smoothed over the rough wood when I sat, skipping over the crevices in the surface.

Mom's voice chattered in my head. "Step on a crack, break your mother's back!" she'd sing as we walked down the sidewalk when I was very young. *Before.* "Never walk under a ladder!"

She'd been a creature of habit, never leaving the house without makeup, without wearing something mauve. So much of her wardrobe was anchored in it. Mauve shoes. Mauve dresses. I used to think if I cut her open, her blood would be the same color.

I spoke almost directly into the sagging breasts of the only waitress—Magda—to order my usual: smoked salmon, cucumbers, and cream cheese on black bread. She waddled toward the kitchen to set the ancient cook into motion.

Magda's hair reminded me of the color of the moon. I always half-wondered if space dust would swirl out if I patted the heavy bun at the base of her neck.

I dug around in my bag and retrieved a book.

"A little Fyodor Dostoyevsky will cure what ails you!" Mrs. Gerhardt had crowed when I'd checked it out at the library over the weekend. Always with a word about what I read, always a comment about…something. She'd been thrilled when I went through a Victorian phase in high school, always pushing the Brontë sisters at me. It had been impossible to tell her how much I hated them. The silliness of Jane Eyre and her tenderness for Mr. Rochester. All her resources, and she did nothing of worth with the money. A life wasted. I couldn't tell Mrs. Gerhardt a lot of things, though, like the fact that Meehan had been reading *Crime and Punishment*. There was an irony to it.

I could not imagine that Mrs. Gerhardt would agree with the concept of killing or breaking and entering for a higher purpose. The good of a horrible action outweighing the bad.

I was not Raskolnikov. If I ever had to kill someone, it would be for the good of mankind, not due to my own petty wants and desires. Every law I broke benefited mankind.

A shadow obscured the light from the dusty ceiling lamps. I glanced up, my polite smile ready for Magda, but a stranger smiled down at me.

"Are you here alone?" he asked. "If you are, may I sit with you? I hate to eat by myself." His words held the rich vowels and guttural syllables of a heavy Eastern European accent, similar to the owner and wait staff but different in a way I couldn't quite name.

My heart shook the cage of my ribs, but I jabbed my finger toward the empty seat across from me. What had I done?

"I am Zory," he said, his back erect in the unnaturally perfect posture of an electric chair.

"Lela," I muttered. Something nagged at the back of my mind, like a word balancing precariously on my tongue.

"Thank you, Lela."

I nodded again. The broadness of his chest was intimidating in that way that only strong men can be, bringing to mind the warnings Dad had always drilled into my head as a teenager.

Don't talk to strangers.
Know your surroundings.
Be careful.

The man cleared his throat. My head jerked up, eyes now focused on his angular chin. Light brown goatee and mustache, neatly trimmed.

I memorized the shape of his razor-edged nose and elfin ears. The gray eyes—just the color of the barrel of a gun—peered beneath bushy eyebrows. Maybe he knew about my mission and planned to kill me. I'd always thought there had to be someone working against me.

Newton's third law. *For every action there is an equal and opposite reaction.* And my work was too important not to attract the attention of an opposite reaction.

Maybe Trina, maybe someone else.

"I am new to Houston." The words hung there, almost without movement from his thin lips. "Have you lived here long?"

Getting to know me before luring me to his car to chop me into tiny bits. That seemed rather cruel.

"All my life," I said, gauging the distance and time it would take to bolt out the door.

The teacup in Magda's hand clattered as she set it on the table. I whipped my head toward her in time to see her shrewd eyes go soft while examining the man, slackening the usual tight curve of her mouth.

She spoke a few words to him in Russian; the line of her lips hinted at flirtation. In English, Magda informed me, "It is real honor to have Mr. Korchagin choose teahouse for lunch. He is national hero in Russia."

A national hero? *Korcha*—

My mouth dropped open. Zory Korchagin. The man sitting at my table was Zory Korchagin. Russian cosmonaut. Oh God, training for the *Empire* mission.

He said, "She exaggerates."

Magda turned, and this time, instead of her slow lumber, her generous hips tipped side to side, the rocking of a great ship in tumultuous seas, on her way back to the kitchen.

"I am…" He ducked his head and fiddled with the yellow packets of sugar substitute on the table. "I am here to work with NASA."

"Well, Mr. Korchagin, it was certainly nice to meet you." My voice sounded high, unnatural, but my cheerful smile slid into place, slick as grease. "I should go, leave you to your lunch." My chair screeched across the floor.

He stopped me with his burning fingers. Had he touched me like this five minutes ago, I might have screamed and flung my tea in his face. Now all I could do was freeze.

Being personally acquainted with a subject on this level would ruin my objectivity. It might upset the delicate balance I needed to successfully complete an observation. How could I sit outside his house to investigate his comings and goings if he'd recognize me? Any contact at all with me in his waking hours might have a detrimental effect on him and his mission, and I couldn't risk the fall-out.

But what if leaving has a more heinous effect? a child-like voice hissed.

I sat, jerking my arm away in the gentlest possible way.

"Please, call me Zory," he said.

My hands clutched the edge of the table, and I perched on the seat, staring until finally I said, "Okay, *Zory*." The words ripped at my throat, but my voice remained friendly.

"Lela. Such a pretty name."

"Thank you." Breath in my lungs, moving in and out.

"A family name?"

Why did he even care? Perhaps it was just small talk. Maybe he was lonely or bored. "No. Just a name. What about yours?" I forced myself to ask, still grinning like an idiot. "Zory's an interesting name."

"It is my grandfather's name. If you see my passport, it is Zory Pavlovich Korchagin."

"Oh?" I knew that; it was a piece of information I'd already obtained.

"Yes, the patronymic, you understand. My father's name is Pavel. I know this is different than how you Americans do." His brows crooked. "Do you work close by?"

"Yes," I said. "Just down the block."

"Oh? What is your job? I mean, what do you do for a living?" He smiled apologetically, although I wasn't sure why he might be sorry. I was probably regretful enough for both of us.

"I'm a sleep-lab tech."

His shaggy eyebrows rose. "What is that?"

"I watch people sleep," I said. Magda plunked down another teacup and smiled, crooked teeth like tilted tombstones. "For scientific purposes," I added. "Mostly if they're having problems."

"Trouble sleeping?"

I sipped the tea, incinerating my tongue and wishing my entire body would burst into flames. "Kind of. People who sleepwalk or have bad nightmares. Sometimes it's people who have breathing problems like sleep apnea. We watch them, take notes."

He reached for the container of jam on the table and stirred a teaspoon into his tea. Odd. "Do you like your job?"

"Yes. Do you like yours? A satisfying work life is important to overall happiness, you know?"

Breathe. Four-three-two-one-in, four-three-two-one-out.

"Mmm hmm. I get to see space. What else is there?"

Magda returned with my sandwich. The plate in front of Zory held a plain boiled chicken breast with a side of turnips. The menu contained no such dish. I suspected Magda would have insisted the cook make him anything he requested.

He attacked the chicken like a man who hadn't eaten in weeks. "This is good," he announced the second he swallowed. Magda backed away, grinning.

The way he ate was fascinating. Methodical. A sawing of his knife, a stab of his fork, a piece of chicken or turnip popped into his mouth, alternating each with every bite. After every third bit of food, a sip of tea. Would he sleep in the same way: aggressively? Purposefully?

I didn't touch my sandwich. I couldn't. Every attempt at asking a question froze on my lips, so I continued to beam at him. Maybe he'd think I was mentally unbalanced and run away.

"You are reading a Russian." He nodded toward my book. "*The Idiot* has always been one of my favorites from Dostoyevsky."

"Oh?"

"Yes. How far into the novel have you got?"

"Not far. I just started reading it the other day." *Breathe. Breathe.* I willed my heart to beat slower, pulse quieter. "I must say I don't understand Prince Myshkin's assertion that the worst thing about a death sentence is the prisoner's loss of hope. Does he not understand that sometimes people must die for the good of society?"

"An interesting thought," Zory said. "I look forward to discussing it when you have finished. I have heard it said it relates to his innocence… perhaps his madness." When I didn't answer, his mouth loosened and widened, generous and full. "We Russians have a very different relationship to madness—idiocy, as Dostoyevsky says—than you Americans." His eyes lightened, and his lips jerked as though fighting a smile.

"Oh?"

"Depression is not looked upon so suspiciously in my country. You will not find so many Russians," he puffed up his chest at this, "calling themselves by your technical names for diseases of the mind, but there is no shame in it. Here, you have embarrassment, you take drugs to hide it." He paused. "I do not wish to…well, you will tell me of how you feel about it when you are finished reading."

I counted the pits denting the table, hoping to distract myself from the intensity of his stare.

"Do you like Houston?" He broke the heavy silence, his accent a warm caress against the cold air.

"Yes." My face was beginning to ache. "It's a great place—great for families and lots of room to stretch out."

A small smile played at his lips. "What fun is there here?"

"Oh. Uh, well…" I had no idea what people did for fun in Houston. "Food. I mean, there are good restaurants. My coworkers sometimes go out for drinks."

"Do you? Go out for drinks, I mean?"

"No, not really." My glasses slipped down my nose by a millimeter, and I shoved them back into place. "I have obligations at home." I allowed for a measured but chummy chuckle and checked my body language: turned toward him but not leaning in. Friendly but not too friendly. He would forget me the second I walked out the door.

"Do you…are you married?"

"No."

"No boyfriend?"

I shook my head and glanced at my watch.

"I have no wife or girlfriend either." For a moment his lips drooped, but the expression in his eyes solidified into a determined stare.

"Oh. I'm sorry to hear that." For just a moment, I thought of babbling on, imitating Trina as a way to eat up the dead air between us. She was just the kind of girl a guy like Zory would be interested in.

He stared, twisting his lips into a half smile. "Would you like to go to dinner tonight? With me?"

I'd seen a movie once where an alien chewed its way through a man's ribcage before bursting forth. In that moment, the gnawing dismay gummed at a similar breach near my solar plexus as my breath caught in damaged lungs.

"No. I'm sorry, but I have a study. So nice to meet you, though. Take care now."

I grasped at my book and bag, tossing money on the table, before steamrolling through the restaurant and plunging back into the humidity.

Chapter Five

TORNADO-PROOF

T RINA WAS TYPING AWAY AT HER KEYBOARD WHEN I RETURNED. HER ponytail moved in time with her fingers. I'd sprinted back to the office, every few feet glancing back to make sure Korchagin hadn't followed me. Telling him I worked in the area had been stupid.

I sat at my desk, my vision narrowing to a funhouse tunnel.

Breathe. Four-three-two-one-in, four-three-two-one-out.

Trina's desk phone trilled. "Forty Winks Sleep Lab. Trina speaking," she said.

I gritted my teeth and forced myself to block out her voice. Instead I looked over the work schedule for the week.

Trina hung up the phone and called over the cubicle wall, "Lela, you'll never believe it! That was Beth from the front desk. The office is closing in ten minutes. We've been ordered to go."

"What? Why?" I asked. Howls still echoed inside my skull, squealing around the periphery and twisting around my brain stem.

"Houston's under a tornado watch, but apparently the threat's pretty high. Nearly all the study subjects have canceled for tonight. Huge wall of storms coming through. Beth said she already called Mrs. Hernandez to reschedule. Mr. Larsdale decided to close shop to be on the safe side."

"He did?"

"I'm as surprised as anyone else. Want to go get ice cream? There's a place that just opened up a few blocks over, and I hear it's really great!"

She was like a child. An ignorant, willful child. I imagined her stepping outside the doors of the office and getting sucked up into a vortex, landing blocks away in the boughs of a tree. Every bone in her body would be cracked and broken, hair ripped from her head.

"Lela? Ice cream?" she asked. Maybe she was hoping I'd be the one to die.

"No, I'm sorry. You should go home." I stared through my computer screen, through the wall, wishing I could stab her with my eyes. "Don't want you to get caught in the storm," I added, trying to sound sincere. "That's just asking for trouble. Lots of debris with those things. I saw something on the news the other day about someone getting shot clean through by a two by four."

She sighed, and I could almost smell the attack of her rotting breath. "What are the odds that a tornado would actually roll through downtown Houston?" Her head popped up above the partition. "I guess the library will be closed, too, right?"

I smiled—probably too wide—and pushed my glasses up my nose. "You'll have to call Mrs. Gerhardt to check. I'm not scheduled today."

She tittered and whined while I all but ignored her, muttering at pauses between her words. I had to get Korchagin's address before leaving, even though a war brewed in my stomach over whether I should begin my investigation or give him a week to forget my existence. There was no reason for him to remember me. I hadn't done a single thing to stand out.

His account popped up, and I scribbled the information in my notepad. *Clear Lake.* Not too far from Johnson Space Center.

Trina now stared at me from the corridor. "Aren't you coming? I'll walk you out."

"Sure," I said, although the last thing I wanted was to spend time alone together. It would be just my luck if she got the bright idea to push me down the shaft or strangle me; if we were the last to leave, no one would find my body until the next day. *Smile. Nod.* "On my way. Last person out gets a knife in the gut."

She grinned and shook her head. "Better hurry then."

But we weren't by ourselves in the elevator, which should have been a relief but wasn't. The Chin lurked in the corner.

"Hey, Max!" Trina said. "What're you still doing here?"

"Gotta make my rounds, collect the trash," he said. The voice didn't match the rest of him. It reminded me of water over stones, fluid and clear. Beautiful, really. Otherwise, he was short and hunch-backed, and his paunchy stomach rounded out his blue jumpsuit. His thinning hair waved around his head. Tiny piggy eyes set deep in his face, making his chin, which jutted out to give him a noticeable underbite, all the more prominent. "Tornado or no, it don't matter." He paused for two seconds and said, "Heya, Lela."

I nodded at him but didn't speak. The elevator stopped at the lobby level, and Trina pranced out.

That voice, quieter than it'd been even a moment ago, chased me out of the enclosure. "Stay safe, pretty girl."

My lips twisted into a sneer. I kept walking.

The sky had turned an expectant yellow-gray, something I hadn't noticed in my haste to return to the office. Everyone outside moved like swimmers slogging through gelatin. My eyes darted across the lot in case Korchagin lurked.

Trina turned toward me, my mother's smile twisting on her face. "Have a great—"

"Oh, I forgot something inside," I said. "I'll see you tomorrow. You be careful now." Before she could answer, I scurried back into the building.

The Chin held the receptionist's trash can. I nodded to him. "I'll be in your office," I said.

I took the elevator to the second floor, pausing only long enough to ensure no one saw me before ducking into the janitor's closet. The smell of dampness and chemicals made me light-headed.

His heavy footsteps thumped in the hall before the doorknob turned, and then he was there, his thick, chubby fingers fumbling with the buttons on his jumpsuit. I had things to do, but my schedule demanded I keep my regular appointment with The Chin.

I was prepared, underwear clutched in my fist. It took only moments to ready him. He sank into me, and I closed my eyes. He grunted and shoved.

"What's the most toxic cleaning chemical you use?" I asked. His fingers bit into my back, rubbery lips on my neck.

"Don't worry none," he said. "I ain't got nothing on my fingers. Lela, you feel like—"

"The chemical," I prompted.

He groaned. "Ain't sure. Maybe the chlorine bleach. Ammonia, maybe. I got a drain cleaner'll take the paint off a car."

It was pleasant, the feeling. I concentrated on the sensation, the nerve endings. It was like being caught in a dream, even if it was The Chin. Dreams were a rarity for me since my sleep cycles were abbreviated. In anyone else, that would have caused catastrophic consequences, but not for me. I was clearer without the fantasies, without the confusion that came with them. In my childhood there had been nightmares so real it had been difficult to know if I'd been asleep or awake.

Sex was something hybrid, something between worlds.

I opened my eyes. "Those chemicals are potentially fatal, right?"

The Chin pulled back, face slack. The wispy brown strands of his hair wouldn't lie against his skull. His mouth tightened. "Sure enough. Mix the wrong ones together, drink it up. It'll kill ya, all right."

"Which ones?"

"All of 'em. You gotta handle them just so."

It was over just as fast as it started.

The Chin's chapped lips puckered, and his eyes pricked at my skin while I pulled away to jerk my skirt down, trying not to knock into the mops that lined the wall.

"Why don't me and you go out tomorrow? Do somethin' fun?" When I didn't answer, he said, "Come on, I'll take ya to the carnival. We'll have a good time."

"I'm sorry, but I have something else to do."

"What about the next night? It ain't goin' to be too humid."

"I really don't have time." Smile back in place, I said, "I volunteer, you know."

The Chin—I rarely thought of him as Max Fowler—chose silence this time, disposed of the spent condom hanging morosely off his penis, and pulled his boxer shorts up. He hiked his jump suit into place in jerky starts while I ignored the pleading in his eyes, slipping my own underwear up my legs. I scrabbled for shoes with my toes and bumped a bottle of bleach on the floor.

It was nothing special, that bleach. It was the same brand I could buy in the store. Perhaps he'd know if there were such a thing as industrial bleach.

The day I'd met him had been his first day on the job, only a few weeks after I'd started at the sleep lab. One day he dropped a cluster of bluebonnets on my desk, the white eyes of the flowers staring and the leaves beginning to wilt.

"They's illegal to pick in the state of Texas, you know," he'd informed me, chest filling out.

The Chin now wore the same expression as when he'd gifted me with the flowers, but I shifted a half step out of his reach.

His eyes went soft around the edges, but his jaw and underbite pointed the way to the door. I took that as my cue to escape. The dusty air of the supply closet drifted after me as I side-stepped into the hallway, striding back toward the elevator. I was out to the parking lot in seconds.

A car wasn't supposed to be the safest place during a tornado watch, but there was security in it anyway. Away from The Chin, away from Trina. I pulled the note with Korchagin's address from my bag and argued with myself for a solid twenty minutes over whether to head to his place or wait out the storms. In the end I set the GPS to his address and followed the voice onto the interstate, lining up the car a foot to the side of the center divider.

I'd hoped to get information from The Chin that might be useful. *How disappointing*, I thought. Maybe next week I'd be able to obtain something more interesting. For now, though, I had to concentrate. Put him out of my head and focus on Korchagin.

Tall buildings loomed along the edge of the road, rising up almost like soldiers guarding the shorter structures around them. It was possible sentries lurked in the windows, spying through binoculars, logging the passing cars and trucks. For what purpose, I couldn't know, but I felt their eyes on me. Maybe they were spying, monitoring my activity and gearing up to interfere with my mission.

My eyes were on the road, thinking about Dad, about Mrs. Gerhardt. About Nike waiting for me at home, meowing by the door. Wondering if Korchagin would be at his apartment when I arrived.

What had he been doing in town in the middle of the day anyway? Johnson Space Center lay twenty-five miles from downtown Houston. It wasn't exactly a quick jaunt. While Russian food probably wasn't plentiful near his work, I doubted the teahouse was his only option for lunch. Didn't he have training?

Maybe he'd had an appointment.

The sky darkened with each mile until it was the color of smoke underlaid with a sickly olive hue. The leaves on the trees in his neighborhood flapped in the wind. I flipped on the radio and tuned to the weather.

A staticky voice rustled out of the speaker. "The Houston area is under a tornado watch until seven this evening. Communities north and west of the city are already experiencing severe storms, which have left up to fifteen thousand without power. Ellington Airport reports an area of strong rotation."

That wasn't far from Clear Lake.

Korchagin's apartment building was one I'd never been to before. The stucco and terra cotta tile budded up out of a manicured lawn. I parked in the lot near the front door and glanced around.

It was a ghost town.

I shoved the car door, straining against the wind. Each step was a battle, but I reached the arched-over porch, hauling myself along the railing up the stairs.

The tall wooden door into the building shook in its frame. It opened after a brief struggle, and I tossed myself inside, expecting to run into a doorman or neighbor. At least I had an excuse—I could play the damsel in distress, pretend to be scared of the storms. So many of these new constructions had built-in shelters.

But there was no one.

Bright lights bounced off the walkway in a highly polished lobby. Blond woods and dark russet chairs dotted the area. Large green plants lingered in the corners, sprouting out of hefty clay pots. All the while, rushing winds squealed outside the floor-to-ceiling plate glass windows.

I closed my eyes and listened to the ripping and tearing, the weak roar. Even though my body was responding to the fear I knew I should feel, my mind was calm and flat.

My father's voice resonated in my head. "You take cover now, Lela. No arguments." Not long after Mom had gone, we'd been at the library on a stormy day, bad enough for Mrs. Gerhardt to order us into the shelter.

Mrs. Gerhardt and Dad had taken turns reading *Alice in Wonderland* to the kids by flashlight. Their voices trading the lines back and forth echoed in my memory, her reedy voice layering over his deeper baritone.

"No, I'll look first, and see whether it's marked 'poison' or not," Mrs. Gerhardt had whispered, and my father answered with, "if you drink from a bottle marked 'poison,' it is almost certain to disagree with you, sooner or later." He'd grinned at me even as the wind creaked through the foundation. His tall, scarecrow frame barely folded onto the milk crate on which he sat.

Later Mrs. Gerhardt had run me through the science behind tornadoes, and I'd asked a million questions about how to tornado-proof a house. Dad said our house wasn't built to withstand one, but we could weather it out in the bathtub if one ever rolled through our neighborhood. We didn't have stairs, but the library did—and all the books said a reinforced, interior stairwell was one of the safest places to ride out a tornado.

The stairwell in Korchagin's building wasn't as luxurious as the lobby. The concrete risers led up, all very utilitarian. Metal hand rails spiraled up the space. Still, it didn't need to be pretty as long as it was up to safety codes.

I paused at each landing up to the third floor, peering around the corner to make sure Korchagin didn't lurk above. Only once did I see another person—on the second floor, a woman almost fell through the door with a full laundry basket.

"Can't be too careful," she said when I seized her shoulder by reflex to help her stay upright. "I'm always so afraid of getting caught in an elevator during a twister."

I smiled and pretended like my skin wasn't crawling from her touch. She descended the stairs at a jog.

She was right about one thing: it paid to be meticulous. A voice in my head told me I should keep her in mind. Watch her to make sure she didn't know Korchagin. I'd have to come in and out of the building several times without notice. I'd have to find a spot outside with a good view of his apartment. If she recognized me...

The third floor featured a wide hall with soft white walls and wood floors. A beige and gray striped runner stretched the length of the hallway and turned right at the end, leading to what I assumed was either another set of stairs, more apartments, or perhaps the elevator bank. At the bend in the corridor, a small decorative table perched below a high, narrow window.

It was still early—just past three-thirty in the afternoon. If Korchagin's neighbors all had regular schedules (and I hoped they did), most were probably at work. Or perhaps they'd taken shelter somewhere.

I pressed my ear against Korchagin's door, and it was like holding my ear to a conch shell. Whooshing waves ebbed and flowed, pushing me out into deeper water. It was just intensified ambient noise, but the salty ocean air tingled in my nose.

The mechanical clunk of the elevator doors sounded in the distance, the tide hitting the shore.

I retreated to the stairs. It wasn't the cosmonaut who walked around the corner, though. It was a scrawny man in cowboy boots and jeans. He stopped at the door across from Korchagin's and let himself in.

The wind had picked up. A hint of it whisked through the concrete of the stairs. By the time I reached the bottom, faint sirens rang through the emergency door that led outside.

I rushed through the lobby, keeping my face tilted toward the ground. Rain coursed down the plate glass windows in sideways streams, and hail bounced off the sidewalk beyond. A blue sky glowed in the distance. It hung there like a watery mirage off the edge of an impressionist gray cloud shelf.

The second I stepped outside, the rain slammed me back against the door.

It opened, and a strong arm yanked me back. I yelped, panicked at a stranger invading my space, sure it was Korchagin.

But it wasn't. A short man dragged me to a door hidden behind one of the russet chairs.

"We have to seek shelter now," he said, voice clipped. "Tornado's heading right for us. Didn't you hear the sirens?"

"Hands off," I said. "Let me go!" I struggled against his grip, my teeth chattering together so hard I thought my jaw might break.

"Calm down, miss. It's coming, it's coming." The door shut behind us with a click that sounded like death. He was the one—the one who wanted to kill me. An associate of my mother's, maybe. He'd waited all these years, hunted me, watched me, and this was it.

My hands patted over the wall, looking for a weapon. Anything at all. There were only smooth planes.

"Knew I heard someone walking around out there," said another voice. A woman's voice.

"Liam, what's it look like?" asked someone else.

The man who hauled me in answered: "Not good. Hail, heavy rain. Didn't see the tornado, though." A radio crackled. "Liam to caravan two. Liam to caravan two. Status report, please. Over."

I still couldn't make out anything or anyone in the blackness.

Breathe. Four-three-two-one-in, four-three-two-one-out.

"Caravan two reporting. We have a funnel on the ground. I repeat: we have a funnel on the ground. Looks to be a weak one, moving south southeast, parallel to Almond Creek Drive. Over."

And then a familiar voice spoke. "That is good, is it not? This tornado moves away from us."

Oh God, it was Korchagin.

The air in the room went sour, tendrils of it scouring over my tongue. A roar in my head overtook the screaming in my ears. I could almost picture him: wedged into a corner, perfect posture fighting against the slump forced by short ceilings. He would probably run one of his big hands over his crew cut and try to see through the dark to assess the situation. He was a problem solver. All the astronauts were.

He couldn't be working against his own shuttle crew, but maybe he was being watched. The man who forced me into the room surveilled him in the hopes of finding me, and now the danger had come to a head.

"How long should we wait?" the woman asked.

"Sirens are still blaring," the man, Liam, said. "Another one could drop down right on us."

The woman's breath was loud, ragged. Korchagin comforted her in low whispers.

"I think I'll just go check it out," I said, huskying up my voice. Somehow a slurred French accent came out with it, making me sound like a foreign drunk with a pack-a-day smoking habit.

No one answered, including Zory. He obviously hadn't seen my face in the light; he would have said something. If I stayed there was no telling what might happen. This Liam guy would find a way to murder me, and then he might kill Korchagin, too. And if Liam didn't manage to take me out, Korchagin would see me eventually, and I'd be forced to kill him myself.

My hand touched down on the edge of the door. Liam couldn't see me in the dark unless he wore night vision goggles or had some kind of special powers. Neither was out of the realm of possibility. I felt along the seam—

Step on a crack, break your mother's back.

—stopping when my fingers touched the warm metal of the door handle.

He'd stop me if he could see.

The only sound in the room, though, was breathing and murmurs. Korchagin, again, reassuring the nervous woman.

I eased closer to the door and shook my hair into my face. It would have to be quick. Lightning fast. My heart hurtled, pounding so hard it must have been audible to everyone.

After, I would have to bolt like I was on fire. Drive away fast. My car was suited for anonymity, just like me, but it was speedy. If I lingered, waiting for the storm to clear, Korchagin would eventually emerge. And it wouldn't matter how forgettable my car was.

He would see me. Clear as the sky after the rain.

Panic choked and turned in my stomach, adrenaline sprinting through my veins.

He would see me.

He would remember me.

My hands shook. I threw open the door and ran.

Chapter Six

BRAVING THE MONSTERS

MY BEDROOM CLOSET SMELLED OF PAPER, SHOES, AND FABRIC, ALL coalescing into a single fragrance that rooted me to the floor. My dress was still damp, the hem clinging around my knees along with my hands. I rocked back and forth.

Breathe. Four-three-two-one-in, four-three-two-one-out.

The drive home from Korchagin's apartment building had been frantic. One of them—the people in the storm shelter—had probably followed me, so I'd zigged and zagged, angling off the interstate, taking a series of crazy turns, and then speeding back to the main road.

The sky cleared and left me unprotected by the cloud cover.

Nike had met me at the door, cold nose butting against my ankle. He tried to get me to talk, but I couldn't form words. I seized him and beelined for my bedroom, closing us both inside.

Finally, I moaned, "I made a mistake. Such a bad, bad mistake. They're on to me. I ruined everything."

The walls of the closet blistered and peeled.

He lifted his head and blinked up at me with his jewel-tone eyes. *Are you sure?*

"No, of course I'm not sure. I'm pretty sure Korchagin didn't see my face, but his neighbors—I think they've been talking. They've been plotting to stop me. Or maybe it was because I went to lunch with Korchagin that all this happened. It's the universe telling me I put the mission in jeopardy."

Just take care of your schedule for the next few days. See what happens. Exercise caution.

"I will. I mean, I have to. I can't do anything to put the shuttle at risk." I continued to lurch back and forth, waiting for the peace of being near my files to chase off the fear and the panic and the hollow pit that lived in my stomach.

You should take a shower. Perhaps a nap—when was the last time you slept?

"I've had more than enough. And I can't sleep when I've got so much to do—that's silly. But a shower sounds good."

Two steps into the hallway, and the doorbell shrilled, drilling into my ears like an ice pick. Then came a wood-shattering pounding against the front door.

I leaned against the wall, cringing with each blow. It was them— Nike'd been wrong. They'd found me.

"Who is it?"

"Lela? Lela, it's me. Open up!"

My eyes widened. What was Trina doing on my porch?

The metal of the doorknob in my hand smoothed unfamiliar, as though I had emerged from my closet into the wrong house. I threw open the door, cursing myself as I did; I should have retrieved the auto-injector first.

Her blonde hair snarled around her head, and she braced herself against the frame on one solid arm. A large duffel bag squatted at her feet.

"Oh, thank God you're here!" For a moment her pale face reflected pure malice, which disappeared into a relieved grin.

Suspicion ate at me, but I managed to catch myself. "Are you okay? What are you doing here?"

"A tornado touched down in my neighborhood."

"Oh?" I almost asked her if she lived near the airfield but bit back the words just in time. "Are you okay?" I repeated.

"It was unbelievable. The sirens went off, and, well, some guy on my floor was knocking on doors and getting us into the parking garage. So, we're sitting there and then there's this noise! Jesus, it sounded just like they say in movies: like a train was tearing through the place, like twisted metal and stuff. My apartment didn't get hit, but it must have torn open some pipes—water's everywhere! I had just enough time to run up and pack a bag before the police arrived, declared it a hazardous area, and kicked everyone out." She spit out the last word as though she fought for breath. Her dark eyes were like a knife. "Anyway, you don't live that far from me, so I thought maybe you'd let me stay with you until I figure something out." She picked up her bag and wedged past me. "You live alone in this big old house. You must have some room, right?"

I cast a glance toward the sky, hoping this was just a hallucination or dream. When I didn't wake, I spun around and followed Trina into the house. Perhaps this was God's punishment for my sins or carelessness, the retribution I'd been expecting.

Or maybe Trina had finally decided to act on her thoughts. She hated me—it was obvious.

Nike stood in the hallway. *Send her away.*

"Don't worry, though. I won't be a bother at all. Hi, kitty, what's your name?" She bent down to touch Nike's head. He froze for a moment before stalking away. "God, you're such a good friend, Lela," she said. "I'd be stuck without you—Greg and I just planned a trip to Cancun, and buying my plane ticket wiped me out. I don't have the cash for a hotel right now, and I know it'll take weeks to get the insurance company to cough up some money."

I finally managed to get out some words: "How did you...know where I..."

She had the audacity to laugh. "I've had your address in my book for years!"

"Oh." My guts knotted, but I managed the smile I'd been working on. "Well, doesn't that just beat all?"

"Anyway, thanks again for letting me stay. I promise to be out of your hair as quickly as possible, but this'll be great. We can get to know each other better. It'll be a blast!"

Her face made her look grateful and excited, but I saw her fists clench, like she thought of nothing but punching me. Voices in my head screamed, warning me, and I stepped backward.

"I—I don't have a guest room," I stammered. "The couch, maybe."

"Fantastic, Lela," Trina said. She raked her fingers through her frazzled hair, maybe trying to straighten it to her normal style. "That's definitely okay with me."

Dad's voice came to me, clear as day: *Being nice doesn't cost you a thing.*

I turned up the wattage and bleated, "Great!"

Nike's yowl from the next room froze me solid. I stood and stared while Trina made herself comfortable in my living room. Eventually I slunk away to my room, surfacing only when I was sure she was asleep. I only observed for a few minutes, long enough to see her eyes whip back and forth beneath her lids, the evidence of a dream. She whispered "mud puddle" once, reminding me of the dream interpretation book a patient had once given me. Dreaming of dirty water was supposed to be a warning about unscrupulous people. That kind of thing was pure bunk, but Trina was most definitely untrustworthy.

I returned to my room and shimmied a dresser in front of the door. Each hour brought a different scenario. Some other way she planned to make me dead by dawn. To break into my closet and destroy my work. To force me to confess my investigation of Korchagin.

Nike crouched on the dresser next to my father's urn, watching my trajectory across the room. My legs burned with the effort of staying upright. My back ached.

Lie down, Nike blinked.

"I can't," I hissed. "She's out there. What am I going to do?"

Why did you allow her in? I told you to get rid of her.

"I wanted to, but you don't know. Mrs. Gerhardt would be so disappointed."

How would she even know?

"Are you kidding me? You know Trina can't keep her mouth shut. Everyone will find out. And then they'll talk about me more."

Maybe this is an opportunity.

"An opportunity? To do what?"

The universe is telling you to keep your enemies close. You can study her. Find out her true motives. And if you know where she is, she cannot interfere with your study of this cosmonaut. I'll keep an eye on her so you can rest.

I nodded. "Yes, okay. But just for twenty minutes."

My body was light, hovering above the comforter. I was air. Just like the doll at the library, my eyes clicked closed when my head lolled on the pillow. *Slllliccck.*

The dreams descended.

The sky was so clear, shades of blue shifting and rippling: azure, cornflower, ultramarine, turquoise. The sizzle-roar of the propulsion engines on the shuttle and the fiery liftoff. The hollow feeling of my stomach turning sour, sour, and then the pop. The curling columns of smoke and the blackened skin. The screams, the screams.

I woke, gasping and tearing at the skin on my face.

No. They'd been asleep. It could never have happened like that.

The floor was reassuringly solid beneath my feet a few moments later. Nike opened one round eye to glare in my direction, then returned to his post.

Trina flitted around my kitchen just after sunrise. She banged around, and finally I had to see what she was doing. Her hair hung like a sheet to her shoulders, and her mouth stretched wide: too wide. I half expected it to split her cheeks in two and reveal her real face underneath.

"Good morning, Lela! That couch of yours—it's like sleeping on a cloud. What a great night."

"What are you doing in here?"

"Ooo, grouchy in the morning, huh? I'll remember you're not a morning person." Trina poked around in the refrigerator. "You don't have much in here. There's just bottled water and oranges and all these little containers."

"I'm particular about what I eat," I said. My smile was slow to bloom, but I turned toward her and chirped, "You are what you put into your body, you know!"

She'd poisoned my food.

Trina laughed. "It explains why you're so thin. You won't mind if I bring in some groceries, right? I won't take over your fridge or anything—but I've got to have toast and yogurt to the start the day. And coffee! You don't even have any coffee."

She'd been searching through my stuff. Bugs danced over my skin, little legs scampering and poking. I absently scratched at my elbow.

"Caffeine is dangerous," I said. All drugs were. Mom had taken pills—little red capsules she said were her vitamins. And then she'd flushed them down the toilet.

"Don't tell your father," she'd warned, that evil smile sneaking onto her face. Her hair had curled up extra wild around her cheeks, as though even her hair was in rebellion. "Three can keep a secret if two of them are dead," she'd cackled.

Trina's eyes narrowed before going big and round. "I'd just die if I didn't have a cup in the morning. Can't wake up without it. I didn't know you were such a health nut—you probably run or do yoga or something, too, right? You're always so serene. Nothing ever bothers you."

Right. Except for the lunatic assassin in my kitchen.

"I have to get to work." I couldn't leave her alone in the house. My fingers twitched toward the autoinjector, now in the pocket of my pants. "The early bird catches the worm," I said through my teeth.

She clapped her hands. The noise was like a gunshot. "We can carpool. How great will this be?"

The skin on my face pulled into a thin veneer, ready to crack. "Yes. Great. What a treat."

Nike waited in the hallway. *Go with it. I'll set traps while you're at work. Keep her close.*

I nodded and switched the autoinjector into my briefcase. "Will you be ready shortly? Don't want to have to beat someone up for a good parking spot."

"Four minutes," she squealed, bolting past me. "What's in here?" She stopped in front of my dad's bedroom door and pointed.

"I keep that closed off," I said, never looking away from her face. Her eyes shifted into slits. "Storage for my father's things."

She lingered for a second before disappearing into the bathroom.

My mother hadn't slept in the house for twenty-one years, but touches of her still existed in the faded mauve comforter on my dad's bed and a pair of her shoes in the corner, looking as though she'd just kicked them off ten minutes prior. The closets and drawers still held her clothes. My parents' wedding portrait still hung on the wall, Mom in a plain white gown with her ringlets piled on top of her head, and Dad tall and rawboned in an ill-fitting tuxedo. His hair had been dark and thick then, a far cry from the salt and pepper receding hairline he'd sported as he got older.

My mother's floral perfume lingered in the fabric of everything along with Dad's Old Spice, reminding me of climbing between the two of them when I was little. It hadn't happened a lot because Mom yelled, but one night it had been storming badly. The thunder woke me up, and the lightning made the shapes of goblins on my walls.

I'd counted between the boom of a thunder peal and the bright burst of lightning, but the pause never lengthened considerably. After fifteen minutes of counting and cringing and sniffling, I'd braved the monsters under my bed and sprinted to my parents' room. Mom had grunted and rolled over, but Dad had gathered me up, kissing my forehead.

He'd sung quietly, hot breath on my ear as I cowered. The rhythmic rise and fall of his chest lulled me, comforted me. I fell asleep there then, just as I was able to drop into a drowsy half sleep in their bed as an adult sometimes. I vaguely wondered about the length of my sleep latency there versus my own room, rare as my naps were.

Trina didn't even glance at the bedroom a few minutes later when she skittered down the hall.

"Ready?" she asked while smoothing the front of her crisp, white button-down shirt. "Do you want me to drive? I don't mind."

Would it be safer? She didn't dare steer the car into a retaining wall. And pulling into the parking lot at work with my dead body in the front seat would be sure to attract attention.

"Yes, of course. No problem," I said, beaming.

The drive to Forty Winks was excruciating, each moment filled with inane chatter about the weather. About her boyfriend. About how much she liked my house. How grateful she was. Behind her words lay the ever-present malice.

The Chin ambled across the lot just as Trina pulled into a parking space. She almost skipped out of the car and waved. "Hey, Max. Good morning!"

He stopped and waited for us to catch up. Trina arrived first, of course. Hazy sunshine gleamed down on her mauve skirt. It looked familiar.

She orchestrated the air with her hands, poking and chopping. The Chin's mouth lifted into a half smile while she rambled, his bottom teeth glinting in the light. His fleshy jowls wobbled, sweaty. The air already held the hint of lightning that would likely ignite the sky on my drive home later.

Snippets of her words floated back to me: "savior" and "such a doll" and "cute little bungalow."

"Lela's a good woman," The Chin said, small eyes soft and staring. "Real good."

Trina's strong fingers wrapped around my forearm. It took effort to resist jerking away.

"Morning, Lela." The syrup of his voice dripped over my name.

"Good morning," I said.

He stumbled into step next to us. The click of my flats and Trina's high heels echoed off the brick of the building. "How was your night?"

"Okay. And yours?"

"Momma was asking after you."

Trina squeezed my arm. "I didn't realize you two are so close. Wow!"

"Got some things in common, ain't it right?" he asked me. His cheeks reddened.

"I'm not sure what you mean," I said. No one could know about our meetings. It was private.

Trina's tinkling giggle drilled down my spine. "Always keeps things so close to her heart, this one does."

"You ain't kidding."

"She'd never tell a soul someone's secrets, would you?" She turned to grin at me with my mother's mouth. I froze.

"A good woman," he repeated.

He would talk more. He would tell Trina.

He had to be stopped.

If he drove, I'd have found a way to cut the brakes. But he took public transit. There might not be a need to be artful, though. He worked with chemicals. Nail guns. A little accident would barely be a blip on the radar at work. I'd read about the effects of soaking a body in acid. Messy but ultimately effective.

Don't be rash, Lela. Dad's voice was an ice pick. *Breathe.*

Four-three-two-one-in, four-three-two-one-out.

I nodded. Of course, Dad was right.

He'd almost always been right.

I'd been thinking about him more since Mrs. Gerhardt had reminded me of the anniversary. Being generous and smart made him well-loved, and not just by me. The number of people at his funeral should have been comforting. That's what people said anyway.

I'd hated everything about the experience, even with Mrs. Gerhardt's vaguely comforting presence in the back of the parlor. From the large pores pitting the funeral director's nose to the smell of death and form-aldehyde embedded in every surface of the viewing room, it all made everything worse. When I'd complained about the stench, some kid had sprayed lilac-scented air freshener.

I might have been tempted to strangle the boy with the aerosol and chalk it up to one of the stages of grief. Just for a few minutes.

Perhaps the Kübler-Ross model needed to be modified to account for the compulsion to kill those who annoy the mourning. It would be the sixth stage, right after anger.

I shook away the thought and forced myself into the elevator.

Trina had finally released my arm, but now she nudged me. "Max has a thing for you."

"What?"

"Oh, yeah. You see the way he looks at you? He's totally in love with you."

I stared at her reflection in the mirrored elevator doors. The dark blonde hair appeared burnished under the dim lights. "He's just friendly."

"Well, yeah, he's friendly all right. You two should go out. You're single, and I don't think he's ever had a girlfriend in his entire life." Her sharp chuckle was cruel. "A man like that would treat you right, at least."

"A man like that? What does that mean?"

"He's, you know, kind of homely, don't you think? Sweet as pie, but he's shy. I think he still lives with his mother, and he's got to be—what? In his forties?"

"Let's not talk about The...Max, okay?" I said. "That just doesn't seem right." I grinned wide, gritting teeth behind my lips.

Her hands clapped to her mouth and then fell to her sides. "Oh God, Lela, you're right. Listen to me talking about him like he's a dog. He's such a nice man, and I didn't mean anything by it. I'm so sorry for letting go like that. You must think I'm a horrible person."

My mother had worn a mauve skirt just like Trina's. I was sure of it.

"Not at all," I said through a clenched jaw and a fake smile. "We all have to work together, though, so it's not right to speculate. Let everyone's private life stay private."

"Absolutely." My mother's hair bounced around on Trina's bobbing head. When had her hair gotten so curly?

It wouldn't take much effort to cut off her oxygen supply. I'd studied nerve centers and pressure points. She was taller than me, maybe a little heavier, but I could probably incapacitate her. She'd slump down to the elevator floor, and it would give me enough time to—

No.

Not at work, and only if she tried to kill me.

It wasn't right, and that kind of thing wouldn't fly with management, I was pretty sure.

"Do you want to go to lunch together today?" Trina asked.

Thoughts of Korchagin petrified my muscles. Even when the elevator doors banged open, my gait was stilted and slow. I couldn't deviate from my daily ritual of lunch at the tearoom—not too much, anyway. There were conventions that needed to be observed to keep the universe appeased.

But I couldn't allow him to see me. Not again.

Not ever.

A thunderbolt cracked in my head. Smoke trails split behind my eyes, sending two plumes rocketing across a blue blue sky.

Chapter Seven

PLAY BY THE RULES

Each gap between the slabs of sidewalk on the Houston street stretched like a gaping maw, waiting to suck me up, hurtle me into a void. I wondered if it would be like sleep—terrifying and soothing at the same time. Maybe I could get more rest one day when I had less to do. When the astronauts were no longer in danger…if that time ever came.

The teahouse door handle bit into my fingers as I pulled. The owner lounged at the edge of the divider, her meaty arm almost enveloping the curve of the worn wood. Before lumbering toward me, she brushed her limp gray bangs out of her eyes.

"You friend of Zory Korchagin's," she announced in a warbling voice. "I have chef make something special."

The blood drained from my face. He couldn't possibly be here; I had changed my schedule to avoid him. And he wasn't—when she manhandled me into the dining room, only one table was occupied: an elderly man with his face over a bowl of borscht. My table was empty and Korchagin-free.

"I really just want my usual," I said.

The owner harrumphed, her considerable bosom heaving. The relief of seeing Magda waddle across the room with a menu under her arm allowed my gut to relax fully for the first time in hours.

"I have for you." She reached into the pocket of her apron and produced a slip of paper. Her swollen hand plunked it onto the table next to the napkin. "Mr. Zory tells me give to you." She eyed me, then turned her gaze to the paper. "I think he like you."

The note vibrated with menace. He liked me? What was that even supposed to mean? The fact that he'd remembered me was bad enough.

Magda's exasperated sigh pushed the paper closer. She startled at the screech of my chair skittering back as loud as the lightning sizzling under my skin. I caught the puzzled shake of her head while she made her way back toward the kitchen.

I poked at the note, wondering what it said and what his handwriting looked like. Against my better judgment, I snatched it and pried apart the folds. Heavy loops and letters drifted across the space. A whine of anxiety seeped through my clamped lips.

> Dear Lela,
> I did not mean to upset you with my request, wishing only to get to know you. Perhaps you will let me see you again.
> — *Zory*

Under that, a string of Russian characters.

Magda returned with a cup of tea, the chatter of porcelain jarring and high-pitched.

"What does this mean?" I asked, pointing to the letters.

She bent over and squinted into the text. "Bit of poem," she answered. Her wide voice was full of longing as heavy as oil. "It say:

> 'The rim of the sky will be the color of hard crimson, and your heart, as it was then, will be on fire.'"

She clicked her tongue. "He like you lot."

Her lips puckered into a smile. She pivoted on her heel and marched to another table without a backward glance.

I didn't know the poem. Magda wouldn't say a word when she delivered my sandwich and I asked her about the author, instead just shaking her head and chuckling. The food turned to ash in my mouth as I read and reread the note, searching for hidden clues, hoping to decipher its deeper meaning.

Nothing made sense, and not understanding what Zo—*Korchagin*—tried to relay ate at me.

I barely noticed the humidity on my walk back to the office, the note clutched in my hand. Korchagin's angular face existed in the jaw of the security guard at the front desk when I walked through the lobby. His sharp nose took up residence on a woman in the elevator.

He was everywhere and in every thought.

The second I sat at my desk, I pulled up a search engine on my computer. I typed out the words from the poem and was immediately rewarded with the name of the poet: Anna Akhmatova.

"There you are!" Trina's lilting voice speared me in the back of the head, just a touch of antipathy hanging on each syllable. I wiped the search results from the screen with a quick finger. "The Hammond meeting's been moved up an hour. I stalled them as much as I could, but the director wants the analysis in his office before it starts."

"Oh, thanks, Trina." If she picked up on my distraction, she didn't mention it. She only leered out of her round face and sat at her desk. Even from across the partition, I could feel her scheming.

I could barely concentrate while printing the reports on the Hammond case, thinking of red skies and the gray of Zory's eyes reflecting a wall of flames.

✳✳✳

ONE OF THE MOST INTERESTING CASES I'D RUN ACROSS AT FORTY Winks was a man with sleep paralysis. He became conscious in the last seconds of REM sleep, waking to see the demons and monsters that plagued him in dreams.

His heart rate rocketed to dangerous levels. And the screams—it was the most horrifying thing I'd ever heard. Eventually we'd helped him, and I'd ended the study in the positive, but it'd taken months of listening to his shrieks.

All humans have bad dreams, but this was different. Unique.

When I'd explained that women generally have a higher frequency of bad dreams than men, he'd laughed—an uneasy, gruff sound not dissimilar to gravel grating over macadam—and said he found a new reason to thank God for his penis every day.

Living with Trina was a waking nightmare, and there was no treatment. She was everywhere: in my car, in the shower at home, drinking tea in my kitchen, in the coffee room at work. I doubted being a woman made it any worse, but the last time I'd been so terrorized had been before my mother left.

It'd been nearly a week since Trina's invasion. Five days of hiding in my bedroom to protect my files. Five days of answering questions about my life, my parents, Mrs. Gerhardt. I'd worn a path in front of my closet door and sprained all forty-three muscles in my face in the pursuit of appearing friendly. My cranial nerves were shot.

Every moment, Korchagin's face floated behind my eyes, and his red skies wreathed me in agitation. He hadn't been back to the teahouse, and I'd been too scared to go near his apartment building again. I couldn't put it off for much longer, though.

The shuttle mission loomed, and I had to complete my investigation. I had to watch him. The closest I'd probably ever come to a full night of decent sleep was by observing it in someone else.

By the time Saturday morning arrived it was with the greatest relief that I found myself truly alone in the house. Trina had gone to the library for her shift. Nike followed me into Dad's bedroom.

The morning sunshine hazed through the curtains, highlighting the faded comforter and pillow shams. I crawled onto the bed and collapsed onto Dad's pillow. It still smelled like him, even a year later.

Dad collected stories like other people collected state spoons. He used to tell me I took after him, but I couldn't see it. Maybe through the set of my eyes or the color of my hair. Mrs. Gerhardt had once said that even though I looked a lot like my father, I had a lot in common with my mother. I'd begged her to say it wasn't true.

Dad's warmth radiated into a room, gathering people to him and prying their histories out of them. Even me. He loved hearing about the sleep lab, the subjects, and the things they said and did.

Their dreams were particularly of interest—his eyes would grow wide, a smile on his face, as I recounted the murmured, "applesauce spider web" from the CEO of a construction firm during her second REM cycle. Telling him those things likely broke lab rules, but it was just my dad, and he'd never repeat them to anyone.

He'd refused to move anything of my mother's after she left. From my vantage point on the bed, the silver glinted off the back of her hand mirror on the dresser. Her brush lay beside it with strands of curly hair still tangled in the bristles.

Her clothes were in the drawers and the closet. All that mauve. I'd never understood why he kept it all. Now I was the one who couldn't bear to move a thing.

Except the closet door hung ajar.

Nike pounced onto the bed, yellow tail switching. *She's been in here.*

I rolled off the bed. "You should have told me. You were here—you should have seen this. What were you doing the whole time?"

Maybe it was at night when I was in with you.

"Great. Just great," I yelled. My mother's perfume swelled in my nose, choking out everything else. I gagged on the stench. "What's she been doing? It's not her business."

Breathe. Four-three-two-one-in, four-three-two-one-out.

"This crosses the line," I said. "Unacceptable."

Perhaps it's time to eliminate the problem.

"This is not the time," I said, but I wondered how much I believed my own denial. My house was sacred space. My personal life was not to be violated. Rage built and built until I could taste it in the back of my throat like burned toast.

Dad's voice ran a soundtrack behind my thoughts. I wasn't sure if he agreed with Nike or urged me to a new calm. The skin of my fingers crusted over with burns, and in the mirror the fire grew in my pupils. I could not allow this to stand. I had warned her to keep out of the room.

I had warned her.

The next few minutes held a clear silence in which I could picture her rifling through drawers, looking for my secrets. I stalked out of the room and down the hall, shoving my keys and wallet into the back pocket of my pants. Fury made the walls bleed, each droplet cascading into a river of gore collecting at the baseboards. It flowed toward Dad's bedroom, as though the entire house had shifted on its foundation.

Mrs. Gerhardt sat behind the circulation desk when I arrived at the library. Her skin was the color of ash, and her eyes were dull. Perhaps she wasn't getting enough sleep. Still, she smiled in greeting, but it muddled and died on her face when she saw me.

"Lela, what's wrong? Let's go to my office." She beckoned and shuffled toward the room behind her. I followed, whipping my head toward the children's area. If Trina felt my glare, she didn't acknowledge it. She was probably brainwashing the kids…recruiting them to help with her plan. Get them young and build an army. The weight of the idea pressed against my chest, squeezing my heart.

I closed the door behind me and waited until Mrs. Gerhardt had settled into her chair before I sat. My foot tapped out a furious beat, almost in time with my lungs working.

Breathe. Four-three-two-one-in, four-three-two-one-out.

The overhead fluorescents buzzed above and cast harsh shadows across Mrs. Gerhardt's thin face. Her red, red lips seemed to float above her mouth.

"Now what's going on?"

"Trina's been going through my personal things. It's completely inappropriate. A breach of trust. And—"

"Oh, yes," Mrs. Gerhardt said. "Trina was full of compliments this morning about your generosity. You did a very good thing. Reaching out to another person in need is noble. Your father would be delighted to see you helping a friend like this."

"She's not my friend."

"It looks very much like she is, like it or not."

"She's been snooping in the house."

"How do you know?"

"I know. I just do," I said. My eyes were boiled onions, like I might peel them apart, layer by layer, with my nails. I could almost feel the air drifting between the skins, puffing up my pupils until the pressure behind them burst.

Mrs. Gerhardt huffed, breathing hard. "Have you spoken to her about it?"

"No. Not yet."

"I can see you mean to have it out with her." Her face paled further beneath her lipstick. "You're upset—that's obvious. But when you and Trina have this conversation, you'll need to be calm. You could really hu—"

"I just want her out." I squeezed the arms of the chair and thought of the autoinjector. "I want her gone."

"It might be good for you to have some company," she said. "Learn to share the house with someone other than your father."

"Nothing good can come of this. It's like living with a toddler—she has no self control." *And she's spying on me.* "She never listens, and she's always watching me."

"Why don't you let me be there when you meet? I can mediate. Make sure no one loses her temper and says something she doesn't mean."

"You don't understand," I said. The pressure had moved from my eyes to the back of my head. "There are things she has no business—"

"I understand more than you think." Mrs. Gerhardt's eyes crinkled at the edges, mouth turning up into a half smile that wasn't particularly happy. "If you don't want to talk to her now, maybe you should skip your shift today and take a walk. Do something relaxing. Maybe go have tea at that Russian place you like so much."

Korchagin's face scorched under my skull. "Something relaxing? I can barely get my lunch down in that place these days."

"Did something happen?"

I explained about Korchagin. Not everything, of course. Enough for her to understand. Half of me didn't know why I'd even brought it up.

"Do you like this man?" she asked, a cautious note lingering behind the words.

"No. I mean, I'm sure he's perfectly nice, and he insisted on discussing Dostoyevsky, but I can't possibly have any kind of relationship with him."

She leaned across her desk to set the coffee maker to life. The burble of liquid came next, along with Mrs. Gerhardt's stare. "And why not? He has good taste in novels."

"It's a work thing," I said, thinking fast. "There's a clause in my contract that prevents us from fraternizing with clients."

"The heart wants what the heart wants and all that muck," she said. "I know you'd never be unprofessional, and I know you don't like surprises, but perhaps spending time with him and with Trina might be good for you." Her smile trembled, setting her face into motion—a fishbowl with a bright red goldfish swimming in it.

"No. I'm better off alone."

"Alone, hmmm? You're alone too much, if you ask me." She lifted the pot from the burner and poured the coffee, the scent swirling around me.

"It's either that or be fired," I said, fidgeting.

"I'm sure you know best," Mrs. Gerhardt said, pushing the mug across the desk. The way she said it made me think she doubted it, just a little bit. I wrapped my hands around the mug and stared into the depths as though something sensible might lie at the bottom. "You know, when I met my husband, I wanted nothing to do with him."

"You and I are very different people."

"Yes, but people sometimes grow on you. I don't think you liked me very much when you first met me," she said, lips twitching. "And I thought you were a little strange, too."

"Me?" I asked. "Why?"

"What would you think of a ten-year-old girl requesting science journals? We actually had a meeting about you. Called your parents in and everything."

The festering anger was at a bare simmer now. I kept a grasp on it, tenuous. "I don't understand. Did you think I was going to blow up the library or something? Why did I never hear anything about this?"

"Your dad was the one who came in. For all I know, he never even mentioned it to your mother. That was the first time I met him, too—worried about your checking out material too old for you. One of the trustees was sure you were using the journals for an arts and crafts project, but you were such a serious kid—I couldn't imagine you'd destroy library property." Her lips lifted, revealing a smudge of crimson on her front tooth.

"So what happened?"

"Nothing. Your dad vouched for you, and that was that. You and I got used to each other, didn't we? Maybe it'll be the same with this Zory. Or with Trina. She's making such an effort. You just have to give her a chance."

I could feel my mouth drawing in on itself, pulling into a knot. "She's not willing to play by the rules."

Mrs. Gerhardt's brows rose, piling up the wrinkles on her forehead. "Rules?" Her chin swiveled back and forth. "So what are you going to do about her?"

"Let her know she's not welcome to snoop in my things."

"Maybe you misunderstood what she was doing. Promise me you'll talk to her first before accusing her of something, okay?"

"I didn't mistake anything. She was in Dad's room, rifling through the closet. I can't have her doing that." My voice had gone tight, strangled. Trina might as well have stood behind me, slowly cinching a rope around my throat.

"No. No, of course not. You're set in your ways. I understand." She patted my fingers.

I sat back in the chair, just out of her reach. "Maybe you're right. I'll go. You know, take the day off if you're sure you don't need me. By the time Trina gets home, I'm sure I'll have calmed down enough to talk to her."

With every word, the agitation roiled heavier in my stomach. My skin crawled.

I thought maybe she'd smile or look relieved, but if anything her mouth puckered even more. She nodded and pushed herself out of the chair, staggering unsteadily to her feet.

Before she could put her hands on me again, I edged toward the door and yanked it open.

"Everything will be fine," I said, baring my teeth at her and forcing enthusiasm to my face.

Her eyes went wide, and a faint lift at the corner of her mouth drooped almost immediately. I backed out of her office, still smiling as hard as I could, and walked toward the front door with my head down. If Trina saw me, called my name, I might have said something I'd regret Mrs. Gerhardt's overhearing, and she would definitely know my expression was fake.

Smile and the whole world smiles with you. The same probably wasn't true for angry screaming or wanting to eliminate your roommate.

I barely remembered the drive back to my house, so focused on how to handle the situation with Trina I steered without paying attention. It was only when I closed my fingers around the handle of the screen door that I noticed the white paper wedged in the frame.

Korchagin's handwriting flashed out at me, and I wanted to throw my arms across the door to protect it from another terrible invasion. He'd been here. He knew where I lived, stolen my privacy. The resentment twisted my mouth. I shoved the folds out of the note.

> Dear Lela,
> Please meet me at the teahouse on Monday at one o'clock. I'm sorry to have missed you here, but your smile has been on my mind.
> — *Rory*

I sank to my knees, trying to dampen the high-pitched panting coming out of me. A shrieking tone rang in my ears. With each thud of my slamming heart, my goals crumbled.

Above me, a trail of smoke burst apart and snaked across the sky. The corners of the world darkened and tumbled over me, leaving me pink and naked and exposed.

Chapter Eight

CIRCADIAN RHYTHMS

THE SMOOTH PORCELAIN OF THE EMPTY TUB COOLED MY SKIN, although hair still slicked to my forehead. Angry voices, pointed and prickly as the thorns on the bush outside the house where I'd been hiding out earlier that afternoon, carried through the door. I hunkered into the curve along the back slope of the bath, listening to Mom's high-pitched shriek and Dad's deep drawl.

"It's not normal, Gus. She keeps staring at me while I'm sleeping. She's sick. She's trying to steal my soul!"

"Roni, come on now. Lela's ten—there's nothing wrong with her. She's just going through something. Maybe you just need to sleep. You haven't gotten a good night's sleep in a while."

"Going through something? The kid's a wreck."

"Well, you can hardly blame her. You yell at her all the damn time."— The dull thud of something, perhaps a cabinet door closing—"Maybe you should go back to the doctor, have your medication adjusted. You're on edge lately."

"You coddle her too much. Don't you care that she's turned into this weird girl? And what about all the reading? You can't tell me her teacher assigned her medical studies in the fifth grade. She's planning something. Mark my words, that girl's hatching something rotten."

"It's a phase. That's all."

"She's obsessed with the shuttle, and today she's all fascinated by flies and—"

My head dipped to the journal clutched in my hand. *Genetics and Science*. Most of it didn't make much sense. But I did get that fruit flies slept, just like the astronauts did. Just like I did. Well, like I wanted to. There was a lot about circadian rhythms I didn't understand. I'd asked Mrs. Gerhardt about it, and she'd explained that it just meant the activity and rest people go through in a twenty-four-hour period. I had made the mistake of using the phrase while speaking to Mom, and she'd freaked out. She'd accused me of trying to listen to her thoughts.

"You're driving me crazy. Just let the girl be. She'll be right as rain after this passes, interested in something else next month. Just let me call Dr. Harris, get you into see him."

The meat of my lip pressed between my teeth, and I ran my tongue over the skin inside my mouth.

Mom and Dad's raised voices faded to a buzz. I buried myself in the journal, imagining the sleek bodies of fruit flies, their wings wrapped around them like warm down comforters. Mama Fruit Fly would tuck in her babies, sweet and loving. The reedy voice of Papa Fruit Fly would sing them to sleep.

I wanted to be tucked in and sung to sleep. Only Dad held up his end of the fantasy.

The door swept open, Mom's voice loud and grating. "Jesus, Lela—what are you doing in here? Gus—your daughter's reading in the bathtub." She stepped closer and pitched forward until she lay almost over top of me. Her usual wild hair was limp, and she smelled. Her heavy eyeshadow smeared almost above her brows. "I got them," she said, voice low and triumphant. "I got every last one of them. Got 'em fooled, but not you. Oh no, not you. You see right into me with your crazy eyes."

Chapter Nine

RELATIONSHIP TO MADNESS

NIKE WAS SITTING ON MY CHEST WHEN MY EYES POPPED OPEN, AND his pink nose was only inches from my face. My head felt heavy, a balloon filled with cement and quicksand. The fuzziness, the thickness enveloping me, left me confused and uneasy.

Three-quarters of dreams are nightmares, in theory. The subconscious is a funny thing, taking the stress of the day and transforming it into scary, negative fantasies. There was some speculation that dreams were the brain's way of solving problems.

The remnants of the one I'd woken from now stuck to my skin, and my fingers still ached: I'd dug a hole in the backyard just yards from the rose bush under which I'd buried my father's ashes, and there was something to do with screaming and the closet in Dad's room. I couldn't quite remember the details, but instinct told me it had to do with Trina.

She's come and gone, Nike blinked. His irises had gone more brown than topaz.

"Who? How long was I out?" I rubbed the unfamiliar sleep from my eyes. My conversation with Mrs. Gerhardt filtered back, along with finding the door open in Dad's bedroom. Korchagin's note and invasion of my private space screamed through my veins.

Trina.

"Did she take anything?"

He stretched and jumped to the bed. *She left a note. But no, she only packed a bag and left.*

I bolted upright. "A bag? She's gone? And a note? Are you sure it's not the thing from Korchagin? Oh, God. Did he come back? Was he in the house? Did Trina let him in the house?"

The floor was cold under my feet. I sprinted down the hallway, Nike on my heels. Getting to the house and falling into bed yesterday were only vague shadows that filled my entrails with jagged marbles.

Trina's handwriting was puffy and frilly on a sheet of pink paper tucked into the mirror frame in the hall. If I cared to sniff the note, it would probably give off the odor of my mother's perfume. Irritation poked harder—maybe she'd started to smell like my mother because she'd been spritzing herself from the glass flacons on the dresser in Dad's bedroom.

I smoothed the paper and read:

Lela,
Missed you at the library yesterday.

You were so sound asleep when I got home, so I didn't want to wake you, but I'm taking off for Austin for a few days. Greg and I got in a big fight, and we need to work some things out. Not sure how long I'll be gone, but please let work and the library know I need some time off.

Thanks! You're the best!

Trina

"It's just like Trina to leave it to me to break the news about her vacation. She's probably hoping I'll get fired over it."

Nike rubbed up against my ankle. *Maybe you should install a lock on your father's bedroom door. And an additional lock on your closet. It couldn't hurt.*

I nodded. "Yes. I'll do that."

The very air in the house was brighter without Trina's darkness lurking in the corners. The light streaming through the living room window was all wrong for late afternoon, though.

"How long was I asleep?"

It's Sunday morning. Nike glanced up at me, eyes shining.

I collapsed into the armchair. "Really? No wonder I feel so fuzzy—you know too much sleep is bad for my concentration. Why didn't you wake me? Do you think Trina drugged me?"

It's possible. She looked in on you once, but she didn't come in that I saw. Maybe she drugged me, too?

Snakes slithered up my arms, spiraling around my biceps and across my shoulders, tightening around my neck until I thought I might choke on the fear.

I stalked to the kitchen and threw open the lid to the trash can. It was a fresh bag, completely empty. She hid the evidence somewhere. The backyard garbage bins.

The smell of something lingered, but I couldn't quite point out the source. It was a strange kind of sweet, like meat and sugar. Nike watched from the window overlooking the rose bushes while I tore open the bags and rifled through. A jagged piece of broken glass sliced into the meat of my palm, but beyond that there was nothing but old receipts and junk mail.

My research files overflowed with detritus like this. Handwritten lists. Books. Old photographs, although they were tricky. I usually took those only from astronauts who lived in the area permanently. People who stayed here temporarily or during training only brought the essentials, so they'd notice if a photograph turned up missing.

What would Korchagin's apartment look like? I couldn't imagine he'd bother to bring much with him from home—perhaps a few photographs, his clothes. He was on a three-year loan program, so maybe he'd have more of his belongings shipped. But astronauts always had letters and receipts, things that told me about who they were.

I had a policy, a code of conduct important to the accuracy of studies, that governed what was acceptable to take from an astronaut's home. It had taken me years to develop. In fact, I hadn't dared to implement my first study until the policy had been perfect, polished to a sheen, reconsidered a dozen times, and rejiggered. I revisited the code every year in December. It resided in a special file, the color code white.

Blood dripped down the side of my hand. Everything I was and would become lived in that blood…every genetic code, every flaw. My mother resided within me. My father, too.

A bead rolled along the line of my wrist and fell into the grass at my feet. I'd neglected the lawn since Dad died; he'd have been upset. It had gone a little on the brown side, some of the turf uneven and scraggly. It would be a perfect time to mow and trim—too bad the neighbors would complain. So often late at night and early in the morning I felt antsy and compelled to action.

Dad had watered the lawn as often as possible and edged it with precision, almost always in the morning, before the Houston sun blazed. The size of the plot on which our house sat made it silly to use a riding mower, which is what Dad always dreamed of, but his little push model did the job, trimming the grass evenly. He'd call me out after he was done, and we'd walk around barefoot, enjoying the springiness tickling our soles. My feet were tiny and white; his, thick-veined and tanned.

After Mom left, he still kept up on that kind of maintenance, but he never invited me out to the yard. It still made me sad, even after all these years.

He'd trudge into the house and glance at me, his mouth tugging down and his dark eyes drooping. More often than not, he'd have a fistful of roses picked from the bush in the back. He'd stare at them and then me, his face moving through a range of emotions until it settled on a tired grimace. "Mowing takes it out of ya," he'd say, deep voice raspy and beaten.

My hands sifted through the dirt around the rose bushes, my blood mixing with the soil. The stink of the mauve roses assaulted me. I'd thought of pulling them up after the funeral, but Dad had taken such loving care of them. The canes were sturdy and thick with health, gnarled like a fist near the roots.

The bush I'd planted with his ashes—the one that should have produced white blooms—still struggled to thrive. Its branches were spindly, small spots of mildew on the leaves.

I yanked the flowers off the more robust plant, crushing them under my knees, just like I would do to Korchagin's interest in me. It was the only smart option. It was the only way to save the space shuttle...all the astronauts.

The only way to atone for my mother's sin.

Maybe the only way to stop whatever Trina's plan was. Her absence was at once a relief and a cause for suspicion, even though a lingering voice from somewhere deep in my brain told me there was nothing to worry about. I used to listen to that voice, but not anymore. I couldn't even trust myself sometimes.

The next day, mind carefully focused on Korchagin, I stalked toward the teahouse at the appointed time. The acetate lining of my suit pants stuck to my calves in the humidity, and the shoes—my God, the awful shoes—pinched at my toes, ripping at the skin of my heels with each step. The discomfort was worth it because I needed the feel of a powerful business suit. Severe. Black. My hair pulled back into a tight bun. If I'd owned contact lenses—something unnecessary as far as I was concerned—I'd have worn them because I wanted him to clearly see my eyes when I glared, demanding he leave me be.

Maybe I'd remove my glasses to inform him I wasn't interested in seeing him again, but then I couldn't watch his face, see the understanding wash across his features.

And I wanted him to understand. Fully. Without my having to resort to the autoinjector.

The owner rounded the corner from the dining room and smiled, giving me a glimpse of her missing side teeth.

"Come—Zory, he wait for you."

She tethered herself to me, guiding me like an ox, but instead of being led to a pen, I was delivered to my usual table. As advertised, Korchagin hunched over it with a newspaper spread before him.

He glanced up, and my face smoothed into a blank mask. Our interaction needed to be calm. I couldn't allow even a remote bit of the anger searing the inside of my veins to burn through to the surface—I didn't want it to be mistaken for interest.

Mrs. Gerhardt would have been proud. Sort of. After what she'd said the day prior, she probably would have preferred I invite him home for dinner and tell him my life story.

He stood and extended his hand, replacing the teahouse owner's hold on my arm.

"Lela, how good to see you again." When I didn't say anything, he leaned in and kissed me on the cheek. I thought it was over, but he quickly darted around to kiss my other cheek and again where his lips had first touched down: left-right-left.

It was just a greeting—possibly one typical for him, for all I knew—but it wiped clean my intentions. I had to dig the edges of my nails into the palm of my hand to stop thinking about the prickly brush of his facial hair and the smell of soap on his skin.

He gestured to the table. I fought the urge to run, sitting instead, my spine straight as the lines Dad used to carve into our lawn with the mower, and my fists clenched in my lap.

"Would you like some tea?"

My head bobbled. "Mr. Korchagin, I—"

"Please, call me Zory," he interrupted in a low voice. He folded his newspaper precisely in thirds and set it to the floor. "You have a beautiful face—you should wear your hair back more often."

My fingers itched with wanting to tear the pins out of my bun and shroud myself in handfuls of hair.

I jutted my jaw forward and drew up my lips. Just as I opened up my mouth to tell him to leave me alone, he spat out a string of Russian, guttural and thick. Despite the stressed intonation of the words, a tender smile played on his wide lips.

"What was that?"

"A poem. It makes me think of you."

"Kor—I mean, Zory, that makes me very uncomfortable."

He sat back, shovel hands flat on the pitted wood of the table. "The poem? But you do not even know what it's about."

"Magda translated the part of the note in Russian." *And your heart, as it was then, will be on fire.* The line fired around in my brain.

"She did? Well, then. But it is not the poem I was thinking of. You remind me so much of many poems." His gray eyes stared over the table. I nearly flinched away.

"You shouldn't be thinking about me at all, let alone reciting poetry to me."

"But why not? Are you...do you have a boyfriend or a husband? You said you did not."

"No, it's not that. It's just that—"

"Do you have a girlfriend?"

"It's not that either, it's just—"

"Then why should I not think of you the way a man thinks of a woman?"

"I just...well, I don't date. Not anyone."

"But why?"

Oh, God. Why couldn't he just let it go?

"Zory." I steepled my fingers, hoping my thoughts would come out as intended. "We can't go out. It just wouldn't work."

Magda nearly crashed into the table, clinking teacups clutched in her hands. She fussed over Zory in Russian and tongue clicks, smiling at me before turning to go, a great ship sailing across the floor of the dining room in a voluminous blue polyester muumuu-slash-rigging.

Zory stirred a teaspoon of jam into his tea and glanced up, the corner of his mouth crooked upward. "Perhaps you would just let me be your friend?"

I threw up my hands, my fingers knocking into the salt shaker and sending a spray of tiny grains across the table. I sucked in a breath and scrambled for a pinch only to find Zory—*Korchagin*, I chanted in my head—nipping at the salt as well.

Before I could even snap my jaw shut from the surprise that nearly unhinged it, he launched the salt over his left shoulder and mumbled a few words.

"What—I mean, why did you do that?" I sprinkled a few bits of salt over my own shoulder, hoping he wouldn't notice.

The tips of his small ears reddened. "Just this thing we do in my family. It is a superstition."

"Do you do that a lot?"

He shrugged. "Well, if I don't, I might get sick."

"Oh? What else?"

"Hmm? With the salt? No, nothing else with the salt."

"Do you," I paused, trying to figure out how to ask, "have other beliefs? Things your parents taught you?"

"Oh, well, yes. I do not wear a hat in bed or walk under ladders or sleep with my feet pointed toward the door, if those things are what you mean. Very bad luck. On Earth at least—it is much harder to control when I am up there." He pointed toward the ceiling of the teahouse.

My tongue swelled in my mouth, too large to say much of anything. It was just as well: My brain had stopped working.

I'd run into people who believed that black cats and breaking mirrors brought bad luck, but the seriousness with which he confessed led me to believe this was more than just some lighthearted thing he joked about. His beliefs anchored deeply.

"It's also bad luck to ignore a woman like you."

"I'm sorry—what?"

"I like you. You feel very lucky. A charm."

"A charm." I repeated the phrase, my eyes fixed to his forearms, bare in a short-sleeved shirt. His biceps were hills leading to a light dusting of dark hair on his forearms. For a second the veins pulsed with thick, black blood under paper-thin skin. I shook my head free of the vision, letting my eyes travel to his chin.

"Yes. Perhaps if I let you go, bad things will happen. My grandmother tells me the importance of luck and people who bring you luck."

The words rooted me to the chair, and for the first time I doubted my plan.

"What does your grandmother have to do with anything?" I asked. Even I could detect the ice in my voice had melted.

"Very smart woman, my babushka. Revered in the family."

"Because she's lucky?"

He chuckled. "She is at that, but no. She's special. I suppose if she were an American, you might call her crazy. Not so for us."

"Because Russians have a different relationship to madness," I said.

"You remember?" He smiled, clearly delighted. "Perhaps my babushka has a bit of the seer in her after all. She told me I would meet a woman here, someone who would…well, someone new."

Panic pressed all the air out of my lungs, as though a boulder had dropped onto my chest from a great height. I now lay under the giant rock, a trapped rodent flailing and searching for a way out.

"And lucky."

"Yes. Lucky," he said.

"And you believe her? You just said that she's insane."

"Of course I believe her. Insane is just a word…and I said others might consider her crazy, not that I do."

"What does she have?"

He fiddled with the fork lying on the napkin. "Have?"

"She has a mental illness, right?"

"I do not know what it is called here, but she is sometimes very sad, followed by times she is very happy. When her mood is good, she runs around the house, smiling and laughing."

"It sounds like bipolar disorder," I said.

"Perhaps. Before I left to come here I woke to find her in my flat. She stood on the chair in my bedroom, barking like a dog." He grinned, which was odd—I would have thought that would have been frightening, similar to Korchagin's showing up at my house uninvited. It explained why that had seemed acceptable to him at least. The familiar jagged glass under my skin returned, grinding and grating. "And that was when she told me I'd meet someone who would bring me luck."

"Does your grandmother do that often? The sneaking into your apartment thing?"

"She once undressed in the town square, sure the government had done something to her clothes. She threatened to kill the head of the Communist Party in public. I did not see this with my own eyes, you understand. It was before I was born. But it is legend in my family, before the Soviet Union dissolved, of course. It was a bold and potentially dangerous thing."

I couldn't understand why he continued to grin. Had my father committed the same acts, I'd have had him committed. When my mother killed the astronauts, I'd started to think of ways to turn her into the police without having the proof to condemn her. As hard as I searched the house, there was no evidence, and I was just a kid. But something with witnesses, like with Zory's grandmother, that was different. "So what happened to her?"

"Nothing." His laugh was sudden and loud, a pop of sound. I startled in my seat. "I can see what you are thinking, but that is not how things work in Russia. We are not so afraid as you Americans are." The neat goatee bristled. "If my grandmother foresaw you, that is good enough for me. You will keep me safe on the shuttle. I know it."

✸✸✸

I TRIED TO CONTROL MY BREATH. IT WOULDN'T DO FOR ANYONE AT THE office to see me struggling. I ducked behind my computer and closed my eyes, regulating my inhales and exhales.

He believed…more than believed…he said he needed *me* in order to make things go right. It conflicted with everything I'd adhered to over the years: Keep the subjects at a distance, don't involve myself. And now I couldn't reconcile what he wanted and what I knew to be true.

I'd studied him after his grand proclamation, inspecting for any sign of insincerity, any indication of a lie. He was nothing other than pleasant and warm, completely honest and lacking any pretense. Everything about the man made me nervous, sure that every action and reaction from either of us would bear out some horrible scenario that ended with another shuttle explosion.

And the story about his grandmother. He spoke of her with such love and respect. Mentally ill or not, how could he find her so credible? How could I?

Despite it all, I couldn't walk away. Just in case.

The Chin lumbered by my cubicle and stopped under the pretense of checking the garbage cans. His stomach stretched the fabric of his uniform taut.

"Trina ain't here?"

I shook my head and forced myself to stay calm. "No, she had to take a last-minute trip."

"Hope it's somewhere fun. You have a nice weekend? What'd you do to your hands? Ya got scratches all over 'em."

"Just a little gardening," I said. Why was he lingering? Habit now, my mouth bowed up into a smile so hard it hurt my face. Being friendly was painful in every sense of the word. "How about you?"

"Nothing too grand. But ain't nothing like having a lazy weekend." He paused, but before I could come up with my second question, he asked, "You gonna keep our appointment?" He glanced up, lizard tongue poking over thin lips.

Oh.

"Yes. Give me twenty minutes."

He turned away, and I gripped the edge of my desk. Now more than ever I needed the stability of my routine and the specialized knowledge The Chin could provide. I allowed the elevator to swallow him before standing.

Trina's face, stretched into a scream, etched behind my eyelids. Somehow, she was the reason for Korchagin's interest, for the interruption in all I knew. I stalked the hall, hoping she stayed in Austin. The rest I could untangle myself.

Chapter Ten

SIREN'S CALL

H OW WAS YOUR D—"
    I cut The Chin off with a kiss, something not part of our usual routine, but I didn't want to answer more questions. I'd had enough from Korchagin. I had enough of my own.

He fumbled with the buttons of his jump suit, and I shoved my underwear down, stepping out. Before they could get lost in bottles of bleach and air freshener, I grabbed them up, clutching as though they'd spit out the answers I'd been looking for if only I squeezed tight enough.

The Chin's bottom teeth gleamed in the hazy overhead light while he struggled with the condom, eventually sliding it on. Heavy breathing turned to quiet grunts, whispering things I didn't quite catch.

With my eyes closed, I could be anywhere, with anyone, and for a moment I pretended. Before I could stop it, his underbite thinned and receded, his wobbly jaw becoming angular and—

I pushed away the face I didn't want to see, forcing my lids open. A sweaty hand in the curve of my back, hot exhalations on my cheek that smelled of cream cheese. The curving, beak-like nose. Discomfort seeped through my pores. This *thing* was already finished for me. The finality of it cloaked over me in waves. How that might influence my mission, I couldn't be sure, but Nike was right: I didn't need The Chin. I could find another source for information. I could adjust my schedule, work to fill the hole it left.

Another few moments, and it was truly over—with me avoiding his eyes and him smiling. I shrugged his hand away, turning to tug up my underwear. The Chin still grinned, clearly not feeling the bittersweet air circling between us like a shark drawn in by hemorrhaging blood. With my shoes back on, I whirled on him, ready to say the words.

"Mom really wants to meet y—" he began, his small eyes kind and sweet as always. I held up my hand to stop him.

"I need to say something, and I need you to listen. I've been thinking about us, and this isn't," I said, almost wincing when his face went slack, "fair to you." I tried to sound regretful and soft, willing him to accept it with dignity. "I'm not the right woman for you." That was true, although it didn't help ease the clenching of his facial muscles. "You deserve someone you can introduce to your mother and take out, and I'm just not that person."

The Chin's eyes watered, his uniform only half pulled up. "Is it because…" He gestured around the closet, his thick fingers limp. His mousy brown hair lay like a slug across his head.

"No," I said. "I…well, I just can't be serious with anyone right now, and I don't want to hold you back from meeting someone."

Dad had liked to say lying wasn't a sin if it was done in the spirit of saving someone's feelings. In my case, it was more of an issue of ending things so he wouldn't talk about me. No matter how many times he'd assured me that our relationship was still private, I could feel him collecting information about me. Cataloging it and storing it away for future use.

His mouth stilled, and he rubbed his chapped lips, back and forth, with his fingers.

"Oh. Well, okay then. Oh." His voice was dead grass now, crunching and dry. He tucked his arms into the sleeves of his jump suit, buttoning up, slow and deliberate.

He gathered a mop and a bucket, and he left without a word.

I closed my eyes and imagined the darkness of sleep, bunching and then relaxing each part of my body, starting with my feet. The rising control allowed me to see, regain the distance important to my life. I watched. Always watched.

✳✳✳

NIKE AWAITED ME AT HOME, HIS SCREECHING YOWLS URGING ME TO hurry as I filled his food bowl, like it was his last meal. Considering

I'd gone back on my original decision about Korchagin, perhaps God would strike me down for daring to screw with the safety of the shuttle. Cutting The Chin out of my personal life was minor by comparison.

Nike snarfled his food, seemingly unconcerned about the potential for additional divine retribution. His loud purring sawed through the kitchen.

"I think I'm going to have to go out with Korchagin."

The purring cut off, and Nike cast an eye in my direction.

"Don't look at me like that. You don't understand. He—" He turned to bare his rump to me, and I rolled my eyes at his dramatics. "He says he thinks I'm good luck…you know, to *him*. His grandmother allegedly predicted it. What if he's right?"

I trailed after the cat to the living room. The sky had grown darker, and drops of rain ricocheted off the hood of my car outside. The sound carried through the window, a hissing, metallic ping.

"Not that we discussed my research, but he said without a lucky charm things could go wrong—what if…well, it's sort of like my sleep observations, I guess. What I do has repercussions on the safety of the shuttle launch, but I get the feeling he thinks he needs some sort of a charm to ensure that all goes well, too."

Nike turned and blinked, *What has happened to your judgment? He might be an astronaut, but he's also a man. This luck thing—it's a line.* His tongue rasped out, cleaning his hind leg.

"If it is, he's very good. And, I mean, he's nice enough. Even Mrs. Gerhardt said I should at least give him a chance."

This is a bad idea. Any change to your observation routine could be deadly.

"Yes, I know. I've considered that. At this point, though, it's either kill him or keep him close. You can see the wisdom in that, I'm sure. The conservative approach has worked well, but maybe it's time to take a leap of faith."

He nuzzled against my hip, so I laid him across my lap, scratching between his ears.

"It's definitely a time saver. If he invites me over, I can get a peek at his personal space and catalog it. All of this could really jump-start the speed with which I'm able to complete my research."

Only one new astronaut and Korchagin's colleague from Russia were scheduled for the next launch. And there were still a few astronauts in the program I'd not observed who hadn't drawn an assignment yet. Being part of Korchagin's life might increase my productivity.

It could even allow me to sidestep some surveillance if he socialized with his coworkers.

Nike's purr rumbled through my legs. It was obvious he recognized the brilliance of the plan.

I'd thought it through. I told Korchagin I'd consider going out with him, and I had. He'd given me his phone number before we left the tearoom, but calling to announce that I'd date him was silly—the very idea agitated me, a feeling echoed in the wind outside scouring at the windows almost as though it fought to get inside the house.

If Korchagin were serious—and it appeared he was—he would find me again. He knew where I ate lunch. And perhaps I'd ask him about the poem he'd recited. My only recourse now was to let him tell me as much about himself as possible.

With only an hour until the library closed, I found myself hovering outside Mrs. Gerhardt's office. The shuffle of her feet sounded behind me.

"Lela, what are you doing here? I didn't think you were on for a few more days."

"I'm not. I just thought I'd drop by."

She eased behind her desk, breath loud in the silence of the small room. "Is everything okay? You look a little frazzled. Have you been arguing with Trina again?"

"Oh, no. I'm fine. I wanted to drop by, though, to let you know Trina had to go out of town. I'm not sure how long she'll be gone."

"Goodness, you must have scared her the other day." Her fingertips fiddled with the telephone cord. "You didn't hurt her, did you?"

"What? No." My smile slammed back into place. "She was gone when I woke up."

Her eyes widened, and she said, "That's that, then. I'll have to bring in another volunteer to take over her shifts." Her lips fluted while she made a note on a pad of paper. "I guess you'll have some time to yourself at least."

"I suppose. It's nice to come home from work and not have to deal with her rummaging where she doesn't belong." My hands curled into claws. I forced them to relax. "Mrs. Gerhardt, what do you think about luck?"

She glanced up for a moment but kept writing. Her handwriting was perfect. She'd told me once that the nuns in her Catholic elementary school were particular about cursive. "Luck? Well, I think we make our own luck. Why?"

"Just curious. So you don't believe in chance at all?"

"It's not that I don't believe in it entirely," she said, setting down her pen. "There are things that are out of our control. My mother used to say God controls everything, that he has a plan for everyone and everything, but it always seemed to me like that was silly. What would be the use of trying or making an effort to will things to happen if everything we do is futile? And what makes one person lucky but another one unlucky?"

"What does luck have to do with God having a master plan?" I asked.

Mrs. Gerhardt's red lips quirked. "If God has a hand in everything that happens to us, it isn't luck if good things happen, now is it? It's predestination. But let's say God has nothing to do with anything. Doesn't the concept of luck negate the idea? Yet being lucky is like being blessed or favored, I suppose."

"So you're saying luck is like getting direct approval from God?"

"I'm saying I don't believe in luck, God having a plan, or anything like that, which isn't to say I'm right. But everything that happens to us in life is as a direct result of our actions."

I let that settle for a moment before asking, "Dad's dying…that was a result of something I did?"

"That's not what I mean," Mrs. Gerhardt said.

"But you just said—"

"Did you become a lab technician because you worked hard to see that dream come true, or did the opportunity fall into your lap?"

"I worked hard, but that's just one thing. You came here by chance, I think. It's not like you woke up when you were six and decided you wanted to work at this particular library branch, right?"

"This is a very odd conversation, Lela. Why are you asking?"

"If someone said you were a lucky charm to them, would you believe it might be true?" I stared at the framed print above her desk, an image of the Houston skyline.

"Rationally, no. But there's more to luck than that. If you consider a four-leaf clover to be lucky, and you find one, you then become convinced that anything you do will be the right thing. So instead of sitting around and wondering if you should make a move, you might just do the thing you've been thinking. Make sense?"

"Yes, I guess. Luck is in the eye of the beholder."

She grinned. "Now you've got it. Never let any opportunity pass you by—whether I'm right or not, you make your own fate. You're the captain of your ship, so to speak. Are you going to tell me what this is all about?"

I shook my head and counted the questions I'd asked. Definitely more than two, but it wasn't like I had to worry about that most of the time with her. Now that Dad was gone, she was the closest thing I had to real family. For good measure, I commanded my mouth to move again into a smile full of teeth.

✳✳✳

THE HAZE CREPT THROUGH MY BEDROOM WINDOW AT DAWN, stealing in as though it had come to make off with my soul. Maybe it had; a tunnel careened through my innards, sucking in the emptiness. The fog split in two, braiding around my bicep until it inched away, twin snail heads limping off.

I shook my head to clear it. It could have been a dream, but I'd lain awake all night. My brain wouldn't quite stop hashing over what happened with Korchagin the day prior, nor my conversation with Mrs. Gerhardt. Every rustle of movement from the rest of the house had me on alert, sure Trina had returned and stuck her nose where it didn't belong—the family photo albums, Dad's old financial files, or Mom's warped records all lined up in neat rows. I'd been waiting to hear foot-steps in the hall, tiptoeing across the squeaky floorboard just past the bathroom door.

The dull thrum of electricity emanating from my alarm clock drew my eyes for the hundredth time, and I groaned. I had to peel myself out of bed in five minutes.

I'd have to stop at the hardware store and pick up a lock for the other bedroom door and possibly something like a nanny cam. Trina would eventually be back, and if she set traps to kill me, I'd know about it.

I didn't like the idea of leaving her alone in my house again, but the lock would help ensure she didn't invade every aspect of my life...not that there was so much of it left for her to horn in on. And Mrs. Gerhardt was right—being proactive was the only solution. I would make my own luck in this case.

Nike's heavy body thumped on the bed. Finally, he sat on my chest, staring down at me. He sniffed and turned away, leaping to the floor and twitching his tail as he padded out of the room.

The alarm blared through my head, and I smacked at it to stop the noise. The *thunk* from the direction of the floor indicated I'd knocked it off the bedside table.

"Lela, are you up?"

I vaulted off the bed and flung open the door. "What are you doing here? I thought you'd gone to Austin."

Trina laughed with my mother's mouth, only now she looked so much more vivid—as though she'd solidified into this strange, technicolor hybrid. She appeared to have grown taller, wider. She even wore blue eyeshadow over her dark eyes. "Would I leave you alone like that? I came right back after seeing my boyfriend. We made up, and figured since we're going on a trip, I shouldn't take too much time off. Besides, I missed you!" It was nearly a threat, the malice as syrupy as molasses on her tongue. "I'm going to make coffee, if that's okay. Why don't you shower first?"

"That's fine."

She sauntered away, swishing her new hips side to side. I backed down the hall toward the bathroom. My mother's perfume stormed the space.

From outside the door, Trina's voice filtered through. She sang at the top of her lungs, letting loose with a song I'd never heard before, something about suspicion. The sound of it was haunting, almost a siren's call that made me want to go to her. But instead of attraction, it was revulsion: deep, ugly, and necessary.

I bit the inside of my cheek and turned off the water. Without a lot of good options, a wait and watch attitude seemed smart. *Keep your enemies close*, Dad's voice reminded me.

As though my decision evoked her, Trina trilled, "Coffee's ready, Lela! Shake a leg!"

I groaned and buried my head in a towel.

Chapter Eleven

HORRIBLE MONSTERS

I HELD MY BREATH IN THE DARKNESS, AFRAID TO MAKE A SOUND while skulking into my parents' room, a notebook and pen clutched in my hand. Even if the bright pie of the moon hadn't lit the bedroom, the layout of every piece of furniture hovered in my mind—but if I stubbed my toe on the bed frame or tripped over a shoe, I'd make noise. Mom would wake and be mad, and then she and Dad would yell at each other.

I just wanted to watch them sleep.

Dad lay on his side under the covers, one arm slung over Mom's waist. She slept on her back, blonde curls tumbling across her pillow. Her position was supposed to mean she bore leadership traits and had a lot of confidence. The paper I'd read at the library said only eight percent of the population slept that way.

Dad's position was much more common. The research noted that people who slept on their sides were friendly and trusting. He was definitely the nicest person I knew. Mom was a different story. She was evil.

I didn't have a regular sleep position that I knew of, as the crazy state of my hair announced every morning. Instead of lying flat in the back like Mom's or pancaked on one side like Dad's, my hair looked as though squirrels nested in it—a whole family.

The sleep position paper talked about how people who tossed and turned all night were complicated. That didn't hold true at all—nothing about me was fussy. I didn't think so anyway, but Mrs. Gerhardt had cornered me one day to say different.

"You've got an entire world behind those eyes, Lela, my dear," she'd said, sliding a stack of journals over the counter. She'd also included a copy of a book by Roald Dahl, *The Magic Finger* scrolled across the cover. "I have a feeling you'll like this. A little young for you, maybe, but right up your alley." I'd smiled and backed away until my shoulders found the solid backing of the doors, then ran all the way home.

I'd never tell her, but I liked the book. I read it quickly and under the flare of a flashlight and the weight of my covers. That night I'd had a magic finger to punish my mother.

I wasn't as perplexing as Mrs. Gerhardt thought, but maybe needing to watch Mom and Dad sleep wasn't a simple thing. Still, sneaking into their bedroom always proved easy enough.

Not every kid had my interests. I'd observed my classmates—at recess and in class, at story hour at the library. Even at the park. Other kids played and laughed, ignoring the bad things that happened around them. For all I knew, maybe they spent their nights thrashing in their bed sheets while reliving the shuttle explosion, just like me. No one could know my most secret part, so maybe they had secret missions, too.

Something told me I was special, though, and not just because my mother had caused the accident. I could keep the astronauts safe if I learned how. There were clues. I just needed to solve the mystery.

I'd already thought it through—the astronauts probably all slept on their backs like Mom. They had to on the shuttle; there was no other choice once the straps fastened them to their seats.

Panic swelled my tongue. Flames licking at their feet, blistering my skin, blackening their flesh and crackling in my ears. *They didn't have to, didn't have to, didn't have to.* I seized at the calm of my muttering. If it happened again, I would know it was all while the astronauts slept... completely unaware. And the knowing is what stopped it.

Mom smacked her lips, and then her arms shot out from under the blanket, sandwiching her body onto the mattress. Her mauve night-gown wrinkled over her chest. My lids drooped, but I was determined to keep my eyes open. My own sleep could wait. There were too many important things to do.

I held my position to stare at them for another couple of minutes before moving on to the official observation, just like I'd read about. Mrs. Gerhardt had pointed me in the right direction—I'd told her Dad snored really loud.

"This is a very grown up thing for you to read," she'd said, helping me reach the journals high on the rack. "Maybe you can talk to your parents about the studies."

I'd shrugged and grinned.

I sniffed and made a pass around the room. Stinky perfume, Mom's brush, lamp, white dresser scarf. I wrote it all down on the notebook, careful to point out the shoes—mauve sandals—kicked to the side of the bed. Dad's shoes were jumbled by the door, and his jeans draped over the chair in the corner. I could have named every object in their room with my eyes closed, but I was adhering to the scientific method now.

I had to observe, watch, record. My teacher taught us about genetics this year, making us grow pea plants to document. My notes had been perfect; she'd said so.

Dad grunted and rolled closer to Mom, the squeak of a fart sounding from his side of the bed. Mom moved more than he did…her arms and legs, anyway. The rest of her stayed almost eerily still.

I'd seen a movie about vampires, and they'd lain in coffins with their arms crossed over their chests. It was easy to imagine her like that. The moonlight washed out her skin, bloodless and waxy, turning her into a horrible monster. I tilted my head, peering into her slightly opened mouth to search for her fangs.

Her teeth flashed, normal and white, though, the pointy ones seeming the typical length. I wondered if she'd scream and cry if I drove a wooden stake through her heart.

The gray shadows hugged Dad, hiding him away from the light. Even in the dimness, I could still see it when his arms or legs slid this way and that, and I duly marked every twitch and twinge.

The moonlight crept across the floor until the first vestiges of dawn appeared. I stood at the foot of the bed and waited. Watched. Recorded.

Chapter Twelve

SMALL, WHITE FLOWERS

KORCHAGIN ARRIVED AT THE TEAHOUSE TWENTY MINUTES AFTER I did. Had he bribed Magda to alert him when I showed up? Again, I wondered why he wasn't at work—maybe there was a different training protocol for the cosmonauts.

"I did not tell you last time we met, but I like your house," he said.

"Oh, well, thank you. I inherited it from my father." I tried not to let the grimace rise to my face. He couldn't know how much I minded that he'd secreted that note into my door.

"Inherited?"

"My father passed away," I said.

"I am sorry."

"Thank you. It was quick." I could hear the doctor's voice in my head, see the expression on his face as he delivered the news. Dispassionate. Unemotional.

I envied his detachment.

"And your mother?"

An awkward pause stretched between us. I took a deep breath in through my nose, a hint of her floral perfume in the air of the teahouse. I glanced around—for what, I wasn't quite sure—but she didn't magically appear beside me, dressed in mauve with an insult on her tongue. *She's gone, she's gone, she's gone,* I chanted to myself.

Perhaps Trina lurked around a corner. She'd been acting even chummier since her return. I didn't know what to make of it—the changes in her appearance, in her behavior. It was disquieting, to say the least. It was possible her sleeping habits had changed; a study had once shown that the sleep deprived appeared less attractive and healthy than those who got plenty of sleep. But voice and height should not have been affected. It wasn't even possible, but when it came to Trina, anything could happen.

"She's...not in my life," I said.

"Oh, she passed away as well?"

"No. She just, well, she went away when I was ten. She left."

My mother's disappearance was the last thing I wanted to discuss.

Even though I knew the answers, had the research squirreled away in his navy blue folder in my closet cabinet, I asked anyway: "Tell me about your parents?"

"I am named for my father's father. Not a Russian, by the way, which was quite scandalous to the family at the time." During the pause that followed, he raised a bushy eyebrow, and a small smile showed through the trimmed hair of his goatee. "Beyond this, there is not much to tell. My father, he is an electrician by trade, although my mother and father run a small deli together, not too different from this," he said, gesturing toward the kitchen with a flip of his hand.

"Oh? Are the menus similar at your parents' restaurant?"

My instincts told me to hold back and put some distance between us, but the part of me compelled to observe him and calculate the microarousals of his sleep leaned in and smiled, encouraging him to share his life story with me.

"Well," he peeked around, "do not tell anyone, but my mother's borscht is much better. I also miss her chalakhach very much—it is not on the menu here."

"What's that—chal...ak..."

"Chalakhach," he corrected. "It is lamb chops."

"I'm sure Magda would force the cook to make it for you if you asked."

He ducked his head, hand drifting up to stroke the hair on his chin, just the color of nutmeg. "I would not want to take advantage. I just go into space. It is...I believe the expression is *no big deal*. I enjoy it, and I am proud to be a part of it, but I do not think it is important."

"No!" I said. "Being an astronaut is huge!" I cleared my throat and attempted to modulate my excitement. "It's an important accomplishment."

He cocked his close-shorn head to the side, stayed silent.

"While I can't say I know much about the Russian space program," I babbled, "it likely means the same things it means here—you're academically gifted, you possess excellent physicality and ability to withstand extremes in atmosphere and mental pressure, and you likely have superior leadership qualities."

"Do you know many astronauts?"

My entire body locked down. I focused on the collar of his shirt. *Breathe.* Four-three-two-one-in, four-three-two-one-out.

"No. Several have been into the lab for studies, of course, but I've not been in the position to work with them."

The rest of lunch was uneventful. I observed him, noting what he ate, how he phrased things. By the time I went back to the office, I had many things to add to his file, including more about his grandmother. He'd talked about her quite a bit, telling me stories about her antics, the weirdest of which involved nearly getting herself killed when she broke through the crowd during a Soyuz launch. He'd been tucked away inside the capsule, but he'd heard later that she'd thrown rocks at the launch pad and demanded he be released. She'd been sure someone had tinkered with the fuel lines, and that he was in danger.

He chuckled at my reaction, saying only, "It is the love affair with madness."

He couldn't guess that I'd been appalled, and the greater part of me wondered if I had a Russian counterpart looking out for the safety of the cosmonauts. The Russian program had had its share of fatalities over the years, although nothing nearly as catastrophic as NASA, and nothing recent—in fact, not since the early seventies. My gut told me it was more luck than safety by design, though.

Korchagin had also supplied me with his entire itinerary for the week. That night he'd attend a NASA event, some sort of training lecture. I'd even learned he had no security system guarding his apartment against break-ins.

Even work had been pleasant—Trina spent the remainder of the day off in one of the labs running a study, which would keep her there until at least ten at night. After reviewing my research, feeding Nike, and installing the lock on my dad's door, I texted Trina that I was going to visit a sick friend and left for Korchagin's apartment moments before she was due back at my house.

The drive to Clear Lake passed as though the universe approved of my progress, and for the first time in weeks I smiled out of genuine joy.

The weather had broken. While the breeze blowing through the small crack at the top of my car window didn't approach the level of humidity I'd grown used to, it wasn't the cool touch on my face I'd been hoping for. It did smell of jasmine, though, a thick scent that tickled my nose and tempted me to roll down the window even farther.

I'd always loved the smell and the small, white flowers. Dad had always preferred night blooming jasmine, although he never planted it at the house. "It'll compete with the roses," he'd said. Korchagin's apartment complex was surrounded, the buds trumpeting off the shrubs like shooting stars.

But now was not the time to stop and smell the flowers. I had work to do.

Since things between Korchagin and me bordered on less contentious, my brain had centered itself, better able to concentrate. His placid gray eyes and generous mouth still occasionally popped up in my mind, but it wasn't distracting. In some ways Zory and I engaged in almost an old-fashioned and slow courtship—an odd thing to consider given my disinterest in relationships.

Dad told me once about the way he and Mom started dating. She'd come to Houston to go to college. Moving across the country for school was unusual for a woman at the time, and Dad admired her confidence. He'd lived in the dorm next to hers, although he didn't ask her out until the end of their freshman year—he said he wanted to wait for her to date all the other guys on campus sniffing around her.

"Your mother was a force to be reckoned with," he used to say, a fondness in his expression that I never quite understood. Dad never stopped missing her. I used to think he stayed quiet around me sometimes because I reminded him of her.

She'd said yes to him—he'd asked her to the movies. They'd seen a film about demonic possession, and afterwards they'd grabbed something to eat. I wasn't sure how much of that was true; Mom once told me she wasn't impressed with him at first, but he'd finally worn her down. She'd mentioned the two of them "toking up" in her room. At the time she told me that, I didn't understand. Even after I did get it when I grew older, it made even less sense to me.

Dad said that when people didn't have a grip on their faculties, they did stupid things they didn't mean to do. "You of all people should understand that, Lela."

The parking lot was lit only by a few dim lamps, and I parked in the far corner. I cracked open the door of my car as quietly as possible, the hinges barely making a sound, thanks to The Chin's good advice on lubricant. There was no one in the lot to hear a noise anyway—it was deserted.

Two-thirds of American adults are in bed and sleeping by midnight. It was only a quarter after eleven, but prior investigations had taught me the majority of those who kept a typical schedule would be in their apartments for the night. Still, after my last foray into Korchagin's building, I knew at least some of his neighbors had been home during the day. There was no telling what I might encounter.

I tugged on a curly blonde wig and swiped pinkish-purple lipstick over my mouth. It wouldn't do to be recognizable to the woman I'd encountered on the stairs or the man who'd pulled me into the closet during the tornado.

Inside my bag were the usual tools: autoinjector, latex gloves, camera, lock picks, and the clipboard with the observation forms. I'd decided not to develop an assassination scheme yet because Korchagin wouldn't be home for hours, and there might be something learned during this first investigation into his living space that might be useful for putting one together later.

I stepped out of the car and crossed the lot, noting the other flowers growing around the building. Even in the dim light, the hummingbird bushes glowed as though flames licked up around the petals.

Your heart, as it was then, will be on fire.

I shook my head to clear the thought. They were just shrubs, nothing more—green leaves, crimson flowers. Not a hummingbird in sight. Dad's voice came to me: *Just focus, honey.*

A man sat in the lobby, but he didn't even look up from his newspaper when I rushed past. I glanced around the corner into the stairwell. Quiet. The type of quiet that echoed in my ears.

Giggles—perhaps from a few young kids—wafted under the door at the second-floor landing. I readied the autoinjector, but no one came through. What were they even doing up that late? Children required eight to nine hours of sleep each night. The risks if they didn't get enough sleep at that age were severe.

I ticked over the behavioral problems associated with lack of sleep until I stood in front of Korchagin's door. The hallway was dead. Not a movement. Not even the suggestion of another conscious person. I closed my eyes and let my ears pick up the sounds: the hum of air conditioners, the faint chatter of birds beyond the walls, the sound of my own heart pushing blood through my body. With practiced hands, I reached for the knob.

The lock gave in seconds. That was unacceptable. Anyone could break into his apartment. He needed more security, more deadbolts. Yes, it was easier for me to get in, but he had his safety to think about. My observations only extended as far as keeping the shuttle from exploding. I couldn't protect him from harm all the time, particularly if he didn't take responsibility for his own home.

As I'd speculated, his living space was simple and unadorned. Plain furniture that had likely come with the apartment dotted the living room. A small galley kitchen sat just off the living space. His refrigerator was almost as bare as my own: milk, jam, a few take-out containers. He was clean. Every surface in the kitchen sparkled.

The bathroom was messier. Towels were slung over a bar, not folded. Bristles of hair dotted the bottom of the sink, as though he'd trimmed his goatee and left without cleaning up. I indicated the soap and shampoo he used in my notes before moving on to his medicine cabinet. No prescription medications—just a bottle of aspirin and his shaving cream. I snapped a few shots of the room to study later.

The knob to his front door rattled.

I raced to the door, my heart pumping. With my back pressed against the wall next to the frame, I detached the autoinjector from the clipboard and waited.

Breathe. Four-three-two-one-in, four-three-two-one-out.

"The key won't turn." A female voice slurred.

"You have it in there right?" A man, but it wasn't Korchagin. Outrage built in my chest. Were they breaking in? But with a key? Who had given them his key?

They fumbled for another ten minutes, arguing and trying to force the door. How would I incapacitate two of them? The autoinjector held just enough serum for one person—I'd have to aim for the man.

"You ain't even got the right floor!" the man howled. "This is three—you're on four!"

The woman giggled, and the clicking of the knob stopped immediately. Their voices became fainter—moving down the hall, I assumed. I shook my head and allowed myself to relax a fraction. Perhaps Korchagin would consider moving if this was indicative of the quality of his neighbors.

I tiptoed to his bedroom, intent on finishing my first investigation within twenty minutes. These initial explorations were never in-depth. It was mostly to understand the layout of the apartment, determine personality and habits. I'd already gotten a jumpstart on the latter.

His bed was made, a brown comforter pulled tight across the mattress with a bank of pillows leaning against the wooden headboard. Several books were stacked on top of a tall chest of drawers, along with a pile of papers.

His closet door and all the drawers were closed. A pair of pants, folded, rested on the seat of a chair.

I wandered closer to the books and took a photograph. All the titles were in Russian.

A plain black book sat next to the pile of novels. Within were several pictures sandwiched behind an acetate sleeve. A tall skinny man with Korchagin's sharp nose and a shorter woman with short, brown hair—probably his parents since they were standing behind a deli counter. Another shot showed an older lady with a gap-toothed smile and a face like a gargoyle, half hiding behind a stone monument. His grandmother, maybe. She even looked crazy, her clothes mismatched and a short-shorn head.

His drawers and closet were neat without the fastidious attention to detail a typical military man might have had. Tucked in with his boxer briefs were letters, but they were, again, in Russian. Perhaps I could pay a translator to convert them to English. Of course, that would leave a paper trail, which I couldn't afford.

Frustrated, I perched on the edge of his bed. Firm mattress. I curled up, careful to keep my shoes off the comforter. A scent clung to the pillows—musky and woodsy.

Each moment brought new questions about who Korchagin really was. Could he be as forthcoming as he seemed? There was nothing all that useful in the apartment, nothing that could prove or disprove a thing. It was as if Trina had caught wind of my intentions and white-washed the place before I'd gotten here.

I rolled over and sprang from the bed. It was a possibility. There hadn't been any scratches on the lock on my closet door, but I hadn't scrutinized it. If I had learned to pick locks cleanly, she probably had, too.

The lock on Dad's room was useless.

Nike would tell me if she'd broken in, though.

Back in the car, I tried to block out the annoying buzz of street lights while making my final notes. This observation was different in every way. The noise grew and grew, reverberating around me until I had to close my eyes and focus on the small voices whispering my name.

✳✳✳

TRINA ATE HER LAST BITE OF TOAST AND WIPED HER HANDS ON THE napkin tucked into her shirt. After her final gulp, she grinned. That, too, had changed—it was my mother's, through and through, but it was more sinister than I'd ever seen it before. "So, tell me about this boyfriend of yours. I didn't even know you were dating anyone. You can definitely keep a secret."

Three can keep a secret if two of them are dead. It was as though she and my mother had hissed it into my ear, clear as day.

I jack-rabbited out of my chair, all but hurling my teacup into the sink. "Oh, would you look at the time." My voice rose to a squeakiness not even dogs could hear. "I should go. Early meeting about a study and, you know, paperwork."

Not that I considered Zory my boyfriend in any way, but how had she found out I'd decided to let him see me again? She'd been spying. My stomach clenched.

"You're so right! We should get going. Goodness, let me grab my bag."

I endured her chatter on the way to work, waiting for her to drive a knife into my neck or start cackling madly. I glanced over as I drove down the exit ramp. A sparkly barrette hung in her hair. Not my mother's barrette, but something similar. That was new.

The queerest feeling crept through my stomach and up my throat. Even during the elevator ride up to our floor, it scoured my insides.

She was biding her time.

I'd noticed similarities to my mother before, but now…Trina looked more like her than I'd thought possible. The barrette, the now-curly hair, the color of her clothes, the mouth. Even her cheekbones and the set of her eyes were familiar in a frightening way.

Something terrible popped into my head: My mother was back. She'd returned with some relative and sent her to watch me. Instructed her to work against me.

I couldn't think about it now. I had work.

Hours later, the chirp of my office phone dragged me out of an analysis of the data produced by a study I'd overseen a few days ago. A middle-aged man with wiry, electrified ear hair and a bald head had snored with so much gusto that the glass of the observation flexed, a warped-sounding *boing* digging around at the inside of my brain while I checked his oxygen saturation level. In all my years of working at the lab, I'd never heard anything quite so irritating, with the exception of Trina's voice. Snoring was usually an easy fix—it would contribute to the column with my points, and I'd end up ahead for the month. Maybe even enough to mitigate the chance I was taking with Korchagin.

"Forty Winks Science Laboratories. Lela White speaking."

"Lela." The rich, rounded consonants of my name had never sounded quite so luxurious. "It is Zory."

"Oh. Uh, hello."

"Good morning. How are you today?"

What was wrong with the phone number—my personal number—I'd provided for him or the email address I'd written down? Not that I checked my voice mails or email during work hours. Perhaps it was an emergency, although his voice sounded calm yet amused, just as always.

"I would like to take you to lunch. A proper date."

Holding the receiver away from my mouth, I sighed, exasperated. I couldn't say no, and on some level I didn't *want* to. I enjoyed his company more than I liked to admit, and I'd been hoping to see him today for lunch anyway. It was the best way to observe him now that he'd inserted himself into my life.

"Okay, yes. I can meet you at the tearoom shortly."

"Oh. That is fine. Would you like to try someplace new?" he asked. "I suspect you would be quite beautiful in the sunlight."

Not have lunch at my usual spot on a work day? I picked at the eraser on my pencil, tearing it to tiny, mauve shreds. Perhaps it wouldn't be an issue if I just saw the restaurant or if I walked inside and walked right back out. I would still technically be there. Yes, that would work.

"That's fine. Why don't we meet there, though, and make a decision about where to go?"

He hung up after agreeing. I powered down my computer, glancing around in the hopes that Trina wouldn't pop up before I had a chance to leave. The halls stayed silent as I crept out of our space toward the elevator, and I nearly made a clean escape from the building when a heavy hand clamped down on my shoulder.

I spun in the frame of the front door, catching sight of The Chin in street clothes instead of his usual dingy blue jump suit. His fine hair was carefully combed, the part perfect and even.

"Where ya off to, Lela?"

"Oh. I'm meeting a friend for lunch."

He fell into step beside me, even matching my stride, both of us avoiding the cracks in the sidewalk.

Step on a crack, break your mother's back.

The Chin's presence next to me felt wrong, as if I'd forgotten to feed Nike or failed to diagram an astronaut's room during an observation. I wanted him to be taller, thinner, and I tried to pretend his curving nose slimmed and straightened as we walked. The plodding footsteps kept me rooted to the reality.

The heat shimmered the air, a murky, gasoline-soaked haze through which we walked. With every step, I wished one of us would combust, burn to ash.

"You been okay?"

"Me?" My eyes cut toward him. The collar of his white button-down shirt sagged, gray with sweat. "Why would I not be?"

"I…well, I worry about you. Not that you never told me nothing, but I know things. I know your dad died, and you been living in that house by your lonesome for a while now. It ain't right."

"What's not right about that?"

"I don't mean nothing by it, but you shouldn't have to be alone. You say you're not the right woman for me, that it ain't got nothing to do with me being a janitor, but maybe you just didn't give me a fair shake."

Oh, God. This was worse than him thinking I needed to be sheltered and taken care of.

"I like my life as it is." The restaurant loomed at the end of the block. Zory was absent, something for which I was grateful. "And you shouldn't waste your time with someone who can't make room for you."

"I ain't so dumb as you think, you know." His dark eyes narrowed, back hunching even more as he slumped. He shoved a hand in his pants pocket.

"What's that supposed to mean?"

"You ain't never really liked me like I like you. No one never turned me into a stud horse before, and girls like you don't come around every day."

The Chin wasn't slow; I knew that. But he never questioned our weekly sex meeting in the janitor's closet, never pressed for more—not with any degree of urgency—until right before I ended things.

"I thought for a while I could pound you into wantin' me with all the screwing, but," he stopped short, putting his fingers on my arm to halt my progress, "you need to know that I would treat you good. We could have a life together if you'd give me a chance to prove to you the kind of man I am." His hand was the temperature of the sun, of burning rocket fuel.

I yanked away. "I…I don't want that," I sputtered. "Max, you're a good, kind man, and I know you have this vision of me, but I'm not that person."

"You have an awful funny idea about yourself." His hair blew in the sudden whipping wind, and I squeezed my eyes shut against the dust abrading my cheeks. "And me."

"Look, I don't want to stand here and argue. Do yourself a favor: Meet someone nice. You can take her home to meet your mom and go out on dates. Maybe you can even get married and have babies. You want that, right? To get married? Make a family?"

He nodded, eyes downcast.

"That's not what I want. My future does *not* involve weddings or children." *And it doesn't involve you,* I added, searching again for Korchagin. The sidewalk remained free of people, free from eyes that always watched. "It looks like you're dressed for something important— do you have something going on?"

He gaped. "Oh, well, yeah. Taking Mom to her foot doctor appointment. I," he said, inspecting his watch, shoulders slumping, "should get moving. Don't want to be late—she'll be madder than two cats in a sack."

I nodded.

"This isn't over, though, pretty girl. You didn't give me no good reason why we shouldn't go out." He smiled, bottom teeth almost peeking out over his lips and his chin jutting.

"Lela?"

Korchagin's brows ascended the slope of his forehead, gaze landing on The Chin. Before either of us had time to react, he stuck his hand out and grabbed The Chin's palm. It was unclear where he'd appeared from. It was as though he'd materialized from the very air.

Watch me pull a rabbit out of my hat.

"I am Zory Korchagin." In the bright sunlight, his eyes glowed almost dove gray.

"Oh. Well. I'm Max. Max Fowler."

"You are a friend to Lela?"

"Yeah, good friend, and we work together."

"Max was just leaving to see his mother," I said.

"It was nice to meet you, Max. Perhaps I see you again." Korchagin turned, a mischievous grin playing at his mouth, making me wonder what he looked like as a boy. It wasn't hard to picture him climbing over a jungle gym or napping. I was willing to bet he slept like the dead even as a child. "Shall we, Lela?"

The Chin stared at me for a moment, understanding dimming his eyes. "See you," he muttered, waving as he dragged his feet, heading for the corner.

"So," Korchagin brushed some of my hair away from my cheeks, "where can I take you for lunch?"

You will hear thunder and remember me, and think: she wanted storms. My face cracked.

Chapter Thirteen

A FEATHER FLOATING

K ORCHAGIN'S THICK-FINGERED HANDS SHREDDED THE BUN OF HIS sandwich into a mound of flakes at the side of his plate. His tall, wide frame spoke of his strength, but his hands appeared just a touch too big for his body. They belonged on an even larger man—someone who made his living by lifting heavy things or tilling the land to plant crops. They didn't have that worn, chapped look to them, but they still exuded a kind of roughness I wouldn't have associated with an astronaut.

"If I wouldn't have entered the space program? Oh, well, I don't know. An engineer, perhaps."

The bottled water froze my skin, goose flesh wreathing my wrist and spiraling up my forearm. Zory reached across the table and smoothed his thumb over the back of my hand—perhaps in an effort to ease the bumps—and I quelled the compulsion to snatch back my hand, at the same time fighting against the temptation to thread my fingers through his.

He liked to touch people, I'd noticed, and people loved to touch him. I didn't understand it, really. No one hesitated to shake his hand or squeeze his shoulder. It could have been the little boy impishness of his smile or the earnestness in his eyes. The guileless quality of his voice made him less threatening than his appearance suggested. Yet I had no doubt he could inflict physical damage if he wanted to.

Anyone could if the situation warranted.

"What did your parents want you to be?"

He pulled his thumb away, rubbing at the short, bristly hair beneath his lower lip. "I am not sure. I'm not even sure *they* knew. You have to understand growing up in Russia, well, when I was a kid, everything was much different than now."

"What do you mean?"

"It was the Soviet Union when I was very young. The state owned and controlled everything. My parents were lucky—they did not have to share a house with anyone, and they had a permit to own a car, but they did not hope for much. Their expectation was I would go to university some day. I was smart enough, and the school was free…you know, the state paid for it."

"That part sounds nice, at least—the free school."

"I have heard about how the American system works. It is more like this in Russia now, but I do not think it is as expensive."

I shrugged, thinking about my student loans. Dad had helped as much as he could, and I'd lived at home. It wasn't as bad as it could have been.

"I have cousins in university," Zory said. "Moscow State University, the Moscow Conservancy. One attends Belgorod State University. I went to Moscow Institute of Physics and Technology and trained at the Gagarin Cosmonaut Training Center. My babushka knew I would be in the space program when I was a child, even if my parents had not the will to say so." He paused. "What about you—what did your parents want you to be?"

"My father didn't care. He just wanted me to be happy."

"What about your mother? She had ambition for you, did she not? Mothers always do. I think it is tied up in the need to see you succeed. After we had more choice in Russia, my mother used to tell me she spent twenty-three hours in labor, so I had better do something to make her proud." His white teeth peeked through facial hair, a dimple I hadn't noticed before to the side of his mouth. "She even threatened me once when I got a bad grade. Babushka, too. She told me she'd sneak into my room at night and steal my teeth."

"Your grandmother sounds, well, colorful." That was one way to put it. More like it sounded like she belonged in a loony bin. I was growing to accept that Korchagin did not always operate with a rational mind. "I'm not sure my mother gave much thought to what I might grow up to be."

"What was she like? I am told daughters often grow up to be like their mothers."

I shook my head. "No, I hope not, at least in my case. She…well, she was the kind of person who should have never had children—I don't think she liked them very much."

"Did she not like you? How could that be?"

"You don't really know me."

"You help people sleep better. That's generous and loving. And you let me take you out without knowing much about me." He cocked his head to the side. "And you read Russian novelists—which of itself means you cannot be a bad person."

"Oh. So you like poetry, I guess, right?" I readjusted my glasses on my face. "And Dostoyevsky?"

His mouth tightened, almost as if his lips wanted to kiss. "Yes, I do. Given our conversation about *The Idiot*, it makes sense you think I like Dostoyevsky, but why would you think I like poetry?"

His eyes darkened as he leaned forward, the color of his irises morphing from the gray of river stone to the shimmering pewter of a pigeon's feathers.

"You left me that part of a poem on the note at my house. And you mentioned a different poem the other day."

"Mmmm, yes. Many things remind me of you."

The feeling of flying made my stomach bottom out. Men had complimented me before, said pretty things, but I'd never allowed it to affect me. Maybe he was rubbing off on me.

"I looked up the poem. You know, the one you left on my door… after Magda told me the name."

"So you said. How did you like it?" The light smile on Korchagin's face made him years younger.

Angry. Hungry. I considered for a moment before answering, wanting to be sure whatever I chose to say didn't reveal too much.

"It was lovely, but it made me sad."

"Sad? How so?" Two twin wrinkles appeared between his brows, like parallel boughs of a tree.

"Well, the writer talked about not being with the one she loved, right?"

"Mmm hmm, but it is a love poem. You objected to me leaving it for you." He adopted a crescent moon smile, lips clamped shut. And when I nodded, his mouth trembled. "Do you know Akhmatova?"

I was glad he said the poet's name. Even after searching for a pronunciation, I'd had problems trying to figure it out exactly. I'd stared at Trina while she slept (or pretended to sleep), running over and over the possibilities in my mind.

"No. I was much more into science and math in school than things like literature."

"That does not surprise me—you are very precise. I like that about you. Everything is just so, every word carefully chosen." When I didn't say anything, his smile loosened. "Akhmatova is a well-known poet in Russia. Much of her work is quite political."

"Oh?"

"She was critical of Stalin, and she was censored. My parents both revere her. She was the voice of their fear and distrust."

"But the poem you left for me—that didn't have anything to do with—"

He smiled again, less restrained this time. "No, it was a poem about her lover."

Oh.

"Do you write?" I asked.

"Poetry?"

I nodded. His face didn't dim, but he reached for my hand again, this time tracing the outline of my fingers with the tips of his; it tickled. The urge to scuttle backwards was less this time, but still there.

"No, but it has always been part of my studies."

"Is Akhmatova your favorite?"

"I would not say so. She was my ex-girlfriend's favorite. I like Akhmatova very much, but Ilya Kutik is my favorite."

"Ex-girlfriend?" I asked.

"Alyona. We broke up before I came here."

"Oh. Was it serious?" I hated myself for asking. What did it matter? But I was my father's daughter, always asking questions and seeking the truth.

"We were supposed to marry, but she ended things. She did not want me to come to the States, but I could not stay away. We fought about it, but in the end, I had to put the space program first. You are very different from her. You are a puzzle." He paused, the weight of his eyes like a physical caress. "And I am interested in the whole."

I did pull my hand away from his then, under the pretense of eating, not saying a word in the hopes that he'd keep talking about his ex-girlfriend, simultaneously concentrating on ignoring the thrill that ran through me at his words. Despite my efforts, a small fire lit in the embers of my chest, the sparks heating my face. I swore the scent of jet fuel hung in the air below the odor of food.

Eventually he did continue. The achievement of gleaning information from him without having to ask was a strangely victorious feeling, twining with the warmth to lull me into a strange quasi-contentment that also filled me with terror. There was no winning in any of this, but it seemed as though we had yet another thing in common: putting the shuttle before anything else.

"I was surprised to find it didn't hurt in the way I'd expected." His voice drifted between us, a feather floating and landing without a sound.

"Were your parents upset?"

He shrugged and flattened his palms against the table. "Perhaps my mother, but my father understood. He sided with my grandmother, who said Alyona did not feel lucky. Now I could not agree more."

"Again with the luck."

"My father is quick to believe my babushka, just as I am. She has always taken great care to follow the signs, and it stuck with him."

"What does that mean—the signs?"

A flash of white peeked from between his lips. "It means that my babushka believes in the old customs. Americans consider a broken mirror bad luck, yes?"

I nodded.

"She knows this also brings bad luck if you *look* into a broken mirror. A birthday can never be celebrated early, or it will bring bad things to the house."

"What does that have to do with your ex-girlfriend?"

He laughed. "After Alyona left, my babushka pulled me aside to say a woman like that could never be good for me." The pads of his fingers tapped the table three times. "Did you date the man you were with earlier...Max, I think his name was?"

"No."

His laugh came easy. "He is certainly taken with you. I cannot blame him."

"What do you mean?"

"You already know I want to see you."

"We're on a date," I pointed out.

"Yes, but I like you quite a bit." After a moment, he reached over to tuck a strand of hair behind my ear, and I stiffened.

He muttered something under his breath that sounded like Russian.

"What did you say?"

"Oh, there's a bit of a Kutik poem I've been thinking about lately."

"What is it?"

For just a moment his cheeks colored, but then his eyes pinned me. "It is probably not right for me to tell you. It is too forward for you...for us. You know, right now."

"Let me be the judge of that."

He took a deep breath. "Okay, but I warned you. I like you, Lela, and I do not want you to think I am...how you say...coming on too strong."

I hoped my smile appeared encouraging, and it must have because he sat up straighter. In doing so, it put more distance between us, although the moment felt painfully intimate.

"You must sense how my hand's caress travels first along your spine." He broke off, and I swore an icy fingertip skimmed up my back as his words echoed in my head. "From the uppermost vertebrae to your waist, and then inclines back again."

I shivered, the air burning and freezing at the same time. It was his eyes, searing and unguarded, that made me feel as though I should run...give up my plans and escape from the tightness in my chest.

But he continued reciting, and I could do nothing but sit there, petrified and half-aroused. "...in languid absent-mindedness until that moment when the lines all intersect..."

My ears contained an entire hive of bees. Nothing sounded in my head but buzzing until I shook my hair out and heard, "search for its armor's alphabetical chink in all epithelial directions." The stings were a million hypodermic needles.

Maybe Zory was right: I wasn't ready to hear this.

✳✳✳

H AS A MAN EVER RECITED LOVE POETRY TO YOU?" Mrs. Gerhardt snorted and glanced up, an amused smirk etched onto her lips. The library held the stale smell of dust, worse than usual. "Oh, Lela, honey. Is this about your young man?"

I nodded and scanned in the book from the returns pile, thinking of Zory's fingertip on my spine.

"What poem?" She stacked the returns on the cart to be reshelved, her thin arms trembling with the effort.

"Something by Ilya Kutik."

"A Russian?"

"Of course."

The smirk widened. "Well, let's just look up Mr. Kutik, shall we? He must be in 808.1, yes?"

"Probably. But I don't know the name of the poem."

"No matter—we'll find it." She tapped the keys of the computer. "Hmm, okay. So he doesn't have a collection of his own, but several of his works appear in a larger…"

"It's not that important," I said, stamping another book.

"Not important? I daresay it must be. I'm fairly certain I've never seen you blush the entire time I've known you. Not even when your father announced that you'd gotten your period."

That had been humiliating; even then I'd hated anyone knowing my business. For him to announce I'd "become a woman" in the middle of the biweekly volunteer meeting was not something I had been happy about. One of the junior librarians had even tried to give me a silly book about menstruation. I'd glared at her until she went away, book tucked under her arm.

Mrs. Gerhardt tugged at my sleeve, urging me to follow. We wound around the stacks, with me trailing after her at a snail's pace, until we reached the poetry collection. She muttered and scratched her fingertips over the spines of the books.

"Ah, here we are." She slid a slim volume out and flipped to the back, her breathing heavier than it had been just moments before. After a moment, she said, "Not Russian—Ukrainian." She paused. "He went to school in Russia, though."

"Okay."

She flipped back to the front, eyes bouncing across the page. She raised her eyes to mine. "Did the poem mention your nipples?"

"What? No." My arms automatically crossed over my breasts.

"Something about a sparrow?"

I shook my head.

"Oh, this one's sexy. *On your back I trace the letter A.*"

"That's the one."

She read more, and a few moments later she looked up and placed the book in my hands. The pages were thin and brittle, but the words were lush. I could feel her eyes on me as I scanned the lines. Another pass-through, and I shelved the book.

"So this man. What did you say his name is?" she asked.

"Zory."

"This Zory. He has, well, intentions."

"Yes, it seems so."

"How do you feel about that?"

I sank onto the floor, pulling my knees up and leaning back against the shelf. "He's really attractive."

It was a very bad thing that I allowed myself to admit it. But I was determined to complete my observation without letting it get in the way. There was no reason for me to care about such a thing.

"That's not what I asked." She haltingly lowered herself to perch on the step stool in the aisle, almost panting now.

"I don't know. I mean, he's nice. And I like him. But I'm not sure this is a good idea."

"Mmm hmm, I remember you saying that. Sometimes, though, you can't let your head make all the decisions. He's got a good job. You like him."

"It's more complicated than that."

"Explain it to me."

"I can't." God, how I wished I could.

She struggled to stand, and I sprang to my feet, helping her, my hand under her elbow. "I may be an old woman, but I've heard it all. There's nothing you can't tell me, you know?"

"I know," I lied. "But I'd rather keep this to myself. Just for now."

She shook her head. "That's fine. Just know that if you need to chat, you can come to me."

We shuffled around the stacks, heading back to the circulation desk. Her pace was so slow, and she smelled different than she used to: baby powder and an old, mildewy odor rather than the almost gingerbread scent I'd come to associate with her. Her breath rattled in her chest.

My eyes were focused on the back of her head when she turned. "Whatever happens, don't let him rush you into anything."

I grinned. "You don't have to worry about that."

She snorted again in between short gasps. "Mmm. I'll bet. I know you think you're so analytical, missy, but let me tell you—your heart is bigger than you give yourself credit for. For instance, I bet I can convince you to take a shift in the children's section to read to them."

"Think so, do you?"

"You can say no, of course, but I'd think you'd like the chance to prove you're better at it than Trina. The kids like her, but she's kind of silly. Talks down to them. I think you'd be better. Might as well give it a shot before she comes back to the library."

"Wow, you're really being pretty transparent," I said, watching her red lips smile. "What's all this really about?"

"Nothing. Nothing at all." Her head tilted to one side. "You'd make a good reader, that's all. And children are good judges of character. Perhaps you could bring Zory by eventually and let them decide for you if this man is worth your attention."

Leaving the fate of the shuttle program to the girls and boys I'd seen in the reading room. I chuckled. "Yes, I'm sure that's a fine idea. Maybe we can let them run for mayor of Houston while we're at it."

"You don't believe children can be serious?" Mrs. Gerhardt asked. "You were nearly funereal when you were their age."

"So? I was more mature than they were."

"Maybe. You can't imagine what it was like to run across someone like you, but at the same time every child is obsessed with something. Whether it's princesses or trucks or drawing. You were just interested in something more advanced." She flapped a hand toward the shelves. "And maybe all they need is a good role model, someone who will talk to them like adults. You could…I don't know, shepherd along their interests."

"You really think that'll be useful?" I asked.

"I do. And I think being around the kids would be good for you, too."

"In what way?"

"You're still a pretty serious woman," she said. Her face was chalky beneath her face powder. "Hanging out with them now and then might help you remember how to have fun."

"I know how to have fun," I said. It might not have been her idea of a good time, but my mission was all the recreation I needed.

"Then say you'll do a reading. You don't have to commit to it as a regular thing, although I'd love to see that. Just do it once and see how you feel."

I nodded and leaned against the circulation desk. There was something in what she was saying. I wouldn't live forever, and it wasn't likely I'd have children to pass along my legacy. Maybe it was possible to identify someone like me at an early age.

The preparations, the trial and error. None of it would be necessary if I could find an apprentice.

The shuttle program need not ever be in jeopardy again. The thought turned over and over, but I could come to only one conclusion: Nike and I would have to discuss it.

Chapter Fourteen

A MILLION FISTS POUNDING

"He had it coming."

"But, honey, you have to understand that you can't solve all your problems by hitting first and asking questions later." Dad frowned, although his eyes were still kind.

"Dad, you don't get it. He said—"

"It doesn't matter what he said. You could have really hurt the boy. Now you're suspended from school. You're lucky they didn't decide to expel you. How's that going to look when you're applying for college?"

It was a little early to be talking about college—I wasn't even eleven yet. Dad wouldn't let me tell him exactly what happened with Brian Deems, but it was bad. He insulted the astronauts on the *Constitution*, said they weren't heroes. Even Dad wouldn't have been mad about my smacking Brian if he'd only let me explain. Besides, I hadn't hit him hard. He'd hardly even bled.

And really, I barely even remembered doing it. The words had come out of his mouth, my brain went fuzzy, and *bam*! He was on the ground holding his face.

The front door slammed, and Mom's voice screeched, "Lela Farley White! You get your ass in this room right this instant!"

Dad and I sighed at the same moment, and his shoulders sagged.

"Go on," he murmured. "Get it over with."

He walked me out, hand on my shoulder. Before I could even come to a complete stop in front of Mom, a sharp pain rolled across my cheekbone, hot and hard, and my glasses flew off. The crack of her hand against my face ricocheted off the ceiling, and my father's abrupt intake of breath was a dim noise from behind me.

"Jesus Christ, Roni, what the hell do you think you're doing?" He pulled me behind him, although his rangy frame was scant protection. My face had exploded into a flaming wall of skin, the throb ringing on the underside of my skull like a million fists pounding to get out.

"She's running around beating the shit out of little kids, Gus! You baby her, and she'll never learn what's right and wrong!"

"Lela, sweetie." Dad's soft, gravelly voice cut through some of the sting, and his hand patted my hair. My glasses slipped against my fingers as he handed them back to me. "Go to your room, okay? Go lie down."

I was too shocked to cry—and besides, Mom told me crying was for babies—but I had the sense to do what Dad asked. The hallway walls smoothed, too cold and too slick, under my hand as I stumbled, stubbing my toe on the baseboard. Shouting came from the living room, followed by hissing and spitting, like a cat doused in water.

The thump of my heart beat in my face, pounding out a miserable rhythm. It would make reading hard, but I'd picked up a new journal about sleep architecture at the library. Mrs. Gerhardt and I had talked about some of the words I'd need to understand it. Polyphasic sleep. Sleep depth.

Before rounding the corner into my room, I put on my glasses and stopped in the bathroom. Even squinting against the light, I could see a handprint—well, the fingers of it anyway—blooming bright pink against my cheek. Even a cool wash cloth didn't help with the redness or with the pain.

Dad checked in on me a while later, pulling the book out of my still-shaking hands.

"Are you okay?"

I nodded, not really in the mood to talk.

"Your mother's just worried about you—she didn't mean to hurt you like that."

My head bobbed on my neck as though I agreed, but I knew the truth. She had every intention of slapping me. She'd never done it before, but I could see she would have kept hitting if Dad hadn't pulled me away. I was young, not stupid.

"Just keep out of the way for a bit until I can calm her down."

He didn't have to ask. I was content to stay in my room and never see my mother ever again. She hated me. She pretended to like me—sort of—when Dad was around or when she wanted other people to think she was a good mom. When she wasn't in a crap mood, she wasn't all that bad. Most of the time her mood sucked.

It thundered again that night, but I didn't dare sneak into Mom and Dad's bedroom. When I shut my eyes I saw the fire mushrooming in the blue sky, billowing out on itself and trailing to puffy white streams—my usual dream—and I'd blink furiously, trying to push the thought of the charred flesh away. With every gasp, I could almost smell what I imagined to be the odor of shuttle fuel.

Breathe. Four-three-two-one-in, four-three-two-one-out.

The door of my bedroom shushed against the carpet, and I kept my eyes shut, not wanting Dad to know I was awake. The edge of my bed dipped slightly, not heavy enough for his weight. Unless someone had broken into the house—and it was the preferable situation—my mother hovered over me.

"I know you're awake." Her voice competed with the dull hum of the air conditioning, hardly audible over the noise and cold as the air. It pinned me to the bed as effectively as if she sat on my chest. "You think anything you do matters? I burned 'em up, and I'll do it again. You'll see. They need to die."

Hot tears burned at my eyelashes. Even though I didn't want to cry, wetness streaked down my temple.

Mom saw it and laughed, gruff and derisive. My teeth ground together, hurting my jaw. The glittery barrette in her hair twinkled sharply like an angry beacon in the dim glow from the outside streetlamps.

"Don't think you'll get any sympathy from me with those big crocodile tears. I know your tricks. You're ugly—inside and out. An ugly, ugly girl."

With the next flash of lightning, she rushed from my room, and for a moment I wondered if I had imagined the entire thing.

Chapter Fifteen

PASSING ON THE LEGACY

T HE BOOKS STACKED HIGHER AND HIGHER ON THE COUNTER, ONE
after the other, until it seemed as if Mrs. Gerhardt had built a
cellulose and wood pulp wall between us. The part in her light hair
caught the overhead lights, flashing a seam of pale scalp.

"Thanks for coming in this afternoon, Lela. So hard to schedule
volunteers on a weekday sometimes."

"No problem. I've got an overnight study at the lab, so I had some
free time today to make up for it."

"Nothing with your young man?" I could hear the smile in her
voice.

Until that moment when the lines all intersect. Zory's poem had not
referred to those kinds of lines—of fate, of chance—but it didn't stop
his face from returning to me. I couldn't get him or Kutik's words out of
my mind. Even the conversation I'd had with Mrs. Gerhardt about luck
refused to fade out.

"No. Soon, though. Just not today."

She stuck her head out from behind the stack of books. The corners
of her mouth rose. "Any more poetry?

"No."

"That's too bad." She hesitated. "Are you letting him get to know
you?" I opened my mouth to respond but her eyes glaring down the
slope of her nose stopped my words. "The real you."

"I'm getting to know him," I said. That would have to be good enough.

"Hmph. Well. Did you finish the Dostoyevsky?"

"Almost. I like the dichotomy of light to dark, good to bad."

Mrs. Gerhardt turned and smiled. "Yes, I thought you might. What did you think of the prince?"

"I don't know. I mean, I know he's supposed to be this pure and good character, but what's the use? So far he hasn't made anyone's life better at all. It's silly. Sometimes taking a moral stand doesn't accomplish what's needed, and you need to get your hands dirty to make things happen."

"How so?"

The things I couldn't tell her balanced on my tongue. Instead, I said, "It's like what we were talking about before: You make your own luck through taking action."

"Interesting takeaway from the novel," she said. "Have you read *Dr. Jekyll and Mr. Hyde*?"

"Yes, of course. I read it years ago. I was in middle school, I think."

"Consider reading it again, using it to compare and contrast against *The Idiot*."

"Is that an assignment?" I asked. There was a slight gray-blue tinge to her skin. It made her red lips pop off her face.

"No, of course not. I just think you might find it interesting. We also just got some new psychology materials I think you'll like. One in particular was fascinating—a book on personality disorders." Her rheumy eyes studied my face.

I nodded. "So…shelve the books. Anything else you need me to do right now?"

"There will be a few more things. I might ask you to do a bit of paperwork for me this afternoon. And I'd still like you to take a shift in the children's section sometime soon."

She turned and disappeared into her office, and I pushed the book cart down the first aisle, thinking about the conversation Trina and I'd had this morning. She'd asked me not to tell Mrs. Gerhardt she was back. She needed time, she'd said; I hoped she'd spend the time looking for another place to stay. I'd asked her how the insurance and landlord debacles were shaping up. It was as though I'd opened the floodgates. She started to cry, big heaving sobs and snot bubbles and hiccups pouring out of her. In between hysterical outbursts, she wheezed out the story, although all I could make out was "landlord," "asshole," "so slow," and "homeless."

No one had ever prepared me for dealing with crying people. I'd read magazines and books and seen enough movies to know I was supposed to do *something*—be supportive in some way. The atmosphere swirled so uncomfortably between us, though, especially since I was so sure it was an act designed to get me to let my defenses down.

I didn't want to look at her, and there was no way I wanted to hug her. Eventually I'd moved close enough to pat her on the shoulder. I'd shuddered, hoping she didn't see, and moved away, but not fast enough—her hand darted out to grab my shirt, nearly pulling me over with the strength of her neediness. There was nothing else to do but continue patting her while staring at the ceiling. I found myself reciting Korchagin's second poem.

I'm surrounded by some overmuch silly, long and sticky spider web of touch.

Trina's clutching was not the kind of touch the poet—or Korchagin, for that matter—likely intended, but I was trapped, the steel bands of her fingers holding me in place, preventing my escape from the snare of her emotions.

I'd heard about the phenomenon of wanting to chew an arm off to escape awkward situations, and in that moment I seriously considered it, imagining the squeak of my teeth against sinew and muscle, bone and cartilage, tearing and wrenching, an ache in my shoulder radiating down to the stiff fingers patting her.

She was buying time, leaving herself enough of it to figure out a way to kill me. It was obvious. The changes since she'd returned from Austin, and all this increased melodrama…she waited and watched for an opening. My only solution was to cut out sleep altogether and be vigilant.

✳✳✳

THE STREETS OF MY NEIGHBORHOOD TWINKLED LIKE CRUSHED GLASS as I maneuvered through the development. Work had gone quickly, the study interesting—a middle-aged woman with terrible nightmares. Her REM periods, number of awakenings, and respiratory events had been off the charts. Most sleep studies were routine and quiet. Her patterns surprised and excited me. Each limb movement was violent and unexpected; it was fascinating. I couldn't wait to run it through the full analysis. As interesting as it was, I worried I might not be able to help her, which would earn me negative points. Unease gnawed against my ribs.

Nike met me at the door, nudging his yellow head against my ankle hard enough to almost knock me into the wall. I set my briefcase on the small table in the hallway and lifted the cat to lie over my shoulder, enjoying the rumble of his purr against my cheek, like a tiny but persistent lifeboat motor.

Trina pranced out of the bathroom, leering. "Hey, Lela! How was the study?" Some implied threat hung behind her words, although I couldn't quite figure out what she was trying to say.

"It went fine. It was a good one."

"You always get all the great cases."

She passed by me on her way to the kitchen. "I've got to go into the office, but can I make you something? Some toast? Or oatmeal?"

Right, and give her the opportunity she was looking for. I'd seen her in the kitchen pawing at my decoy food.

"No, thanks. I have some things to take care of. You go on ahead."

"Oh yeah? What are you up to today?"

My eyes narrowed. "Just running some errands."

She smiled with my mother's mouth. A small chip marred one of her front teeth, just like Mom's. "You going to the grocery store? Would you mind picking up some milk?"

An extra bit of contempt jolted me, poking at the tough hide of my belly. My mouth unleashed the blinding smile. "If I go, yes. I'll do that."

"Hey, so what would you think about me moving into your parents' room? I'll help you clean it out and everything. Your couch is really comfortable, but I worry about you."

"You worry about me?" *Right.*

"Well, yeah. I mean, your dad's been gone a year, and you're still keeping that room like a museum. It's time to move on, don't you think?"

"No." Maybe she noticed the rage in my eyes, although I hoped I'd cultivated it to look more like sadness when I explained about how carefully kept my mother's space remained and how much I missed my dad.

I played the traumatized daughter well.

When I asked Dad where she'd gone that morning—the morning

she was just gone—he'd stared, perplexed, like he couldn't quite figure out what I was asking. I would never forget his next words or the way he'd said them:

"Lela, are you okay?" he'd asked, like I might shatter into a million pieces.

He would only say she'd gone away, a disturbed set to his mouth, but as I got older I'd wondered why she'd left her clothes. Not that it mattered. Still, I always puzzled over whether there was more to the story—whether she met someone else and left Dad and me, or maybe she just didn't want to be my mom anymore, but Dad continued to see her. I didn't ask, though, because whenever she came up in conversation, Dad got so strange.

Trina moved toward the kitchen door, the strangest expression lighting her round face: victorious and dark. "Whatever you say! I should really get to the library, I guess. See you later. Maybe we can have dinner—I'll cook."

"Uh…maybe." Over my dead body, which wasn't far from what might happen if I agreed. "Did you talk to Mrs. Gerhardt? I told her you'd be away for a while."

If Trina returned to her regular volunteer shift, it might interfere with my plans. If I could recruit an intern or an apprentice from the children's reading group, there'd be a set of eyes on her in the library. Better counter-surveillance, for sure. The idea of spending time with the kids was sounding better and better.

"Oh, she won't care if I pop in," Trina said. "You watch—it'll be just like I never left at all."

She rushed toward the door, and I gripped the edge of the counter. I could hear her fumbling with her shoes, with the door, and then she was gone. The rumble of her engine outside broke the silence.

I stalked back through the hallway to my bedroom and rolled onto my comforter. Nike snuggled into my armpit. He kneaded the pillow under my head, the *snick* of his claws sinking into the cotton resounding in my right ear.

"This thing with Trina is getting out of hand," I said. "But I can't let her be my focus right now." He ignored me in favor of tenderizing his surroundings. He didn't disagree, so that was a good sign. "My attention has to be on Zory." *Korchagin*, I reminded myself.

Nike curled, resting his chin on my shoulder. I could tell he wondered how I felt about Korchagin.

"I don't know. I mean, he's a very nice man, and we do have a few things in common. I've never really dated anyone before, not like this… so I'm unsure of how to proceed. He hasn't attempted to take things in a sexual direction, aside from reciting the poem to me."

Nike closed his eyes, sighing.

"Yes, I know he's a man. He's healthy, so I'm sure he's got normal needs just like everyone else. But aside from a few pecks on the cheek," I said, "there's been nothing."

What about your janitor? How's that going?

"The Chin's been keeping his distance, for the most part. I haven't seen him at all." I smiled and said, "And Mrs. Gerhardt has this fantastic idea about expanding my mission. She wants me to read to the kids on the weekend."

What does that have to do with space shuttle safety? And since when does that woman know anything about your observations?

"I've always thought she must know more than she lets on, but maybe it's not such a bad thing. I can find someone like me, train them up to continue my observations when we're gone. I don't know why I never thought of it before. I wonder if any of the children in the group are up for adoption. It would mean that the shuttle is never without protection."

The purple-black light of the sky morphed into a lighter dusky hue, throwing the elm tree in the neighbor's yard into profile. Korchagin had insisted on picking me up at the house, intent on surprising me with whatever we were going to do. I still had six hours until he'd show up, more than enough time for a nap.

I lay awake and counted the cracks in the ceiling, thinking about passing on my legacy.

Chapter Sixteen

THE EYE OF THE BEHOLDER

COOL SHEETS TWISTED AROUND MY LEGS, THE COMFORTER GRASPED in my hands but otherwise not covering me. I shivered in the frigid breeze blowing across my shoulders, my teeth chattering. If I kept this up, I'd chip a tooth.

I reached for my clock and shielded my eyes with my arm: only an hour until Zory was due and a few minutes until the alarm went off.

I still hadn't slept, and Trina hadn't returned yet.

Whorl patterns in my ceiling turned into puffy clouds of vapor and smoke, splitting in two, transforming into the antennae of an ashen snail. Before the flames and pieces of detritus veered off from the formations, I vaulted out of bed, almost tripping on the sheets. The alarm sounded for a single beep before I slammed it off.

Up and at 'em, Dad's voice chirped in my head.

The sense of freedom of having the house to myself again—even if it was just for a few hours—returned in a gush of joy that blitzed down my throat and tickled my lungs. For the first time I could remember in, well, ever, I sang in the shower, my usually quiet voice filling the space with my tuneless yodel. I'd never enjoyed singing, even in private. There was something about the act that seemed so…personal.

Every syllable forced out of my throat prickled at my skin as though I bared my soul to the air particles, to Nike, to the toilet. My sixth-grade teacher had attempted to get me to sing in chorus; I couldn't even sing above a whisper when she tried to determine my voice range. That morning in the shower, though—it was as if I were nine years old again, before life had forced me into collecting myself so carefully.

There had been times we'd been a happy family, but Mom's weirdness as I got older made sure we didn't stay that way. There was something that had constricted its grip on me after she was gone, too. The shuttle disaster, her role in it, my mother's leaving…it all had something to do with the way my skin hugged me like a straitjacket.

Everyone had something to hide.

But now the possibility existed that I might find a kid who needed a purpose in life. Mrs. Gerhardt was almost an ally in my mission. It was as if the universe smiled on me, handing me more tools to ensure the shuttle's safety. It wasn't the time to focus on my recruitment process. I would think of it later.

Zory arrived with a bouquet of red flowers and a warm smile to accompany his normal greeting. Left peck, right peck, left peck, although the last kiss lingered a bit longer than normal, his short goatee tickling against my freshly showered skin.

"You look nice," he said, his hand on my elbow almost as though leading me to my own kitchen, the direction I headed to sink the flowers in water.

"Lela?" His forehead creased as he hovered over me. I wasn't a short woman, but he still stood at least a foot taller.

My fingers loosened. The flowers landed with a barely audible swish, scattering over the shabby linoleum, half poking into Nike's water dish.

A small, almost apologetic smile crept over my mouth while he bent to collect them. Our legs touched when he kneeled to help gather the flowers.

"Are you okay? Is something wrong?" He brushed the hair out of my face, the pads of his fingertips burning my skin.

"Yes. Yes, of course I'm okay." I tried to straighten, the stems clutched tightly in my hand this time, but he wrapped one hand around my wrist to keep me in place. "Thank you—for the flowers, I mean. They're very nice."

"You seem nervous. Do I scare you?"

No. Yes.

"No. I'm not scared." The lie bubbled out of my throat like vomit, my fear hiding just beneath the surface.

Before I could say another word, the manacle of his hand released me but slid up my arm to touch my chin, outline the hard bone of my jaw. A slight shift, and his facial hair scratched my cheek again, only this time his lips found my mouth.

I quit breathing, my lungs paralyzed in fear.

At the same time, I responded. I kissed him back, the rim of my glasses pressing into my cheekbone for just a moment. His musk and soap scent intensified, and his palm cradled the back of my neck. I surrendered for a few moments to enjoy the sensation of his warmth.

He pulled back when I stiffened and helped me to my feet. "May I?" He gestured toward the flowers in my hand. I passed them over without a word, all the while expecting an earthquake to rip the house apart and swallow us both whole. It was like I had *sinned* by bringing him here and then forgetting to keep him at a distance. "Do you have a vase?"

I searched the cabinet under the sink. Coming up empty-handed, I offered a smile. "No. Will a glass do? I have a big cup."

He nodded. "I will bring you a proper vase next time." He plunked the stems into the cup and filled it with water from the sink. In the light coming in the kitchen window, his hair glowed almost like he wore a fiery crown.

Zory touched the petal of a flower and smiled. "Fifteen red carnations."

"Oh? They're very pretty."

He laughed. "You do not get my meaning. There are fifteen." He stressed the number, as though it were important, and smirked. "It is Russian belief," he continued. "Never give a woman an even number of flowers, and never give yellow flowers."

"Why?"

"Yellow flowers assume we will argue, and an even number of flowers are only given at a funeral."

"Is that right?" My nerves calmed as he spoke.

"My babushka would, how you say, *have my head* if I did not give my lucky charm the right flowers."

I turned away, wondering if I should offer him a drink or something. Of course, Trina had poisoned all the bottled water I'd left in the refrigerator, and she'd likely done something to the tap as well.

Nike came swishing into the room, his long fur bushy and perturbed.

"You have a cat." Zory bent over to pull Nike into his arms, and the cat purred.

"Yes, this is Nike."

"Like the shoe?"

"No, like the Greek goddess. She was the winged goddess of victory," I said.

"Mmm, you know, NASA named a few of its early rockets after her—Nike Apache and Nike Cajun."

"And Nike Hawk, Malamute, and Tomahawk," I said, almost on instinct. My fingers clamped over my lips.

He laughed, stroking his big hands over Nike's yellow coat. "That's right. How do you know? Surely you must have picked it up from one of the astronauts in for a sleep study, yes?"

"The question is how do *you* know? I wouldn't have imagined a Russian cosmonaut would know all that much about the American program." I took a step forward, scratching Nike under the chin.

"Bah!" He waved his hand before returning it to Nike. "I know everything about the history of space flight in this country. When I found out I had been invited to participate in the mission, I did not want to be left at a disadvantage."

Zory appeared too comfortable leaning against my kitchen counter. The nerves fizzled again, and I held on to a weak smile, trying to solidify it on my face.

"You will show me your library?" he asked, setting the cat on the floor. Nike glared, swishing away.

"My library?"

"Your book collection. Something tells me it will reveal much about you."

"I don't really have very many books in the house," I said. "I volunteer at a library, so most of what I read is borrowed."

"Ah, a thrifty woman. So you are still reading the Dostoyevsky?"

I nodded, leading him to the living room. "I'm close to finishing."

"And what do you think? You will have read other Russians?"

"The librarian I work with has always had me on a reading list—it's a lot like we have our own private book club. *The Idiot* isn't one of my favorites so far, but yes. I've read the major Russian writers. I have to say that in quite a few, I don't like how women are portrayed."

"In what way?" he asked.

"So many of the female characters are weak for no other reason than that they're women."

"You must be speaking of Sonya in *Crime and Punishment*," he said, fingers rubbing his goatee.

"In part." I pointed to a small stack on the tall table near the door. "Here's the stack of other things in the pipeline. No Russians."

He bent to read the titles, muttering to himself. "*An Artist of the Floating World. Paradise Lost. House of Leaves. The Age of Innocence.*" He paused and glanced up, his sharp nose leading. "Interesting. *House of Leaves*—I do not know this book. Tell me about it?"

I busied myself straightening the pile. "It came highly recommended." Mrs. Gerhardt had suggested it to me years ago, but I had only just checked it out. "A psychological horror novel."

He thumbed the pile of science journals next to the books. "What is your favorite?"

"I don't think I have a favorite, but I admit to having a strange fondness for Chuck Palahniuk." I turned to face him, his expression surprised. I didn't blame him; it felt odd to be speaking about myself so freely. "What's yours?"

"Mmm. *The Master and Margarita*, perhaps. You know, Bulgakov. It is hard to choose. One day maybe you will see my library. It is sizeable."

"Er, yes. Maybe. Perhaps we should get going?" I said, attempting to avoid any talk of the future. Who knew what could happen. What *might* happen.

"Mmm hmm, all right. I guess we should."

I sighed. "Where are we going?"

"Do you like art?"

"You mean like paintings?"

"Not exactly." The corners of his mouth twitched, and he walked to the front door, waiting for me while I fumbled with my keys that hung on a hook just inside the kitchen.

"Not exactly? What does that mean?"

He opened the door and stepped out to the porch. I followed, locking the knob and deadbolt behind me.

"You shall see." He took my hand just as naturally as breathing, as if we held hands every day. "But you never answered my question."

Zory's dark red car waited on the street. He opened the door for me, and I slipped into the passenger seat. Within seconds, his hot breath, almost as steamy as the outside air, clouded around me. He pulled the seat belt across my chest. His forehead bumped my shoulder as he clicked the mechanism together.

My father used to fasten my seat belt for me when I was little. He'd bundle me into his small black car, laughing when I couldn't manage to secure the end into the buckle. The deep sound of his chuckle rang in my ears.

The feel of a hand brushing against my hip startled me, and my bones jostled all at once. The corner of Zory's eyes crinkled. He crouched beside me, hands now resting on his knees.

"Do you?"

"Do I what?"

"Like art. I will give you a hint—it is not traditional art. Hold the thought."

The door closed, and he moved around to the driver's side, getting in before I could think too hard about what was and wasn't art and where we might be going.

"So?"

He turned the key, and the engine coughed to life, weak and sputtering. The car had been alone on the street, so anyone could have tampered with it. Trina could have circled back and cut the brake line.

"Yes, I like art."

"What kind do you like?" he asked. "I like found object art. I think it is how you call it."

"Found object art?"

He pulled out onto the street and navigated past the playground I'd avoided as a child. I held my breath until he stopped at an intersection, sure we'd barrel through with no way of slowing down. "Maybe I do not have the right term. It is when artists take things they find—you know, on the street or in the garbage, and make it into something…perhaps sculpture. I have a cousin, Adelaïda, who is this kind of artist."

What if knowing him—really knowing him—was the thing that would negate the blessings I'd brought to NASA. It might invalidate my studies and the protection that my work built around the missions. He'd already been to my house, and that was something I'd been sure would be problematic.

I needed a test. Something to prove this was okay.

"And your cousin does sculpture? Using...what? Old tires or used tissues?" I shuddered at the thought, focusing my attention back on the road as I worked over theories in my head, experiments I could put into motion.

Zory laughed and turned onto the freeway. "I do not think I've ever known her to use tissues, but she did use pieces of tires—I am sure of it. Much of her work is welded-together metal she finds. My parents are not fans, but my grandmother finds the chaos of the work soothing. Adelaïda is exhibiting some of her pieces in Kazakhstan right now."

"Near the Cosmodrone?" I asked.

His eyes bored a hole into my cheek before he spoke. "No, not really. Kazakhstan is a very large country, although not as big as the States." He paused as he passed a truck. "How do you know about the Cosmodrone?"

My hands tightened into claws. "Oh, well, you know—it's Houston. When you live in such close proximity to the Johnson Space Center, and then with all the astronauts coming into the lab...you hear things."

"I'm surprised to hear anyone talking about Baikonur. Our program has a long, proud history, but—well, forgive me for saying so, but Americans are conditioned to think you are the best at everything. We Russians launched the first animals into space. We had the first spacewalk. We even sent women into space before you did, but do we get any credit at all? No." He shook his head in what I assumed was disgust, although the pleasant expression never left his face.

I said nothing, but he obviously took my silence as an offended quiet—he added, "The United States has done much to further space exploration. I'm excited to be part of the next launch."

"Yes. I understand the *Empire* mission is going to be quite exciting." My voice barely carried over the guttural noise of the engine. My mouth wouldn't shut off. "You'll be delivering a robot to the space station, right?"

"Mmm hmm. There are several interesting experiments being carried out."

Zory began detailing the finer points of the upcoming mission, and I zoned out—I probably knew the plans as well as he did. His voice drifted like a fog into my brain, and I thought out my problem: My observational objectivity was threatened by Zory's presence, both in my life generally and in my house specifically. This loss of integrity might threaten the effectiveness of my studies as well as the safety of the next shuttle mission. Since Zory was on that mission, I couldn't very well stop seeing him because I needed to evaluate his sleep habits.

Given all that, what could I do to test my luck and Zory's safety? There was no real way to conduct a fair test. It wasn't as though I could send a fake shuttle into space.

An idea formed in my head, which solidified into a workable hypothesis. If I could somehow put Zory in danger and he came out unscathed, the shuttle mission would surely not be at risk from our relationship. It made sense—I was the underlying factor. He thought I was good luck, so why not put it to the challenge? And if having him in my house had doomed him, his fate now hung sealed anyway.

Even Mrs. Gerhardt would see the logic. I would not be leaving the fate of the shuttle up to chance. No, I would be the captain of my own ship, as she'd said. My actions would contribute to the success of the mission, and mine alone. It would be a good lesson to pass along to my apprentice, whenever I found her...or him. And if Trina caught wind of it, it would give her some idea of my tenacity and professionalism. She wouldn't stop me easily.

Determining how to test might be a little tricky. A situation would have to present itself, making it impossible to plan and control the conditions. Still, it was worth a shot.

Zory took an exit off the freeway, revealing his intended location: The Heights. The squat bungalows, like giant tree stumps, whizzed by as we drove down the street, giving way to industrial gray and then apartment complexes. He parked, backing into a giant space on the street.

"Where are we?"

His white teeth flashed. "We are going to look at cars."

"Cars? I thought this had to do with art?"

A few moments later we stood in front of a strange-looking silver building, and as we approached a portico, a metallic car came into view.

"What is that?" I asked. The hood stretched out like a long hallway, ending in a hammer-shaped front. "Are those..."

"It looks like a gargoyle, does it not?" Zory grabbed my hand again, squeezing it. "And maybe," he squinted at the car, "a pig."

"What is this place?" Another car behind it gleamed pink in the sunlight. The pearl of seashells covered every available surface, but the windshield gave it the appearance of a marooned reef.

"You have heard of the annual parade of decorated cars in Houston?"
I shook my head. There could be a yearly cavalcade of dolphins in
bikinis waltzing around Main Street Square, and I'd never know it. Every
spare moment I had was dedicated to my specialized research or library
work.

Dad's voice echoed in my head: *Don't ever give up, Lela—take your
goals by the shoulders and wrestle them into submission.*

"This is a museum that displays some of those cars, but I've heard
there are other exhibits, too."

"And this is art?"

"Art is in the eye of the beholder, is it not?" He grinned, running
his hand over the brown fur of a car featuring a dog's face on its hood,
complete with a giant, pink tongue lolling out of the front grill.

Inside the building, my eyes drew to a car covered in beads, each
layer swirling around its curves. Orange and white billiard balls dotted
the chrome planes; each bore the number thirteen. I shuddered. Beside
me, Zory crossed himself.

I glanced at him out of the corner of my eye. He shrugged. "The
number thirteen. Unlucky."

His words, his superstitions, helped me breathe more easily while
considering and rejecting testing scenarios. We moved through the
exhibits, Zory continuing to hold my hand.

"Think of it as recycling. My cousin, she finds pieces of cars, parts of
buildings, and instead of these things littering the ground, they get made
into something…well, perhaps not beautiful, but it certainly provokes
thought. And isn't that what art does?"

I understood his point of view, although I didn't necessarily agree.
While some of the cars in the museum were pretty—a small car decorated in an eddy of yellow, orange, and red mosaic tiles, the patterns
morphing into fiery licks of sunshine and flames—it didn't approach the
level of the *Mona Lisa* in terms of importance.

"Would you like to get something to eat?" he asked.

He released my hand and smoothed his palm against the small of
my back, sending an unexpected rush of warmth from my toes, up my
legs, and across my back.

You must sense how my hand's caress travels first along your spine.

"Yes, that sounds good." I smiled, hoping it appeared genuine.

I wasn't hungry, but I wasn't an idiot; eating is what people did on normal dates. They sat and talked and ate.

Outside, the humidity layered over me, too close, too cloying. My hair stuck to my neck, and my glasses fogged and slipped down my nose at the same time. I removed them, squinting against the sun.

"I do not know if I will ever get used to this heat," Zory said from behind me.

I turned. "It gets hot in Volgograd, though, doesn't it?"

He peered down, smiling, eyes soft. "Sometimes, but not like this." His fingertip skimmed down my arm, sending up a rash of gooseflesh despite the sweat at the back of my neck. "You look like a flower."

The heat rose beneath my dress, sucking the cotton to my skin. I didn't know where to aim my eyes. With my vision fuzzy, the edges of Zory's face blurred but sharpened as he moved closer.

His fingers on my neck trapped the clammy air against my skin. Perhaps I should have protested his touching me…at least until after the test. His mouth touched mine, soft and searching. The thought shriveled into a small, burned thing.

His tongue sneaked past my lips, the hair on his upper lip and chin tickling my face. The slick of saliva and a click of teeth, the jagged scorch of his mouth—I forgot everything except that.

My world shrank to the pinpoint of a kiss. A good kiss, but I struggled for air and for clarity, trying to remember the important things. My testing. My hypothesis. Trying to get Zory killed.

✷✷✷

MRS. GERHARDT SAT IN HER OFFICE, SORTING PAPERWORK, WHEN I visited after my date. Now that she was an inexorable part of the mission, it felt right to brief her, keep her in the loop.

The tip of her hair peeked above the back of her chair, the telephone cord stretching behind it. I knocked, just hard enough to alert her to my presence, and pushed the door open.

She glanced behind her and gestured toward the chair in front of her desk.

"Yes, yes, of course. I'll come in tomorrow. Thank you. Yes, see you then." She set the phone back in its cradle and shook her head as though to clear away the cobwebs. The skin around her eyes crinkled when she smiled at me, but that was as far as it went—the expression in them stayed serious. "What are you doing here," she asked.

"I just wanted to check in," I said. "What's going on?"

"What do you mean?"

"You look upset."

"Oh, it's nothing. I have to go to the doctor tomorrow. A follow-up. Nothing new."

"If you say so."

"I do." She let her hands fall to the blotter on top of her desk and blew out a gust of air. "So how's everything going with your young man?"

Zory. God, I was torn between giddiness and horror at what I had to do in order to keep seeing him. "Pretty well. We went out—our first real date."

"Where did he take you?" Mrs. Gerhardt busied herself with the files on her desk, but she didn't fool me for a second; every ounce of her attention was focused on the answer.

"We went to the Art Car Museum—you know, in The Heights? And then to a late lunch. It was nice."

"Nice, huh? I daresay the look on your face tells me it was quite a bit more than nice. Used that Kutik poem on you again, did he?" Her smile became a lascivious smirk.

"Mrs. Gerhardt! No, of course not. It was our first date."

Possibly our only date, depending on how things went with the plan I was formulating.

"Mmm, well. Despite that, I think you like him quite a bit more than you're saying, am I right?"

I nodded, my eyebrows drawing together. Whether I genuinely liked him or not was irrelevant.

"How did the date end?"

"You are a lecherous woman," I said.

"Give an old woman a break. I'm living vicariously through you, which I never get to do." She set her pen down and pushed the papers away. "You know, I had my doubts that you and Trina would last two weeks as roommates without hearing on the news that you'd beaten her up or something, but I think she's been good for you."

"You think Trina has something to do with Zory?"

It was her turn to laugh. "No, that's not what I mean. It's just that she moved in with you, and all of a sudden you're mooning over a man."

"Trust me. Trina's got nothing to do with anything. And for the record, she *does* drive me insane."

"Not surprising, really. You do like things your way—remember the incident with the comb?"

I rolled my eyes. "Oh, come on. I was fourteen!" I couldn't be held responsible for the stupid things I'd done in middle school, especially when it came to punishing a girl for taking what was mine.

"Yes, well." She checked her watch. "It's time to close up shop, missy. Would you help me make a sweep?"

My knees flexed, pushing me upright. "Of course"

Her hands gripped the arms of the chair hard, pressing the frail bones beneath her skin into the skin of her fingers. She rose slowly, her eyes closed for a moment. The things I'd noticed—the change in her smell, her slow gait, the color of her face—echoed in my mind, entangling with this doctor's call on a Sunday. I slipped my hand under her elbow and helped her around the desk and out the door, although she stepped away from me on the main floor.

She kept up a steady stream of banter as we made our rounds—slowly, haltingly—to the corners of the library, checking the doors and making sure all the patrons were out.

Mrs. Gerhardt asked me to lock the front doors, talking about the newest order of books to come in. The air around her paled and shimmered, and I narrowed my eyes. Smoke plumes rose from the white ends of her hair and split in two before they crawled across the space above her head. The scent of charred flesh clawed its way into my nostrils. I opened my mouth, gulping in air, and then it was gone.

"Yolanda had a handful with those kids by herself," she said.

My eyes focused back on her pale, ashy face. "By herself? Trina wasn't here?"

Her thin brows drew together. "Isn't she still off with her boyfriend?"

I shrugged, but inside my body a fire seared. If she hadn't been at the library, where had she been?

"Have you thought more about taking a shift with the children? I could really use a reader tomorrow."

I smiled. "Yes, of course I'll do it."

The future of the shuttle program depended on it.

Chapter Seventeen

LITTLE MONSTERS

THIRTEEN SETS OF EYES STARED AT ME. THE LITTLE GIRL I'D SEEN during Trina's shift in the children's section was twisted into a ball in the middle of the mat, curled up with a ratty brown teddy bear. The other kids fidgeted and squirmed.

I cleared my throat. My mouth slammed into the brightest, shiniest smile. A small boy sitting at my feet sucked in a gasp, and his chin trembled. His wail started as a thin, high-pitched hiss and crescendoed to a curling scream. The girl next to him covered her ears with her hands until the boy's mother—or so I assumed—scooped him up and dragged him away.

The top of Mrs. Gerhardt's head was just visible over the low wall separating the section from the wider part of the library. I left it to her to police the parents. There were more important things at hand, like finding my protégé.

"Today we'll be reading *Robby of the Rocket.*" I held up the book. I hadn't been sure if it was a good idea to show the kids a book about an orangutan manning the space shuttle, but Mrs. Gerhardt said it would be okay, that none of thetm would think a primate really had the ability to steer a spacecraft, but I wasn't so sure about that. At the very least, any children I might identify as viable candidates for my training program would never been dumb enough to fall for something so preposterous.

I flipped the page and showed the illustration to the boys and girls. "Robby hooted at the stars. His smile was wide."

The girl with the bear had fallen asleep. I continued to read, eyes falling on each kid on the floor. Five boys and eight girls. Well, four boys, not counting the boy who'd been carried out. If Zory had been around, he'd have likely commented on the total number of them. I could almost hear him: *Thirteen is unlucky, Lela.*

Ages were hard to determine. The book said it was for three to five year olds, but some of the children were tall. None of them seemed particularly bright. A girl in a purple sweater picked her nose. The boy to the other side of her had a wandering eye and his hand down his pants. No one paid close attention to the story, but at least they were quiet.

Erin scurried to the front of the room when I finished and clapped. "What an exciting story, Lela! I think it's time for milk and cookies, don't you?"

The children certainly perked up at the mention of the cookies. She whispered to me, "Twenty minutes for snacks, and then it's nap time for these little monsters."

I raised an eyebrow. The little boy who'd cried barreled back into the room and tripped over the edge of a mat, which sent him into hysterics again. "I have to consult with Mrs. Gerhardt on something," I said. "You don't need me to pass out snacks, right?"

Before she could answer I sprinted across the room and past the divider. Mrs. Gerhardt's chin jerked up when I slapped my palms on the circulation desk. The skin of her face was even paler than it had been when I arrived, as if it lacked any blood at all. The clock on the wall behind her ticked loud and fast.

"Oh, Lela," she said, voice fluttering, "how's it going in there? As bad as you thought?"

"Finding intelligent life in the universe isn't easy."

"Come on now." She laughed. "They're little kids."

"I thought it would be easier."

"Easier? To do what?" She might have been playing dumb, but the spark in Mrs. Gerhardt's eyes said she knew exactly what I was talking about. "I hope you'll accept another shift. It can take some time to get into the swing of things when you're working with children. They can sense fear, you know?"

"I'm not afraid of them." And I wasn't. But I also wasn't interested in wasting time on the search if all the kids I met were the same uninteresting snot noses.

"That was a joke," she said. "About the fear, that is. I'm serious when I say that it can take a few weeks to feel comfortable with them. But every shift will be different. Different kids, different books. Maybe the astronaut book wasn't the best choice—you should experiment."

"Right. Because being successful doesn't necessarily correlate to an interest in wanting to *be* an astronaut," I muttered. Louder, I said, "That's brilliant! Maybe next time I'll focus on some other discipline. Do they make polysomnography books for children?"

One corner of her mouth lifted. "I don't know. I'll look into it for you, okay? But for now, Erin will need help watching all those kids. Children without the proper number of chaperones is a recipe for disaster."

I thought about winking, but it didn't seem quite right. Instead I nodded and grinned before heading back toward the children's section.

Today wouldn't be a total waste. I could still watch them sleep and think more about my plans for trying to kill Zory. A black haze tugged at the edges of my brain, pulling my lids down like gravity, but I ignored the call. It was no time for my own rest.

✳✳✳

ZORY STUDIED THE MENU. HE'D EXPRESSED SURPRISE WITH A QUIET raise of his brows—a predictable sign with him, I'd noticed—when I'd insisted on the bar with the entire gang's worth of motorcycles parked in the gravel lot littered with beer cans.

He'd probably assumed I knew something about the food at this place, despite the several times before I'd told him that I didn't know the city that well.

This was not the tearoom—no chance of getting a decent salad or sandwich. Judging by the greasy smears on the laminated menus, cracked with either age or too many bar fights, it was either a burger and fries or nothing at all. Reading the menu only confirmed it. The only thing not deep-fried, covered in cheese, or full of fat was the sweet tea… and even that was suspect.

My stomach turned.

A hard-looking woman in too-tight, fluorescent capri pants shimmied to the table, her bright pink nails peeking out of open-toed sandals. She didn't say a word—just stood with her hip jutted out, lips drawn into a scowl, and the pen in her hand poised over a worn pad of paper while she stared at us.

I considered telling her that her clothes made her look as though she wore a sausage casing in an effort to spur an attack, sure Zory would come to my rescue, but it wouldn't do to turn up to work with bruises. Trina would ask questions, and I didn't feel like sharing any more of my personal life with her than I had to. And Mrs. Gerhardt—she'd be concerned, although maybe she'd figure out it was something mission-related.

I ordered a tuna melt and a Coke (because there was no bottled water).

"What kind?" The waitress's dark hair gathered her skin back tightly, but her jowls still shook when she spoke. She'd probably been pretty once. Now she wore years of hard work on her face, each pockmark and line representing what I could only assume were failed marriages and heartbreak. It was what happened when you didn't have a purpose in life.

Something about her eyes reminded me of my mother. I sank into the chair, wondering what she'd look like after all this time. I still half suspected Trina might be a relative of some sort.

"Do you have Sprite?"

An abrupt nod, and then the waitress turned to Zory, who ordered, offering her his usual warm smile, which wasn't returned.

A crowd of grizzled men in denim and leather eyed him from the bar. My heart rate picked up, the beat of it keeping time with my internal voices, screaming at me and each other to do something, anything, to drum up some drama to start a fight.

The stale air was a wet sheet without a breeze, unmoving and heavy. My legs shifted under the table, and my feet bumped into Zory's. He picked up my hand and laid it palm-up on the table, tracing the lines down my skin. I shivered and tried to fight back the rush of affection that heated me from within.

"Do you believe in palmistry?" he asked. One side of his mouth pulled up.

"No."

"I did not think you would—a woman of science." The pad of his finger pressed into the flesh at the base of my thumb and then traced the groove above it. "I have a cousin who reads palms."

"A cousin who builds sculpture, a cousin who reads palms." I smirked. "You don't really buy into all that, do you? You're as much a scientist as I am."

He shrugged. "You have to understand—this type of thing is a part of life. As much as I would not admit this to anyone else, there's something about living in Russia. It is very much a mix of modern life, technology, progress, mixed with a type of old world certainty of unseen and unknowable things. It is strange to think that even my babushka has an email address now."

I stared. "So, you do. Believe, I mean."

I thought again of the photograph of his grandmother. I could almost hear her babbling in Russian, telling Zory she'd steal his teeth if he didn't do as she said.

He smiled again, a small chuckle burbling over the table. "A little. Take your life line, for instance." He retraced his path down the line near my thumb.

"Let me guess—I'm going to live a long life full of excitement?" My intended sarcasm came out more like gentle teasing.

"Is your life full of excitement?" he joked back. The tip of his finger skimmed up the line for the third time. "But no, it's not about how long you may live. Catryn says it reveals health, bearing out marks for the major things that happen to you. Yours intersects with your destiny line." He pointed to a different line, the one rising up the middle of my palm.

"And what is that supposed to mean?"

"Hmm. Well, I may be wrong, but I think it has something to do with spending time as a child satisfying your parents."

"What else?"

His fingernail drew across my skin. "I know this is the heart line."

"And?"

"Yours begins below your index finger. You give away your heart too easily, but you don't really know love."

I hiccupped in surprise. One of the guys at the bar turned again to cast an eye in our direction. Above the eyes, his brows grew together.

My mother's voice screeched in my head: "Trust not the man whose eyebrows meet, for in his heart you'll find deceit."

"No, that does not sound like you," Zory admitted, never taking his eyes off my palm. "You hide yourself, your heart. Afraid of getting hurt, maybe. You have broken lines here, so that shows an emotional loss.

Your mother and father, likely."

"Spend a lot of time with your cousin?" I asked, tugging at my hand. He held on tighter. I glanced at the man at the bar, then back at Zory. He raised his eyes, sweeping up my arm and up the expanse of my neck and face until he pinned me, too intense to look away.

"Yes. You would like her. Catryn reminds me of you very much."

If I harbored affection for Zory it made the situation that much worse. I didn't quite know what that meant for me, but for Zory it was impossible. I'd doomed him just by allowing him to court me, or whatever it was we were doing.

A bar fight wouldn't do to prove that this wouldn't take the whole shuttle down. More options laid themselves out in front of me—my own form of palmistry or voodoo, although more reliable—as he spoke about summers with his cousin, learning about her interests. Too bad my initial search for a protégé hadn't turned up anyone even remotely intelligent. We could have brainstormed ideas.

"Do you not have any other family?" Zory asked, interrupting my thoughts. A snail trail of smoke and water vapor curled behind my eyes.

"No. My dad's parents died before I was born, and Mom's parents died shortly before she left. Neither had brothers or sisters."

"Too bad. I have just the one brother, but my cousins always spent much time at our home." His hands ticked off cousins and other relatives in a complicated family tree, and I went back to my own deliberations.

If breaking things off with Zory wasn't a viable option—and it seemed like the least attractive of my choices—I could do what I had intended before admitting I liked him: keep seeing him.

Still, small-scale danger probably wouldn't tell me if my personal involvement with Zory put the entire shuttle mission at risk. It would need to be something major, a catastrophe, and if he lived, I'd consider that perhaps everything would be okay. If he died, that would take care of the risk all together.

The anxiety of that option turned my feet numb.

I examined his face, noting the chin, the small ears, the permanent stress lines etched in his forehead. Too many for a man of thirty-five. I cataloged the flaws before moving on to the beautiful things—although in truth, even the imperfect things made him handsome. His light eyes, bearing flecks of blue and black, widened when he noticed my staring.

"Do I have something on my face?"

"No." The waitress shuffled back with our drinks, sloshing them on the table. Without a word, she left, leaving the stink of acrid perfume behind. I hadn't noticed it before.

The glass in front of him gave me an idea; perhaps I could slip something into his drink next time we went out—if he managed to live, I could take it as a sign. "Just wondering who you favor more—your mother or father," I lied.

"I do not know." The fingers of his large hands came up to stroke his goatee. "I can tell you that my mother and I share the same eye color, and my father had my hair color when he was young."

"When he was young?"

"Well, he does not have any hair now." Teeth flashed through his thin lips. "He went bald many years ago."

"Will you go bald?" I tried to imagine him, head bare and gleaming. A vision of the hair burnt off his scalp flashed in my brain, and my stomach clenched, roiling to protest the attending smell of charred flesh.

The phantom odor stayed with me through the weekend. Monday came too soon, but at least cleaning chemicals replaced the smoke in my nose. I hadn't even been in the office for an hour before The Chin cornered me in the hallway around the corner from my cubicle.

"You told me you wasn't seein' no one else," The Chin said. His voice was a little too loud and his posture a little too aggressive to be casual. I straightened up to my full height.

"I had no intention of seeing anyone else when we broke things off."

"You lied. You're going out with that guy I seen you with."

"What is the problem here?" I clenched my jaw and bared my teeth in a dazzling smile.

"The problem?" he asked, face twisting into a confused expression.

I'd been kind to him, going out of my way to end things nicely, but this was too much.

"I know you think you can convince me that we're meant to be together or something, but I can assure you that is just not going to happen. I like you, but we were not meant for one another."

"Well, I'd say that's a problem right there." His underbite grew larger as he jutted his chin. "He's wrong for you."

"Please. Stop this. You just need some time to see I know what I'm talking about." I pushed past him, willing him not to follow. His hand landed on my arm. "Don't touch me," I spit, balling my fists so hard my fingernails cut into my palm.

He pulled back as if stung by the seething steam likely rising through my jacket. "I didn't mean nothing by it."

I whirled on him. "Of course you didn't. Please understand: I do not want to see you."

Breathe. Four-three-two-one-in, four-three-two-one-out.

His eyes clouded over, but that didn't stop him from smirking. "I don't believe a word that comes out of your mouth. We go way back, you and me, and you'll see that I'm the guy. Maybe not now, but you will."

"Are you finished?" Sparks popped in front of my eyes as my focus sharpened and dimmed. Bile rose in my throat. Something in the air reached for me, a heavy presence that wanted me to close my eyes, to give in. I fought against it and broke above the voices, now screaming inside my head.

"For now."

"Good. I have to go."

I stalked down the hallway, eager to get away, willing my heart to calm, my nerves to ease. I didn't need The Chin making a scene at work.

I'd spent the better part of a week ignoring my feelings for Zory, trying to bury them, and trying to develop a plan for how to proceed. I'd spent my lunch hours at the teahouse avoiding Magda's curious eyes while sorting through ideas. I'd made lists of potential disasters I could orchestrate, considered accidents I could arrange.

At night I diagrammed and studied, planned and thought each idea through its logical conclusion.

With each option I added, my attitude worsened and yet control over the shuttle project expanded and solidified. It might tear me up—if I let it—to possibly get him killed, but there was no help for it.

If I went with poison, it would need to be something that wouldn't permanently injure him if he lived. That meant caustic cleaning products were out.

Over the years I'd researched the types of poisonous plants grown in the area, and there were a few—foxglove, wisteria, castor beans—but it might take some effort to prepare them and feed him enough to make a difference. There were ways to make homemade ricin and cyanide, and those were reasonable options. Purified nicotine also remained on the list.

The autoinjector was out. There was no possibility of survival.

And then another list formed—a list of less subtle possibilities. Finding a way to drown him, setting a fire in his apartment building. I'd watched a documentary about professional assassins; while I didn't want to kill him, it would be possible to hire someone to kidnap him and put him in the path of an oncoming train or place him in a cage full of lions at the zoo.

There were simpler options—sneaking into his house and greasing the bottom of his bathtub or feeding him something to which he was allergic, like I'd planned with Meehan.

For once, I wished Trina wasn't the enemy. She'd probably have good ideas, things I hadn't thought of. The irony of the situation wasn't lost on me: I wished I could talk to a killer, someone I was sure was actively trying to murder me, about how to put a man I was pretending to date in mortal danger.

The universe had the strangest sense of humor.

Chapter Eighteen

DREAMING OF TEETH

T HE HALLWAY ADJACENT TO MY OFFICE SPACE APPEARED PALER, whiter than usual, with dim patterns dancing below the paint. How odd. It brought to mind a short story Mrs. Gerhardt had put on my reading list when I was in college—"The Yellow Wallpaper."

This wasn't the Victorian era, though, and I wasn't crazy.

"So you've been seeing a lot of this Zory guy," Trina remarked, smiling and doing this thing with her eyes that made it seem like she knew what I was up to. The glittery barrette in her hair winked and sparkled, glaring at me. I hated the thing, but it'd taken up permanent residence in her hair since she'd gotten back from Austin. "It's serious, huh? You should bring him over so I can meet him."

The weeks Trina had been invading my personal space frayed the ends of my nerves like a wire stripped of its protective coating. The woman couldn't take a hint. No matter how many times I asked about her insurance or if she'd started searching for apartments, she either choose not to notice my agitation, or she didn't care.

Or maybe it was her intention, hoping it would make me careless.

"Uh, yes, maybe. I'm sure he'll be around sometime soon." I ignored her assessment of my relationship with Zory. It was none of her business, not that it mattered. She'd told everyone at the lab about my house.

"I bet he's gorgeous. Russian, right? You haven't told me a thing about him other than that. What's he like?" She peeked over her computer and stared.

"He's tall."

Her eyes widened, and she slapped her palm on the desk, laughing. "Lela White, you're holding out on me!"

I didn't know what to say to that, so I shrugged and popped out my gleaming smile.

"I'm going to find a way to get you to open up one day," she said, giggling. "I mean, I don't even know anything about your family other than that your parents are both gone. It's been so long, I'm surprised you still keep their bedroom. I mean, it's bigger than yours and—"

"How do you know that?"

"What?"

"How do you know my dad's bedroom is bigger than mine? I keep the door locked." I wanted to vault across the partition and slap her, even though she was finally admitting she'd gone snooping in the room.

"Well, you know, I poked my head in once when I first moved in. I was just curious. I mean, I just wanted to see where I was living and all. You could really—"

I gripped the arms of my chair and said in the calmest voice I could muster, "I'm sorry, Trina—that room is off limits."

"Huh?"

"The room. My dad's room. We've discussed this before: I'm not ready to handle that, and it needs to stay as-is."

"I didn't hurt anything. It was just that once."

My fingers itched to shake her until she screamed. "Uh huh." Those two syllables were the only ones I could squeeze past my tense throat.

My mother's hair disappeared behind her monitor, barrette and all. Still, the ends of it waved around above the partition, moving like it was alive on her head, undulating and snapping. "Hey, I meant to ask you— why do you have a lock on your closet door? It reminds me of being a kid and thinking a monster lived in my closet. I begged my mom to put a lock in, but she fed me this line about…"

Trina rambled on about what I assumed was her idyllic family life, complete with a loving mother and father and family outings that didn't end in tears or screaming or murder, but I couldn't listen. I didn't give a crap about whatever alleged monster lived in her childhood closet.

"Your mom was really pretty, by the way."

My head snapped up, and my eyes bored a hole through my computer monitor. "What?"

"Your mom. You look just like her, you know. What do you use on your skin, by the way? I pawed through your medicine cabinet but couldn't find your moisturizer. You must keep your makeup bag in your bedroom, and I didn't want to go rooting around in your private space like that."

She rambled on while the pressure inside my head built. Maybe her entire plan was to stress me out to the point of having a heart attack. Or an aneurysm, like my father.

I turned back to the list I'd been making—all the ways I could try to get Zory killed. My breathing eased as I read the prospectus. Only one choice offered a somewhat simple, clean solution.

I'd still need to research…consult books on arson investigations to both make sure the fire caught and ensure no evidence pointed toward me afterward. I'd require supplies, but I couldn't imagine there'd be anything too hard to find or too difficult to obtain.

So, it would be fire. I circled the word on the checklist, stared at it, and chewed on the inside of my cheek. Trina's high-pitched voice droned just outside my thoughts. I clicked my pen shut and stood, notebook and briefcase in hand.

"I'm heading out," I announced. Before Trina could reply, I was halfway down the hall. The Chin grinned at me from in front of the elevator bank.

I took the stairs.

✳✳✳

"MY BABUSHKA SAID SHE DREAMED OF HER TEETH FALLING OUT last night." Zory spooned jam into his tea, leaning forward with his elbows on the table. Magda tsked and crossed herself as she backed away.

"What does that mean?" I thought of the gas cans locked in my closet. I'd bought them with cash, and I'd worn a blonde wig for the transaction, my scalp sweating and prickly beneath the synthetic hair.

The last few days had been rushed. After deciding on the plan and putting in the research to make it successful, I'd been gathering necessities; a large-brimmed baseball cap and latex gloves lay beside the fuel. I'd had to move my dresser against my closet door after the walls behind my filing cabinets had pulsed and dripped for five minutes.

"It is a sign of a death," he said, his tone solemn and quiet. "She thinks I'm going to die."

"A dream? And now she's convinced…"

He nodded. "She asked me to be careful, and I will."

"Okay. In that case, yes, please do. Did she say anything else?"

"Not about that. But my mother said my grandmother has been talking to herself lately. She does that sometimes when she is in one of her moods." The fondness in his voice was unmistakable. "Perhaps they will come here to see the shuttle land. My grandmother would like you very much."

"But you'll be careful?"

"Yes, of course."

I hoped being cautious didn't include asking management to upgrade the sprinkler or fire alarm systems at his apartment building. After leaving his apartment the night before (noting a few minor additions to his décor since the first time I'd been there), I'd sneaked down into the complex-wide utility room to check it out. It seemed relatively simple, although I'd ordered user manuals for each, just to be sure.

"I should tell you that I think your friend Max is following you…or us. I cannot be sure."

He had my full attention with those words. "What do you mean?"

"Look out the window, but do it slowly. He is across the street, watching from the edge of the building."

Sure enough, The Chin's pale profile—dominated by his jaw—shadowed the marble of the office on the opposite corner. He still wore his jumpsuit from work. When he noticed my gaze he turned, shoving his hands into pockets and almost running in his haste to get away.

"What on…" I scrutinized his back as he fled.

"I have seen him quite a few times over the last week or two. He's not very good at hiding. Do you know why he would be trailing you?"

"Maybe he's crazy."

"You should report him at work. Does he act that way there? It is not safe for you."

"Yes. Maybe I'll do that. Report him, I mean." I pulled my eyes away from The Chin's retreating figure, mind ticking off excuses to downplay his actions. "I'm sure he's just worried about me. Well, concerned more about you."

"Me? Why?"

My mind spun like a Tilt-a-Whirl, and the accompanying vomit burned at the back of my throat. This was the last thing I needed to worry about. I was already concerned about Mrs. Gerhardt; although she had come back to the library after her doctor's appointment and insisted nothing was wrong, I didn't quite believe her. Doubt and worry lodged behind my ribs.

My concern over The Chin was greater, however. "I...well, he... thinks I should be careful dating you."

"Does he think I am a bad man for you?" He turned his head and craned his neck, watching for The Chin, but I was sure Max was gone by now.

I shrugged. "I don't know. So, what do you want to do this weekend?"

My throat burned like a hot poker had been shoved down into my esophagus. I'd need to deal with The Chin quickly.

Breathe. Four-three-two-one-in, four-three-two-one-out.

"What business is it of his anyway?" Zory asked. My attempt to change the subject hadn't worked.

"He might have a crush on me." Too close. Too true.

"Well, this I already know, but that is no reason to follow you like a puppy. Or me, for that matter."

"I'll talk to him—I didn't know he was doing that."

"Do you want *me* to talk to him? I can explain the situation to him."

"What situation?"

"Us. I mean, I will tell him you are my girlfriend."

For just a moment I forgot about the arson and The Chin and Trina and everything else. "I am?"

"Well, yes. Do you not think so? I like you very much. I think you like me."

"Oh. I...I guess I am." For a moment, the irritation lifted. I smiled, but it immediately died on my lips.

I planned to torch my boyfriend's apartment building and try to kill him. Dad and Mrs. Gerhardt wouldn't like that one bit.

His sudden grin took me off guard. "That is a relief. I was beginning to think you considered me only a friend. One who occasionally kisses you."

He reached across the table and brought my hand to his lips, kissing the palm. Nerves fluttered in my stomach. A string of thick, Russian words came out of his mouth, and I cocked my head.

"More of that Ilya Kutik poem," he explained. "*I trace that circle with my nail on your back 'til O throbs hot over all your limbs.* Perhaps you are getting closer to being ready to hear it?" His mouth settled into a smirk, and he kissed my wrist this time, goatee brushing my skin. Gooseflesh erupted up my arm, my heart stuttering.

What was he trying to do? The remainder of the poem echoed inside my skull.

"There is a picnic, you know, an event for work next weekend. Perhaps you will come with me? And maybe after, you might consider spending the night?" He never took his eyes off me, but he laid my hand on the table, wrapping it in his.

My intestines roiled. If my plan worked, he might be dead by then.

✳✳✳

THREE TEENAGE GIRLS ROUNDED THE CORNER AT A SPRINT, GIGGLING behind their hands. Mrs. Gerhardt shushed them, her skeletal index finger pressed against her lips. Properly chastened, they slowed their gait.

I shook my head, forgetting about them while I got into a rhythm: choose a book and flip to the back cover, scan it in, stamp the card, pass it to the right. Over and over. It was meditative, and my mind wandered, thinking of Zory. Mrs. Gerhardt shuffled up behind me.

"How's everything going?" I asked, not interrupting my work.

"Just fine. I am going into the hospital tomorrow—routine testing."

Her voice was all wrong. I couldn't quite pinpoint it, but something was there, lying just below the surface.

"Oh? Didn't you just have a doctor's appointment?"

"Yes. This is nothing out of the ordinary, though. I'm fit as a fiddle. Nothing to be concerned about."

"If you say so."

Her hand squeezed my shoulder, and it took every ounce of will-power not to turn and throw myself into her arms. The compulsion jerked at my skin, unfamiliar and raw.

I shut the last book and pressed my hands flat against the counter. Nothing to be concerned about. *Right.*

Breathe. Breathe. Breathe.

"Coincidentally," she said, "I got the evaluations back on your shift with the reading hour. The parents felt safe leaving the kids, but the children themselves found you a little scary."

"What? How was I scary?" I asked. "I read the story. It's not like I told them the truth about what happens during a shuttle liftoff. That would have scared them to death, but I held off."

She chuckled. "Well, I think maybe you're a bit too abrupt with them. Next time try to loosen up a bit. You don't have to be so serious all the time—it's okay to laugh or be silly."

"I'll keep that in mind."

There was a time and place for that kind of behavior, but now was not it. Every day my body was rotting. Every day I was a step closer to the end. Now that I'd recognized it, it ate at me, and the importance of finding someone to carry on my work…well, it wasn't my number one priority or even my number two, but it was something that needed my attention.

The next day at work, the digital numbers on my desk phone blinked, counting down to break time. The Chin would likely be in his office, and I needed to speak with him. Privately.

Trina's side of the office space had remained quiet all afternoon on account of a client meeting. I took full advantage, plowing through an analysis in silence. Every fifteen minutes I glanced at the time, anxious to get this out of the way. The last minute ticked by, and I pushed back from my desk.

Every step toward the janitorial supply closet felt like one pace closer to my execution. The ghost of a noose around my neck rubbed and irritated, tightening as I approached. Without bothering to knock, I threw open the door and stepped inside, sweeping it closed behind me. The Chin, startled, glanced at me and smiled.

"Come to your senses, huh?"

"What are you doing?" Our words jumbled together, my seething hiss over his low, attractive voice.

"What do you mean?"

"Why are you following Zory?" I crossed my arms over my chest, keeping my spot near the door. He drifted closer, the excited smile on his face dimming.

"I ain't—I'm following you. Seen some pretty interesting things, too. You been busy."

"Doing what, exactly? And why? Get a kick out of seeing me buy deodorant and apples?" Every molecule in my body stood at alert.

"Now, don't go getting all mad." He took a step forward. I skittered back, knocking into the wall. "I'm just—"

"Look, I don't really care why you're doing it. Just stop. Stop following me, and stop turning up on my dates."

Normally my height never gave me a second thought, although in that moment I wished to have a more menacing and threatening presence so I could hover over him instead of glare face to face.

"I should be your boyfriend, not him. He's all wrong for a girl like you."

"How would you know?"

"That place he takes you to? You deserve better 'an that. And he's only going to leave you to go back to that country of his after the space shuttle launches. What then?"

"What then? It's none of your business, that's what then. This is none of your concern. Leave me alone." *Breathe*, I reminded myself. Voices in the back of my head urged me to *burn*, but I ignored them.

Breathe. Four-three-two-one-in, four-three-two-one-out.

"Nope. Don't think I will." He wiped his hands on a rag from his pocket. "You think you know what's good for you, but you ain't got no clue."

"Trust me when I say you're *not* the best thing for me." My vision fuzzed around the edges while my hands shook.

"We'll see."

Every ounce of self-control I possessed congealed in my gut. If I weren't on a schedule, I might have done something to put him out of commission—flatten his tires or—

That set off an alarm in my head. The Chin didn't have a car; he used public transit. How was he even getting around? He'd been outside the restaurant today, but Zory had said he'd seen him other places, too. That could only mean The Chin had bought or borrowed a car. Maybe I could do something to the engine, keep him stationary.

I gave him my sparkling-toothed smile. "Don't talk to me. Don't follow me. I don't want anything to do with you, and I will make you very sorry if you have the audacity to keep this up."

His brows drew together. He inched forward, reached out a hand toward me, but drew back like he'd been stung. "Think so, huh?"

"Take another step, and you'll regret it."

"Why you so…I don't know. Are you mad? I just want you to give me a shot."

"A shot? I could kill you right now!" Until this point, I'd been able to keep my voice low, but now the volume escalated. As much as I wanted to, it was hard to pull myself back, keep myself in control. Another five minutes of this, and my head might explode. "Leave me alone!"

Now his hands waved in front of him, attempting to soothe. The knob from the door pressed against my side, and I focused on it, breathing and counting to keep myself from launching across the space and doing *something*.

My toe nudged a bottle of bleach. If I could incapacitate him in some way, it would only take a few seconds to force the liquid down his throat.

"All right, all right. Calm down, Lela. I just want ya to think about it." The curve of his nose seemed more hook-like than normal. He looped his thumbs in his pockets and rocked back on his heels.

"I can promise you I won't give it even a second of thought if you keep chasing me all over Houston. This is not funny." I glared through my smile before tearing out of the door and rushing out into the hallway. Thank God no one appeared to be in the vicinity.

My shaking hands ceased to tremble the farther I got away from the janitor's closet, but the irritation still poked at my heart, threatening to cut loose the organ to flail in my chest.

With my plan to put Zory in mortal peril and the initiative to find a protégé, it probably wasn't prudent to devise an additional incident. Stretching myself too thin was a bad idea. Perhaps I could manage this thing with The Chin in another way.

Trina grinned at me—her meeting over—my mother's mouth on display. The stale office air smacked into my teeth when I smiled. It was almost perfect now. I'd been practicing in the mirror and could produce a gum-baring, overexcited smile in seconds. I sank into my desk chair and picked up the phone, pretending to dial. Maybe she'd think I was listening to messages.

The phone still pressed to my ear, I checked my email. Only one new message—from Zory.

Looking forward to seeing you this weekend. So glad you agreed to come with me.

I'll see you soon.

Love,
Zory

I deleted the message without replying and hung up.

"You'll never believe the client chat I just had!" Trina gushed the second she heard the click. She described every detail of her case, and I zoned out, thinking about the oxygenation concentration percentage needed for a good fire and how I might keep The Chin from ruining everything.

Chapter Nineteen

THIRD LAW

THE SULFURY ODOR OF DIESEL FUEL SINGED MY NOSE HAIRS, EVEN through the bandana blocking my nostrils and mouth. I'd doused the edge of the hallway runners on the second and fifth floors, right at the edge of the propped-open doors to the stairwell, with a little too much, but I wanted to be sure this went according to plan. I squatted in the doorway of the third floor, my gloved hand steadying the gas can at my side.

Laying fuel-soaked rags right up against Zory's door seemed like a smart idea, but I didn't want to arouse suspicion that he was the target of the arson. My itinerary called for precision to light up the whole place instead. With the air conditioning on in most of the apartment units, there likely wouldn't be enough oxygen supply to really feed the fire, so I'd propped open the door to the roof. It had taken a surprising amount of strength—the solid, heavy metal of the door kept pushing my props out of the way until I wedged a sweatshirt I'd found in the complex's trash under the door and crammed a stray garbage can in between the knob and the door frame.

It also occurred to me during the planning process that perhaps I should drill holes through the concrete in the stairwell to facilitate the oxygen saturation rate, but it wasn't feasible—loud and time consuming and probably impossible. I compensated by bracing the stairwell doors open, even on the floors where I hadn't splashed any fuel.

In addition, I opened the windows at the far end of the hallways, dousing the tables below in diesel fuel.

The air from the window would draw the fire toward it, feed it, and make it grow. If anyone was out and about at three in the morning, it might cut the fire short if they saw the smoke, but it had to be risked.

Everything had to be risked.

Dad's voice hummed in my head: *An ounce of prevention is worth a pound of cure, Lela. Take precautions, and do everything right the first time.*

Between all the work that I'd done and my father's constant advice, whoever ended up being my protégé would have a wealth of training. Every second of this trial would become part of my legacy.

The diesel came from five gas stations, the containers purchased one at a time from different Houston locations. Everything I'd bought had been paid for in cash, and I'd worn a new disguise for each shopping trip. I'd taken a day off from work to gather the last of my required supplies.

The car I'd used to transport everything from my house to the apartment building…well, I'd borrowed it. Mrs. Zehner, the ancient woman who used to flirt with Dad before he'd died, had an equally elderly station wagon. It hibernated in her driveway like a slumbering bear, except for the rare weekends when someone—her son? Her grandson, maybe—took it for a spin. I never thought that weird tidbit of knowledge would ever come in handy. I'd researched methods of hot-wiring that particular model as well as how to unlock the door, both of which turned out to be surprisingly simple.

If my itinerary remained solid—and I had every reason to think it would, since I'd timed it out in my own car the night prior (I'd also cut the chain to the sprinkler cap at that time)—I'd return home before dawn.

As a precaution against anyone recognizing the vehicle in the event Mrs. Zehner woke and reported it missing, I taped over the five in her license plate number to resemble a six.

Trina definitely wouldn't be awake. For all her plans to kill me and thwart my mission, she slept like I'd darted her. Come ten at night, she collapsed on the couch and didn't start emerging from sleep until six. She was a back sleeper, just like my mother.

I glanced at Zory's door, my guts squirming. I backed into the stairwell and descended.

Exactly seventy-two minutes. That's how long it took from the time

I entered the building to the time I exited. Well, almost. I stood at the precipice of the mostly hidden side door.

It had taken some time to lug each gas can into place—I'd figured on ten gallons for the total job, dribbled down the stairwell, dripped down the hall of every other floor. There was no need to take the empty cans with me, so I backed awayand lit a road flare, tossing it into the puddle inside. Before I could even feel the heat of the fire, I was across the lot.

The plan left nothing to load into the car, so I found myself back on the freeway within ten minutes. The drive home went off without a mishap, although my minor hyperventilation over Zory's fate almost ran me off the road until I got it under control. I replaced the station wagon as planned, easing it back into its spot, the lights turned off. The neighborhood was, as I'd anticipated, quiet.

It was almost too simple.

I snapped off my latex gloves before nudging open the front door of the house and tiptoeing past Trina and down the hallway, my heart jackhammering in my chest. Dad's voice murmured to me, so quiet I couldn't discern the words over the pounding beneath my ribcage.

Nike followed me into my bedroom, leaping to the top of my dresser and staring. I stripped out of my smelly clothes and into a clean top and jeans.

"She stayed asleep, just like always," I noted in a hissing whisper. "Good job, Nike." I'd asked him to look after Trina, keep her out of the way on the off chance she woke up. Not that his job was so tough.

He ducked his head. *You're welcome. I take it your plan was sound?*

"Oh, yes! Everything went great tonight. Not a thing happened to knock me off my itinerary. The gas smell on my clothes and hands isn't great, but that'll come out. I…I am thinking about Zory, though."

You are allowing yourself to become too close to this man. I can see it in your face.

I chewed the inside of my cheek, embarrassed. "I do like him a lot. Liked, I guess. *Liked* him a lot."

You did what you had to do.

"Does it make me a bad person if I hope he got out? I hate to think of him burned or dead. I mean, I know if he is, it's my own fault for not putting my foot down when he first showed interest, but there was no real way out of it without drawing attention."

I swore Nike rolled his wide cat eyes before licking his paw.

"Well, there wasn't! Look, I'm not going to defend myself to you. I know it needed to be done, so I did it, regardless of my feelings."

I scooted off the bed, sliding my foot from underneath Nike's rear end. He curled up in the warm spot where I'd just been sitting and blinked. After an hour of staring at the ceiling, my thoughts drifted to my last shift at the library.

"Nike, you awake?"

The blink of his eyes was visible in the moon shining through the window. *Of course.*

"What do you think of the idea of finding a trainee for the astronaut observations?"

I'm surprised it took you this long to talk to me about it. It's an absolute necessity. Think about it—we already know Trina is, in all likelihood, your counterbalance in all this. Her group probably has dozens of operatives. They must have a succession plan. You should, too.

"Do you...let's just say, for the sake of argument, that Zory survives. That's the universe giving me a clear signal that proceeding with our relationship is a good idea. What if I produced a protégé? Myself?"

Are you suggesting that you have a child with the cosmonaut?

"Yes. It's a perfect scenario, really. I could maybe clue Zory into my mis—"

Have you taken leave of your senses? That could put everything we've worked for in jeopardy! Nike glared, and his tail rattled in agitation.

"It's not like I would tell him without the proper precautions. It might be a gradual thing, perhaps even after the child is born. Perhaps not even until he or she is ready to begin training in earnest. I can insist on exposing my successor to the things necessary to be good at the job—self-defense, chemistry, sleep science. After tonight I'm well-versed in arson. And we'd have the natural advantage of having Zory to provide context to the space program itself. The child would have a natural inclination toward science of all disciplines."

Are you sure that's the optimal option?

"No, of course not. How can I be sure about that? Mrs. Gerhardt seems certain I can locate someone in the reading hour, someone I can mentor."

That seems like a better bet. At least you could have the surety of being able to observe and choose a child based on ability. Even though you and Zory would produce genetically gifted offspring, there are no guarantees—your child might have a learning disability or have a disinterest in your mission. How would you handle it if your bouncing baby girl grew up to have an interest in something distasteful, like cheerleading or chess club?

"I hadn't thought of that. Maybe you're right. It's largely theoretical now anyway. Zory is probably dead," I said, and a strange ache weighed in my chest at the words. "I suppose I could procreate with The Chin, but it would be a DNA crapshoot."

You're better off conducting the search at the library, Nike surmised. *More control over the process. But in general, yes, it's a must. I will not last forever, either, you know. It's important you have someone who can advise you.*

I nodded, taking note of the heaviness in my bones. From my toes to the tip of my skull, fatigue had set in and left me in an unpleasant drowsy state. My thoughts swirled like dreams. There would be no sleep, but a vague ether into which I'd drift between light and dark.

Babies took time and effort. Zory would be an excellent father, no doubt, but he wouldn't accept full responsibility for the care of a human being. I would be too busy to properly do so. Nike was right, as usual. Babies weren't like cats. It was inappropriate to leave them for days at a time with large bowls of food and water and a clean litterbox.

Recommitting to the search via the library patrons was the better plan. Zory's face filtered behind my eyelids, but I shut it out, thinking instead of what the training and recruiting protocols might look like. Before long, I could see a young girl trailing me to watch the astronauts sleep.

✳✳✳

Yes, Mrs. Ramos. I promise it won't hurt." I faked a smile, trying to reassure the small woman sitting across the desk in the conference room. I'd edged out of bed at dawn, head pounding from the smell of diesel still strong in my nostrils.

"Okay. Well then, I guess…tomorrow night?"

The unexpected case had come my way, but I couldn't say I minded. The woman—Mrs. Ramos—hadn't been able to sleep all the way through the night in five years. We'd been trying to work her into the schedule for weeks. The best part for me: I could go home after our meeting and take most of the next day off to make up for working overnight.

I'd avoided watching or listening to any news prior to coming into work, but like a dog with a bone, I couldn't leave it be. The second I sat down at my desk, I checked online to see if I could find any mention of the fire. The apartment building had been heavily damaged with several fatalities reported. No word on identities, though.

Anyone who'd burned was a hero; dying can be poetic or painful, useless or meaningful. The dead never chose their fates, but who did? No one would ever wake up one morning and say, "I think I'll die today to save the space shuttle."

The phantom smell of seared flesh tickled my nostrils, strips of blackened flesh blistering and cracking. It would peel away and crumble into soot.

Mrs. Ramos smiled in relief, and I moved to shake her hand. Her palm stuck to mine, tacky and moist with sweat.

We walked down to the lobby while I tried to make small talk.

"Thanks for going over the procedure with me," she said when we reached the front doors. "It makes all of this so much easier."

"Of course, Mrs. Ramos. Anytime. I'll see you tomorrow night."

She shuffled out the doors, dark hair gleaming in the light from the overcast sky. The sound of her heels clicking against the macadam echoed back, even through the glass-enclosed lobby. It sounded like a ticking clock, counting down the time until the news would release Zory's name among the dead.

The Chin stood several feet away in the hallway, watching through eyes narrowed to coin slots. He maintained his position while I moved closer to the elevator. His lips pressed together.

I waited for the doors to open so I could escape the weight of his stare.

"Heya, Lela."

I nodded in his direction, relieved when the alert bell dinged. "Good morning."

"Have a nice night?"

Several people streamed off the car, and I stalked on without answering, pressing the "close door" button rapidly in the hopes The Chin wouldn't follow me. He didn't.

The air inside closed in, pushing at me, until I wanted nothing more than to cower in the corner. I hadn't the time, though. If Zory was gone, there would be contingency plans to be made, another astronaut to vet.

My desk phone rang just as I sat down.

Please let it be Zory. Please let it be Zory. Please let it be Zory.

"Forty Winks Science Labs. Lela White speaking."

"Miss White? This is Dr. Adam Tetsuro from Memorial Hermann City Medical Center. I'm calling about Marjorie Gerhardt. You're listed on medical forms as her preferred contact."

"Yes. Is there something wrong?"

"I'm afraid I can't disclose anything over the phone. Can you come to the hospital?"

"Yes. Yes, of course. I'll be right there."

The receiver thudded onto the desk, my mind blanking on everything except the instruction to suck air into my lungs and push it out again, over and over until the feeling began to return to my body.

My colt legs could barely stand without wobbling, knees buckling with every third step. I paused in the hallway, trying to deaden the quicksilver emotion in my veins.

Trina stepped out of the elevator and beelined for me. She wore my mother's clothes, plain as day—a mauve dress and shoes. Her hair curled up, flipping around her head.

"Are you okay?" she asked, inspecting my face. "You look like death."

"Yes." Except I wasn't. "No. I mean, I'm okay." This wasn't about me. "I need to go to the hospital."

My eyesight dimmed, the office walls coming over dark red. I clutched my bag, forcing myself to take a step.

"The hospital? What's wrong? Should I drive you? I should drive you. Come on—I'll call the HR office on the way."

I almost agreed, but she didn't belong in my private life. Or Mrs. Gerhardt's, for that matter. She'd probably just use it against us.

I swallowed back bile and loosened my hands, daring my face to defy my order to smile. "No. No, I'm okay. I just…well, a friend has taken ill." I gritted my teeth and propelled myself toward the elevator.

The scent of my mother's perfume chased behind me, and goose flesh broke over every inch of my flesh. "Go. Don't worry about a thing," she said, sneering.

I sprinted into an open elevator, my mind on autopilot until I found myself in the emergency room, Dr. Tetsuro standing in front of me. The broad plane of his cheekbones made for a wide face, but his mouth was small, almost as if he wore Kewpie doll lips all drawn up into a permanent pucker.

"Thank you for coming. I'm sure you're aware that Marjorie has been in heart failure for some time." He paused, almost as though allowing me time for a show of emotion. When I said nothing, he continued. "The paramedics were called to her place of employment today, and she was delivered here. We did all we could for her, but I'm afraid her heart was just too damaged. She passed away at 11:16 this morning."

A strange voice howled in my head, and I bit the inside of my mouth, forcing it quiet. It didn't listen, though. It grew into a wild scream so loud the pale yellow walls shook and tangled.

"Oh," I said. My jaw clenched to keep the keening behind my teeth.

"Yes, well. There are some forms you should sign. Has Marjorie indicated to you what she'd prefer to have done with her remains?"

I shook my head, my eyes feeling foreign in their sockets. *Marjorie.* That wasn't her name. Dead. Something was very, very wrong.

"Right this way, Ms. White."

Each step crossed a tile, and I placed my feet, avoiding the seams. Mom's voice cackled in my head, lower than the other—"Step on a crack, break your mother's back."

I moved through the space like a ghost, my thoughts wispy. I signed papers, and people spoke to me in soothing voices. My cell phone rang several times until I turned it off without looking at the ID screen. Static buzzed in my ears.

Without realizing I'd left the hospital or even that I had been driving, I suddenly saw my house outside the car window. The brakes screeched when I slammed my foot down to stop, and my head whipped forward. Nothing felt real or right. The concrete of the front walk caught on my shoes. I nearly tripped over the front step and the feet planted there.

Feet.

My chin jerked. Zory. He sat on my front steps, leaning back and braced on his elbows, face turned to the sky, now pulsing red and yellow. A noise almost like a wounded animal bleated out of my mouth. He tilted his head to look at me. The whites of his eyes were shot through with angry, red blood vessels, his face pale and wan.

I sat next to him, his body reassuring and solid. I considered moving away to put some physical distance between us, but I couldn't make myself do it. Now that he had survived the fire, maybe it didn't matter. The universe had given its permission, but maybe it wasn't so much a free pass as an exchange. One life in exchange. Zory lived, and Mrs. Gerhardt died.

My fault.

"Are you okay? What happened?" I asked. It was all I could do to keep my voice steady and the noose from choking off my seared throat. The very air around me shimmered and sparked.

He groaned and slipped his arm around my waist, resting his cheek against my hair. "Horrible fire."

"Where?"

"My apartment building." His arm tightened around me. "Can we go inside?"

"Yes, of course." I stood and took his hand, hauling him up from the step. The weariness on his face pulled at my heart, the thought of Mrs. Gerhardt lying cold on a slab tearing it in two. "Are you hurt?"

"The medics say just a little bit of smoke inhalation. Nothing of concern."

I ground my teeth together, gnashing and tearing. Yes, nothing of concern.

He followed me into the living room after I unlocked the door. "I was lucky."

He sank into the couch, old coils groaning under the sudden weight. I took his outstretched hand and let him pull me onto his lap.

"Lucky?" I asked, fighting the inappropriate giggles tickling my uvula. Yeah, he was lucky, all right—lucky every action I took had an opposite and equal reaction with the universe. I was the living embodiment of Newton's Third Law of Motion in the most warped, awful way.

"I do not know what woke me, but I smelled smoke. The carpet in the hallway was on fire. One of the other neighbors and I knocked on doors and helped get people out of the building. Not everyone made it out, though…and a few people were burned." He shuddered, dragging me closer until he hugged me, his arms strong around my ribs and hips.

I looped my arm behind him, rubbing my fingers against the back of his tense neck. He didn't notice my own body had moved into rigor mortis in solidarity with Mrs. Gerhardt's now-decomposing corpse.

"But you're okay."

He nodded and scrunched his face against my shoulder blade. "Yes. An old woman who lived on one of the upper floors died. Her and her cat. I do not know who else."

I killed a cat. Nike jogged into the room and glared at me. He had overheard. We'd have to have a chat about it later. I killed a cat and the closest thing I had to a mother in a single twenty-four hour period. The bitter tang of sin licked at my gut, grooving its tongue around my intestines and tasting my disgust.

"What about your apartment?"

"What of it?"

"Well, was the building destroyed?"

He shrugged. "It looked pretty bad last night. It is still standing, but I do not know if anything inside remains."

My calculations must have been off. "Do you...where are you staying?" My conscience almost got the best of me, an invitation to stay at my house almost flying out of my mouth.

It was bad enough with Trina underfoot all the time. She'd said something the other day about the insurance company sending her a check, so she'd start searching for an apartment soon. Maybe she'd decided to back off, cancel her plans, or maybe she figured the element of surprise would be a better option to put the space shuttle in danger.

The taste of solitude was so close. So close. I could barely enjoy the momentary glee with the weight of all I'd done crushing my larynx.

"A hotel. The people at Johnson will find a space for me at another apartment building—they're good about it. I am feeling very fortunate, though. I did not lose much. Just some clothes, my computer. The furniture was not mine, and I did not bring much with me from home."

"That's good," I agreed. Mrs. Gerhardt was gone. Every time I thought the words, they seemed less true. "You look so tired."

"I am. I have not slept yet."

"You should make an effort," I said. "Your brain needs a rest, particularly after such a traumatic event. Without enough sleep, the neurons are interrupted..."

We lapsed into silence. I stayed in his lap, running my fingers through his hair and thinking about Mrs. Gerhardt and the poor cat.

Zory's breath evened out, and when I tilted my head down, his eyes had closed. The lines in his brow eased. It was my first opportunity to observe him sleeping. Grief tore at me, but I couldn't allow the moment to pass.

I eased out of his hold and shifted him until he lay on the couch. His big body didn't fit: his legs dangled off the arm. He looked like a giant reclining on a piece of doll furniture. The cool air of the house wasn't freezing, but I tucked a blanket around him anyway.

He slept hard at first, never moving or even twitching. I considered getting an observation form to mark up, but how would I explain it if he woke up or Trina came home? Instead, I sat on the floor, crossed my legs in front of me, and held vigil over him, lest the universe decide it needed more payment for my transgressions. I could annotate his file later.

His eyelids twitched approximately twenty-six minutes after that, and his eyeballs jerked back and forth beneath them. His whole body stiffened for a moment and then relaxed into the couch, although he threw his arm out once. The dream appeared to last for sixteen minutes. Without monitoring his brain activity, I couldn't be one hundred percent sure. He had two more dreams in the space of three hours, and I found myself timing my breaths to match his.

The air circulated in my lungs. More giggles fizzed up my throat, but they wedged in my pharynx. How would I find my successor now? Obviously the library wouldn't close down without Mrs. Gerhardt, but no one else would funnel kids interested in science into my children's section volunteer shift.

The front door opened and closed, and Trina appeared. I untangled my legs and stood, pressing a finger to my lips as I led her to the kitchen.

"Oh my God, is that Zory?" she asked, her voice hushed. Not like that fooled me. There was a sparkle of excitement lurking in her eyes—maybe she thought she could take out both of us at once. "Was he in the hospital?"

"His apartment building burned down last night. He's exhausted. But no, he wasn't why I had to go."

"Then…what is going on?"

"It's Mrs. Gerhardt."

"Oh! Is she okay? I mean, you looked so shocked at work. Is she still at the hospital, or did you drop her at home? I should take her a casserole." She picked at the mauve skirt she'd obviously taken from my mother's closet. The skin on her arms bubbled and waved.

I closed my eyes for a second before answering, trying not let the distress settle in my face. "She's dead."

Her hands fluttered in front of her, but I caught the satisfied smile that flashed over her face. "Oh God. What was it? She wasn't even that old."

"No. She…it was her heart."

"Do you, I mean, are you okay? Do we need to call her family? Can I help you do anything?"

I nearly cackled. Yes, she could move out immediately. Take my poisoned water with her. I'd resorted to keeping a case of water, cans of tuna, and a bag of oranges locked in my closet.

"No, thank you."

She nodded and padded down the hall to the bathroom. I returned to the living room to watch over Zory.

He was a good sleeper.

Eventually, though, real life intruded. The chirp of my cell phone pulled me back to the kitchen. Mrs. Gerhardt's lawyer assured me he would take care of the arrangements for her body—she requested a cremation, no memorial service or funeral.

By the time I hung up, Trina sat beside me at the table, uncharacteristically quiet but everything about her screaming happiness.

Finally, she said, "What a horrible day for you." Her tone was almost taunting, but I didn't let her evoke a reaction.

"For me?"

"Well, yeah. I mean, your boyfriend loses his home, and now this thing with Mrs. Gerhardt. I know you two were really close. You know, maybe Zory could stay here. You have room."

I watched her face—my mother's face. "No, I don't think so. Speaking of which, any luck on apartment hunting?"

Her eyes widened and then narrowed. "I haven't really had a chance to look, but I definitely will this weekend. My boyfriend said I should move to Austin again to be with him, but I just don't want to move without having a commitment, you know?" She paused and craned her neck, straining toward the living room. "He's really hot."

"Who?"

"Who? Zory, that's who! What does he do? A big guy like that—I bet he must be a construction worker or something, huh?"

"Yeah. Or something."

A thump came from the living room. Trina smiled and stood. "I'll let you two have some privacy." She disappeared moments later, only the sound of the front door marking her departure. She'd left behind the sour smell of her delight, though. I wrinkled my nose and wished the universe had decided to take Trina in the exchange instead.

Zory came stumbling toward me, rubbing the sleep from his eyes. "Why did you let me nap, Lela—I did not want to bore you." He kissed my cheek.

"You just missed my house guest," I said.

"The mysterious Trina."

I nodded.

He studied my face, brows drawing together. "You look upset. Is something the matter?" He took my hand.

"A friend, she…died this morning."

"Oh. Oh, Lela—I am so very sorry. Had I known, I would not have burdened you. I should go."

Part of me wanted him to, but another part worried if he left my presence he'd be snatched, killed in transit to his hotel. "No." I smiled grimly. "Please stay for a while."

Chapter Twenty

STRIKE A MATCH

THE HAIRBRUSH SNAPPED THROUGH MY HAIR, PAIN RADIATING FROM
my scalp with each yank of Mom's arm. I mashed my lips together,
determined not to make a sound. Not a peep. I'd have rather died than
let her know she hurt me. With every pass, I prayed she wouldn't hit a
snarl because I doubted she'd take the time to untangle it.

"Doesn't matter what I do," she complained, glaring at me in the
mirror over the dresser. "Still looks like hell."

Little fuzzies dotted her turtleneck sweater, and the color had faded
from the original mauve to a pale lilac. I focused on a snag near the arm
seam so I didn't have to see her perfectly made-up face, her lipgloss shiny
and sticky and her eye lids shimmering blue below her usual barrette.

"I don't know why your father insists on all of us going out to dinner.
You're just going to sit there and stare at us. Yeah, poor little Lela, she
has it so bad."

My silence must have made her even madder; she got rougher and
rougher until the bristles nearly gouged flesh off my skull.

Only babies cry, only babies cry, only babies cry.

Her crazed eyes darted and scattered, wide and scary. She stopped
brushing and tore at the hair that had come loose in the brush.

"Dirty." She pursed her lips in disgust. "We must burn it. Unlucky
to throw it away. Burn it."

Mom stomped out of the room, and my whole body sagged. My
head ached, but there was no time to think about that—Dad expected

us to be ready to go when he got back from work. He'd be home soon, which didn't give Mom much time to stop being so weird. She usually acted much meaner when he wasn't around, but this was worse than normal.

She rushed back in, a pack of long matches clutched in her hand.

"Get off the bed, Lela!" she shrieked, her face sweaty and red. She threw the handful of my hair she'd pulled out of the brush onto the middle of my comforter and struck a match against the rough pad on the box. "Can't throw it away…have to burn it. Breathe. Four-three-two-one-in, four-three-two-one-out."

Chapter Twenty-One

THE REPLACEMENT

M RS. GERHARDT'S PRESENCE LOOMED IN THE STACKS OF THE library despite her physical absence. Every time I turned a corner I expected to find her shelving a book, but a mortician was probably prepping her for cremation even as I thought of her.

A cremation fire was stoked to 1,700 degrees, give or take. She could only have weighed 120 pounds—most of her bones would burn to dust in an hour. Another thirty minutes, and she'd be ready to pour into the urn. I hadn't had to pick one out; her lawyer had seen to that.

"Lela, so glad I caught up with you." It was the interim librarian, a mousy woman with a thick waist and broad shoulders whose name I could never quite remember. I'd never seen her in anything other than matronly print dresses and black loafers. "Mind if I pick your brain about a few things?"

"Sure. What can I help you with?" I asked.

"To start with, there are some personal things in Mrs. Gerhardt's office I thought you might want. But secondly, I want to talk to you about the volunteer schedule. She never really went over this kind of stuff with me, and until the board can hire someone to take over for her, I want to make sure we have continuity. You've been here longer than anyone, so I'm hoping you can help me figure it out."

I shrugged. "Sure."

The relief on her face was almost comical. "Give me twenty minutes. We're supposed to get a delivery of interlibrary loans in a few minutes."

She scurried off toward the front of the library, and I continued wandering.

Maybe I should have felt guilty for not shelving books or doing other work, but with all that was going on, I needed to simply *be* in the library and think to get my focus back. I had the all-clear to continue seeing Korchagin, and Trina seemed to be backing off her quest to tinker with my mission, but now my protégé program was off track.

Five minutes later voices echoed out of the back corner, a lonely alcove full of reference books rarely sought. I heard a high-pitched laugh, a tinge of cruelty to it, followed by a thud.

"Quit it," a boy said.

"Don't be such a fag." A girl that time, maybe the same who'd laughed. The crack of books slamming into the floor sounded next. "How much do you have on you? Give it."

Another boy now: "Look at that—five dollars. Bet you got more."

"Backpack," the girl barked.

Now I could see them. The girl was thin with dark hair pulled up in a ponytail. A tall boy with shaggy blonde hair had a shorter one with a red bowl cut by the shirt, holding him against the shelf. None of them could have been any more than ten or eleven, but the redhead might have been a little younger. He was definitely shorter and weaker than the other two.

"Is there a problem here?" I asked. "This isn't a playground." Mrs. Gerhardt had mentioned this kind of thing from time to time—kids using the library to roughhouse or pick on little kids. She'd scheduled anti-bullying programs, but the ones who acted up weren't the kids who attended.

The girl smirked at me. "Naw. Just talking. Ain't that right?"

The kid with the red hair jerked away from the taller boy but said nothing. The blond boy folded his arms over his chest and said, "Yeah, just talking."

"Well," I said, giving them my best tooth-baring smile. "Let's talk." I walked over to the girl and laid a hand on her shoulder. She flinched, and I dug my fingers into her flesh. "For instance, did you know that a grown woman could choke the life out of a little girl like you with very little effort?"

The tall boy paled and backed up. The girl sneered and said, "You'd get in trouble. I'll tell. The cops'd come and haul your fat ass to jail."

"Would they now?" I asked. I ducked down so our noses nearly touched. Her hazel eyes widened. "Did you also know that I can kill you without leaving so much as a mark? And I very seriously doubt this boy," I gestured toward the shorter boy, "would corroborate any story you might tell. I suspect very much he'd call you a liar and a thief, especially since you have his five dollars clutched in your silly little hand. And this one," I jerked my thumb at the other boy, now frozen in place, "will be useless as well—I do have a bad habit of following up on my threats."

The girl swallowed, a movement that sent a spasm through her entire body. She stayed silent.

I forced my smile wider and squeezed tighter with my hand before straightening. "I think the two of you should go now, but remember what I said. And give the kid his money. If I see you bothering him or anyone else in this library again, we're going to have a nice, long chat."

Mrs. Gerhardt had her way of doing things, and I had mine.

The girl hurled the bill at the small kid and ran past the taller boy. Sprinted was more like it. He pivoted and followed, looking back only once. I stared until they turned down the corridor. I allowed a smile and turned back.

"Okay?" I asked.

The redhead was already snickering. "Wow, lady. You've got some balls."

"Language," I snapped, and his face pinched. "Have some respect."

"Uh, sorry. I mean, I'm very sorry." He stuck out his hand. "My name's Dave."

I took it—his fingers were small and clammy. "Dave. I'm—" I almost told him my first name until I remembered Mrs. Gerhardt's rule about working with children. "I'm Miss White. Is this a regular occurrence?"

"Don't know. Haven't lived here long enough to find out."

"You're new to the area?"

He nodded. "Yeah." He stooped to pick up the books that had fallen or been thrown.

I studied him, noting his faded jeans and blue hooded sweatshirt. His t-shirt was plain and red, his sneakers dirty but not raggedy. A constellation of freckles dotted his nose and cheeks, his brows a ruddy auburn. He set the book on the table, and I could feel my forehead wrinkling.

"Isn't that a little advanced for you?" I asked. My pulse picked up. "I have a few books more appropriate to your age group."

He scowled and jerked up his chin. "I'm not a baby."

"You're studying astronomy for fun?"

"S'school project."

My stomach flipped over and over. "Do you like space?"

He nodded, still not moving.

"And you like to read?"

"Yes, ma'am."

It was as though Mrs. Gerhardt's ghost stood next to me, whispering in my ear. *Watch him.* "Well. I have a special interest in space travel and related sciences. If you need something, come find me. You know, if you need to talk about books or terminology. I'm happy to help you."

"Okay. I mean, thanks."

I watched him go, my mind racing. If I could carve out some time, I'd start an observation. A sleep study on a boy might not be that easy—it wasn't like he was at an age where he had his own place or his parents probably left him alone overnight too often. I'd have to find a way into his house, or maybe as a first step I could convince him to come to the reading program in the children's section. He was too old, of course, but if he was truly my protégé, maybe he'd instinctively know why I was asking, just as Mrs. Gerhardt had understood without my having to tell her.

Nike and I would have to begin immediately. I'd need a test. Maybe putting this boy in danger was the answer, like it was with Zory. There was no one left in my life to take in payment.

There was almost a skip to my step as I made my way toward Mrs. Gerhardt's office. The interim librarian sat behind the circulation desk, sorting through the delivery.

"Do you know the boy who just checked out *A Beginner's Guide to the Universe*? Red hair?" I asked.

"Oh, uh, hang on." She tapped on the keyboard and said, "That's Davey Enders."

"Davey," I said.

"Mmm hmm. Why, is he giving you trouble? I saw those bratty Zimmerman kids run out of here like someone was chasing them. Hope he's not taking up with those two. We've gotten more complain—"

"No, not at all," I said. "Seems like a smart kid."

She nodded. "Ready to tackle the office and the schedule?"

Anticipation and hope warmed me. Maybe my succession planning wouldn't have to be put on hold after all.

I held on to the thought for the next several days, mapping out the best route to take to Davey Enders' house. There was no time to do an initial investigation, though, because there was planning for my first full-scale observation with Zory. He'd asked and I'd agreed to attend a NASA event, standing dutifully at his side while he introduced me to men and women I'd watched sleep and trying to purge the panic of having them so close.

It was only on the drive to his hotel that I managed to unclench my jaw but only slightly: hotels made me uncomfortable. I always worried about the organisms, germs, and bodily fluids lurking in the corners, on the walls, under the mattress.

The comforter spread ugly daisies across the surface of the bed, a matching print glaring at me from above the headboard. I set my overnight bag inside the door and perched on the edge of a worn blue velour chair in the corner.

"Did you have fun today?" Zory asked. He tugged his shirttails out of his khaki pants.

I sat, my hands clenched on my lap. "Yes, of course."

"Really?" His lips curved into an incredulous half moon. "I am sure no one else noticed, but I know that you are still upset about Mrs. Gerhardt."

"Well, yes. Of course. But I was with you—and it's a help to have a break from Trina."

Upset wasn't quite the word I'd have used. Frazzled. Anxious. Even worried. *Upset* didn't cover it, especially not with so many people at the event talking behind my back and scheming. It was the first thing I'd noticed, and it was worrisome. Had they figured out that I'd been to their homes?

He ran his fingertip along my jaw. His smile grew, and he shook his head. "She is an odd choice of roommate for you. I almost feel like I know her from the way you talk about her."

"It's not intentional," I answered, faking a grin. "We're very different."

"Ah, I know." He sat opposite of me at the edge of the bed. "You say she is…enthusiastic. You are careful, always holding yourself just so." He leaned down to ease off his shoes, never taking his eyes from me. "I like it," he said, his voice loud in the silence of the room, despite his low tone. He kissed my knuckles, lighting a smolder in my veins even as anxiety clawed at my throat. "You do not need to be so afraid with me. And you do not have to stay the night." Zory's gentle smile warmed his face, bristling the hair on his chin. "Or, if you do stay, nothing must happen between us. There is no need to rush if—"

I cut him off, my lips on his and his grunt of surprise hanging heavy in the air. His fingers bit into my hip bones, maneuvering me closer. The solidness of his hands grounded me, kept my mind from wandering too far. He'd asked me to stay and I would. It was an excellent opportunity.

The want fizzed in my belly, rushing from my navel to the very tips of my limbs, focusing me on the connection between the two of us at our lips. His shoulders pressed against my ribs, bone to bone. He laid a trail of kisses down my chin, the column of my throat. His saliva on my skin. Maybe it should have bothered me, but the universe had said yes… now I did, too.

His hands put a few inches of distance between us, his thumbs traveling up my ribs. Another squeeze, and he nuzzled his forehead into my chest. The hair of his goatee prickled at my skin through the thin fabric of my dress. My fingers skimmed up his arm to the shifting muscles of his back. Deltoid. Trapezius. Levator scapulae. The fabric of his shirt collar—the blue of cornflowers—contrasted against the whiteness of my forearm.

Frigid air eddied around me, sensitive on my skin as the hem of my dress rose, draping over Zory's elbows. The heat of his palms curving up the back of my thigh stoked a furnace, flames licking up the small of my back. And after that, each piece of clothing either of us wore slipped off, littering the floor, hanging off the bed.

His lips nipped at the skin below my collarbone, the space between my breasts, the ledge of my belly button, repeating the circuit with his mouth and hands. I discovered the sparse hair of his chest, along with the parabola-shaped scar on his pelvis.

I didn't stop to ask about the scar, but I thought about it, wondering if it'd been a training accident. Or maybe someone working against the space program had intentionally injured him. Trina or one of her friends.

"Focus, Lela," Mrs. Gerhardt whispered to me. "The hard work starts tomorrow. Recruitment efforts are crucial. Davey might be a good choice, but there are other options."

I nodded and paid attention to his skin on my skin. The rip of a condom package, whispered words to me in Russian—I caught a few recognizable phrases, but my thoughts lay elsewhere—and we moved together, tender in such an unfamiliar way.

Zory's hands collected my hair at the nape of my neck, tugging gently. He kissed me until I couldn't breathe. Quiet sighs and needful grunts exchanged between us, rocking, pulling, pushing. Too close, too close, and yet not close enough. The tension rose, burst, and spread, quick and surprising, just as shocking as the feelings rasping across the inside of my chest. He shook, his strength held in check, and then he stilled, the two of us wrapped around each other.

He excused himself, the mattress springing back along with thoughts of the germs on the bedding. When he returned I had hidden under the sheets. He joined me, bowing around my back, his hand resting on my breast.

"Tell me something," he murmured, his nose tracing the crook of my neck before positioning a kiss on my bare shoulder.

"What?"

"Anything. Tell me something I do not yet know." His breath hushed over my neck, rounded syllables tracing the curve of my ear.

I forced myself to stay relaxed. He must have felt my muscles tense, though, because his hand shifted to tighten around my hip, sliding back and forth as though attempting to comfort me.

"You want me to…tell you a story? About me?"

"Mmm hmm." The words vibrated through my back. "I want to know more of you."

A nervous giggle tore out of my throat. What would he want to hear about first—that my work kept the space shuttle and the crew safe? That my pursuit of him had cost me Mrs. Gerhardt? It wasn't safe for conversation. I lived an unusual life, a special life. A life with purpose.

"My mother left us when I was ten," I said. It probably wasn't the happy story he'd been expecting, but nothing else was appropriate. Her leering face morphed into Trina's, and a hand squeezed my intestines.

"I remember you told me that when we first met."

"I woke up one morning, and she was gone. Dad said she'd left, but he never really said where she went."

"And she never came back? Did she call?"

I shook my head. "No."

"Did she ever get in touch with your father? To ask for a divorce, perhaps?"

"No, she didn't even take her clothes. Her suitcase...it's still in the closet. Everything is."

"That is odd."

"Is it?"

"I don't know. Yes. Where would she go without her clothes?" His thumb brushed the same pass of flesh against my hip bone, over and over. "Do you miss her?"

"No."

"What was she like? You said that she did not like children, yes?"

"Just, well, she wasn't always mean. I remember having fun with her when I was younger."

"What happened?"

"Not sure." It felt strange to want to tell him these things. Anything but the fact that she killed his colleagues. "Just one day she..."

"Did she hit you?"

"She hated me."

Zory's silence answered me, but he held me a little tighter, his arms squeezing and releasing like a never-ending cycle. After a few minutes, he spoke again. "Did your dad not step in to protect you?"

"He didn't know. Well, he didn't know how bad it was anyway. And it was my responsibility to watch her, keep her in check."

"I do not understand what you say. Do you..."

"What?"

"Do you think your dad could have sent her away? Maybe he knew more than you think. I would do anything to protect my family...my daughter, if I had one. Kill, even. My babushka has said often enough that there is nobility in guarding those you love. She once fought off a man that tried to hurt my mother."

Dad never saw much, although maybe he did have some idea. But Dad would never...no. Could he? No. An uncomfortable finger of doubt wriggled at the base of my brain, but I stamped on it, choosing to concentrate on the lines of Zory's body instead.

Maybe I'd visit Mrs. Gerhardt's small house to see if I might find some sort of evidence about what she knew about my mother and father. A diary of some sort.

Now that the depth of her quiet knowledge had been exposed to me, it made me think she knew more about everything than she'd let on. It was entirely possible that *I'd* been *her* replacement in the race to keep the space shuttle safe. If that were the case, she must have lapsed on the job at least once.

The more I thought about it, the more sense it made. She'd been the one to point me toward the sleep journals, explained terminology to me. But maybe I'd never know…if she were careful like me.

I sighed and twisted in Zory's arms, kissing his throat.

Chapter Twenty-Two

A FINE CANDIDATE

M Y SHOULDER ACHED FROM BEING CRAMPED IN ONE POSITION FOR so long—cuddling after sex had never been part of my experience, owing to hasty redressing and quick escapes. Zory's body emitted heat as though the fire I'd set at his building still raged inside the confines of his veins. I wriggled, uncomfortable and too warm.

Everything clustered too close, not close enough. I still lay awake, calculating and observing every twitch and breath.

His sleep onset latency ranged to sixteen minutes. Falling asleep in that period of time scored as excellent on the Multiple Sleep Latency Test, although to get a true reading I'd need to note the time it took during the day. Not that it mattered—he likely wasn't sleep deprived. The man slept hard, his breath long and deep in my ear, just the barest hint of a snore sawing beneath the exhalations.

His arms locked me into place, tightening as I squirmed against his strength, but I finally managed to free myself without bothering him too much.

I sighed when cold air took the place of his heat, struggling into a t-shirt from my bag and pulling back the curtains just enough to let in a glow from the moon and street lights. The rough fabric of the armchair scratched against the underside of my legs, and I pulled the shirt to cover my knees after I sat with a sleep observation form and pencil.

I had come prepared.

Completing a full study was easy this way—getting sexually involved with all the astronauts would make things so simple. It would cut the time it took to complete an observation. Granted, going about my usual routine seemed like less trouble, and it might look suspicious—maybe they'd just think of me as a groupie. Did astronauts have groupies?

The more I thought about it, the less attractive it seemed. Zory was the only one I wanted. There was something about him that chased away my normal reticence to be close to a new person. Besides, if I could somehow figure out a way to tell him what I was doing one day, he might be of help with his NASA contacts. He could be the one to make friends, and I would reap the benefits. The silent partner.

"Lela," Zory murmured, his arm reaching across the bed.

I lowered my observation paperwork, hiding it under the bed and waiting to see if he fully awoke. He drew my pillow into his arms and hugged it to his chest. I thought about adding a note to the form about his action but stopped when a shocking thought popped into my head: it was cute. *Cute*, which was strange, considering I never really thought in those terms. Zory was an attractive man, and I liked him.

I'd miss him when he returned to Russia. If he returned. When he left, I'd be alone. Really alone this time without Mrs. Gerhardt to talk to. Nike and I were perfectly capable of designing the training sessions, but having both of them with me would have been helpful.

Dad used to tell me, "the heart wants what the heart wants." Mrs. Gerhardt had told me that, too. I never really understood until that moment.

Zory spoke again—a moan this time, followed by the word "fire." I tightened my grip on the pencil, the annotation on his chart barely legible.

Each hour brought a new quirk, some spasm of his leg or a different tone to his breathing. He swore a few times in Russian, and once he hissed out some words I didn't know and descended into unintelligible muttering.

I could picture him trussed up, strapped to the seat in the shuttle during takeoff. I wouldn't describe him as a restless sleeper—not at all. Ge'd only talked in his sleep and moved a bit more after I got out of bed.

For the next thirty-seven minutes I stared, memorizing the curve of his bicep and the three freckles across his collarbone that formed a jagged line. Within minutes I swore I could see Mrs. Gerhardt's profile in the shape. His arm jerked again, obliterating her face. There was nothing left to learn from watching—at least not in that moment—so I stowed the evidence of my observation and pivoted onto the mattress, easing under the covers and back between his arms.

It was possible I'd never get a true observation on Zory. He had no natural habitat now that I'd burned down his apartment. But maybe the universe had given me more when it took Mrs. Gerhardt—maybe the study process could be truncated. Hmm.

He tensed against me, nuzzling his nose against my neck. He kissed my shoulder and whispered, voice thick with sleep, "Where did you go?"

"Nowhere. Go back to sleep."

Hours later I was back at the library. The benefit of helping with the volunteer schedule was being able to take shifts when I needed an excuse to be somewhere else. As much as I enjoyed Zory's company and having access to that much information, too much of a good thing was probably taking advantage of the universe's gift to me. The smell of him clung to me, though, a powerful reminder of my mission.

I wheeled the cart down the aisle, Mrs. Gerhardt's voice calling out the Dewey Decimal call numbers for each book that needed reshelving. I was in the 500s hunting down the location of a quantum physics book when I heard footsteps behind me.

"Miss White?"

Davey Enders stood behind me, fidgeting his weight from foot to foot. His hair was shorter, making it look brighter, almost like the shine of a new penny.

"Davey," I said. "What can I do for you?"

"Dave," he corrected. "Can you…I mean, my mom doesn't…would you read my paper?"

My brows rose. "Why would you want me to do that?"

"I wanna get a good grade. And you said—"

"Yes, I remember what I said. Why don't you sit down?"

He scrambled into a chair at the nearest corral and dropped his backpack at his feet. I pulled up a chair and sat next to him. "Any trouble with those kids again?" I asked.

His mouth twisted up, like he was trying not to smile. "Nu uh. You scared the sh—I mean, crap out of them. No one's bugged me at all." His whole body seemed to shudder. "You were just kidding, right? About all that?"

I could feel Mrs. Gerhardt hovering over my shoulder. "He's not in your program yet, Lela," she said. "Remember your public face."

"Of course," I said. "Just wanted to give them a taste of their own medicine."

Clearly satisfied, he allowed the grin to take over his face. "Thought so, but my mom says you can't ever be too sure."

"You told your mother what happened?"

"Uh uh. She thinks there's nothing but pervs and killers around, though. She didn't even wanna let me walk to the library or to school by myself. Dad told her to chill."

"I see. Do you like Houston?"

"It's okay."

I watched him scrape his cuticles, big eyes glancing around. "I'll tell you what," I said. "I'll read your paper, but you have to tell me what your favorite subjects are. You do well in school, right?"

"Good job," Mrs. Gerhardt said. "You're doing really great at getting him talking."

"Yeah. I get all As. Well, some Bs."

"Some Bs? You should study harder. What's your best subject?"

"I like science."

"Did you like the book you checked out?" I asked.

"Yeah. It was good."

"And you understood it?"

"Some of it."

"That's great. Do you ever check out science journals? For instance, if you like astronomy, there's *Astronomy Now* or the *Journal of Cosmology*. We can get them for you, you know, if you're interested in research."

"That's cool. Maybe."

"Do you like the space shuttle?"

"Yeah," he said. His face was turning pink under the freckles. "It'd be awesome to blast off and go to the moon or whatever. I bet they see aliens."

We sat and talked for another fifteen minutes. His paper was simplistic but accurate. He'd make a fine candidate for my program. Even Mrs. Gerhardt agreed.

✳✳✳

A N UNEXPECTED BREEZE SWIRLED MY SKIRT AROUND MY LEGS AS I stepped out of my car Monday morning, skimming the fabric across my kneecaps. The change in the temperature of the air concerned me. My eyelids drooped.

Nike and I had worked all night on protocols. I still had some work to do on devising a plan for observations, but the ideas we'd come up with for shadowing and training were excellent. It felt odd to be so excited about something while I still grieved Mrs. Gerhardt, but she was with me. Not all the time, but she'd been helpful during my initial interview with Davey Enders.

"Morning." The Chin's voice cut through the thoughts banging around inside my head, and I opened my eyes. He stood several feet away. The Forty Winks building looming tall behind him, his thumbs hooked into the pockets of his uniform. The wind ruffled his thin hair.

"What do you want?" A glance around the parking lot confirmed no one near enough to overhear. I didn't feel it necessary anymore to feign polite interest or niceties. Stalking was against the law, and I wanted to make it clear I didn't condone his following me or Zory.

"Nothing. Just sayin' hi." He pursed his lips and took a step closer. "It's a real pretty morning, ain't it?"

"Yes, I guess." The caged animal inside me, boxed in and agitated, paced.

"Do anything interesting this past week?"

"No."

He rocked back on his heels and grinned. "Is that so?"

"Yeah, that's so."

An uncomfortable silence stretched between us. I stared at the pavement. There would definitely be a module in successor training that covered personal relationships. I'd brought this on myself by getting involved with The Chin in the first place. Dave—if he turned out to be the one—would learn from my mistakes. A howling rose out of the pavement and wound around my ankles.

"Well, me…I took me a scenic drive not long ago. Late at night. Took in the sights."

"That's great. Good for you."

"Have a light?"

I snapped my head toward him. "What?"

"You know, fire. You like fire, don't ya?"

My ribs contracted, each muscle in my body shrinking, ready to attack. I patted my pockets, hoping I'd absent-mindedly left the autoinjector there, but there was nothing.

Breathe. Four-three-two-one-in, four-three-two-one-out.

The Chin snickered and marched across the macadam. "Catch you later, Lela," he called over his shoulder. "Say hey to your boyfriend for me."

"What an insolent young man!" Mrs. Gerhardt yelled.

There was no way he could know. His words had to...no. Anxiety swelled below my skin, ballooning out and punching holes through me. My entire body sagged at the first blow, the metal of my car cool and hard beneath my back. My vision fuzzed, dimming and narrowing until only a pinprick of light remained.

"Oh my God, Lela! Are you okay?" The last person I wanted to see darted around me, patting my shoulder and pulling my hair back. My knees buckled, lungs fighting to take in the correct amount of air. "Put your head between your knees. Oh my God. Talk to me. Are you hurt?"

I wanted to kick Trina, but my legs refused to function. The rasping sound grating in my ears turned out to be my own breathing, which I noticed when the blood pulsating through my head dimmed to a dull drone.

"Oh, crap! Lela, say something. Anything!"

Zory's face came unbidden into my mind, and my breathing calmed enough for me to flap my hand, fingers barely moving. At the same time, it brought back The Chin's words. How could he know about the fire?

"That man's been spying on you, Lela!" Mrs. Gerhardt said.

I forced air into my lungs, forced the snapping turtles in my gut to step back. *Breathe.* Four-three-two-one-in, four-three-two-one-out.

God, breathe. Breathe. *Breathe.*

I fluttered my hand again, this time grasping Trina's wrist. The bones of her wrist cracked and clicked.

"Okay, okay," she said. "I need to get you into the car. Can you stand up?"

I leaned back, turning my face to the sky. The bright sun mocked my anxiety, laying bare my apprehension. Mrs. Gerhardt stood behind Trina, shaking her head. Her lips moved, but no words came.

I rocked back and forth, hands clamped over my ears and The Chin's words echoing behind my fingers.

Trina backed away and ran for the building. Mrs. Gerhardt coaxed me into my car, but the drive home was a blur. It took all the energy I had to stagger up the walk and into my house. I scurried along the walls, pressing close, until my fingers fumbled with the lock on my closet door.

My filing cabinet was cool against my skin. Needles pricked at me, stabbing and stinging, as I stewed over The Chin's words. The silence buzzed around me like a cloud of locusts, the hoard pulsing and receding. The same sound clogged my ears. I scratched at the inside of my closet door.

I was fine. Everything was okay. Nothing threatened the space shuttle. No one threatened me. The Chin's words had simply been a coincidence. He didn't know a thing. Trina was going to move out without ever having found a way to stop my work.

Mrs. Gerhardt had returned, and I'd even identified a potential successor.

Breathe. Four-three-two-one-in, four-three-two-one-out.

I wanted to call Zory and absorb the warmth of his voice, but he was at a training session. The snail trails split apart behind my lids. Smoke stung my eyes.

God, I was pathetic. The next shuttle mission would go off safely because of me, because of my dedication to observing the astronauts to make sure they could sleep during launch. I had to trust the ground crew would do their jobs, and I would do mine.

I'd need to deal with The Chin. Permanently. I'd solve the problem. Maybe I'd encourage my new recruit to go into chemistry. That would bring a wealth of benefits to my program. The assassination plans would improve by leaps, but that was far into the future. I needed solutions more immediately.

And I needed to focus, get my head back in the job.

One by one, I plucked folders from the drawers and reviewed the contents. In my hand was Meehan's file. I repeated what I knew about him, what I'd discovered during my observation of him. Calm calm calm.

My phone rang.

"Lela, it is Zory."

"Yes. Hello."

"Would you mind if I come to visit with you later? I am free for the night, and I find myself missing you very much."

"No, not at all."

With every word he said, I calmed, knowing the universe had already approved my course of action with Zory. And I'd already identified a potential trainee. Nothing The Chin did or said could derail my work. I worried for nothing.

I had the tools at my disposal to ensure he didn't interrupt anything. Ensure he didn't get in my way.

I emerged from my closet into the sun streaming through my bedroom window.

Trina clambered through the front door an hour later. I hadn't noticed earlier, but she wore another of my mother's outfits—a mauve skirt and sleeveless sweater.

"Oh God, are you okay? I went to let people know you and I needed the day off, and when I came back you'd already gone. Do you know what could have happened?" The satisfied smirk on her face said what her words didn't: she wished something terrible had happened.

"I'm fine." I beamed at her, smiling as hard as I could.

"You're fine? You really need to take some time off and properly deal with losing Mrs. Gerhardt."

Wishful thinking on her part. "I'm just overly tired."

"Tired? Tired my ass! That was a full-blown panic attack, and I should know. My sister's been rocking the Xanax for years to deal with hers, but I don't see any medication at all for you in the bathroom. I wanted to search your purse this morning, but I know you're a private person."

"No, really. It wasn't—"

She cut me off again, and this time her eyes glowed with an evil fury. "You should see a doctor. I mean, what if I hadn't been there when—"

"Trina!" It wasn't a yell, but my voice rose over hers. Still calm.

"What?" She stopped, her hands still fluttering around me. As with The Chin, so it was with Trina—nothing she could do could damn the mission.

"Stop. Everything is fine. I'm fine."

"I don't believe that. Just promise me you'll at least take a day off," she demanded, finally stilling.

"That girl doesn't have a bit of sense," Dad said.

Mrs. Gerhardt answered, "My fault, my fault. I should have seen the danger Trina posed to Lela's work."

"Okay, I promise," I lied and silently shushed Dad and Mrs. Gerhardt. "Look, Zory's on his way, and I'd rather he didn't know anything about what happened. Can we keep it to ourselves? You know, between us?"

"Yes, of course. But—"

"Any luck on the apartment hunt yet?" I asked.

"Well, no. But maybe I shouldn't move out yet. I mean, you're in the middle of a personal crisis. I should stay. You need someone to look after you. When I think of what could have happened—"

"No," I said, my voice a little too sharp. "This isn't…" I took a deep breath and started again, modulating my tone. "You need your space. You should keep searching."

She giggled. "Oh, Lela. You're always looking out for me." Her smile dimmed. "For a minute this morning, I thought Max had upset you."

"Let me make this clear: Th—I mean, Max had nothing to do with it." I stared at her, irritated by her attempts to trip me up.

"Oh. Well, it looked like you and he had a fight."

"No."

"Okay." She shrugged and grinned again. "So Zory's coming? You've been seeing a lot of him. Do you think maybe he'll move in after I move out? I mean, things are pretty serious."

"No. He'll move back to Russia."

"He likes you, though. A lot. And I can tell you like him, too."

"He'll go back to Russia." Maybe he would, maybe he wouldn't, but the lie might buy me some time.

She smiled…that same smile I'd been suspicious of since the day I'd met her.

"If you're sure you're okay."

"I am," I said. "You should go back to work. No need for you to lose another day of work."

She nodded. "Yeah. I mean, they're already watching me because of taking off like that when I went to Austin. You're sure, though? I don't want to leave you if you need me here."

I nearly shoved her out the door. All I wanted were the clear thoughts that came with being near my research.

Zory arrived that night. He stepped into the living room, a bunch of red carnations clutched in his hand. He passed them to me and kissed my cheek, caressing the small of my back with his palm.

"For you."

I took them and grinned into the flowers. The crimson petals bled onto his fingers. My eyes blinked it away. "Let me guess—fifteen?"

He laughed. "Of course."

Trina's clothes, pillows, and blankets covered every inch of the living room. With no choice, I led Zory to my bedroom, wary of his being too close to my life's work. The observation files were locked inside my closet, though, the key hidden in the glove compartment of my car.

The old springs of my mattress protested Zory's weight. I turned and leaned against the now-closed door and glanced between his body lounging on my bed and the door of my closet.

"I can see how living with Trina could drive you mad. She's quite messy."

I smiled and crossed the small space between my dresser and bed, perching at the edge of the mattress. "That's one way to put it. I'm used to living on my own, so having her here has been difficult."

"For a long time I lived in my parents' house, all of us together. Adelaïda was with us for a summer once, and of course my babushka has stayed there off and on." He touched my arm. "I know it can be hard. An invasion of your space."

"Yes." I reclined beside him, twisting to face him.

"And yet you do not seem to mind me being here, knowing about you."

I could almost hear the rustle of paper beckoning me from the files behind my closet door. Mrs. Gerhardt's ashes now resided in the closet as well. Her last wishes were to be scattered on a beach in Port Aransas. It would have to wait until after the shuttle launch, if I went through with it at all. I'd heard her voice—she'd spoken to me. The ashes couldn't be hers. Of course, maybe it was necessary. If the others were watching, it made sense to throw them off the trail.

"Where did you go?" His hand cupping my cheek snapped me back into the present.

"Nowhere. Just thinking."

"About what?" He traced designs down my arm, letters of the Cyrillic alphabet, I imagined, just like the poem he'd recited.

"Nothing, really. It's strange to have you here."

Yes, I know that the body's a locked up safe. The poetry lurked behind his eyes, soft and yielding.

"In your bed?"

"My childhood bed."

"Is this okay? I do not want to make you uncomfortable." The heat from his palm curved around my elbow, migrating to my hip. The expression under his goatee vacillated between serious and slightly amused.

My fingers rested just at the bottom of his ribs, sandwiched between his torso and arm. "Yes. I'm not a baby," I teased, a quiet smile on my face. Davey had said those same words to me.

"I am under no delusion about that, Miss White." His grin spread, and he rolled to kiss me on the forehead. "I only meant that I do not want to do anything here if you do not wish it, especially if your room-mate returns home."

"She's probably listening right now." She probably had a glass pressed up to the door, a trick I'd read about as a child.

"Mmmm. Maybe." He closed his eyes, the smile still a ghost on his lips. "But there is no urgency with us."

Despite the lights in the room, he slipped off to sleep just as quickly as he had the first night we'd spent together. I considered waking him and telling him to go. He was fine just where he was, though. Having him so close to the information I'd collected on him jolted a panicked and nervous stuttering in my sternum, but he fit perfectly on my bed, leaving me just enough room to curl up next to him.

Maybe he'd stay with me.

Chapter Twenty-Three

A DOCILE LAMB

NIKE'S YOWL SENT ME SKITTERING OFF THE MATTRESS. THE FLOOR-boards were frozen under my bare feet. The night had passed with what I believed to be four perfect REM cycles for Zory. I'd come close to falling asleep once, pulled under the tide by the symmetry of his deep breaths, but a pounding pulse rattled the walls and jolted me alert.

"Come back to bed," Zory muttered. He pulled the covers over his shoulder, maybe fighting the chill from the air conditioner, and rolled into the space I'd just vacated.

I stumbled over my feet and rushed to open the door before Nike made more noise. A quick glance at the clock revealed an hour remained before I got up, whether I worked or not. Zory had never made mention of the time his workday started, but it had to be early—astronauts worked hard to train and simulate situations, especially this close to the launch. Even if he had different protocols than NASA astronauts, he'd be buried in preparations.

Nike gifted me with a reproachful glare as he switched into the room and leaped up onto the bed. He snuggled around the top of Zory's head, and Zory's thick-fingered hands drifted to pet the cat's nose. The smack of his lips was audible over the wall-shaking pounding, although even that was fading now that I was in no danger of falling asleep.

"Come back to bed," he repeated, opening one eye. The dim light cast him in shadows, almost obscuring his face.

I did as he commanded, easing against him and resting my head on his bicep. "What time do you need to get up?"

He kissed the top of my head. "Not for another forty-five minutes, golubushka. The alarm is set on my watch. Sleep now. Or kiss me. Either way." I could feel him smile, his cheeks shifting against my hair. The rumble of his laugh vibrated through my chest.

I pressed my lips to his Adam's apple. His heartbeat throbbed there, almost in time to the noise in the room. Nike's stare weighed on me. Even though I couldn't see him above Zory's head, I could feel it.

"*Get him out of this room!*" a voice hissed. "*He cannot be this close to your research. It'll ruin everything.*" It was Nike. Speaking out loud.

I jerked against Zory, wondering if he'd heard the words, too. He hadn't reacted, so I hoped he hadn't noticed my reaction. Nike had always communicated via blinks. This was new. Had he always been able to talk like that?

Prickles of electricity ran currents up my legs, across my stomach and chest, and down my arms, but I held perfectly still, sure that if I moved, Zory would feel it.

"*You see? You put him in danger.*"

"Don't be silly," I argued silently. "I've already tested that hypothesis."

Nike left me alone, long enough for Zory's breathing to ease again, but his sleep was anything but peaceful.

"Lela!" It was more of a shout but probably not loud enough to wake Trina. Still, Zory's yell echoed in my room, the vestiges of it suspended in the air, light as molecules. His legs criss-crossed back and forth, bumping me across the mattress, and his whole body jerked.

"Are you okay?"

"Mmm hmmm. Sorry, I must have fallen asleep again. I did not sleep so well last night."

"You seemed to be out pretty solidly." My voice held a note of caution. Perception was not fact, yet I didn't want to discount his own observations. The autoinjector was tucked into the top drawer of my bedside table, and I'd use it if necessary. Of course, one ten-minute episode wouldn't override the depth of his sleep over my last two investigations of his habits. Not unless further examinations proved it the rule instead of the exception.

"I kept waking," he said. "It is probably just being in a new place." He snaked his arm across my waist, squeezing at my skin with his fingers.

Nike's voice—much different than the timbre of his high-pitched meow and other cat noises—screamed in my ear. *"Get him out of here! You're going to ruin everything—he can't sleep!"*

I rocketed out of bed with startling speed, Nike following as though poked with something sharp. Zory sat abruptly, and I could just make out the hands scrubbing his face.

"I...you...I have to get to work early," I stammered. "You should go."

"Oh. Yes, of course." His accent was thicker than normal, the consonants broad and sibilant, hissing through the murk as fast as the cat. "Are you well? You seem upset."

"No, no. Just a busy day." My lie came out as a half-panicked but whispered shriek. My body sagged. Mrs. Gerhardt's lawyer wanted to talk later. Nike and I needed to talk more about the educational program and Davey. It really *would* be a busy day.

Both of us had remained fully dressed with the exception of our shoes—I'd never bothered to change into pajamas the night before, and Zory never undressed—so getting him out of the house in a hurry wasn't a problem. Outside on the front porch, he hugged me, his arms locking around my ribcage.

"When can I see you again?" he asked. Birds tittered, welcoming the morning. The tinges of the normal humidity returned with the sun. A lone car rolled by, but there was no other movement in the neighborhood—just me and Zory. I had a feeling, though, that Trina or The Chin spied from behind a shed somewhere close. Their eyes were on me, prickling at my skin.

"Tomorrow maybe?"

He nodded, knocking into my shoulder with his chin, and pulled away to look at me. "I like waking to you."

"He's a smooth-talker, that one," Mrs. Gerhardt said. I was wondering where she'd been.

For a brief moment, I wondered if maybe Dad's death was related to my observations. Perhaps back then I'd done something that put the shuttle program at risk, something I hadn't recognized, and he'd paid the price. A life for a life, like Mrs. Gerhardt.

"It's possible," she said. "Those friends of yours are sneaky."

I forced a smile to my face. "But you didn't sleep well, you said."

He leaned in to run his fingertips down the length of my cheek-bone. "But that had nothing to do with you. I sleep like a rock usually."

"Just an anomaly then?"

He chuckled, the sound startling in the quiet of the still-dim morning. "Yes, my little scientist. Just an anomaly."

His lips were soft on mine then, insistent. Before my brain could engage, my arms twisted around him like tree roots, anchoring him to me. I almost invited him back, wanting to strip him of clothes and be close, but then Nike's words rattled in my ears. My own reservations returned, reminding me of the potential danger.

"I have to work tonight, but maybe tomorrow?" I winced, sure he'd pick up on the fact that I lied about going in early when I had lab work scheduled overnight.

His kisses warmed my ear. "Yes. I wish I could meet you for lunch, but we are scheduled so heavy right now. We're doing underwater work today. Simulating a walk. Tomorrow night? I can take you to dinner?"

As much as I wanted to say no for his own protection, I agreed. There were other things out there more dangerous than me. "Yes. Can I stay with you?"

"At the hotel?"

I nodded, and his mouth found mine again. He took a step away, still kissing me. "I would like that very much, golubushka." Another step toward his car. "I should go so you are not late."

He turned away but grinned over his shoulder. He'd called me… whatever that was…twice now. I had no idea what it meant. My Russian didn't extend very far.

He drove away, and I walked back into the house, closing the door behind me as quietly as possible.

"Was that Zory?" Even just awake, Trina's voice ricocheted around the space, alert and bubbly. It crowded out the air in the room, sucking up all the oxygen. It was hard to make my lungs work.

Nike poked his head out the door and laser-beamed me. *Watch her carefully.*

"You guys are really great together," she gushed. The rustling of her bedclothes drifted out to the foyer where I leaned against the door. "Are you sure you don't want him to move in here? You two…it seems pretty intense."

She herself appeared in the doorway a second later, a comforter wrapped around her narrow shoulders. The dawning light brightened behind her. My mother's barrette flashed in that hair, almost as bright as the glittering ruthlessness baked into her face.

"He'll go back to Russia." The words created a hollow space around my heart, compressing it until I thought I might start panting. He'd go, and I'd have my life back. And yet I would miss him, something I never thought I'd say about a man other than my father. He might stay if I asked, but I'd never tell Trina that. She had to think he'd leave. She had to think I had no stake in protecting him.

"Well, maybe. Hey, you're on the Connacht study tonight, right?"

"Yes."

"We'll be working together then. I traded with Amy—she had to go to a dinner with her husband."

So much for a peaceful observation. Still, maybe it wouldn't turn out to be so bad. Wherever she was on the timeline of her plan, it might be good to keep an eye on her.

"Oh. Okay."

"Since we don't have to be at the lab until a little later, do you want to grab lunch together? It'll be really fun—we can try that new barbecue joint that just opened up down the street."

"I can't—I'm trying to fit lunch in with Mrs. Gerhardt's lawyer. Paperwork to sign, that sort of thing." And I had no desire to ingest whatever she'd be sure to slip into my food.

"Oh, that's too bad. Do you miss her?"

"Yes." I glared. Talking to her about Mrs. Gerhardt was blasphemy.

"Maybe you should get a little more sleep. I bet you're really tired. If I had a hunk like Zory in my bed, you can bet I wouldn't get a bit of rest. I don't know how you manage to even let him leave the house. He looks like he'd be good with his hands. Is he?" She grinned.

More sleep. I nearly snorted. Oh, she was good, trying to throw me off my game. "I'm not going to discuss what Zory and I do privately." Nike strolled between us, rubbing at her ankles. He tilted his head toward me.

"Keep an eye on her. She knows. She knows something."

The yellow fur of his tail bushed out, the hair along his spine cresting into a mohawk as he curled like a charmed snake around her legs. On each pass over her foot, he blinked furiously, a patter of Morse code this time.

Keep an eye on her. She knows. She knows something.

Nike's words of warning repeated on a loop, crawling along my skin and tattooing themselves below the surface.

Instead of retreating to the couch as I'd hoped she'd do, Trina cranked up a ferocious smile. "You're the best friend on this planet, Lela, really. You're so protective over the privacy of everyone around you. I'm just…I know if I ever needed to share something serious, you wouldn't say a peep to anyone."

I brushed past her, trying to ignore the sparks shooting off the ends of her fingertips and hair.

"I'm going to do something special for you," she called after me.

I shivered and muttered, "Thanks for the warning." I'd take the autoinjector to work just in case.

✳✳✳

THE OBSERVATION HAD BEEN ONE OF THE BORING TYPES—A MAN who routinely fell asleep at the wheel of his car. Despite the usual agitation of sleeping in a laboratory setting while being watched by strangers, he was out cold within thirty minutes and didn't do anything out of the ordinary. I sat there, monitoring his EKG and EEG and notating even the smallest of twitches, while Trina rambled.

I mostly tuned her out, wondering when Mrs. Gerhardt would make a reappearance and if I could count this observation toward my positive column. The extra luck would come in handy.

We left the building at ten in the morning, and I squinted against the bright sun burning a hole through my retinas.

"We should go get a drink!" Trina exploded into a frenzy of excitement, her smile blinding and her hands clapping an obnoxious beat.

"What?" That was impolite.

Dad's voice descended on me: "Keep your enemies close, Lela."

I cleared my throat. As much as I had no interest in spending time with her, Dad was right. "What about a drink?"

"We should! Let's go out and get Bloody Marys. It'll be fun, and we can blow off some steam."

"I'm tired. I should just go home and get some sleep," I said, although I knew there would be none of that for me. Not while Trina still lived there. But if I agreed too readily, she'd know I was up to something.

"No, no! Come with—one drink. We'll have a good time, and then I promise to let you go right after. You won't see me all day. I have appointments to look at a few apartments this afternoon."

"Really? How soon are they available?" That was good news.

"Oh, questions now?" She laughed. "Have a drink, and I'll tell you all about it."

A finger of irritation poked at my side. "Yes, okay. Some place close to the house, though." I could scrutinize every move she made, make sure she didn't poison my drink.

She nodded and beelined for my car. My mother's hair slithered around her head while she waited for me to unlock the doors.

Every mile we drove made Trina more animated, and twenty minutes later she was engrossed in telling a story that involved waving her arms around in front of her. All it would take was a slip of her hand, and she could steer us into the next lane of traffic. Or maybe she was practicing her sleight of hand. Distract me, direct my attention elsewhere, and there'd be drugs in my glass.

Nike's suspicions hadn't been definitive, but he was adamant. A hissing voice whispered, "every action has an equal and opposite reaction," the sentence stuck in a loop.

I muttered the sentence aloud.

"What was that?" Trina asked.

"Oh, nothing. Just talking to myself."

"I do that all the time. Nothing wrong with it! Take this exit. The bar's just off the exit."

I'd never seen the damage to Trina's apartment; she could have done it herself. My jaw clenched. It made a certain amount of sense. Nike's understanding of nuance and hidden agenda was finer-tuned than my own.

With a new sense of urgency playing across my skin, I pulled into the parking lot, gravel crunching under the tires.

She popped out of the car and slammed the door behind her. "Come on, Lela."

I followed without a word while I avoided cracks—

Step on a crack, break your mother's back.

—in the aged walkway, my mind racing and trying to arrange my face into some semblance of an open expression. I really wanted to tackle her to the ground and choke her until she confessed—finally—but that didn't seem like the most prudent way to handle the situation.

Plus, it would draw attention. Dad and Mrs. Gerhardt wouldn't like that at all.

A few old men bellied up to the bar, their backs hunched over pints of beer. Leave it to Trina to know a place that would be open and serving booze at this hour of the morning. Unless she'd set it up. She could know the owner. I'd have to watch the bartender.

As we took a seat at a table near the back of the bar, I calculated in my head. With my current weight and the alcohol in a cocktail…if I had just one, I'd be okay. Drink half a Bloody Mary and then a glass of water. I doubted we'd spend more than an hour in the bar, so it wouldn't matter. I'd promised to have one with her, although my need for answers had multiplied. It might take longer.

Keep an eye on her. She knows. She knows something.

"I'm going to the ladies room—will you order? You know, I've never seen you drink a thing," Trina said, grinning. I imagined the corners of her lips ripping apart, a raw crevice cracking across her skin and creating a fault line up her cheekbones. The blood seeped from the fissure in her screaming jaw, landing with a satisfying *plop* on the sticky table surface. And then she was just herself again, smiling stupidly.

She headed for the back of the bar, leaving me to wonder about her past—she'd told me she had a boyfriend in Austin and they were going to Cancun, but that was the only thing that stuck in my memory. All my suspicions came back—that she was working against me, that she planned my death, that she was working with my mother.

All of it was not only possible, it was probable. With only Nike as a help for brainstorming, I was alone in all of it.

The man from behind the bar delivered two drinks, although I didn't remember ordering. Maybe Trina had stopped on her way to the restroom. Suspicion wedged under my shoulder blades.

Moments later she side stepped around to slide into her chair. "The guys at the bar are wondering if we're strippers."

"What?"

"I heard them talking. I guess most of the women who come in first thing in the morning are strippers just getting off the night shift." She laughed and sipped her beer. I stared at her face until I realized she had a small scar above her eyebrow, just like my mother. "Hey, so are you seeing Zory tonight?"

"Why?" I brought the glass to my mouth and tilted it, but there was no way I dared to take a drink. If the bartender himself hadn't dosed the drink, Trina had—I was sure of it.

"Just wondering." She watched me through slitted eyes. "You like him? I mean, really like him? He seems like such a great guy."

She had to think I was confiding in her, so I answered truthfully: "Yes. I do. And he is. Great, I mean. He's very…special."

"Wow, that's the most I've heard you say about him—you've really been holding out on me."

"No, not at all. I'm just, you know—"

"Private," Trina interrupted. "Yeah, I know. Seriously, it's like pulling teeth to get you to talk, like you've got all these secrets. Three can keep a secret if two of them are dead, right?"

I pretended to suck more of the drink through the tiny straw, trying not to bite it in half. "What was that?"

"Huh? Oh, just something my mother used to say."

"Used to?"

"You know, when I lived at home. I don't visit too often now."

"Why not?" I asked. "Come to think of it, I've never even heard you on the phone with your mother or your father. What are they like?"

Trina shrugged. "They're just regular parents. Probably no different than yours."

Probably exactly like mine. At least her mother. They were probably all in on it together: my mother, her parents. Maybe a huge network intent on killing astronauts.

"They'd probably really like you, Lela. You're so great. People at work are so curious. They know you're really great at your job, but they don't know a thing. I heard someone ask Max about you once, but he didn't say a word either. No wonder you talk to him."

"Someone asked Th—I mean, Max—about me? Who?" I asked. The lining of my stomach felt like it was shriveling in on itself.

"Oh, I don't know. It was a while ago."

"Why would someone go to Max for information about me? We hardly know each other."

Trina smirked. Yes, she definitely knew something. "Well, that's probably true, but he's one of the few people I've ever seen you speak to at work when you didn't need to. People notice. Even some of the other volunteers at the library have been asking about you, but I think that has more to do with Mrs. Gerhardt."

Something was happening to my face—my lips were numbing, the cold extending into my brain. "Oh, well. How unfortunate."

"It doesn't matter. I've spread it around that you're really awesome. I can't tell you how much I like working with you."

Right. I could see right through her.

"So, how to did you start working at Forty Winks?" I asked. I jammed a smile onto my face until I could feel the ache in my cheeks above the numbness. I would charm the information right out of her, no matter the cost.

"I've never told you? Oh my gosh! I started out as the receptionist, if you can believe it. I was fresh out of college and didn't know what I wanted to do. I saw all the cool work being done and ended up completing all the certification work. They hired me on, and that was that."

"What was your major in college?" Maybe it wouldn't matter—there was likely no way to discern her motives from just that information. It wasn't as though she could have specialized in How To Destroy The Space Shuttle or something like that, just as I hadn't majored in How to Save Astronauts. I startled to realize I would in fact be running just such a program. And soon.

She laughed, allowing me a view of my mother's mouth. "Business."

I kept positioning the glass at my mouth and faking sips. It wasn't until my thoughts turned sluggish that I realized she'd somehow managed to drug me after all. My limbs were heavy and clumsy. A dull panic banged in my head

"But what about you?" she asked. "How did you start at the lab?"

"Oh, it was planned." What the hell did I say that for? Was she... had she given me sodium thiopental? I could barely run through the formulation of the drug.

"Really? You always wanted to be a sleep tech?"

"Well, yes." My voice sounded far away. "Our lab works with NASA."

"Holy shit! You're a NASA groupie? I would have never figured you for one." She laughed. "It's always the quiet ones. I bet Zory's not the first astronaut you've gone out with, huh?"

More proof that Trina had been spying—I'd never told her that Zory was an astronaut.

"What? No. I don't date astronauts. Well, except Zory." A voice in my head, a very quiet but insistent voice, told me to shut up. Just stand and leave her there.

"You're just a fan of the space program? Yeah, I get that—it's a cool job. Working with NASA really looks good on your resume, too. What do you want to do next?"

"No, I don't plan to leave. It's good for my work," I said.

She shrugged, and I squeezed my fingers together as a means of attempting more control. I had to force myself onto a safer topic.

Keep an eye on her. She knows. She knows something.

"What about this apartment?"

"Oh, yeah! Well, there are two. If I see one I like, I can move in immediately." She spun her glass on the table. "They're a little closer to the lab, so that's good. I mean, I love living with you, and I like this part of Houston—I've lived here for, like, four years, and my volunteer work is here. Still, change is good. It might be cool to get to know another neighborhood. You know how it is."

I wrinkled my nose, the skin crispy and strange. "No. Not with my Dad's ashes scattered with one of the rose bushes out back."

"Ew, Lela!" Trina said. "That's illegal, isn't it?"

"Dad wanted to be buried there. He told me he wanted to be closer to my mother, so to put his ashes there."

"What—don't tell me your mother's buried out there, too," she joked, drinking the last of her cocktail.

My head pounded, and my heart constricted until I thought both might implode. My mother was probably only blocks away, listening into our conversation somehow.

Breathe. Four-three-two-one-in, four-three-two-one-out.

"Your dad must have really missed her, huh? Well, you too, I guess. I'm not going out to the backyard anymore, that's for sure. I don't want to walk on your dad."

"He's dead," I said, indignant.

"You're not going to bury Mrs. Gerhardt's ashes out there, are you?"

I shook my head, my equilibrium off.

"Don't tell her I'm not dead," Mrs. Gerhardt said.

"I won't, I swear," I said, smirking.

"What?" Trina giggled. "You're tipsy, aren't you?"

"Me? No. Of course not. You drugged me. Just admit it."

Her triumphant cackle peeled the aging paint off the walls. "Come on, I'll get you home."

"You can't drive my car. You'll try to…"

She stood and threw down a couple bills onto the table, and I fumbled with my wallet.

"No, don't worry about it," she said, grinning. "I owe you majorly for even letting me stay at your house. Ready?"

I pushed out of my chair, ready to bolt. She caught my elbow as I stumbled. My damaged balance had turned me graceless. The protest in my head never made it to my lips. She steered me toward the door, a docile lamb. Now that I was standing, the room rotated like a too-fast carnival ride, fingers pinching at my scalp.

"All right, Lela, let's go." She snickered and wrapped her fingers around my wrist. I kept tripping, and even in the air conditioning I was too warm. She pushed outside, hustling me to the car.

The driver's side door opened, and Trina appeared in the seat a second later. "Huh."

"What?"

"I think I just saw Max."

Through the haze clogging my head, I knew that should alarm me. "He has a mole on his shoulder."

Her head swiveled toward me, a smile playing at her lips. "What? Like, a hairy mole? Wait—how do you know?"

"The janitor's closet smells like bleach."

"Lela, you're a regular little chatterbox," Mrs. Gerhardt admonished. "I daresay you might want to reconsider. A lady never tells."

"Huh?"

"I don't like his underwear." Even with Mrs. Gerhardt's warning, the words wouldn't stop.

"Whoa. Hold the phone. Are you telling me what I think you're telling me? You and *Max*?" Her mouth opened and closed, no sound coming out.

I nodded once but stopped because it interfered with my ability to focus my eyes. *Must stare at the brick wall in front of the car.*

"Why?"

"It was…never mind." The words couldn't be dammed. "I think he's been following me."

"Really?" Now her eyes had widened, and I couldn't feel my feet. "Do you think he's stalking you?"

"Uh huh. There's just...Zory's apartment...and the gas station... fire..." I leaned against the head rest, breathing deeply to combat the heat shrinking my skin. Everything felt too tight, too close. *Breathe.* Four-three-two-one-in, four-three-two-one-out. My vision fuzzed. "But you, you already know all of that."

As if she didn't know everything about that night.

Chapter Twenty-Four

FINDING WINGS

SHE SPASMED. NOT JUST HER LEG OR HER ARM BUT HER WHOLE BODY. The mauve throw still curled around Mom's shoulders, although the edge had fallen from her legs when she jolted. I considered folding the blanket around her knees but didn't want her to wake up. Not during an observation.

I'd managed to take a full examination four times, carefully noting how long she usually stayed asleep—the sleep duration, I recited—and how often she woke, even if she just came out of it for a second or two. I hid my notes under the mattress. She yelled so loud when she'd caught me the last time I got better at judging the signs that she was waking. She'd slapped me a few times, too. I didn't want to be around her unless she slept.

Her breath hitched, and I backed away until most of my body hid behind the doorway. The snort she pushed through her nose indicated she'd likely be asleep again within a few minutes, so I waited and then crept closer, placing my feet exactly so I didn't make any noise.

Her body relaxed, face slack, not at all like the mean woman who'd started screaming even at Dad. Last night at dinner she'd thrown the ketchup at his head and yelled that she just had to breathe, and that she knew we were both up to something.

I'd heard Dad on the phone later. He never said the name of the person on the line, but he sounded sad. He said there was something wrong with Mom, and he didn't know what to do. He didn't know the worst of it.

I nodded toward my notes and wrote a few more things about the way Mom breathed—mouth hung open, sucking down air, and then pushing it out through her nose. Kind of a snuffling sound. When I glanced back up, her eyes were wide, glaring.

"You little bitch," she whispered. "You're watching me again. Did you ever stop?"

She flung off the blanket, the cloying rose in her perfume whipping past, and jumped to her feet. I stumbled backward. The loud thump as I landed on my behind shook the floor.

"Why are you watching? Everyone's watching, watching, watching." Now she laughed, a keening noise that made me think of a witch's cackle. She turned on me again, face a mask of fear and then rage, alternating like she couldn't decide how to feel. Eventually rage won, and she threw herself on top of me. Her weight hammered my tailbone into the floor.

"Mom, no!" I yelled, struggling against her. Her thinness gave way to a force I couldn't move. My feet smacked on the padded side of the couch as I flailed.

"Why do you watch?" she spit out between convulsing gasps of air. She shook my shoulders, and my head cracked with each heave. Wetness coated my face and neck. I worried I bled from somewhere, but then my nose filled, and I knew I had to be crying. "You're a baby! You cry and you watch, you and your father."

Her hands slipped up my shoulders and settled around my throat. Panic lodged in my chest like the momma bird I'd seen earlier in the week flopping around and squawking because her baby had fallen out of the nest. How I wished it would have been me. Away from all of this. Away…

She screamed, the pure volume of it nearly deafening me. My body wouldn't stop fighting. Her fingers tightened.

"Mom!" My voice came out as more of a wheezing whisper than the shout I'd intended. It snapped her back to an eerie quiet. Triumph washed over her face. Her hands squeezed, slow and steady. My ears popped, amplifying the noises in my head—a juicy crackling I couldn't identify, the raspy sounds of my breathing, all as though I lay underwater. I flung my hands in desperation, forcing air through my narrowed throat.

"Stop watching!" she seethed, teeth clenched.

I closed my eyes, but she didn't let up. My cheekbones grew heavy, my forehead giant and full of cotton. My hand bumped into something cool and thin—and wobbly. The floor lamp, maybe.

Mom grunted above me. Choking barks whimpered out of my mouth. I hit at her with the hand not wrapped around…whatever it was…and I pulled with every bit of strength I had left. It smacked off the back of her head at the same time my fingers hooked into her mouth. It loosened her grip enough to roll her to the side.

The air gulped into my lungs, filling the empty, sucking spaces. A frenzied instinct took hold of me even though my head still throbbed. It must have weighed a million pounds—my neck strained to hold it up. The tall lamp I often read next to lay broken on the floor, the heavy wrought iron top snapped off and rocking just a bit. Without my permission, my hand picked it up. My body swiveled, and I smacked Mom across the face with it.

She yowled and sat up, clutching at her cheek. Blood seeped between her fingers. A small voice screamed at me to stop, that I'd be in trouble when Dad came home. Something else controlled me, hitting her again with the top of the lamp. Its weight felt good, justified in my hand. The sick satisfaction when it knocked her sideways warmed my gut.

A bubble of confusion and terror grew in my head. My vision fuzzed. Still my body moved, my hand and arm now sticky and wet. Harsh breathing. Moist gurgling. Dull thuds. The sound of the front door slamming. Dad's voice. The blackness spiraled around me, taking me, sucking me under.

I slept. I slept. And I dreamed. Dad's whispering and muttering was ever present, his words far away and meaningless. He carried me through meadows, bright green with tall grass, Spanish moss hanging low and sweeping over my arms and legs. He baptized me in a murky pink river, asking me questions I couldn't answer. And when I woke, the familiar scent of my sheets wrapped around me. My head still held a few bags worth of cotton, the inside of my throat burned raw.

Had I imagined the entire thing? I regarded my hands—my joints screamed, but no blood soaked my skin. My pajamas were clean: blue with little purple cartoon cats. My enormous head tilted to the side, and I kept moving with it, falling until I sprawled on the floor. My bedroom door opened. I peeked through an eyelid, praying to God it wasn't Mom. I wanted Dad, needed him.

"Lela," he said, his tone careful. His gentle hands propped me up, pushed me back into bed. "Are you…"

"I feel…" It came out just air, barely a sound to it. I tried again. "Dad…I…" A strangled squeak but nothing else. My hands moved to my throat, following the path Mom's hands had in my dream. My skin burned, feverish. "I'm sick."

"Jesus, Lela, what happened?" His eyes were shot through with tiny red lines, his forehead creased.

I stared at him. What? "Where's Mom?" I whispered.

"Lela, are you okay?" he asked in a halting voice. "Mom's gone."

My eyes focused on the door and then him. I tried my voice again, but nothing came out. I grabbed a notebook off my bedside table and wrote instead, my handwriting messy and tired.

She's gone? Gone where?

He pulled his hands back like he'd touched a hot stove. "You don't… uh, Lela, honey, Mom's not coming back. You…"

I didn't know what he was saying. My throat burned.

Did she go to the store? I want juice. I'm thirsty.

"I'll get you a glass of water," he said. His words rushed together. "Do you remember? Before?"

Before what?

"Did she…? Did you two get in a fight?"

I didn't write anything this time—she always yelled at me, hit me, but she said Dad wouldn't care. He'd send me away. The bird was back, its high-pitched chirp sounding through the window. I hoped the baby bird had found its wings and flown away.

Chapter Twenty-Five

RELATIVE SAFETY

THE PILLOWCASE WAS COOL AND SCRATCHY BENEATH MY CHEEK, and I groaned. My mouth scratched like someone had purged it with sand paper. Light streamed through the blinds in my window.

Oh, God. The memory of the bar rushed back at me. I barely remembered my conversation with Trina, but I recalled babbling and admitting to this business with The Chin.

If she were planning my downfall or death, she had some new ammunition now.

I sat up and held my head to keep it upright. Through the slits in my fingers, the paint on my bedroom walls peeled and cracked, leaving bloodstained plaster behind. It faded back to the normal orange. I sighed, hoping Trina had decided to take the first apartment she saw.

I groaned again when I snuck a peek at the alarm clock. One in the afternoon. Too much sleep. It tangled my brain into a crazy mess.

The floor boards chilled under my bare feet. The air conditioning had lowered the temperature to that of a meat locker. I stumbled to the door, wrenched it open, and staggered down the hall to the kitchen. Trina sat at the table, reading the paper. She flashed me a happy smile when I walked in. A glittery barrette sparkled in her hair.

"Hey, sunshine! How're you feeling?" Nike lay curled around her foot. He cast a reproachful glance in my direction.

"What are you doing here?" I asked, hoping my voice didn't sound as dead as I felt.

"Oh, I didn't need to look at the second apartment—I took the first! Oh my God, Lela, wait until you see it! It's just fantastic—it's over in the Westchase area, near the Galleria. The apartment is a loft space—really great. Everything is really wide open, and, well, the space isn't huge, but it feels big. These giant floor-to-ceiling windows line one side. The view isn't anything to write home about, but who cares?" Her eyes glowed wickedly in the mid-afternoon light, and her hair lit up. "Looks like I'll be out of here within a few days."

"*Careful,*" Nike said. "*It's a trap.*"

The silence in the air thickened. Finally, I said, "That's great, Trina." We both seemed to be tiptoeing around the fact that she'd drugged me.

"*Don't bring it up,*" Nike warned. "*She's waiting for you to do it so she can tell everyone how crazy you are. She'll get you fired. She'll turn everyone against you.*"

A smirk pressed her lips together, and victory lit her eyes into smoldering coals. "We'll have to make sure we still get together after I move out. You've been such a gracious hostess. We should do something regularly. Go drinking again. That was fun. And informative."

"That girl is pure evil," Mrs. Gerhardt said. "Can't believe I allowed her in my library."

"Maybe we'll do that." Even to my ears, the threat in my words was present.

Trina tilted her head, that ridiculous smile of hers breaking the edges my mother's face. She bent down to run her hand along Nike's back. "I'll really miss it here. You'll be lucky if I don't scoop this one up and take him with me." She laughed, a sound that drilled straight down my spine. "Well, I'm heading over to the new apartment for a few hours—I have to measure for curtains."

I nodded dumbly, tucked Nike under my arm, and fled for the relative safety of my room.

✳✳✳

THERE COMES A TIME WHEN IT'S IMPERATIVE TO PUT A PLAN INTO motion. With Trina taking her plan to the next level, there was no other option than to begin my observation of Dave Enders. Based on where he lived, there could only be one elementary school he attended, and it was parked across the street that I watched him cross the street at the end of his school day.

It was like he wore a flaming crown on his head. Fire licked up from his red hair and singed the sky, and it was beautiful. Dave was too young for me to judge whether he'd grow up to be handsome. He was short and slight with a smudge of a nose and a mouthful of crooked teeth. His shoulders bowed under the weight of a heavy backpack.

It was the sign of a serious student, and I knew he had an interest in science in general, but what else might be in there? If he had a head full of poetry, like Zory, that might not be so useful to me.

He spoke to no one on his walk home, didn't even look up to check for traffic when he crossed the street. He looked like a man with a mission. Well, a boy with a mission anyway, and that was promising. I followed on foot, staying half a block behind him. He never once looked back.

His family's house was a little saltbox of a place with a pointed front gable like a gingerbread cottage. With no indication that his parents were home, he climbed the three concrete stairs to the long porch and fiddled with the front door.

I sneaked past the trimmed trees at the side of the house and slunk along the windows. They were too high off the ground to see much, but I did find a potential vantage point to scope out the interior—at the back of the house, the lawn opened up to the back of a strip mall. If I could figure out how to access the shopping center roof, I'd have a good view through binoculars.

A glance at my watch had me hurrying back to my car. Zory waited, and it would take well over an hour to get to his hotel at that hour.

"I'm glad to see you taking the initiative," Mrs. Gerhardt said. "I know you're not one for making impulsive decisions, but it doesn't hurt to get moving. Especially since Trina's not waiting to make her move."

I steered around a sprawling pothole on the freeway. "Well, Nike and I did some work the other day. We're far from finished with the coursework plans, but it's a good start. As for recruitment, we plan to identify at least five boys and girls, although I'm not sure how to narrow it down yet."

"I'm sure you'll come up with something," she said. "You're nothing if not industrious."

"Do you think Nike will be okay?"

"Oh, I don't think you have anything to worry about there. It was a good idea to lock him in your room. There's no telling what Trina might try to do to him. She really is a piece of work."

When I arrived at Zory's hotel, he smiled and darted forward for a kiss. He pulled back, breathless, and tugged me into his room before shutting the door firmly behind him.

"I have been thinking about you all day, golubushka."

"What does that mean—that word? You called me that the other day."

He twined his fingers with mine, kissing my knuckles. "It means *my darling*." His lips puckered on my wrist. "I hope you do not mind. You do not seem the type for nicknames."

"No, I…like it." I really did, and it was a relief to be with him, even worried as I was about what might be going on at my house. "So were you really so bored today that you had nothing better to do than fixate on me?" I teased.

He laughed and guided me to sit on his lap. "We were in the pool. It is my least favorite part of all this—all the scuba gear and being wet all day."

"Simulations?"

Zory nodded before coasting a hand across my hip, rubbing his thumb just under the hem of my shirt. "We are working through—well, never mind. I do not want to bore you with the details. I did spend some time with the food people today."

"Oh?"

"Mmm hmm." His lips skimmed up my neck. I shivered, snuggling closer. I put Trina out of my head. For now I had to focus on Zory, on my mission. Maybe it had been her plan all along simply to be a distraction. "We must all meet with them prior to liftoff to give them our meal preferences."

He fumbled with the buttons of my shirt, my fingers sifting through the short hair on his head. "Are the choices that much different from the options in Russia?"

His laugh rumbled, deep and amused. "Do you really want to talk about freeze-dried borscht, or would you like me to take you to bed?"

A hissing dulled in the back of my head, and I didn't know whether to be concerned about that or the blood oozing out of the pores on his face. I shook my head, the gore gone in a moment. Maybe I'd been working too hard. Maybe it was just too much sleep—another component of Trina's plan?

I stood and finished the rest of my buttons, smiling at him. "I don't really like borscht."

Chapter Twenty-Six

THE CONSTRICTOR KNOT

THE AIR IN THE ROOM HELD A HINT OF SOMETHING FLORAL—NOT quite roses, but the chemical odor of artificial freshener of a sort, with an undercurrent of sex. Zory lay warm next to me. His big hands held me still against him, and his lips touched my shoulder.

"You have to work tomorrow, yes?" His breath blew over my neck.

"Yes. Trina and I worked an observation last night, but it's back to a regular schedule tomorrow for both of us." I shifted, settling in to absorb more of his heat. "She's—Trina, I mean—moving out, by the way."

"That's good."

"Yes." I shivered and thought of Nike alone in my bedroom.

"Perhaps after she has gone we can spend some time at your house. I am supposed to move to an apartment tomorrow after work, but your place seems so home-like. There is something about being somewhere that feels like family—I guess I am homesick." He chuckled.

I twisted around and wedged my leg between his. "That's inconvenient, considering you'll be in space for a week. I can't imagine a place that feels less like home."

Dad's voice resonated in my skull. "Remember, Lela: the want for home lives in everybody."

A small divot dimpled on his cheek when he smiled. "You get used to it."

"Do you have a sleeping preference on the space station? You've been there a few times before, right?" I'd seen him sleep, so I had no problem imagining him, his eyes closed and the usual peaceful expression he wore.

He nodded. "I forget sometimes you know so much about the program." He shifted forward to kiss me, a lingering touch. "I do not like to sleep in the berths. I'm not…I do not like to sleep in such an enclosed space."

"Your young man doesn't flail in his sleep, does he?" Mrs. Gerhardt asked. "That could make bedtime uncomfortable. Of course, I know you don't sleep much, so maybe it doesn't matter. You always thought you could hide that from me, but I could tell. I could always tell."

I ignored her and said, "I don't blame you. I've seen the measurements."

"A little girl like you would not have such a problem."

"I'm not that little!"

"You are a small woman, Lela. Taller than some, perhaps, but…" He circled my wrist with his meaty fingers and grinned.

I laughed. "Well, where do you sleep then?"

"I get into a sleeping bag and Velcro myself to the wall outside the sleeping area. If I wake up quickly, I do not bang against the inside of the berths. Yuriy does not use the bags at all. He prefers to float, you know, just fastened to something at the waist."

"Do most of the astronauts avoid the berths?" The longer we talked about the subject, the more natural it seemed.

"No," he said. His hand rested at the small of my back. "Some people like them, and some do not."

"What about on the shuttle?"

"Well, I do not know—I have not yet traveled on the U.S. shuttle or with this crew. But there are sleeping bags. The norm is to sleep in your seat."

I nodded. "That makes sense. I mean, you're probably in one right from the start because of being asleep during liftoff."

His forehead furrowed. "We are not asleep for that."

"It's okay—I know all about it," I assured him. "I know NASA says the astronauts are awake and everything, but you'll be out. I mean, nothing will happen to the shuttle. If something did, though, you'll be asleep so you don't feel anything."

"Lela, we must be awake. There are things to do. Besides, it is quite a bumpy, rough ride for the first few minutes until the rocket boosters fall away. The Soyuz is the same way. And I would not want to miss a moment. It is quite excit—"

"No, you're asleep." The agitation returned. Why would he bother to lie? It wasn't like I planned to inform the media.

He propped himself up on one elbow and smiled at me. "I can assure you this is not true at all. Where did you hear such a thing?"

I stared at him, the muscles in my face twisting. "I'm not just anyone, you know." My fists clutched the comforter.

His lips turned down. "Are you okay? You look white as a sheet."

My skin burned, flames worming through my bones. "Why are you saying...I mean, I know..."

Zory tried to free the comforter and pull me toward him. I writhed and slid away, taking it with me.

"What is wrong?" His alarmed tone rang to the corners of the room.

I couldn't stop the panting breaths that ripped out of my throat. Zory's brows drew together. His eyes followed me as I tore around the room, getting dressed. Screaming panic pounded the inside of my skull.

"I have to go!" I spit out, sliding on my shoes. "I can't accept this!"

He moved toward me as I edged to the door. "What did I say?"

"This changes everything! My data, everything I've worked for!" My vision dimmed until all I could see was a tiny pinprick of bright light inside a dark tunnel, and the point pulsed, expanding and contracting. I had to go...think. Make a new plan. Nike would know what to do. God, the people who had died for this—Dad, Mrs. Gerhardt.

I touched around the room, stunned and fumbling, and the cool roundness of the doorknob smacked into my hand.

"Lela, what is—" His voice came from behind me. I scrabbled at the door and yanked it open.

"No, stay. I mean, don't touch m—have to go!"

Before he could say another word, I darted out, the light growing until I could see a bit better. It was enough to make it back to my car without falling. I almost wrenched the door off the hinges in my haste to get inside.

Breathe. Four-three-two-one-in, four-three-two-one-out.

Breathe. Four-three-two-one-in, four-three-two-one-out.

Breathe. Four-three-two-one-in, four-three-two-one-out.

My heaving gasps filled the inside of the car, moments passing until the air came easier. I shoved the keys into the ignition and craned my neck—Zory hurried down the sidewalk, pulling a t-shirt over his head. Before he could reach me, I slammed into reverse. A quiet space would help me make sense of what Zory had said.

Vapor streams from the space shuttle's splitting apart played over and over behind my eyes, the puffy whiteness curling and expanding into antennae—a giant, roiling snail head. Oh God, they had been alive. Panicked, wide eyes and fingers groping with straps. Charred skin. The smell, the smell!

My mother's voice cackled in my head, followed by my Dad's soothing tones. Even Mrs. Gerhardt was there, telling me not to be so hard on myself. They didn't know. They couldn't know.

Every mile I put between me and Zory brought new and terrible ideas—the astronauts praying as they fried, agonized screams, blood. The car tire slammed up the curb, the crunch as the front end smacked into the tree in my yard echoing through the car. I stumbled out and scrambled into the house.

The agitation drove me down the hall to my bedroom. The door to my Dad's room lay open, the lock broken. A bright circle of light shined onto the worn carpet outside the door. Trina's voice carried from inside, her off-key voice loud and braying.

I half-stumbled into the room, gasping and bracing my arms against the frame of the door. She crouched at the dresser with a cardboard box, pulling a stack of mauve shirts out of a drawer.

"What are you doing?" I screamed.

She'd smiled when she saw me, but at my words her mouth drew into my mother's mocking frown. "I…well, I told you I was going to do something special."

"Get out of this room!"

"I'm just trying to help."

"You're not helping! You can't help!" A fissure cracked deep in my guts.

She rose to her feet and crept backward, around the edge of the bed. "Lela, it's nothing. I only packed up some shoes." She pointed to a cardboard box next to the tall dresser. "I can unpack them."

Nike's voice sounded in my head, but I couldn't make out the words. My dad, Mom, Mrs. Gerhardt, even Zory—their murmurs joined in, just below my own wailing. My fists clawed, and I grabbed the first thing I could lay hands on. Mom's hand mirror went sailing toward Trina and bounced off her shoulder. "You've ruined everything!"

"Hey!"

"Why are you here? You come in and act all happy, but you've been watching and waiting and spying and even Nike knows!"

"So disappointing," Mrs. Gerhardt said. "I should have listened to you, Lela."

A perfume bottle hit Trina's chin, and she squeaked. The walls behind her swelled, bulging and rippling. My hand closed around something else, something heavy, and I swung out and caught her in the face. Her hand drifted up like she fought against the heaviness of quicksand, her eyes wide and her mouth open. Her index finger crooked. She touched her cheekbones and wobbled side to side before sinking, sprawling on the comforter.

"Hit her again."

"Nike, not now," I growled, my head throbbing. Terror fuzzed around the edges of my brain, a black curtain growing heavier over my eyes as the panic rose. I stumbled backward and sank to my knees.

Breathe. Four-three-two-one-in, four-three-two-one-out.

Dad's voice again, this time telling me he'd get me a glass of water. I leaned back against the dresser, fighting bile. Just rest, just rest. Everything swelled in my head and then dimmed.

A rushing sound in my ears, echoes like I held a shell to my ear, roused me, rough fibers poking against my cheek. At first the noise was the only thing I could focus on, followed by the realization my body lay curled on the floor. Shivers wracked my shoulders and legs. Something elusive lurked just below the surface of my circling confusion. I couldn't quite get my hands around it.

I pushed myself upright. My head weighed a million pounds. Nike butted my hip, his screechy meow plaintive and distressed. Shadowy whispers touched off my skin, dim murmurs like neurons firing sluggishly in my brain. Zory. Something to do with Zory. Fear and the taste of dread, metallic on my tongue.

Seconds after that, my thoughts sharpened. Oh God, the astronauts! My sobs sounded more like a hiccup turning into a wild animal howl. The tip of a toe dangled in my periphery. Not…wait, it was hot pink. Hot pink toes.

Trina. I'd hit her. She fell.

A sense of accomplishment swirled along with a sick dread in my stomach until I remembered we both lay in Dad's room, and then outrage returned. I crawled to the bed and clawed my way up the spread. Figuring out what to do about the shuttle mission, about Zory, was priority number one.

"*She knows. She knows something.*"

I nodded in Nike's direction.

"I know. There's no other explanation."

"*Tie her up. Put her in the closet.*"

"What are you even doing here? I put you in my room."

He turned his nose up, his tail lashing back and forth. "*Did you really think I couldn't get out? As soon as I heard her unlock the door, I did my part. Now tie her up.*"

"Nike's right," Mrs. Gerhardt said. "She obviously can't be trusted. Look at all the trouble she's caused for you. In light of your other problems, I really don't think you have a choice."

"All right," I said, clasping my hands in my lap. "There's just so much in my head right now. There's got to be some way to keep the shuttle from blowing up."

"*Tie her up. Now.*"

I jumped off the bed and flung open one of Mom's drawers to sort through her mauve and beige bras, the silkiness skimming over my fingers.

We had never been a house where people walked around in their underwear. The only time I'd seen her lingerie was when she folded laundry. The color didn't surprise me, but it triggered a niggling anxiety that wiggled in my chest. Why hadn't she taken her underthings when she left? I'd never given it much thought, and now—in the midst of everything—part of me obsessed about it.

Maybe she'd always meant to return.

Dad said, "Now Lela, it doesn't matter at all what your mother intended. I've got faith in you that you can handle anything."

"Thanks, Dad," I murmured.

The next drawer down held dozens of pairs of underwear and crumbled balls of nylons. Trina's breathing roughened, and her hands twitched. I could use the panty hose to tie her.

I struggled against the dead weight of her legs, hoisting the rest of her body onto the bed. The bones of her ankles ground together, creaking and grumbling, as I bound them.

Why hadn't my mother packed the rest of her clothing?

Trina's arm flopped, a dead fish, the inside of her wrist pale as the moon.

"Behind or in front?" I asked.

"*Behind,*" Nike said. "*Less chance for her use her hands.*"

"Tie a good knot," Dad said. "Nice and tight."

Mrs. Gerhardt butted in. "The Morrow Guide to Knots indicates a constrictor knot is your best bet."

A calm fogged over me. I pulled her arms together, positioned her hands as if she were in prayer, and wound the nylons around her wrists. My lip caught in my teeth. Tie the knot as though everything depended on it. And it did: if Trina got loose, she could…

"*She'll scream.*"

Right. Right. I glanced around, nothing hurried now. The duct tape in Dad's tool kit.

"Watch her," I told Nike.

It took me less than a minute to retrieve the tape, especially with Dad's voice in my ear, telling me where to find it. I cut off a strip with the manicure scissors laid out on the dresser. A squeak sounded from behind me.

"What happened?" Trina whined, low and thick. "What—holy shit!" She wriggled on the bed, back up toward the headboard.

"I know who you are and what you're here to do," I said.

Her breaths morphed into pants. She batted at me as I struggled to position the tape over her mouth. I shook my head and threw myself over her torso. Trina's screams were so loud they hurt my ears.

"Shut up!"

She wheezed, but the shouting cut out. Her eyes widened so much I thought they might fall out of her head. With only a bit more struggle, the tape was in place, but with her arms and legs kicking out, I'd have to restrain her further.

I yanked her off the bed. Her legs thumped off the floor, and I dragged her into the closet. Before shutting the door, I duct taped the tie at her ankles to the tie at her wrists. The heel of her foot caught me in the jaw twice.

"Watch her."

Nike nodded and stared at the door.

"Yes, you're right—I need to think. Maybe I should lie down."

"Are you sure that's wise?"

"Don't worry. It's not like I'm going to sleep. You'll help me figure out what to do tomorrow?"

"Yes, of course."

Trina's dull thumps faded behind me. I struggled with the buttons of my shirt, clicked on the light near my bed, and glanced toward the closet—lots of research to do. It might take hours, but there had to be a way to make everything right again.

I threw on a t-shirt and pajama pants. The cool press of sheets against my skin calmed me further, but my brain whirred and clicked. I heaved over onto my side, seeking the softness of my pillow.

Sleep pressed close, but I resisted. Still, the puffy clouds and vapor trails were vivid behind my eyelids. I could feel Mrs. Gerhardt and Dad, watching in silence.

Chapter Twenty-Seven

A MOTHER'S LEGACY

THE BRAIN CONSUMES TWENTY PERCENT OF THE OXYGEN IN THE body, despite accounting for only five percent of the body's total weight. When I finally emerged from my bedroom, the morning brought with it a clarity I'd never experienced before, which spoke to my mind's capacity to function on no sleep.

When all this was over, perhaps I'd write a paper on it.

I sucked in a deep breath. Without even bothering to take a shower, I dove back into my filing cabinets—between the information I'd collected and Nike's wisdom, the answers to my problems would appear.

"You have superior research skills," Mrs. Gerhardt said. "It may take some time, but you'll find a solution."

Dad said, "Do what you do, Lela. Focused and smart."

The night before, after a brief rest, I had set the urns from my closet on the dresser and began with the blue and red files, lined up in alphabetical order. I began with the As—Janet R. Adams. I remembered the dark brown walls of her bedroom, the way the room had folded around me, inviting and snug. The white furniture stood out so nicely, and even though interior design never mattered to me, I'd taken a few extra photos of the room simply because I liked it. She'd gone into space on the last shuttle and then retired from the program, moving back to California. Her house in Houston had photographs of her large family all over, and they looked like a nice bunch of people, all smiley and arms draped over one another.

"Zero in on the facts," Mrs. Gerhardt reminded me. "The similarities, not the differences."

I read over each note, examined every photo for an answer. If Zory told the truth, if the astronauts really remained awake during liftoff, something here would stand out and tell me what to do. There hadn't been a shuttle disaster since I'd turned ten; surely I'd contributed to that.

As much as my own mother had caused the last explosion.

Dad said, "I wish you'd have told me about that. I could have helped you there."

Now I was midway through my file inventory and review. It occurred to me that perhaps it didn't matter if they slept during takeoff. It didn't make a difference—although it ruined my desperate childhood wishes that the astronauts on the *Constitution* hadn't suffered at all. The very act of my investigations negated the need for them to sleep. My mission ensured the shuttle's safety…not because it had anything to do with sleep, but because of the act itself.

The battle against my mother's legacy.

"I'm sorry you had to die for this," I said to Mrs. Gerhardt.

I allowed myself a tender smile, thinking of our talks about Zory. The shrill ring of the phone cut through the room, and I picked it up on the second ring.

"Lela, this is Jenny Comte from Forty Winks."

"Oh. What can I do for you?" I glanced around. Maybe Trina had placed hidden cameras when she barged into my house. A glint of glass—perhaps the lens of a camera—sparked in my vision. I narrowed my eyes and lowered the folder clutched in my hands, closing it in case the cameras had a view.

"Well, you're not here, and you're scheduled. It's not like you to just not show up."

"Lela!" Dad hollered. "That's not the girl I raised."

Guilt blossomed in my face for a moment before worry set in. If they'd been watching, they already knew I'd had to lock Trina in the closet. Wouldn't they have sent in a team to set her free by now? Maybe she was expendable. Maybe she'd already escaped. My intestines writhed, tying themselves into uncomfortable knots.

"I'm so sorry—I must have accidentally turned off my alarm." I adopted my most contrite voice, hoping she'd buy the lie. "I'm sick with some sort of stomach flu. Been throwing up all night." I covered the receiver with my hand and sprinted to the closet in Dad's room.

Trina's blood-shot eyes widened and blinked against the sudden light. She squeaked and wriggled around, and I closed the door. I hunted around the room but found no cameras. It was probably that they'd hidden them well—I'd do a more complete search later after I'd finished reviewing my files.

"Ugh," Jenny said, her tone sympathetic. "I know how that goes. Well, take care of yourself, and make sure you let us know if you'll be in tomorrow."

"I'll definitely do that." Like I'd have to—they probably had this place rigged and bugged. It didn't matter now. Unless I could figure out what to do with Trina and clean up her spies at the lab, I couldn't go back there. My mission was out in the open, and I couldn't be sure how many people knew.

How was I going to handle this business with the traitor in the closet?

"By the way, have you heard from Trina?" Jenny asked.

It was a test—I was sure of it.

"Yes, she's sick, too."

Sicker than I had imagined.

"Oh," she said, voice surprised. "Have her call us when she's up to it. There are some Human Resources issues to resolve as soon as possible."

I hung up and returned to my room.

Nike waited for me, sprawled across the blue file for Shaun Monaghan, Ph.D., an electrical engineer who flew three shuttle missions. He'd lived with his wife in Clear Lake, along with a Labrador retriever, not far from Korchagin's old building. That observation had taken several weeks longer than normal because I'd had to make friends with the dog first. My initial break-ins were spent petting him and giving him treats before I could explore the house.

Nike had been so angry when I returned home with the scent of dog on me those first few times, but he got over it. He knew it was a necessary part of the job. Now he stared at me, his bright eyes glowing.

"She can't stay in that closet forever."

"Yes, I know. What do you suggest?"

"You don't have many options."

I shrugged and ran my finger along the edge of a file. "Maybe I can reason with her? I mean, maybe she just doesn't understand what she's doing is wrong. Maybe my mother has brainwashed her?"

Nike spared a glance that let me know he thought I was insane. *"She's been working against you from the beginning. And not very effectively, I might add. Nothing's gone wrong with the shuttle in a long time."*

I nodded. "Yes, that's true. It probably wouldn't do me any good to have her working with me, but it's better than the alternative. You said it yourself: I can't leave her in the closet." I grimaced. "Well, I guess I could—I could feed her, but her muscles would atrophy."

"You have to kill her. There's no other way. You might have to kill Zory, too."

"Now that's just not true," Mrs. Gerhardt said. "The cosmonaut has done nothing wrong."

"I don't think it matters that the astronauts aren't asleep," I said. "I think—"

"Zory is the common denominator in all of this. If he wouldn't have insisted on seeing you and making you have these…feelings for him, none of this would have happened. The mission is in jeopardy because of him." Nike's expression was pure disgust.

I crossed my arms over my chest. "Absolutely not. Trina, maybe. But Zory is innocent in this, and the universe wouldn't have let him live through the fire if he were a threat."

"I agree," Mrs. Gerhardt said. "She's done everything necessary."

"Please listen to reason—"

"I really think if I just continue with my observations, that's the thing," I said. "I just have to study Zory again one last time, just to be sure I've covered all my bases."

My feet made shuffling noises against the carpet as I walked back and forth in the small space of my bedroom.

Nothing had changed since I was kid—the rug bore the marks of lots of pacing over the years, but that was the extent of it. The walls remained a bright orange, a color I'd loved as a child. I rarely pulled the blinds up, so the hue hadn't faded in the harsh sun that had washed out some of the color of the drapes in the living room.

My hands shook at my sides, so I clasped them together in front of me, hoping to calm the prickling that crept across my skin, swept down my arms and legs.

I'd read up on color choice years ago as a way of trying to add something to astronaut observations, but after learning more, it had to be a sham. People who like orange were supposed to be intense. They were social and hated to be alone. Considering Nike and Mrs. Gerhardt had been the only constants in my life since Dad died, that didn't seem to be true for me. The solitude had only helped me complete the studies I'd undertaken, though, and I appreciated the silence of my work.

I'd have to ask Davey about his favorite color.

My mother never told me why she liked mauve so much. But during research, an allegedly scientific study indicated that people who like mauve enjoyed culture and refined things, noble causes, but they didn't want to do the dirty work. They were supposed to exhibit creativity and charm, wit. Maybe Mom fooled some, but I knew she hated everyone.

"You fixed her wagon," Dad said, chuckling. "Can't really say it's a surprise she's still around with her hand in all this. She always was on the crafty side."

Nike slinked around my feet, tangling in my legs. I stumbled into the dresser. The edge caught the edge of my ribs. The pain shot through my torso, a dry snap crackling.

I inhaled and gasped at the tightness in my chest. The cat smiled at me, a calculating expression on his pointed face. Smug.

"What are you doing?" I asked.

"I had to get your attention. You have to end this thing with Zory. You're not thinking of the mission—you're only thinking about yourself. But he's just going to go back to Russia after the mission ends, and you won't see him anyway. Do you really think he cares about you? He'll just leave."

"That's no reason to kill him. And yes, I do think he has feelings for me. He told me so." I clapped my hands to my ribs. A deep throb set up under my fingers, keeping time with my galloping heart. "And he'll help me with succession planning. I just know it."

You will hear thunder and remember me.

Nike said, *"After all of this, do you really think he'll still like you? Trina will get to him. She'll tell him lies."*

"No, she won't. She'll be dead. But—"

"He'll know something is going on."

"But she's supposed to move out anyway—I told him last night. And I really think if I explain to him about the mission, he'll be on board. You'll see." Sparks lit the edges of my vision as my heart picked up speed again.

A shrill ring circled in my head. It took a moment to understand it came from the phone. There was no reason for Trina's conspirators at the office to call again. The sound pulsed behind my eyes, the high-pitched scream of a desperate woman, digging and digging. I grabbed for the phone, just to make it stop.

"Lela, it is Zory."

Oh, God—was Zory in on it? I whipped around but still didn't see any cameras—the shine I'd seen earlier had only been a picture frame. Unless the camera was in the frame…

"Are you there?"

"Oh, yes," I answered.

"Are you okay? You ran out last night in such a hurry—you seemed so shaken."

"Yes, everything is fine." My lie sounded false even to my own ears. "Just…" The synapses in my brain ceased to fire, stuck on the idea that perhaps Zory and Trina had been working together. What if…God, what if they had killed Mrs. Gerhardt? "Sudden migraine. Sometimes I get migraines."

"And to think I defended him," Mrs. Gerhardt said. "I take it back."

"Headaches?" Zory asked.

"Yes." My stomach lurched.

It had been a distraction. They'd killed her—it wouldn't be hard to fake a heart attack, especially if Mrs. Gerhardt had an underlying heart condition. They knew I'd be a mess, unable to concentrate on my observations.

"I don't like that one bit," Mrs. Gerhardt said. "They used us, Gus."

Dad said, "It does look that way, doesn't it?"

Zory made a noise, a cross between a snort and a sigh. "But you are okay now?"

"Sure." A horrible thought popped into my mind: what if Trina and Zory were actually in on *more* together? I had no claim on him, but the idea of his sleeping with her boiled a rage under my skin so potent I blistered and burned.

"Can I come over later to see you? I want to spend as much time with you as I can before I have to go to Florida for pre-launch."

"Yes, fine." I had to find out the truth. Maybe Nike was right—maybe I'd have to kill Zory, too.

I imagined I could hear his smile over the phone, but I didn't know if it was his genuine interest in seeing me or mad joy at having more opportunity to spy on me, turn my mission into a game.

Thank God I kept to myself—there wasn't anyone else he or Trina could take from me.

Except Nike. She'd already threatened it. I searched for him, my eyes frantic. My muscles relaxed when I caught sight of the tip of his bushy tail. No one would hurt him—I'd make sure of it.

"What time should I expect you?" I asked. The seed of a plan germinated in my mind, its roots winding around my brain stem.

"I should be there around six. We are in the pool again today, but Gene said something about getting out early if we make it through this sim."

I nodded, glancing back at Nike. The corners of his mouth turned up into a mysterious feline grin.

In a book Mrs. Gerhardt had given me there'd been a note about cats once being thought to control the weather. I didn't doubt it—even now the wind howled outside. The morning sun had given way to clouds that cast a gloom into the house.

"See you then," I said.

I stalked back into Dad's room and stared at the closet door for a few long moments, my side aching, before throwing it open. I settled on the floor in front of Trina and crossed my legs. Tears squeezed out of her eyes and left shiny tracks across the duct tape keeping her mouth quiet. Her neck twisted at an odd angle as she sagged against the wall, Dad's old pants falling around her hair from their perch on the hangers above.

Nike hunched next to me, half-sitting, half-ready to pounce. His tail slapped my hip. I wondered if he could raise lightning and throw it.

"How well do you know Zory?" I asked, ignoring the seeping pain in my side.

She shifted and fell forward into the doorframe before whimpering. Removing the tape wouldn't do anything other than let her spout lies. Waiting to speak with Zory—*Mission Specialist Korchagin*, I corrected— to get answers made more sense.

"I'll tell you what I think." I clenched my fist and balanced it, flesh to knee, concentrating on the sharp sensation of my nails biting into the flesh of my palm to focus attention. Calm had returned, but I had to concentrate to keep my breathing even over the tightening in my ribs. "You started working at the lab because you knew I worked there, knew about the mission, right? My mother recruited you to work against me."

"Oooo, you're good, Lela. She's going to break," Mrs. Gerhardt said.

Dad said, "That's my girl."

Trina shook her head, her chin jerking and her limp hair plastered to her temple. More squeaking.

"Don't bother denying it." I used a soothing voice, the syllables long and soft. "You must have followed me to find out where I went to lunch and somehow talked Zory into inserting himself into my life."

Trina settled back against the wall again, her near-silent sobs sending a shower of snot after her tears.

"I knew he was too insistent. It didn't make sense, but now it does." My heart squeezed out the last of my feelings for him. "I just don't get it. I mean, why would he knowingly contribute toward a disaster for his crew? That's really the only part I can't figure out."

"Maybe he entered the Russian space program for a reason. For this reason."

I stared at Nike. "Huh. I hadn't really considered that. You could be right. That's kind of convoluted, though. I mean, become a cosmonaut in Russia in hopes of going out on loan to the U.S. program?"

He yawned, flashing me his pink gums and white teeth. *"You have another explanation?"*

"Well, no, but—"

Trina coughed up a strange, choking noise. With all that snot, maybe she couldn't breathe. I sighed and leaned in. "Not a word," I warned her.

I wheedled the edge of the tape from her skin and ripped. Her sobs came louder now, the noise like chirping birds in the morning.

"Lela, please, whatever you think—" Her voice was nasal and hoarse, rough as though someone had sandpapered her vocal cords.

"Just don't speak. So, how did you meet Zor—I mean, Korchagin? I'm really interested in your recruitment efforts."

She pressed her lips together, her breathing heavier now.

"Good choice. Calm down—I'm not going to do anything right now. Just listen. I want you to know that I don't blame you. Destiny chooses us. My life would have probably been much different if this weight… everything I do has such an impact. I guess everything you do does, too, huh? For totally different reasons."

The roll of duct tape lay across the room on the bureau. I stood and snagged it, along with the scissors. Her eyes went wide again, following the points as I set them beside me.

"I can't say I like you very much. Well, especially now, but even before this." I picked at the tape, separating the layer and pulling it up, the stuttering noise loud in the small space. "Breathe, okay?"

She nodded, never letting her gaze wander from the scissors. I picked them up and made a cut, fingering the sticky backside of the tape. "Can you breathe through your nose?"

She paused and nodded again. At least I thought she nodded—it could have been a twitch. She squealed, shaking her head as I lurched toward her.

"Okay. Hold still." She shrank back from me and stuttered something unintelligible. I managed to reseal her mouth with a minimum of effort, although my focus lay at least partially with my aches. "And don't cry again—your nose will get stuffed up. Granted, it would solve one of my problems if you suffocated, but I might have more questions."

I situated myself back on the floor, pulling my knees up and clasping my arms around them. "Zory's a pretty good actor, I'll give him that. I never suspected a thing. But now that I do know, I'll see if he slips up. I found some tranquilizers in the bathroom—yours, I guess? I have to go take a shower, so when I'm done I'll grind up some of the pills. Might not have to use them, but I like to be prepared."

"You weren't so prepared this time."

"No. No, I suppose I wasn't." I ran my hand down Nike's back.

I let out a little huff and glanced at Nike, then Trina.

"I never considered the two of you might kill Mrs. Gerhardt."

I could feel Mrs. Gerhardt's eyes on the back of my neck. Whether Trina saw her, or whether she was nervous, I couldn't tell, but she squeaked, her eyes bugging, and scooted away. A pair of black slacks swung in front of her.

"Good," Dad said. "She's scared—she should be."

I unwound my legs and pushed off the floor, closing the closet. The cat trailed after me, meowing his approval. I blocked out the sound of Trina's thumps against the door and smiled.

Chapter Twenty-Eight

DRAW THE LINE

I AM GLAD YOU ARE FEELING BETTER, GOLUBUSHKA." ZORY—
Korchagin, I reminded myself—reached for my hand. His skin was
cold from the condensation on the glass of tea I'd prepared.

Hearing the term of endearment on his lips sparked a flame up my
spine. I smiled anyway, clenching my teeth behind lips stretched wide.
"Are you? Well, thanks."

I folded one leg under me, the throb in my ribs not so bad after
taking a pain killer—another find in Trina's medicine bag—and pushed
my glasses up by the nose piece. His touch made me jittery, bugs skittering across my flesh. I shifted away.

"I missed you last night. I thought you were going to stay with me."

I glanced in his direction and watched him drink. "So you moved
into your new apartment?"

He probably weighed around two hundred pounds, maybe a little
more. One gram of Valium wouldn't kill him, but I didn't want him in a
coma, either. I'd been careful to stir quite a bit less than that into his tea.
I could adjust upward if necessary later on.

Before he'd come over, I'd studied the signs of an overdose—confusion, tremors, hiccups, nystagmus. If he exhibited any of these symp-
toms prior to passing out, well, I'd deal with it. I needed him to answer
my questions before dying.

During the time it took to finish my shower and Zory—*Korchagin*,
I reminded myself again—to arrive, I'd settled on trying to trip him

up with leading questions that didn't make a lot of sense. He probably wouldn't break—Trina and the people in charge would have trained him much better than that.

He'd lied about the astronauts sleeping during liftoff to rattle me. They'd known I was close to completing my observations and wanted to distract me further. Apparently killing off Mrs. Gerhardt hadn't been enough. They hadn't counted on Nike's superior instincts or my good deductive reasoning, though. Fool me once, shame on you, and all that.

"Mmm hmm. It is not very far from the hotel." Where once I'd found the broad vowels and consonants of his accent attractive, now I just heard lies. Dirty lies. Part of me wondered if he was really even Russian.

"I'm glad you figured it out now," Dad said. "No son-in-law of mine is going to treat my girl badly."

If Zory'd been recruited early on and groomed for the Russian space program, he could have been anything—Irish, German, Greek. How hard would it be to fake an accent, learn Russian, and plant an entire family in the country? I wasn't sure of the logistics, but no doubt it could be accomplished with enough money and the right personnel.

"That's good. Not far to take your things," I said.

"Trina found an apartment, you said?"

My lips twisted, gratified the extra precautions I'd taken to keep her quiet seemed to work. I'd forced her to drink water containing ground-up Valium prior to Zory's arrival, although not nearly the amount I'd given to him. She could only weigh 115 or 120 pounds at most. I planned to kill her, but it didn't seem like a prudent time to do it. Zo—*Korchagin*—had questions to answer first.

"Yes. She said she'd be gone within the month."

"That is good. You must be relieved to have the house to yourself again." He grinned and rubbed his thumb over the top of my hand. "It is a shame she will not be out sooner, though."

I returned his smile, forcing my face into a mask of mock happiness. "Yes, that *is* a shame. I'll be happy to be back by myself, the way things used to be, when she's gone." God, was that the truth.

"I have been meaning to ask you—are you interested in coming to Florida to see the shuttle off? You know quite a bit about the program, but I do not think you have ever been present for such a thing, have you? I may not have a lot of time to myself in the last week. You know, I may not be able to call you much…so I would very much like to have you with me there on-site."

The gall of this man! I was not an idiot. I thought of Mrs. Gerhardt and burned.

"Maybe. I'll have to check my work schedule to see if I can take some time off."

"Really?" His faked excitement appeared so real. I should have known from his very first approach in the teahouse that he'd lied. "You would be willing to come with me?"

Dad grumbled and said, "He thinks he can have his way with you and then kill you? You should have never let him sit with you. Of all the…"

Mrs. Gerhardt shushed him.

I said, "Sure. After all, you said I felt lucky to you once. I wouldn't deny you your rabbit's foot on launch day." I wondered if anything that had ever come out of his mouth had been true.

He tangled his fingers in my hair. For a second I thought he might throw me across the room. I debated whether he knew Trina lay bound in my parents' closet. Her spies might have called him. I couldn't be sure. He pulled me closer, though, and whispered a string of Russian words into my ear, thick and guttural.

For all I knew, he'd just said the code word meant to alert a team of highly trained assassins to invade my house and take me out.

"Stay low and go for the eyes," Dad advised.

I froze, waiting for the onslaught, but it never came. He kissed my cheek, angling my face up to move his lips across my skin. I cleared my throat and shimmied back, garnering a curious expression.

"So, tell me about the difference between launch day…you know, with the shuttle and the Soyuz capsule," I said, settling back.

He raised his eyebrows and launched into a description, all the while never taking his gaze off my face. Ten minutes later, his words came slower, his body sagging into the couch cushions. Another five minutes, and he could hardly keep his eyelids propped up.

"Why don't we go to my bedroom?" I suggested, dreading trying to drag his dead weight from the couch to my mattress. It had taken quite a bit of strength to lug the containers of diesel fuel up the stairwell of his building—how I wished he'd died in that blaze now!—but I didn't think I had the muscles to efficiently move him, and breathing was difficult if

I did anything other than sit still.

Mrs. Gerhardt cleared her throat. "Don't forget to lift from the knees. Never your back."

"Slow and steady, that's all," Dad said.

"Okay," Zory said, voice sluggish.

I stood and pulled him to his feet, his weight heavy against my shoulder as I led him down the hallway. A faint thump drifted through the closed door of my Dad's room, but he didn't appear to notice. We shifted into my bedroom, and I aimed him at the comforter. He fell with grace for such a big man. He groaned and rolled over, clutching a pillow between his hands.

"Come and take a nap with me, Lela." The skin on his forehead smoothed. His mouth went slack.

"Yes." I perched at the edge of the mattress and clamped my arm over my side, staring at the reflection in the mirror above my dresser. My skin stood out paler than normal. My mouth cut a straight, grim line across my face.

I looked haunted, and maybe I was.

Mrs. Gerhardt's faux remains rested just on the other side of the door—I'd returned the urns to the space when I'd re-filed my research. Better out of harm's way for what lay ahead. She and Dad had both been through enough because of me. The beginnings of tears prickled in the corners of my eyes.

"Now, now," Mrs. Gerhardt said. "It was an honor to be part of the mission, even indirectly."

Dad said, "This is just a hiccup. Nothing major, you'll see."

Korchagin's arm snaked around the curve of my hips, holding me in place. No real strength lay behind the effort—I could have wiggled loose, and I would as soon as I knew for sure he was asleep. It only took another fifteen minutes before his breathing evened, not shallow enough for me to worry about. The snore I'd once found cute intruded into the silence, annoying and terrible.

I threw off his arm and stalked into my dad's room to retrieve the duct tape. The thumps didn't grow in volume, so perhaps Trina had just shifted in her sleep, not that she had much leeway.

Restraining Korchagin was ten times easier than taping up Trina, mostly because he lay docile on the bed. By the time I'd finished, his legs were fastened together, ankles affixed to the foot of the bed frame. I tied each wrist to the square posts of my headboard.

He could move, but unless he knew tricks—and I couldn't rule that out; there was no telling what kinds of things he'd learned after recruitment to the group intent on bringing the shuttle down—he'd stay put where I placed him. Knot tying would definitely be part of the protégé curriculum. Maybe I'd use the book Mrs. Gerhardt had recommended.

Thank God NASA had a whole cadre of backup astronauts ready to take Korchagin's place on the shuttle. I'd find a way to explain his absence. It wasn't a secret we'd been dating, so the authorities would find their way to me. The explanation might be as simple as telling them Korchagin had gotten homesick and had returned to his country without fanfare or notice.

He wouldn't be the first—I'd read a few stories about astronauts washing out of the program for any number of reasons. It might look a little conspicuous so close to the mission, but it wouldn't cause a problem.

With Korchagin napping on my bed and Trina restrained in the closet across the hall, I unlocked the door to my filing room. The metal cabinet cooled my warm face as I lay my cheek against the surface. I stayed motionless for a few moments and then removed the folder with all of my notes and forms on Korchagin.

I stared, wondering what I should do with the information. Getting rid of it all together might set some other bad luck into motion, but I couldn't keep it in with the real astronauts.

I reached into my supply basket, rifling through until I pulled out a mauve file that had come as a sample in a pack of red folders. My nails dug under the name label on his blue file, and I click-clacked out a new one with my label maker. His information would go in the file marked by the bad color.

After filing it away in an unused drawer, I relocked the closet and heaved myself up to sit on the dresser to watch Korchagin.

For what might be the last time, he slept.

And I waited, watching and cataloging, just as I always did.

His broad chest rose and fell with each deep breath, but he lay otherwise motionless. A small voice demanded I cover him with a blanket and tuck the edge under his chin, but I forced my body still, concentrating on the air in my lungs and the blood in my veins. The panic I thought

I'd feel had gone, replaced only by a coldness that froze my innards but crystallized my thoughts to a fine point.

He twitched and let out a low groan. Several moments after that, he sighed a long, hissing breath. His eyelashes fluttered. His body tried to shift. It was then his eyelids popped open, arms tugging against the restraints. He muttered in Russian.

"Bet he's not spouting poetry now," Mrs. Gerhardt said.

"Mmm. No, probably not," I answered.

I hopped off the dresser, landing with a quiet thud and a wince. Korchagin's head whipped in my direction. "What is going on?"

"Well, Mr. Korchagin, I think I'd like to know that, too. You and Trina and all your little friends, you almost had me."

"What are you talking about?" He struggled against the duct tape. "Why—"

"Is your real name Zory Korchagin?"

His legs bucked. "Is this a joke? Yuriy told me you Americans have a strange sense of humor, but—"

"Answer the question."

A sound like the striking of a match against sandpaper sounded across the room…Nike, wanting to be let in. I cracked the door, enough to allow the cat to slink into the room. He skimmed across the bottom of the bed frame, his tail *thwapping* against the mattress.

"*He's stalling.*"

"Yes, I know." Perhaps Nike should join Mrs. Gerhardt in the closet—to keep them both safe.

"You know? Know what? Is this a sex thing?"

The note of hope in his voice made me chuckle. "No. If you hadn't turned out to be a traitor and a spy, perhaps we could have discussed that sort of thing, but it's too late now."

"What did I do?"

He seemed to have inherited the panic I'd been feeling since meeting him, since he interrupted my clockwork observations. It served him right. Everything I'd worked for was at risk now because of him and Trina.

Each launch since the *Constitution* disaster—ninety seven in total— had gone off beautifully. Each shuttle ascended amid fuel-shimmered air, flames licking out the bottom of the rocket boosters, billowing white clouds mushrooming below. The boosters would fall away, taking the fire and white plumes with them, and tumble back to the Earth against a sky so blue it hurt my eyes to stare. The lights disappearing into the sky repeated if I concentrated hard enough, even if I also saw the debris trailing from an explosion so awful I didn't want to imagine it again.

"Cut the lying. It doesn't become you, and it only insults me."

"Just tell me what you think I have done, golubushka."

"Don't call me that," I said, my voice flat.

"Okay, I am sorry." He pulled against the restraints again, wrists glowing dark pink with the effort. "Whatever you think it is that I have done to you, I am sorry."

I snorted. "Yes, I'm sure you are. Sorry killing Mrs. Gerhardt didn't sideline me quite enough. Are you also sleeping with Trina?" His eyes widened, and he shook his head, protesting. "In the grand scheme of things, it doesn't really matter, but I have to admit that if you are, that makes it somewhat worse."

"Trina?" His head wobbled from side to side again. "No. I do not even know her. Why would you even think so?"

"I understand—you work with someone for so long to accomplish your mission, and things happen," I said and moved close enough to run my fingers across the short hair above his forehead. "In some ways, I suppose you're to be admired—you're like a kamikaze fighter, ready to sacrifice yourself for what you believe in. But taking down the shuttle and all the rest of the crew…well, I guess that was all part of your mission, wasn't it?"

Dad and Mrs. Gerhardt held their breaths, no doubt waiting for the answer.

Korchagin's brows rose and pulled together. "What are you talking about? Lela, just untie me, and we will talk about all this. We will go call Trina and straighten everything out."

"He's not going to break, you know?"

"I know, I know," I muttered. The hum of a car passing outside distracted me for a moment. A clicking underlaid the sound. Nike didn't seem perturbed, so I returned to the matter at hand.

"What do you know? I can help—we can get the answers together."

"You should just end it." Nike wound around my legs, nuzzling his head against my calf.

"What if killing him dooms the mission anyway? What if it triggers the rest of their group to move forward with another plan? I'm fairly sure that Trina is the ringleader. If I just keep them here, maybe this mission goes off without a hitch?"

Korchagin returned to rambling in excited Russian.

"*I don't like it.*"

"The cat's got a point," Dad said.

"I don't have another choice," I said. "What can I do? It isn't as though I've been able to think through the best plan for disposal. If I have to kill two people, I will, but I don't want to be implicated."

"Takin' a life is where I draw the line," a satiny voice said from behind me.

Chapter Twenty-Nine

EXPEDIENT SOLUTIONS

I WHIRLED. MY HEART STUTTERED AND LURCHED IN MY CHEST, WHICH only broadened the ache in my ribs. The Chin braced his hands against the frame of the door, leaning in.

"Been watching for weeks now, and I kept my trap shut about the fire. Didn't know what the hell you were doing, but this…" He gestured toward the bed. "Ain't no way I'm lettin' you do this."

The sharp point of clarity I'd clung to extinguished, replaced by a howling rage that clawed up my esophagus and emerged as a shriek. The pain in my ribs vanished in a millisecond.

Everything happened in slow motion—the buzzing of angry locusts blocked out sound and thought until my vision pulsed, The Chin and the rest of the room shaking and intensifying in color until a crimson glow streaked and rocketed around the walls, thundering and lightning like the first poem Zory had given me.

The rim of the sky will be the color of hard crimson, and your heart, as it was then, will be on fire.

I went airborne, flying flying, until I slammed into a soft body and forced it backward. The Chin under me…a gabbling laugh, high-pitched and mocking…not sure where it came from. In the background, Nike hissed and growled. I fought, but The Chin did, too, stronger than he appeared.

The air around me grew louder, all the noises so loud—ripping in my head, dry cracks, and shouting in the room, the thick syllables of Russian-accented English and urgent grunts.

"Knock it off," The Chin panted, struggling, grabbing at my arms and shimmying me off his chest. I threw my fists and barked out words that made no sense.

I'd heard of people speaking in tongues during moments of religious ecstasy, but I didn't see God—I saw a murderer to my left and an idiot in front of me. I sank my teeth into The Chin's arm, the taste of something metallic and wet coating my mouth, and he swore before pushing me away.

I scrambled backward, retreating to the far side of the bed. My breath heaved out in stuttering gasps.

Breathe. Four-three-two-one-in, four-three-two-one-out.

"Think calm, Lela," Dad urged.

"How?" I screeched.

The Chin, now slumped and holding his forearm on the other side of the room, kept shrinking and stretching by turns—the queasy motion picked at me, gouging chunks from my skin, flaying me alive.

"Stop that!" I yelled, trying to catch my breath, needing the torture to end, spare my body. "Stop growing...just stop!"

Korchagin kicked at the tape holding his feet, keeping up a steady soundtrack of Russian. Every sound he made sliced into the skin of my chest just over my heart.

"And you!" I shoved against his shoulder. "Shut up! I can't hear myself think! Same goes for you two." I pointed at Mrs. Gerhardt and Dad.

Zory ignored me, continuing his litany. The cuts on my skin burned and sizzled, the edges of each laceration blackening and twisting.

"Why are you here?" I demanded, stabbing my finger in The Chin's direction. Breathe breathe breathe. His underbite expanded, dominating his features, and his teeth shot up, white and fang-like.

I shook my head. It all receded, but I didn't trust my eyes. Something lay beneath the surface of his face; some dangerous beast lurked. Why hadn't I noticed it before? "Oh my God! You're in on it!" My hand shook, and I backed away from the bed. All of them. All of them killed Mrs. Gerhardt, maybe my father...the mission.

Nike leaped onto the dresser. I tried to convey a command to the cat, silently begging him to spring, to sink his claws into that ever-changing face. He remained in place.

"Pretty girl, you're havin' the vapors or something." The Chin shuffled forward, his face wobbling. I skittered another foot in the opposite direction. His voice held the low, soft tone I'd use to talk to a small child. "Just...let's you and me take a step back. Ain't a reason in the world for this."

"When did she get to you—before or after we started having sex?"

Korchagin's eyes swung toward me, and his babbling stopped. "You have been having sex with this man?"

The Chin kept staring as though he hadn't heard—or if he did, he wasn't paying any attention. A welt reddened on his forehead. Another burned across his neck. At least I'd gotten in one or two good shots. Succession training would need to include a module on hand-to-hand combat. Maybe martial arts.

The bodies were going to pile up when all of this was said and done. Maybe Nike had some ideas about how to hide them. Maybe it was a good idea to incorporate a class on that as well.

Dad said, "I don't know about the how, but I might have some ideas about where."

"That's nice, Dad," I muttered.

"*You have to kill Zory, too.*"

"Yes, I know." I glanced at Nike and narrowed my eyes. Did the cat think I was stupid? The evidence had stared me in the face all along. I should have known when The Chin wanted more than sex. I should have figured it out when Korchagin showed up at my table in the teahouse.

Was Magda in on it, too? The cook? The owner? God, maybe even the few patrons always in the restaurant. It explained why the teahouse continued to operate even though no one ate there. No restaurant could stay open for years under those conditions. Jesus—*years* they'd been watching me. It would have been so easy for them to get to Dad.

"You know *what*?" The Chin asked. "See my point? You ain't making a lick of sense, but me and you, we'll untie your boyfriend here and sit down and talk. Whaddya say?"

"What do I *say*?" My voice rose an octave, indignant. "I say you're a traitor! You and your friends. How can you live with yourselves? The space program is vital. We're talking about the lives of astronauts here, and you're working to kill them. Kill them! And my family! Mrs. Gerhardt!"

"Killing the astronauts? I do not understand." Korchagin's voice had grown hoarse.

"Hey, hey, hey," The Chin soothed at the same time Korchagin partially freed one ankle from the tape.

"No!" I hunted around for a weapon. If he managed to get loose, he and The Chin would kill me for sure.

"Why are you doing this to me, Lela?" Korchagin writhed on the bed, working the tape at his other ankle as he stared at me. The veins of his arms bulged, speckling up with black blood. It oozed out and disappeared. Oh God. "Why can't you just let me go?"

Mrs. Gerhardt snorted. "Umm hmm. That's a great idea."

"Hey, uh, why don't you just back off there, cowboy," The Chin warned, his palms out. "You ain't helping by runnin' your mouth."

"Yes, because you are doing such a great job yourself," Korchagin snarled back and turned his head to look at me. "You do not need to do this," he said, his voice much more gentle. "Let me call Johnson. I will let you speak to anyone you would like—the commander of the shuttle, the head NASA administrator, someone from Baikonur, whoever you want. You will see that everything is okay."

My eyes vaulted back and forth between Korchagin and The Chin, gauging the strength of each man. The Chin's thick waist and lethargic movements—even as he tried to corral me—led me to believe I could likely make it past him out the door of my bedroom if I had to. He'd almost been able to get control after I jumped on him, but I was smaller and quicker.

If Korchagin managed to get loose, I'd have less of a chance. He'd trained all his life for space travel, pushing himself into peak condition. I'd been afraid of him when we'd first met, and now I understood why.

"Save your breath." I shook my head, disgusted. "I can't believe I fell for your act. There's something wrong with me. I'm gullible and stupid. Not anymore. Thank God I figured it out before it was too late…well, too late for Dad and Mrs. Gerhardt, but at least I can protect the shuttle."

Korchagin never lifted his stare from me, even as he continued to tug at his wrists and ankle.

The Chin shifted. "Nothing about you's stupid or gullible, Lela. This ain't what this is about. You're tired, is all. You just need some sleep. Lemme grab a pillow for ya. We'll let this guy up, and you can—"

"Sleep!" I screeched. "It's all about sleep! All of this."

"Whatddya mean? Slow down and talk to me. Tell—"

"Don't pretend you don't know the importance of my sleep studies.

You as much as told me you watched me break into Korchagin's apartment, and—"

"What?" Zory interrupted. "You broke into my apartment? But why?"

"What does that have to do with the lab?" The Chin asked.

"Not work, you idiot!"

"Why don't you explain exactly what you were doing when you set that fire?"

"The fire is your fault?" Korchagin's body tensed, his face twisted. "Why would you—"

"Shut up! I had to—I had to know, although I'm sure—you and your spies. Trina. I don't know why you didn't die. I planned everything, and—"

"People burned to death, Lela!" Zory shouted, straining further against the duct tape. "You *killed* people! You—"

"You should have died!" The air left my lungs in an abrupt rush, noodling out the last word in a strangled squeak. My ribs had begun to twinge again, breathing so difficult now. "You will today—you and Trina and—"

"Trina? She here?" The Chin asked, the urgency of his voice triggering a dry laugh that got stuck in my throat.

"What, do you think you and your group can save her? They can't save any of you. Unless I kill all three of you, the shuttle's going to explode. I know you don't care, but I do!"

Korchagin's other ankle came free, and he twisted on the bed, yanking his wrists.

"You see what he's doing, don't you, Lela?" Dad asked. "You got to do something quick."

I'd have to find something heavy. If I could knock The Chin out, I could retie Korchagin. I didn't want to set fire to the house and lose the last memories of Dad, but it seemed the most expedient solution. It wouldn't take long to transfer all my files out to my car, pack up Nike, Mrs. Gerhardt, and take a few keepsakes.

When the fire investigators came, I'd tell them they'd been making dinner…a pre-housewarming/congratulations party for Trina.

I stepped toward the door, toward The Chin. He didn't move but kept his eyes on me, his hand shifting in my direction.

"Hey, let's just forget all this, okay?" The Chin said. His mouth bowed into a brittle smile. "It don't matter to me what you done. Just let Zory and Trina go. I'll take care of you. We'll leave. We'll do whatever you want. You wanna go break into houses? No problem. I'll help ya do it. You'll see—let me take care of you."

"This is the man you were fooling around with?" Mrs. Gerhardt asked. "I'll never understand you young people."

Dad shook his head. "You couldn't do any better than this?"

I rolled my eyes and hissed at them both.

Korchagin had gone quiet, working hard to loosen his wrists, sawing the tape against the edge of the bedpost. It had to be now—the tape holding his left arm stretched. I edged closer to my dresser, intent on getting my hands on the lamp at the end of it. The Chin's eyes narrowed further, slits in his constantly changing face.

I sucked in a breath, taking in as much air as I could, even as my lungs and ribs protested. My knees flexed. Fire jetted through every muscle in my body as I waited for even a second for The Chin to glance away. And then it happened: Korchagin freed an arm, drawing The Chin's attention.

I rocked onto the balls of my feet. My fist closed around the neck of the lamp, cool beneath my fingers. A high-pitched keening echoed in the room. It roiled in my ears so loud I winced. I sprang and swung the base of the lamp in an arc. It caught The Chin in the jaw.

Korchagin swung off the bed. He lunged at me as far his remaining restraint allowed. I dodged out of his way. I closed my eyes for a split second, enough to register a flash of royal blue sky dotted with debris, trails of billowy black and white smoke. The Chin had staggered back from the hit, but it hadn't stopped him. I swiveled and flashed the lamp out again. It narrowly missed his face.

"Why can't you just stop?" I spit out between convulsing gasps of air.

The Chin listed forward. He was faster than I could have imagined but still slow. He knocked into me. I faltered, but it was enough—Korchagin's giant hands snaked across my ribs. The sharp tang of bile rose in my throat as my side lit up in searing agony. I held my breath and thrust my body toward The Chin as hard as possible, reaching for him, smiling when my hands closed around his neck.

He gurgled and tried to pull away. My fingers tightened. Strength coursed through me. The skin of his neck warmed under my grip, so shockingly warm. The cords of his neck tensed, spongy yet hard, fitting perfectly into the notch between my thumb and pointer.

"Let go," Korchagin demanded from behind, squeezing my ribs tighter. A breathy wheeze hissed out of me. A weight settled on my breastbone and the edges of my vision fuzzed. Still, it was so easy to adjust my grip, press my palms harder against The Chin's throat. His fingers pried at mine. His face flushed the color of Mom's favorite turtleneck sweater.

Cackles burst out of me, the entire room pulsing with noise.

My hands flexed, tightening. Gabbled choking joined my laughter, even as Korchagin yanked in the opposite direction. And just like that, my hands scraped over The Chin's throat. My fingertips clawed until they held nothing.

A screech filled my ears. Hands shoved my shoulders. It all had me spiraling around, pirouetting, but I saw everything. Splinters of bright light slid into me, and then it all turned black, taking me away.

Chapter Thirty

POINT TWIST

A BOVE, ALL WAS SAPPHIRE BRIGHT. MY EYEBALLS SPANNED IN EVERY direction out the window. My body weighed a million pounds, my head yanked back into a hard cushion, held by gravity. A heavy white jumpsuit stretched tight across my body—my last name embroidered in black on the patch over my heart.

What was this? I tried to lift a hand to scratch my face, pinch my thigh…all to prove I wasn't fast asleep. It didn't do a bit of good, though; my wrist was fastened to the armrest as if stitched in with heavy thread. Maybe the g-forces.

In the next moment, I sat cross-legged in my old elementary school, staring up at a large-screened television. Jet fuel flames burned beneath the shuttle on the launch pad, the vehicle lifting as if by God's own will.

My hand lifted easily this time to wipe the tears on my face. Why was I crying? Mom said not to cry. Crying was for babies, but Mrs. Gerhardt said it was okay. My body was not my own—instead of sitting quietly as we'd been instructed, I jumped up. My scream echoed off the walls of the hallway, and all sound and activity stopped with the exception of me. I sprinted to the television and swiped at the screen.

"Oh, God!" I pounded at the rickety metal rolling cabinet that held the television. "Stop!"

Large arms—much too large—wrapped around my ribs, and I hurtled backward, flying down the corridor, my limbs outstretched toward the shuttle, now exploding, breaking up. Even from this distance, the splitting and curling streams of smoke were visible, wafting in the hall now.

I screamed again and landed with a jolt, flat on my back, staring out that same window. All that blue, only now rumbles shook through my body, chattering my teeth with a violence that should have left them shattered. Too much, too much. The chair I sat in crumbled apart, and I fell, sinking fast, grasping at anything I could as it whizzed by. The growing heat below me roared, flames rushing up and burning my toes, hotter and faster than the searing macadam through shoes on a sunny day.

The air roiled with smoke and fire, everything so very loud and yet the quietest I could ever remember hearing. The light burst, yellow-red-orange. Black and black and black.

"We've been keeping her sedated." A voice—a female voice, I thought—whispered in the darkness. "Every time we take her meds down even a little, she comes to screaming at the top of her lungs."

"Please call me if she gets to the point where she can answer questions." This one was a man, deep. Deep and gruff. Other voices danced just below the sound.

"Yes, of course, officer." The click of shoes sounded, the echo so loud I wanted to wince, but no part of me felt connected anymore. "But it doesn't look good. This one has some long-standing issues."

Shrill ringing pierced the hazy whispers. "Brentwood."

The blinding sky swirled around me again, drowning me in its thick heat.

"No, she's still out…yeah…I know, but there's not much I can do about it. I asked the nurse to call…did you get DNA on the bones in the backyard yet?"

The bones in the backyard? Whose backyard? We'd buried a cat in mine when I was little—a big black cat named Apollo that just got old. Mom and Dad dug a hole in the back corner after wrapping him in an old towel.

"He'll fertilize my roses," Mom had told me, her sad smile strangely comforting. "You'll see—the bush will be big and healthy. It's just like reincarnation."

"Roni, she's six years old," Dad had said with a laugh, holding my hand. "Don't go talking about stuff like that to her."

Mom had flapped her hand and shoveled a spadeful of dirt over the hole. The sun beat down that day, drying everything out. I'd waved goodbye, my last farewell.

"And you say it matches up to White? Her father? Records say he was cremated, though…wait, female? A sister, maybe?"

Breathe. Four-three-two-one-in, four-three-two-one-out.

The murmurs in my head grew louder, more distinct, chanting a directive, little cheerleaders waving pom poms. "Burn burn burn burn burnburnburnburnburn."

"Well, no. The body in the closet was easy to identify, although it took forever to get it out of all that plastic sheeting and duct tape, which explains why no one seems to have noticed the smell. Trina Shook was never reported missing. She was supposed to have been in Austin with a boyfriend, but he says they never made any such arrangement. Says he's been trying to reach her for weeks, which fits: The medical examiner said she'd been dead for at least fourteen days. Yeah, we have Austin PD talking to him. Well, apparently, it was White who told everyone Shook needed the time off from work. A woman at the library where she volunteers says White was all ticked off about something one day—heard her screaming to the librarian about having it out with Shook—and then that's all she wrote. No one ever saw her again. Korchagin says White was talking about the woman like she was there all along, so who knows what was going on during that time. I mean, there's evidence the body was moved around just a few days ago, maybe the night she attacked Korchagin and Fowler. All right, well, I'll go back down there tonight. Forensics is finished going over the scene…yeah, well, it's been a week— they better be finished. The ashes were those of a Marjorie Gerhardt. That's the librarian. Witnesses say they were close. Yeah, we processed Gerhardt's house and her old office, but there was nothing important there…White's house has been processed, too, but I asked them to leave me the contents of those cabinets. I want to go through all of it and see if I can make any sense—"

The man sucked in air, and I imagined him flopping like a fish out of water, great big gills opening and closing wetly in the side of his neck. I couldn't open my eyes—someone must have glued them shut—but he probably had pursed guppy lips and silver and green hair that shimmered like scales under water. A big fish with lots of scars from hooks and boat propellers.

Where were Dad and Mrs. Gerhardt?

"No, he's fine. They both are. A little shook up maybe…no, he's gone to Florida, plans to be on that shuttle come hell or high water. The other one, Max…Fowler. Yeah. He's been busting down the door to get in here to see this woman. Yeah, I know, I thought it was weird, too. I mean, she tried to kill him. My gut says there's something more to that guy's story, but he's not saying much. He just wants to see White. Beats me. I mean, we didn't find anything about the guy in her files, but we found plenty about Korchagin."

In an instant I was back in the fire, my body writhing, my blistered, blackened skin peeling off in long, crackling layers.

"I don't want to speculate until I'm finished looking through those files, but I'm thinking at least two counts of attempted murder, plus an arson charge and maybe two premeditated homicides. Who knows— maybe more, depending on what we can figure out about those bones in the yard."

Bones. I wanted to tell him about my old cat, but my lips wouldn't budge. A face formed in my mind—a woman, hair like my mother. Oh, Trina. With a start, I wondered if the guppy man spoke of her…all those charges. A rich sense of satisfaction beat through me. She hadn't fooled the cops, not for a second.

She'd go to prison. For killing Mrs. Gerhardt. But who else had she killed? I would be one of the cases of attempted murder.

An edge of irritation beat over the inside of my ribs, but it couldn't take root. Trina and The Chin. And Korchagin. All of them in it together. Words struggled at my mouth, but nothing happened.

"No, Gerhardt died of natural causes." Yeah, natural causes. Right. Hollowness grew and grew, swallowing me whole until the blackness at the horizon took me.

My heart thumped. For each beat, a year passed. For each year, a thousand roots grew out the ground and held me down. Hands shook me, and with a start, my eyes popped open. Flames whooshed around me, but below was a face.

It was Dave. Davey Enders. His hair licked at the air, and the smell of ozone snapped around me. He smiled, putting his crooked teeth on display.

"Wake up," he said. "There's still so much to do."

I glanced around. Beyond the door to my room was the circulation desk and Mrs. Gerhardt's office. She sat on the counter with a book in her hand, red lipstick glowing like a beacon. "How did I get here?"

"I brought you here," she said. "You and Davey should get busy."

"What for?" I asked. "The shuttle is doomed, and it's all my fault. I heard the man say that Korchagin is already in Florida for the launch."

Nike strolled through the door. His tail twitched, and his white whiskers dipped. "*It's never too late.*"

Dave pulled a large, cloth-bound book from his backpack and tossed it to me. "Open it to page three hundred."

I leafed through and flattened the book, bringing it closer to my face. "You will hear thunder," I read. My chin jerked up. "I don't understand. How will this help me save the astronauts?"

Rain hissed down and doused the fire. Dave's smile grew until his face cracked, and a torrent of black blood poured out. Thunder was like the rending of metal in a junkyard. The room burst apart, taking with it Dave and Mrs. Gerhardt and the books. All the books.

I was a fierce column of coals with nothing and no one.

✳✳✳

I SURFACED TO A WHITE CEILING, MY THOUGHTS FLAT AND DULL AS the paint. Trina and her people had gotten Dave, my only succession nominee, and now Mrs. Gerhardt was really gone. I blinked, the inside of my eyelids feeling as though someone had scoured them.

"She didn't scream yesterday when we tried it at this dosage, so I figured we could give it a go."

The guppy man had come back. "Thank you, I appreciate it. Can we question her alone?"

"Sure. I mean, you won't really be alone, though—there's a monitor over there so we can observe all the patients from the nurses' station. And I'll be outside with a sedative, just in case."

My eyes rolled around in my head, finally settling on a man in a blue shirt and red tie. No gills, but without my glasses, I couldn't tell for sure. The details were hazy, but I saw it when he waved off the nurse—I assumed she was a nurse anyway: she wore pink scrubs. Almost mauve.

"Don't worry about it."

She smiled and turned around. I didn't see where she went because I was focused on the guy who hadn't spoken yet—heavyset, blurry, with a full, black beard.

"This won't be admissible, you know, Brentwood."

I couldn't feel my toes, but they wiggled when I wanted them to. Weird. My brain fogged and fought, spinning and buzzing like a sluggish hive of angry bees, hypnotized by smoke.

Guppy man shrugged. "Yeah, I know. But really, there isn't any way in hell any of these charges are going to stick—she's mad as a hatter."

"Are you talking about Trina?" I asked in a voice that didn't sound like mine—it rumbled from my tight chest. My skeleton had grown too big for my skin. And slow, so slow—my words burbled out of me in their own time.

"Oh, Miss White." Guppy man smiled and pulled out a thin notebook. The click of his pen made my ears hurt. I winced, surprised my body obeyed my brain commands. "My name is Aaron Brentwood. This is my partner, Miles Timoney. We're with the Houston Police Department. We'd like to ask you a few questions."

"O-okay." My mouth dried, stuffed with cotton. "Can I…where are my glasses?"

He leaned over next to my bed, and I turned my head. A small table. He plucked something from the surface and handed me—my glasses. I slid them on, the edges solidifying, clearing.

"You mentioned Trina. Is that Trina Shook?"

"Have you found her yet?" I asked.

The two men glanced at each other. "Yes, in a closet in your home."

A puff of a laugh pushed out of me. The air was not my own. "Good. Be sure you hold her—she's dangerous, and she'll tell you lies."

"Do you remember the events of October second and third?"

The dates seemed important, and a dim trio of voices whispered something I couldn't quite catch. My head wouldn't focus on anything except the voices. "No. Maybe. Should I remember?"

The man with the beard spoke. "Do you know Maxwell Fowler and Zory Korchagin?"

I nodded and immediately regretted it—even slow as my body moved, the ache that came with the movement sucked the air from my burning lungs. "Yes. I hope you arrested them, too."

The two men glanced at each other. "And why is that?" Guppy man asked. His lips did sort of look fish-like.

"All three of them were c - c -c," my brain couldn't manage the word I wanted. It locked down, swirling, and the voices swelled, yelling, "Burn

burn burn burnburnburnburn," and soon I muttered it too. Over and over.

"Okay," Guppy lips said, soft and reassuring. "We won't talk about that now."

"My cat," I said. "Where's Nike?"

"Uh…the cat. I think they took it to an animal shelter."

"I can still get him back when I get out of here, right?"

Guppy lips frowned. "That's something you should discuss with your doctor."

Nike. Good, he'd find a way to escape and finish my work, protégé or not. Maybe he could even take over recruiting. He could figure out a way to stop the shuttle from exploding this time and ensure its safety into the future. And when I found my way back to him, we'd build on my mission, complete the training program.

The bearded man moved closer. "Do you recognize these?" He pulled out two pieces of white paper, streaked with reddish-brown smears. My child-like handwriting covered them. Written across the top read, "Sleep—Mom."

I could almost feel the papers in my hand after all these years, the pencil clutched in my fingers, and I traced the words *sleep duration* as though writing in the emptiness of the air. I smiled at him.

"Yes. I—"

I couldn't tell this man about my observations, could I? Those sheets, some of my earliest studies. I didn't know what day it was, but the shuttle might not have launched yet. Anything I did could ruin it a—

Oh, God. My feet twitched, and something bubbled up through my veins, some unnamable emotion, threatening the flat calm. I clamped my lips shut.

"Well, I'm hoping you can tell us something about the contents of the file we found these papers in, Miss White." Guppy man pulled a clear bag out of a case and held it close. A snarl of hair, long and curly, and a barrette. "The DNA matches up to bones we found—"

The force of my screams should have been enough to blow the room apart.

The men backed away while I wrestled with my bed sheets. Something held me down—first Mom, then Korchagin. The blue of the sky filtered through my howls, a sharp sting in my arm, and a bland dullness swimming like a lethargic fish through my veins, guppy man oozing through me.

The blackness swirled across the white, white ceiling, sealing me inside my body. The screams echoed even there.

✳✳✳

THE DOCTOR SMILED THE MOMENT I WALKED INTO HIS OFFICE. HIS teeth were too white, too gleaming under the lights.

The nurse released my shoulders and gestured toward the chair. "Lela?"

My head drifted toward her. Her pupils had grown huge. "I'll be back for you, and then we'll go for medication. Okay?"

"Yes." My voice had no life for her, and no matter how I tried I couldn't find myself.

She patted my back and walked out. The door shutting was an exclamation point. The doctor nodded at me, and I tried to clasp my hands on my lap, but my fingers wouldn't cooperate.

"My name is Dr. Tremblay," he said. "You and I will spend some time together during your stay with us. I understand you had an episode recently."

"Did I?"

"Well, let us start from the beginning, and we can delve into that later on. Let's begin with you," he said. "I see from your file that you're thirty-two and never married. Have you always lived in Houston?"

"Yes."

"Tell me about your family."

The words oozed out of my mouth, detailing what I could. He didn't get it all though. With each word I said, the voices in my head howled. He was in on it. He was keeping me from Korchagin, from doing what I had to do in order to keep the shuttle from blowing apart during liftoff. I thought of Nike, doing what he had to in order to make it to Cape Canaveral. He would make it on time—I knew he would.

Dr. Tremblay asked me question after question, about me, about my life, about what he called "my condition." I had no condition—whatever he thought, he was wrong. He poked and poked until I wanted to squeeze the air from his lungs…if I could move fast enough.

"Tell me how you feel in social situations. Do you seek out others, or are you on the shy side?" he asked.

My lips pursed. "I'm probably no different than anyone else."

"And what do you consider normal?"

I glanced away, studying the window in his office.

His sigh resonated in the room. "Let's try something. Maybe a few true or false questions, shall we?"

"When am I going to get out of here?" I asked. My eyes wandered away from the window to the framed diplomas and certificates on the wall and finally to the doctor himself. His white coat was rumpled around the neck, a blue and white striped shirt beneath it. His blue tie knotted up around his throat, a loose wattle of fat pushing over it. His lips were thin, so narrow his mouth looked only like a single thin line across his face. Heavy-lidded eyes pinned me to the chair. He scratched his head, reaching through his styled brown hair to do so.

He was crafty, I could tell.

"That remains to be seen, but I must tell you that your options are not good. If you're found to be sane, you'll be transferred to a maximum security prison." He steepled his fingers in front of him. "I don't think you understand the severity of the charges against you, which speaks to the degree of your psychosis."

"I don't have a psychosis."

"Miss White, you believe your actions directly influence something you couldn't possibly have a hand in. You routinely converse with your cat and two dead people. The police have evidence that you murdered a person, and they suspect you killed one other. You kidnapped an astronaut, and there's detailed evidence to suggest a long-term habit of stalking as well as breaking and entering. There's an eyewitness who says you burned down an apartment building where there were fatalities and injuries."

What was he saying? I'd told him no such thing, and it was an ugly interpretation of my mission. What I did was graceful and good. He made it sound like a crime.

I shook my head and slumped in the chair. "You don't know what you're talking about. Trina Shook is the one who should be arrested. She and Zory Korchagin. Maybe even The Chin—they've all been..."

"What have they been doing, Miss White?" He leaned forward, elbows on his desk. "You realize Trina Shook is dead, do you not? The police maintain that you killed—" He pressed his lips together. "None of that matters right now. We can discuss it another time after I learn more about you." He glanced at his watch. "Our hour is almost up.

You're scheduled to see me three times this week, and I'd like you to think about your relationship with your mother before our next session. We'll be spending quite a bit of time on that."

"Why do you care about my mother?" I asked. Numbness ascended my legs, shaking at my knees and making my thighs heavy.

"I want to know everything about you, Miss White. You're a very interesting case."

The nurse plodded in and recaptured me in her orbit. When I turned around, the doctor was on the phone. I swore I heard him say, "Miss Shook. Yes, she just left. We'll keep her here indefinitely."

My eyes burned. Everyone here was helping Trina. My eyes stung, and screams built up in my head, bursting up my throat until I was yelling, too.

✳✳✳

WELL, MISS WHITE," THE DOCTOR SAID. HIS NAME STARTED WITH a T, I thought, but now I couldn't remember. It was so hard to hold on to my thoughts. "You're looking well this morning. How do you feel?"

I walked through the bright white halls in this place in a perpetual fog, even with my glasses on. Nothing quite solid, nothing quite clear.

His mouth drew up, and he folded gnarled hands on the desk blotter.

I picked at a loose thread at the edge of my sweater. Maybe my sweater. The color—lavender, too close to mauve—chomped at the uneasy calm that weighted my body, held me to the Earth, heavier than I'd been before.

Some fact tried to surface…something about the density of bones and weightlessness. It slipped away, elusive and slimy.

My feet scuffed the tile under my feet. The flooring had once been bright white, now faded to dirty dishwater. I positioned the tip of my toes in the middle of a tile to avoid the cracks.

Step on a crack, break your mother's back.

"I feel fine," I said, offering my tooth-crammed grin.

Dad chided me. "Now, there's no need to lie, pumpkin."

The corner of my lip tugged. Mrs. Gerhardt echoed his sentiment. They'd both come back last week. Just popped into my brain one day, and there they stayed.

"May I have some hot tea? And some jam, if you have it. I'd like tea with jam."

Each breath easing into my lungs lasted five seconds, each exhale the same. Measured. Careful. I waited for Nike's advice to come, but it never did. I prayed for his safety; if anything had happened to him…

"I'll inquire about that in the cafeteria for you. As to how you're feeling, that's wonderful—good to hear it. You've been doing well. Surprisingly well, given your psychotic episode."

"Thank you." I held onto the thread of a wispy thought, just one thing: I had to get out of here. Even with Nike possibly able to do my work, I had a mission, something important to do. The idea had popped into my head, and it felt so right. Like one true thing, and yet I fumbled with the concept, holding it like a soap bubble. "Do you really think I'm still psychotic, though? I've been working so hard."

Inside I snorted. These people were so easy to fool.

"Let's take it one step at a time, shall we? How about this—I'd like you to read something." He fumbled with an envelope, removing and unfolding a white paper.

"Okay." I pushed up the nosepiece of my glasses.

"Your friend, Zory Korchagin." I nodded, and he continued. "He's been in Florida for some time now to prepare for the space shuttle launch, but he asked me to make sure you received a letter. Now, we cannot allow you to take the letter back to your room, but I can keep it for you after you've read it if you like. Do you understand? And just to be clear, I've read the letter. We'll discuss the contents when you're finished."

I nodded and took the paper. Korchagin's face materialized in my memory—the gray eyes, the goatee, the sharp line of his nose. Turbulence bubbled just below the surface of my skin, a wind current of fury. The space shuttle. Murderer.

I wanted to shake my head, but if I did I'd scream…maybe. The feel of it plucked at my vocal cords, but my body sagged with exhaustion, unable to generate the energy needed to even agitate the tide.

The doctor sat back in his chair and watched me, so I concentrated on keeping my face blank while I glanced at the words written in Korchagin's heavy loops.

Dear Lela,

Now more than ever you remind me of my babushka. Still, I do not quite know what to say to you after all that has happened. There is no way for me to know what made you think…whatever it is that you think. The police will not tell me much, although my grandmother assures me that you had nothing but the best of intentions. I, too, know you didn't mean to hurt anyone—it is not in your nature. I know it because I know you.

I leave in the morning to prepare for the flight, and I want to see you. The doctor tells me that you cannot have visitors. I just want to make sure you are well before the launch. Please do not worry about my safety. I have trained for this mission—we all have. Nothing will go wrong. You will see.

When I return, I will come for you. Your bad year is ending; I feel it in my heart. I have feelings for you still and will think of you while I am away. I pray you think of me too. I will come for you, and we will be together.

Yours,

Bory

Underneath that, a string of Russian characters bled across the page. He'd translated the letters below. *Your heart, as it was then, will be on fire.* The familiar words rose the hair on my arms, although I couldn't fit a memory into meaning.

The barest tremor shook my hands, but I clasped them together on top of the letter in my lap, determined not to let the doctor see.

The doctor watched—always watching—and marked a notation on papers lying on the desk. My chart probably. He observed me. The thought generated the beginnings of a laugh, just a heaviness in my throat that wanted to erupt, but the compulsion dampened almost immediately.

"How do you feel about Mr. Korchagin's letter?"

I stared back, wondering what the right answer was. "He's concerned about me."

"Yes." The doctor's brows elevated just a fraction. "He does not understand the American psychiatric and justice system, so he worries we'll release you."

"What are you talking about? He's coming back for me when he returns."

The doctor's eyes widened. "Is that what you perceive? You believe the letter says he plans to pursue a romantic relationship with you?"

"You read it, so you already know. He's an excellent liar. The shuttle's not coming ba—" My mouth snapped shut. "I mean, I'm sure all will go well with the launch. No problems at all. And when he comes back for me, we'll talk. He'll be my boyfriend again." I stretched my mouth into a smile. Oh, everyone was waiting for me to say something, to say more. I'd fool them all.

"I see." The doctor bobbed his head and made another mark on his notes.

"Do you still think he's trying to sabotage the shuttle mission?"

Yes. "No."

"Well, then you are, indeed, making fast progress." He said it, but there was something in his voice, some catch, like he didn't quite trust the words. "And what about Maxwell Fowler?"

"What about him?"

"Can you think of a reason why he might be so adamant about seeing you? More to the point, would you like to see him?"

I shrugged. "He's not important."

He wrote something else, and I leaned forward, trying to discern a word. My body responded so slowly, though. He flipped the file closed before I could get close enough to read. "Well, that's certainly interesting." He paused, his eyes poking into me just as if he'd used a knife. "I'd like us to watch the shuttle launch together. Just you and me and Miss Shields."

He stood and walked around the desk, opening the door. He called out, and a woman stepped into the office, a nurse. My mother's hair curled around her face, Trina's eyes staring out. Her fist curled around something long.

The doctor turned back to me. "Would you like that, Miss White? To watch the shuttle launch?"

"Yes."

"Good, good. It's happening shortly."

"Today?" The word had been sharp on my tongue, and yet it slurred out of my mouth at a snail's pace. With Davey and his flames gone, only Nike could keep my mission alive. It was a dangerous trip. Over a thousand miles. I'd heard of stories before where animals traveled long distances and survived, but something terrible lodged in my throat.

"Yes, that's right. Is that okay?"

"Of course."

The doctor nodded at Nurse Shields, just a quick movement. He flipped on a television I hadn't noticed behind me, and the white shuttle appeared, a voice speaking in the background. Information about the shuttle.

My calves bunched and released, biting cramps. I closed my eyes and breathed through the pain as quietly as possible. Stealth. My eyes roamed around the room, searching for something else to focus on.

"Right on time, doctor," the nurse said.

"Yes, yes. Miss White, how are you feeling?"

"Fine," I forced out between clenched teeth.

"No secrets here," the doctor said.

"Three can keep a secret if two of them are dead," I said, smiling again.

"What an interesting expression." That was the doctor, but I refused to look at him. I couldn't take my eyes off the button on the bottom of the television until the announcer's voice rose in excitement. "And the shuttle *Empire* has achieved liftoff." The man blathered on, but I stared in horror at the blue, blue sky, squinting against the brightness.

Something in me broke, sheared away from the deadened calm, boiling up, bubbling over. I jumped out of my chair, faster than I thought I could move, my vision sizzling around the edges, and a high-pitched keening pounded in my ears.

The doctor startled—too slow, too slow. I kicked the chair at him, and he tripped. Voices rose out of the darkness, shrieking and babbling, and I screamed with them, throwing myself at the screen.

"Grab her! Use that needle, Shields!"

I threw my arm out, smacking into something soft over hard, whirling until I was nose-to-nose with the television. My fingers clawed at the shuttle as it rose and rose through the air, the rocket boosters falling away.

The howling grew louder. Fingers closing in on my arms and pulled me away. Still I fought to keep watching. Something sharp in my bicep, and then a sting.

I staggered backward, mourning the shuttle as the dim heaviness took me, gravity pulling at me just as surely as it would take the shuttle down any second.

My lips trembled out a prayer for the astronauts to be asleep, for NASA to have mercy. My mission incomplete. Everything shattered. Dad. Mrs. Gerhardt. Davey. Nike, for all I knew.

I screamed louder, shaking and reaching until the blackness at the horizon swallowed me whole.

Oh God, save them.

My eyelids trembled, the noise dimming. Dad waved frantically from the corner. Mrs. Gerhardt smiled, something sad and final, head nodding. I fought, but my feet moved forward: Sleep now beckoned with seared and blistered fingers.

Nicole Wolverton

fears many things, chief amongst them that something lurks in the dark. Her short stories have appeared in *Black Heart Magazine, The Molotov Cocktail*, and *Penduline,* among others. She also moderates "5 Minute Fiction," a weekly international flash fiction challenge. *The Trajectory of Dreams* is her first novel. She resides in the Philadelphia area with her husband and small cadre of pets, and when she isn't writing, you can find her on the Schuylkill River paddling with the Philadelphia Flying Phoenix women's dragon boat team, sky diving over New Jersey, or digging around in her gardens. Visit her website at www.nicolewolverton.com.

Acknowledgements

When you write a book, you never really do it on your own. I'm super thankful to the following:

- Chase Nottingham, my critique partner. He's an amazing writer, editor, and friend, and I'm grateful to have his eyes on everything I write.
- Randi Segal, Julie Zangara, Gilly Wright, and Suzanne Sanders, the first to look over this manuscript (and excellent women). There are others who read parts of this manuscript at various points, so thanks to all!
- Bitingduck Press. Thanks to my editor for working with me to shine up the story. Thanks to the editor-in-chief for seeing something in the manuscript.
- Everyone who contributed to research. Thanks to the Philadelphia Science Festival—because of PSF, I was able to attend talks by science writer Mary Roach and Guion Bluford, Jr., a retired astronaut from West Philly (and the first African-American in space, I might add), both of which were useful for the space travel parts of this novel. Mike White, an old friend from high school, helped with the arson research. I promise to only use the knowledge for good, Mike! Thanks, too, to everyone who answered my questions about sleep clinics and sleep research.
- Sarah Adamec, Kymberlie McGuire, and Christine Tremoulet. These Houstonites have always been really generous, letting me crash in their apartments and driving me around Houston over the years. Drinks are on me next time I'm in town! Tiaras are optional.
- Regency Café in Lansdowne, PA. I wrote a fair amount of Trajectory sitting in Regency, and their great coffee, excellent food, free-flowing wifi, and friendly staff made that possible.

Lastly, thanks to my mom for letting me read whatever I wanted as a kid. I'd like to think early exposure to Kurt Vonnegut, Ray Bradbury, abnormal psychology texts, and those weird Time-Life paranormal books made me the well-adjusted woman I am today. Ma, stop laughing.

Reprint Permissions

"On Your Back I Trace the Letter A" by Ilya Kutik reprinted from *Third Wave: The New Russian Poetry,* edited by Kent Johnson and Stephen M. Ashby (Ann Arbor: The University of Michigan Press, 1992). © 1992, The University of Michigan Press, and used with permission.

"You Will Hear Thunder" taken from *Selected Poems by Anna Akhmatova,* translated by D. M. Thomas, published by Vintage Classics. Reprinted by permission of The Random House Group Limited (print rights). Electronic reproduction is by permission of Johnson&Alcock, Ltd. Copyright ©Anna Akhmatova, trans. by D. M. Thomas, "You Will Hear Thunder," Everyman's Library Pocket Poets, 2006.

Disclaimer
This is a work of fiction. Any resemblance to real persons or events is purely coincidental.